THE FURIES

Katie Lowe

HarperCollins*Publishers*

HarperCollins*Publishers* Ltd
1 London Bridge Street,
London SE1 9GF

www.harpercollins.co.uk

First published by HarperCollins*Publishers* 2019
1

A catalogue record for this book is available from the British Library

ISBN: 978-0-00-828897-6 (HB)
ISBN: 978-0-00-828898-3 (TPB)

This novel is entirely a work of fiction.
The names, characters and incidents portrayed in it are
the work of the author's imagination. Any resemblance to
actual persons, living or dead, events or localities is
entirely coincidental.

Set in Electra LT Std 12/16.65 pt by
Palimpsest Book Production Limited, Falkirk, Stirlingshire

Printed and bound in the UK by CPI Group (UK) Ltd, Croydon CR0 4YY

MIX
Paper from
responsible sources
FSC
www.fsc.org **FSC™ C007454**

This book is produced from independently certified FSC™ paper
to ensure responsible forest management.

For more information visit: www.harpercollins.co.uk/green

THE FURIES

For Maria

While all melts under our feet, we may well grasp at any exquisite passion, or any contribution to knowledge that seems by a lifted horizon to set the spirit free for a moment, or any stirring of the senses, strange dyes, strange colours, and curious odours, or work of the artist's hands, or the face of one's friend. Not to discriminate every moment some passionate attitude in those about us, and in the very brilliancy of their gifts some tragic dividing of forces on their ways, is, on this short day of frost and sun, to sleep before evening.

Walter Pater, *The Renaissance: Studies in Art and Poetry*, 1868

Observe these generation of Witches, if they be at any time abused by being called Whore, Theefe, &c, by any where they live, they are the readiest to cry and wring their hands, and shed tears in abundance & run with full and right sorrowfull acclamations to some Justice of the Peace, and with many teares make their complaints: but now behold their stupidity; nature or the elements reflection from them, when they are accused for this horrible and damnable sin of Witchcraft, they never alter or change their countenances nor let one Teare fall.

Matthew Hopkins, *The Discovery of Witches*, 1647

The strange thing, they said, wringing their hands and whispering as though we couldn't hear, or weren't listening through extension phones or cracks in the walls, was that there was no known cause of death.

Inconclusive, they said, as though that changed the fact of it, which was this: a sixteen-year-old girl, dead on school property, without a single clue to suggest why or how. No unexplained prints on the body, the forensic examination finding no trace of violence, nor rape, nor a single fibre that could not be linked to the girl, her friends, or her mother, whom she had hugged for the last time that morning as she left for school. It was as though her heart had simply stopped, her blood stilled in her veins, preserving her forever in a single moment, watchful as the dawn.

The papers blurred it out, took suggestive photographs of the screen the police erected around the scene, an implicit acknowledgement of the horrors that lay within. But by that time, I'd already seen it. I see it now, sometimes, when I'm struggling to sleep. It's etched there, in my mind, not because it was horrific, nor due to some long-standing, unresolved trauma. No, my feeling is quite the opposite: a thrill, cold and sweet, in the recall.

I think of the scene, now, because it was so perfectly composed, like a Renaissance painting, the girl's neck angled slightly, like *La Pietà*, though I did not see that, then. It was over a decade later, on a tour of the Vatican, that I first realized the likeness. My students, for obvious reasons, thought that my solitary teardrop as I explained the history of the sculpture belied some exquisite taste on my part, a visceral response to the beauty of Michelangelo's work; I did nothing to disabuse them of that notion.

She was beautiful when she was alive – a child just discovering her power, knowing herself, all collarbones and blooming flesh – but death, it must be said, gave her something of the sublime. A little like the poem, 'La Gioconda' by Michael Field: 'Historic, side-long, implicating eyes; / A smile of velvet's lustre on the cheek; / Calm lips the smile leads upward; hand that lies / Glowing and soft, the patience in its rest / Of cruelty that waits and doth not seek / For prey . . . ' An underrated duo to my mind. How I love those words, even now.

In this pose they found her, eyes open, sitting upright on a swing. Immaculately put together, alive but for the blue threads of deoxygenated blood in place of youth's blush; the impossibly delicate silver threads that tied her hands to the chains, the stiffness of her back, the result of rigor mortis, by the time she was found on the still gently rocking swing. Feet crossed at the ankles, ladylike, though one of her shoes had fallen to the ground below. All this, in a thin, white dress, turned almost see-through by the morning dew. A modern masterpiece, precise and profound.

'So tragic,' they said. 'Another angel taken home,' written

on cards taped to store-bought bouquets, ink dripping in the rain. In the markets, beet farmers and fishermen muttered under their breaths; the local newspapers – whose usual focus was limited to the town's growing seagull population and the many, endless failures of the one-way system – were filled with photos of her for weeks, her school photo tacked on their banner, 'Never Forget', in an incongruously jaunty font beneath. The news reporters – the *real* reporters, national, international, such was the allure of the image – lurked among the townspeople for weeks, listening for hushed conversations, searching for clues. Hotels saw a dramatic uplift in room occupancy; restaurateurs joked grimly that death should visit more often. That it had been, by all accounts, a very good year.

'Every possible measure will be taken to get to the bottom of this case, and to prevent anything like this happening in our community again,' the police chief said, chest puffed, parading peacock-like for the camera. I watched it with my mother, first, and then years later, at home, alone, after an unknown voyeur uploaded it online, grainy in a way that echoed the great tragedies of the TV era. Something about it reminded me of a video I'd found of the Kennedy shooting, the solemn delivery, the echo of the head thrown back. 'We will investigate every angle, every lead, and every person in contact with this young lady to ascertain the exact circumstances leading up to her tragic death,' he said.

They didn't, of course. They ruled out the usual suspects – boyfriends, ex-boyfriends, a deranged parent – all to no avail. Even now, if you search for her name, you'll find amateur sleuths on message boards posting their own theories – sometimes unhinged, sometimes surprisingly accurate. In the small hours of the night curiosity leads me there, when the darkness falls heavy and my need to see her swells. I'm grateful to the voyeurs of the internet, to the stranger who uploaded the crime scene photos, decades after the fact. They turn my nerves electric, the memory radiating white hot, clear.

For, despite all that followed – the investigation, the questions, the on-camera tears and plaintive words wailed at drooling reporters – even after all these years, I struggle with this one, unspeakable truth: I don't feel bad about what we did. Any of it. Somehow, I can't. It's a crime, of course, and the fear of retribution naturally haunts me. But still, guilt is not the feeling I associate with her death.

Because, in the year I knew her, and in all the events leading up to her death – her murder – I felt more alive than I ever have, before or since. 'To burn always with this hard, gem-like flame—' a quote I repeat to my students regularly, though it never seems to capture their imaginations as it did ours – that, Pater said, is success in life. And in the memory of her, I feel that flame burn, hard and bright.

We were close to the divine. We touched gods, felt them flow through our veins. Felt lust, envy, greed, quicken our hearts – but for a while, we were truly, spectacularly alive. It might have been any of us, sitting there like the Madonna on the gently rocking swing. Sheer luck made it her, not me.

Autumn

Chapter 1

Visitors joked that it was the kind of place people came to die. A town at the end of the world, at the end of the century: the absolute end of the line.

The population ageing, sick and tired: the remains of the old brickworks hollowed by the wind. A little south, a well-known suicide spot, white cliffs that drew the despairing up and then over into the cool, grey sea. Train tracks that stopped abruptly, roads that led to no place but here . . . These were the obvious signs, I suppose: the root of the joke. But it wasn't just that.

It was the rain-battered shop fronts with peeling signs; pavilions caked in bird-shit and graffiti. The grey beaches, equal parts sand and shards of glass, crumpled beer cans and plastic bags. The arcades on the promenade, Caesar's Palace, Golden Ticket, Lucky Strike, carpets damp with beer and bleach, copper coins rattling on tin; men smoking in the fruit machines' lurid glow, hypnotized by the roll and ring. The pale fields of burned grass, barbed wire and brick. The shipping yards, great metal tombs arranged by mechanical beasts; the wilful, leering stench of the fish market. The corrugated bomb shelters, the stone mermaid, face worn away by the wind.

This is where I spent my youth, and found myself fixed, like a figure painted in oils; decay still rolling on, the shore dragged away by the sea. One day it will all be gone, and the world will be better for it.

There is little to tell of the years before I turned fifteen, my childhood quiet and dull, days and years blurring without consequences. My mum stayed home, taught me to read, watched me grow; my dad ran a small shop which, as far as I could tell, sold everything. I would hide in the cool, dark storerooms, plucking neon pens and glittering pencil sharpeners from scratched plastic trays and damp cardboard boxes. Board games, tested by me, playing my shadow. Books read, carefully, spines unbroken, pages held lightly as ancient runes. It sounds lonely, I imagine, but it was a comfort.

When I was eight, Mum said we'd been blessed with a special Christmas gift, and rubbed her swollen belly. I went to the encyclopaedia. Imagined her insides stretching, fists clutching tendons, amniotic sac bursting, tiny fingers crawling out. It's one of the only Christmases I remember now, as an adult.

It was a girl. A writhing, red-faced, screaming girl with a mass of black hair and cold, grey eyes. She was possessed, her whole life, with a look that suggested she knew more than she let on, little keeper of secrets. She was seven when Dad's car slipped under the wheels of a truck as he drove us to the beach. He died instantly, she lingering for four days, though she barely looked like herself. Barely looked like a person at all, really, her skin mottled blue, wet stitches carved into her skull.

I, for my part, climbed out of the car, a smudge of blood on my arm (not mine), plucked a damp fragment of bone from my hair (nor this). Brushed away the frost of glass that clung to my skin. Walked away, feeling like I'd woken from a long, dull, dream.

And that, I suppose, was the end. Or the beginning, depending on how you look at it.

Their lives ended, and Mum's life stopped. Even decades later, when I returned to clean the house after her death, everything remained as it was that day. Wallpaper greying, carpets scorched with wear. The same books on the shelves, same VHS tapes unboxed under the old TV, still emitting a low, static hum. Same tie hanging in a loose knot on the bedroom door, same crumpled papers in the bin, the same last words abandoned mid-sentence on a yellowing page.

'Perhaps we might consider an alternative approach,' my dad's last recorded thought in smudged, black ink. Everything was placed there with memories attached, my dad's fingerprints and sister's laugh still covering everything, like a skin that wouldn't shed.

I, however, felt nothing. Leaving the hospital, nothing; throwing a clod of damp soil into the pit, soft thump on varnished pine, nothing. Mum weeping on the sofa, clawing at my hair, pressing damp, hot palms to my face, clinging to my life: still, nothing.

Weeks later, I woke on the sofa to find her staring at me as one might take in a half-expected ghost, lip bitten to the jelly beneath. 'I thought she was . . . I thought you were gone too,' she said, her eyes wet with tears, pointing at a face on the screen that looked like mine, but for the details. Hair dull blonde, hers shining, mine textured, split, like old rope; eyes close as one might find to black, but for a chink of amber in her left iris; lips round, always a little too full for lipstick, which gave me the distinct look of a circus clown. Mine were chipped and ridged white with medicinal balm, a compulsive picking I couldn't shake, hers blush pink, smooth and smiling to reveal white, un-chipped teeth. I thought, watching her face flicker on the screen, that she was a better version of me – the one I longed to be. The artist's ideal, brush softly smoothing my faults, delicate touch between the lines.

'Renewed concerns for the missing teenager Emily Frost, who disappeared exactly one month ago today. Her whereabouts remain unknown, and her family have issued a new appeal for any information relating to her disappearance.'

I watched the stock footage, the familiar cliffs, the too-familiar edge. Nobody bothered to count the suicides these days. Emily had last been seen walking there, at the highest point.

'Mum, I'm here. That isn't me. She's just a jumper,' I said, reaching for the remote. 'They always are.'

'We just want you to come home,' her dad said, staring down the lens. 'We miss you, Emily. Please, please come home.'

I changed the channel and went back to sleep.

If there can be said to be an up-side to miraculously surviving a car wreck, apart from the immediately obvious, it's that nobody expects you to go to school.

'Not until you're ready,' Mum said. The therapist nodded sagely behind, a cornflake stuck to his moustache, a fat finger-print smudge on his glasses. 'You don't have to do anything you don't want to. Just take your time.'

And so I did. I took my time: skipped school right through to my final exams, declaring myself 'home-schooled'. I sat in a silent hall, surrounded by people I knew, my former classmates whispering as I walked in and right out again: 'I thought she was dead,' one said, pointing at me with a bloody, bitten nail.

I had already planned my future, or at least, had drawn a basic sketch. I would leave – though where to, I wasn't sure. I'd get a job. A waitress in a quiet café, where interesting visitors would tell me thrilling lies. A bookshop clerk, offering new worlds to bored children; an assistant in a gallery, maybe. I could learn to sing, or play guitar. I could write a book, life ticking quietly along around me. It wouldn't be glamorous, sure, but it would be enough. Anywhere, really, would be better than here, this town in which the greys of the old houses, sky and sea seeped into your heart and turned irrep-arably it black.

But on the day of my results, I came home to find Mum at the kitchen table, papers clenched in white-knuckled fists. 'It's what they would've wanted,' she said, handing me the entry forms for Elm Hollow Academy – a private girls' college on the outskirts of town. 'It's a privilege,' she said: one afforded to me by the unspeakably large settlement offered by the haulage company under whose articulated truck our car had been crushed.

School, to me, was all taped-up windows, boxy buildings

cracking at the edges, grey even in sunlight; freezing porta-cabins, graffitied bathroom mirrors and the loamy stink of teenage sweat. 'I don't want to,' I said, and left.

She didn't argue. But the papers sat on the kitchen table for weeks, and each time I passed I found myself drawn to the glossy pictures on the cover of the brochure: looming, red-brick buildings set against a too-blue sky, sunlight needling through pearly clouds behind a Gothic arch. There was a decadent, honey-sweet richness to it – one that I knew wasn't for me, but seemed, in the flickering kitchen light, the stifling damp in the air, to be another world entirely.

And so – reluctantly, at least as far as my mum was concerned – I agreed to give it a try. Our dilapidated Volvo purred behind me at the gates, and I turned to wave her away, though she – thinking herself unobserved – was staring down at the steering wheel, grin a steely rictus beneath strings of dirty hair. I winced, and turned away, catching the eye of a passing girl watching, embarrassed for us both.

I walked towards the school quickly, looking up at the looming clock tower – the Campanile, I would soon be corrected, inspired by the reds and creamy whites of Tuscan cousins, gleaming in sunlight – and dipped under the arches, into the main building. Students gathered on the steps in clusters, whispering.

I passed wholly unnoticed, and told a stout, grey-haired woman – Boturismo made flesh – my name three times. She stared at me, blankly, through the glass partition, muddy with prints and unsettling scratches. Without a word, she slid a sheaf of papers through the gap and pointed to a row of seats. As I sat staring numbly at the endless list of extra-curricular

activities and advanced classes, none of which I had any
interest in taking, a girl loped by, hair bottle-red, ladders torn
artfully into her tights. She waved with two fingers and smiled,
a rolled-up cigarette teetering on the edge of her lip. I stared
until the last second before she disappeared into the crowd,
when I at last mustered a weak, lost smile.

She must've been smiling at somebody else, I thought. But
as I looked around, back to the wall, this seemed unlikely. I
sat, dazed, among the marble busts and gloomy portraits of
long-dead headmasters until the bell rang, and the crowd
dispersed. I waited, peering down the empty corridors,
wondering whether I might have been forgotten.

A door creaked behind; I heard my name, and stood. The
man in the doorway was tall, though not imposingly so, a
little pot-bellied; tweed and sweater, horn-rimmed glasses; skin
possessed of the waxy paleness common to those who spend
too much time indoors. He stared at me, blinked, coughed;
held out a hand, fingers clubbed and ink-stained. 'Come on
in,' he said, softly.

He moved a stack of books and spilled papers from a wide,
worn armchair next to the desk and I took a seat. The office
was warm, if a little stuffy, books piled high under sediment
layers of dust, framed prints of medieval etchings covering the
walls. 'Cup of tea?' he said. Caught staring, I shook my head
and picked at a loose thread on my folder.

'So, let me begin with my usual spiel, and then we'll get
to know each other,' he said, taking a seat by the desk and
leaning forward, his elbows resting on his knees. He took a
deep breath: tang of stale coffee on it, sour.

'On behalf of the faculty of Elm Hollow, I'd like to welcome you to our student population.' He paused, smiling. 'We're a small school with a varied and prestigious history, and we're proud to have among our alumni leaders across a range of disciplines, including the sciences and the arts.' There was a brief pause as he waited for me to respond; I nodded, and he went on, his smile the kind one might offer to a well-trained dog.

'Our teaching staff includes many of these professionals, and our students are given the opportunity to follow in their footsteps with a wide array of curriculum-based and vocational courses. My name is Matthew Holmsworth, and I'm the Dean of Students here at Elm Hollow. I teach among the Medieval History faculty, primarily, but I'm also responsible for ensuring welfare among the student body, and, of course, welcoming new students such as yourself. You can call me Matthew – though I'd suggest calling the rest of the faculty Dr Whatever-Their-Name-Is until you've reached that level of informality, though, to be quite honest, that isn't likely to happen with all of them . . . I, however, prefer to be called Matthew.'

He paused, drew breath, and smiled again. I looked away. In the weeks and months after the crash, I'd become somewhat accustomed to people looking at me like this, the 'tragic miracle' look, as though the fact of me confused them. I found it nauseating. 'So what brings you here, Violet?' he asked, though judging by this look, he already knew.

'I need to get my A-Levels,' I said, flatly, voice little more than a croak.

'Great. That's great. I'm told you were self-taught last year – is that right?' I heard the creak of his chair as he leaned farther forward, and looked up.

'Yeah. I . . . Yeah.'

'That's a very impressive achievement. You must be quite proud.' I nodded. He looked down at my file, and almost imperceptibly raised his brow. I knew, for all my teenage claims of apathy that I'd done well; better, certainly, than anyone had expected. 'Well, I can see you've got an interest in the arts,' he continued, apparently choosing not to comment. I blushed at having expected more, a knot of shame coiling, sharp.

'We have an outstanding arts faculty – our English programme is second to none, and most of our Music students go on to spectacular things at various conservatoires here and in Europe, so both of those would be solid choices. You might also consider one of our Fine Art courses, too – Annabel is highly selective, but I'd be happy to recommend she review your transcripts, if you're interested . . . '

As he spoke, he ran a finger absent-mindedly over the glass of a framed etching lying on the desk. I followed the path, black ink on creamy paper: a woman tied at the stake, staring into the eyes of some great hulking beast with curling, twisted horns and broad wings. Behind her, three ghouls, arms reaching for her neck.

A silence fell. I realized he was waiting for a response. 'That sounds . . . Great.'

'Super,' he said, with all the brightness of a department store Father Christmas. 'And do you have any questions for me?'

'Can I have a look at that?' I said, reaching for the picture. I caught myself and pulled my hand away.

'This? Well, of course.' He paused. 'It only arrived this morning. I've been wanting to procure a copy since I joined the faculty.' He handed me the frame, and I placed it on my lap, leaning in to examine the beast's feathers and scales, his mad, wild eyes, his used-car salesman smile. The flames curled up and around the woman's feet, rising to meet the hair that fell long down her back. 'Margaret Boucher,' he said, after a moment. 'I suppose you've heard the history of Elm Hollow, haven't you?'

I looked up. 'I've read the prospectus.'

'Oh, no. The prospectus is the sales brochure. Accurate, of course,' he said, with a wry smile. 'But it's the rather sanitised version. Most of the faculty are drawn to this place for one reason or another from our school's history – it's tempting ground for the academic.' He lowered his voice, a confidential whisper. 'My interests, for instance, lie in the witch trials that took place on the grounds in the seventeenth century. Quite possibly in this very spot where we're sitting now.'

'Are you serious?'

'Oh, quite serious, yes. The wych elm you passed on your way in marks the spot where she was burned.' I stared at him, but he went on, cheerfully. 'It was believed – though I'd stress that this is medieval belief, not fact – that this was fertile ground for all kinds of sorcery. Many well-known folk myths originated here, though the references to Elm Hollow have faded away with time. A very good PR job on the school's behalf, I think.'

'Really?'

'Absolutely. It was a real frenzy, for a time. And occasionally, so they say, since – though that's not really my area, being a medievalist and all. Still, it's not uncommon for curious guests to arrive on the grounds, seeking an audience with the Devil himself.' He chuckled, and leaned back in his chair. 'Instead, they meet Mrs Coxon on reception, and they don't seem to hang around long after that.'

He let out a sudden cough, as though catching himself. 'Anyway – this piece is one I've been trying to procure for quite some time. A copy, mind, but a very good one. But don't worry,' he said, with a smile. 'It's not all devils and roaming beasts around here, at least as far as I'm aware. Let's get your timetable sorted and find out what the future has in store for you.'

I left the office clutching an oddly sparse timetable. 'We expect our students to fill these free hours with pursuits which will help them to become well-rounded young women,' the Dean had said as I stared down at it, confused.

I'd enrolled in both the practical Visual Arts class, and Aesthetics, a more theoretical module – as well as English Literature and Classics, a subject not offered at my previous school, but which I'd loved as a child, when Dad would fill my mind with tales of Medusas and Minotaurs as I drifted into sleep. I had taken the maximum four courses students were permitted to study, and wondered what I'd do with all that spare time; imagined myself friendless, hiding behind books.

The corridor stretching towards the English department – a class for which I was by now a good twenty minutes late – was an area where the school showed its age, though it seemed still to possess a shabby dignity, an almost sombre blankness, as though pulled from another time.

Gone were the sex-ed pamphlets in wire racks, the sugar paper displays in childish lettering; gone were the painted breeze-blocks and papier-mâché displays, the keyed lockers and scuffed linoleum floors. Instead, I walked a warm, low-ceilinged corridor with step-worn carpets, passing wooden doors with office hours taped beneath each tutor's name.

It was far too warm for September – but the heating, I would soon discover, was turned on only from September to Christmas, leaving us to spend the first few months of the academic year sweating through our shirts, the second peering at teachers through the mist of our breaths.

Finding the class, I was uncomfortably aware of a thin sheen of sweat on my brow, jumper stuck grimly to the skin under my backpack. I knocked on the door, and peered inside.

The students stared at me, eyes assessing, judging my place in the natural order. I gripped the door a little tighter, fingers turning red, then white. The tutor – Professor Malcolm, the only tutor I have encountered before or since who insisted on such a title, though with what qualification I am still yet to find out – was a squat, balding man with oddly tiny features, a button nose top-and-tailed by thin lips and black, bird-like eyes.

'I'm . . . I'm new,' I said, nervously.

'Well, sit then. And try to learn something.' He turned back to the board, resuming his talk, as I shuffled between the rows and took a seat. I tried to catch up, glancing at the open books and scrawled notes on the desks beside me. 'And, as Blake concludes, "Thus men forgot that All deities reside in the human breast." What do we think this means?'

Met with silence, he sighed. I raised my hand. He sighed again. 'Yes?'

' . . . Blake finds morality and religion too . . . Too restrictive. He thinks it goes against the spirit of man.' I blushed, furiously, realizing as I spoke what I'd done. The silence was cool, relentless – one of the many weapons, I would learn, that the students of Elm Hollow possessed.

He paused. 'And you are?'

'Violet,' I whispered, my betrayal hanging heavy on the air.

He cupped a hand to his ear. 'Excuse me?'

'My name is Violet,' I said again, a little louder: a croak.

He nodded, and went on, as I shrank into my chair.

'Man is a wild and occasionally savage, sexual thing,' he said, affecting his previous drone which seemed designed to counteract the content of his words, the emphasis falling always on the wrong beat. I looked around, surprised at the absence of titters or comments in response to the mention of sex, but the class was silent. Only then did I see the girl from before – the girl with the bright, red hair – three seats away, staring back.

I looked back down at the desk, names and doodles carved into the wood. When I finally met her eye she raised an eyebrow and smiled. I felt myself about to become a punch-line – but, unable to see anyone else watching, braced for the laughs, I returned a dim half-smile, a weak attempt at nonchalance.

She pointed at the tutor, rolling her eyes, and smiled; mouthed 'dickhead,' and turned back to face the board. She slid lower into her chair, and began rolling a cigarette from a tin hidden on her lap beneath the desk, perfectly still, but for the dexterous, whipping movement of her pale, thin fingers, chipped black nails catching tobacco scraps beneath.

I lost myself in thought, the class dull, air growing thick with impatience. By the time the bell rang, I was in something like a trance. As I slid my notebook and pen back into my backpack, I looked around, feeling myself watched. But it seemed I had been forgotten, my presence no longer of interest – and the girl with the red hair was gone.

Wednesday afternoons were reserved for extra-curriculars, and as I had none, I spent the rest of the day exploring my new campus, wandering by the grand Great Hall where the choir practised some mournful, gorgeous song.

I walked the long, high-ceilinged corridors of the Arts building, where drama students lurked in thickets, launching into soliloquies, echoes overlapping. In music rooms violinists practised beside pianists, the same rippling passages played time and again, while the warm autumn breeze whistled through the trees outside, shaking leaves which fell in lazy arcs. I can still see them falling like outstretched hands, hear them crunching underfoot. It is a scene, a mood, still fresh and bright in my mind, recalled with the bittersweet taste of youth, of lilacs and lavender in the air: the campus entirely idyllic, and utterly charming.

Except, that is, for the dining hall. There is good reason

why this area is never shown on the prospectus or to visiting parents: it is the underbelly of the school, necessary and crude, one of the few parts of campus where function is allowed to outweigh form.

The fluorescent-lit canteen rattled and hissed, emitting the rancid tang of meat in rendered fat; the vending machines rang and rattled with constant use. Students gathered in heaving clusters around laminate tables, surrounded by an odd mixture of cheap plastic chairs and a repurposed pew dragged up from the basement for a drama rehearsal several years before. It is still in place now, decades later, more cracked and bruised still.

I settled into a corner, watching my classmates hungrily, mining them as one might an anthropological study – this approach perhaps indicative of one of the many reasons why, while not entirely isolated at my previous school, I had still found it a struggle to make friends.

I looked at the casual way they'd adapted their uniforms – all made, it seemed, from materials designed to scratch and needle the skin beneath – Doc Martens, black, red and tan; butterfly clips in pastel shades holding fraying braids. Tartan, denim jackets tied tight at the hips. Velvet headbands, earrings, strings of beads and silver chains, all signifying personalities and secrets which I – wearing my uniform simply as the handbook prescribed – seemingly did not possess. I felt woefully underdressed, and hid lower behind my book (a novel whose simpering heroine I had begun to find irritating, and which I would soon abandon, never to be finished).

Still, it seemed I had not gone entirely unnoticed. I felt the eyes of the girls on me, though each time I looked up, they'd already looked away; heard, too, the whispered words 'She looks like . . . ' passing from one group to the next. I could imagine their thrust. Some creature, a farm animal: dog, pig, or cow. As the clock tower rolled one slow minute to the next, the whispering seemed to grow louder still, a growing hiss, a menace, as I blushed and sat lower, longing to disappear.

As I blinked away tears, staring blankly at the words on the page, three figures passed by the large windows at the other side of the cafeteria. My eyes followed the shock of red hair as the girl bobbed alongside two others, who smiled and talked as they kicked the fallen leaves underfoot.

I imagined them turning back to look at me; willed the girl to give me the same, playful smile she'd offered earlier, and shuffled in my seat, my pose determinedly relaxed.

But she didn't turn back, and they walked on, disappearing into the sunlight, their shadows trailing tall and proud behind.

Chapter 2

The studio was covered in creamy paper, pastel drawings crawling from corners like creeping clouds of smoke. I felt a cool smudge at my elbow, a violet stain smeared across the cuff of my shirt.

Over the course of the week, those of us in the practical classes had filled the space, until it was impossible to leave the room without a coating of pink and blue chalk on our uniforms. Our hands left pastel prints in homage across the school: library books with green thumbs, a peach palm around a test tube, blue lips printed on coffee cups and each other's cheeks. The lesson, I suppose (Annabel, the art tutor, rarely leading us to an obvious conclusion – or any conclusion at all) was that the artist leaves her mark on everything she touches. It would be many years before I would realize just how true that would turn out to be.

She sat on the edge of the desk, feet swinging just above the floor, while those of us in her Aesthetics class sat breathless, waiting for her to begin. Dressed entirely in black, her hair in silvery curls that hung heavily over her shoulders, she seemed drawn from another world. Even in memory, she seems possessed of a wordless authority: the power of one who could silence a room with a single breath.

'Oscar Wilde,' she began, at last, 'described the discipline of Aestheticism as "a search after the signs of the beautiful. It is the science of the beautiful through which men seek the correlation of the arts. It is, to speak more exactly, the search after the secret of life." And that is what we are here to do. Make no mistake. You may be young, and time may seem to be endless, but you'll learn – hopefully before it's too late – that those singular moments of illumination are what make life worth living. It is up to you to seek them out, to see them for what they are. And the sooner you begin, the richer your life will be.'

The door clicked open, a short, blonde girl in sports colours muttering a hushed apology as she entered. She sat in the empty seat beside me, mouthing 'hi.' I smiled numbly back, surprised to be greeted at all. Annabel looked at her coldly, and the girl looked away, abashed.

'You should be developing your aesthetic appreciation of what is beautiful, or worthy of your attention,' Annabel went on, 'by creating your own philosophy – your own theory of art – that serves to explain your tastes, and the way these intersect with the rest of your life experience.' She leaned back, rolling her shoulders; her silver pendant sparkled in the light.

'After all, this is not a course for the lazy student who wishes to sit around and have me talk at them for four hours a week.

Quite the opposite, in fact. I expect you to posit your own judgements, and explore your subjective appreciation of art. Those of you taking my practical course – which I believe is most of you – should take the opportunity to develop these ideas beyond what Wittgenstein called the "limits of language", which, I am sure, you will grow familiar with in this class.'

A ripple of excitement ran through the room. For all their bitterness and dramatics, it is a fact known only to the very best of educators that teenagers are uniquely susceptible to the poignant phrase, the encouragement of their own, individual talents. It may be a cliché – but I am sure a great many creative spirits have been forged through the power of a single glimmer of inspiration at this age.

Certainly in the moment, it seemed as though each of us was alive with potential, though none of us knew, for instance, who Wittgenstein was (even now, I will admit my knowledge is rudimentary at best, his theories a little esoteric for my tastes), or why such a limit to language might exist. Or, for that matter, why a group of sixteen- and seventeen-year-olds might be somewhat unqualified (to say the least) to create our own theories of art. No – in the light of this encouragement, we saw ourselves anew, thrilled with the sense of possibility.

'Marie,' she said, turning to face a dark-haired girl – recognizable as she spoke for her reedy, high-pitched voice, the shadow of a nervous laugh familiar from the canteen. 'Give me an example of a work you find beautiful.'

'Michelangelo's *David*,' she said, confidently.

'Why?' Annabel said, wry smile revealing gums almost white, fading into teeth.

'Because it's a symbol of strength and human beauty.'

Annabel said nothing, the silence deathly, yawning like a trap.

'Is that what you think, or what I think parroted back to me?' she said, finally, as she leaned over the desk and peeled away a sheet of paper, her book on Renaissance sculpture open underneath. The girl stared down, turning pale. 'Though other members of the faculty may enjoy it when their students mindlessly repeat phrases they do not believe, the point of *this* class,' she said, turning her back on the girl, 'is not to give me the answer you think is right. It is to tell me what you really think. I already know what I believe, and I don't need you to remind me.' She looked around the room, eyes cast on each of us in turn. I felt my stomach lurch as she settled her gaze on me.

'Violet.'

'Yes, Miss.' My breath caught a little, nerves shaking through. It was the first time she'd spoken to me directly in either class. There was some brightness to her, that seemed almost to glow from within; as though her blood ran silver in her veins, instead of blue, lighting her skin from below. When I look back, now, I wonder if she could ever have been quite as we saw her, or whether we simply imposed the light upon her, the force of our wanting turning her into something half-divine. On cool days – rational days, when the grey hush of autumn seeps into everything – the obvious occurs. It might simply have been a trick of the light.

'Annabel, please,' she said, without smiling. 'Tell me, what would you choose?'

I felt the class turn to face me, expectantly. Marie glared, her fury at Annabel boring into me. I thought of things I'd read about, seen, their names lost to me in my panic. Finally, I alighted on an image: women laughing, raving furiously, at a town far below; the wild-eyed devil gnawing limbs. 'Goya's Black Paintings,' I said, the words catching on my tongue.

She drew three circles in the air with her fingers, teasing out my meaning. 'There's just . . . There's something about them I really like.'

'You really like?' Annabel said, eyebrow raised. 'Surely you can go a little deeper than that.'

I felt my heart tumbling in my chest. The truth was, I'd seen them in a book when I was five, maybe six years old, and felt a strange thrill at the horror of it all. Mum had ripped the book from my hands almost immediately, but the images had stuck. Years later, I'd stolen the book from a second-hand shop, too ashamed to admit how much I wanted it, cruel faces grinning deathly from the cover. Three days after that, wracked with guilt, I'd returned with a stack of my dad's old books – a donation that would cover the cost several times over.

'Well, it's not really an aesthetic thing,' I said, slowly. 'But he painted them on the walls of his house, just for him. So, even though he was known for his portraits, which are nice, but . . . Well, kind of boring . . . ' At this a flicker of a smile crossed her face, willing me on. 'When he was on his own, he wanted to paint these horrifying things, like the devil eating a man, or the descent into madness. It was like a release he could only get when he was alone.'

She nodded, brushed a curl of white hair behind her ear.

I almost felt as though she turned a little towards me, as though the better to hear something unsaid. 'I assume you know *The Sleep of Reason Produces Monsters?*'

I blanched. 'Sorry?'

'The etching. From a very similar period.'

'Oh,' I said. 'No. I haven't seen it.'

'Look it up. You'll like it.' She turned away. 'In fact, bring a copy with you next time, and we'll discuss as a group.'

As she went on, I felt the girl's eyes on me; tried, but failed to resist the temptation to look back. The red-headed girl from my English class chewed thoughtfully at a thumbnail, grimacing as the chalk covered her tongue; catching my eye, she laughed, and I laughed too, an echo.

She turned back to face Annabel, and I did the same, though the rest of the class passed in a haze, the fact of having met Annabel's approval – a least briefly – leaving me dazed with relief.

The bell rang, and I began to pack my bag, while the red-headed girl and her friends gathered by Annabel's desk, voices lowered in hushed conversation. The tall girl glanced at me, pointedly lowering her voice further. When it became clear the three of them were waiting for me to leave (my cheeks flushing hot with the realization) I scooped up my bag and walked towards the door.

'Hey, wait,' a voice called after me. 'Fancy a smoke?' I turned to see the red-head grinning at me, slyly; the other girls – and Annabel – looked at me, their expressions blank, mask-like.

I didn't smoke, but – taken by surprise, I would later claim, though in fact merely desperate to make a friend – I nodded.

In the corridor, we walked in step. 'So how do you like Elm Hollow?'

'It seems okay. Everyone's been pretty nice so far.'

She pushed the door, the fresh air outside exhilarating. I felt the sweat droplets freeze and dry on my brow as we walked in silence to a graffitied smoking shelter hidden behind the main building, away from the car park, and away from disapproving eyes. A cheer drifted by on the wind from the playing fields; swallows circled overhead in bursts, as though catching themselves mid-flight.

'So . . . I'm Robin, by the way – thanks for asking.' She grinned, waving away my clumsy apology, the words still unspoken. 'Where are you from?' she said, clicking the lighter repeatedly before giving it a firm shake. Finally, it lit.

'Well, I was at the Kirkwood before,' I said. 'But last year I stayed home.'

'Like, home-schooled?' She raised a pencilled brow sharply, red pinpricks blooming beneath.

'Kind of, I guess. But I sort of taught myself.'

'No way,' she said. 'How come?'

'I . . . Well, my dad died. They said take as much time as I needed, so . . .'

'Hey!' she said, brightly. 'My dad's dead too.' She paused. 'I mean, so, you know. I get it.'

'Oh. That's horrible. Sorry.'

'No, no, it's cool. I didn't really know him. Mum says he was kind of an asshole.'

'Oh,' I said. 'Well . . . Sorry anyway, I guess.'

She smiled, looked away. In the daylight, she was freckled

31

and long-lashed, cheeks flushed feverish in the cool autumn air. 'Shit,' she muttered, flinching as the cigarette burned to her fingers. She threw it on the floor and stamped it out with a silver-toed boot. From inside the building, the bell rang.

'Wanna hang out some time?' she said, turning to me.

'Hang out?'

'Yes, dipshit, hang out. You know. Pass time. In company. Among friends.'

I said nothing, dumbstruck. In my silence, she went on. 'I'm going to assume that's a yes, because anything else would be unspeakably rude. Bus stop. Friday. 3:15. Sharp.' She turned and walked away without another word, a cluster of sparrows scattering as she strolled across the grass, while I stood, left behind, paralysed by the encounter.

It couldn't possibly be that simple.

I'd never really *had* friends, though I hadn't been entirely unpopular, either. I drifted in the background, a barely-noticeable side-player, while my fellow classmates turned rebellion into a competitive sport. I, too shy, too nervous, too slow, simply lingered behind, clutching books and feeling the soothing roll of my Walkman in my pocket, pretending not to care. It wasn't that I was incapable of making conversation, or that I was disliked, per se. I simply couldn't work out how one crossed the boundary line from classmates, to friends, as though there were some secret code or sign one had to give to join each little group.

And yet, mere days after joining Elm Hollow – the new girl, late in the semester, with nothing special to recommend me, no gaudy quirks or stylish clothes – I had a friend. A friend, who wanted to 'hang out'. I wondered if I was being set up; became convinced of this, over the hours that followed, when there was no sign of the girls, nor of Annabel, whose studio was empty when I passed, the following day.

Finally, Friday afternoon arrived, and I began the march towards the bus stop, among the hordes of fellow students, who had already focused their attentions elsewhere, now seeming not to see me at all. At the top of the hill, an old playground stood silhouetted in the afternoon light: the younger brothers and sisters of those students being collected squealed and swung, ran circles around their weary parents. I imagined my sister's moon-white face among them, the rubber texture of her swollen skin; shook my head, searched for Robin in the crowd.

'Wasn't sure if you'd show,' she said, grabbing my shoulders from behind, callused fingers brushing my cheek.

'Why?' I stood, frozen. It had been a long time since I'd last been touched, though I hadn't realized it until now. My mother's collarbones pressed against my neck, days after Dad died. That was the last.

'Dunno,' she said. 'You just didn't seem all that into the idea.'

'Oh, no, I was – I just—' I stopped, grateful to be interrupted by a cheer from the crowd by the bus stop; a girl dancing, whirling in circles, so fast she'd become a blur.

Robin and I followed the thinning crowd on to the last bus, her hand still tight around my wrist. She slid in by the window, guitar pressed against her knees; I sat beside her, pressed close as the bus filled up, packed with pale limbs and stale breath.

'So,' she said, turning to me, eyes wide, an exaggeration. 'Where'd you come from?'

'Kirkwood,' I said, again.

'I *know* that. Let me rephrase. Tell me everything. Tell me your story.'

I looked at her, my mind empty of all history, memory erased. 'I . . . I don't know.'

'Interesting,' she said, grinning, a smudge of mulberry brushed under stained lips. She saw me looking, raised a hand to her mouth. 'You're from round here?'

'Yeah.'

'Makes sense, then. Boring, boring, boring.' She paused, narrowed her eyes. 'Not you, I mean. The town. Is boring.'

'Yeah.'

'Yeah,' she said, leaning back against the seat. 'Okay, let's try something else. Pop quiz. Violet's not talking because a) she's shy, b) she's got super interesting things to say but she doesn't want to tell me, or c), she's not that interesting after all and I'm sorely misguided. Go.'

'Not c,' I said, though I felt the sudden flash of a lie. *I'm not that interesting,* I thought. *She's right.*

'I guess a) and b) aren't exactly mutually exclusive. So you *are* interesting, but you're shy and you don't want to tell me your secrets.' She looked at me, smiled. 'I guess that's okay.'

I searched for another way, an easier line of conversation. 'Let's try the other way around. Tell me about you.'

'Oh, me? I'm *super* interesting. Fascinating. A one-woman Pandora's box. But I'm also a lot like you. I don't give it away for free.' She grinned. 'We'll just have to take it slow, huh?'

I smiled. 'You play guitar?'

'Horribly,' she said, squeezing the neck of the case between her fingers. 'Still, it makes me look cool. That's a start.'

'You *are* cool,' I said, and blushed. I hadn't meant to sound so desperate, so eager to please.

She laughed, a bitter snort. 'Well, I guess that's sealed then. You're just about the only person around here that thinks I, Robin Adams, am cool. Which I'm pretty sure makes you my new best friend.' She extended a hand, and we shook, a comical formality that felt strangely intimate in the crowded space. 'Come on,' she said, nudging my arm with her elbow.

The bus shuddered to a halt, and we edged out into the street, where the smell of the sea – something I hadn't noticed was absent from the grounds of the school – whistled between the buildings. The sky had turned from blue to grey over the course of the afternoon, and tiny beads of rain started to fall, so imperceptibly I didn't notice until Robin held a discarded paper over her head and gestured to me to follow, saying 'This rain's going to ruin my hair,' as she bounded off.

I followed her into the grandly named International Coffee Company, with its one dilapidated location in a quiet street, in a town the world forgot. 'Hey, bitches,' she said, announcing herself to the room as we entered. The barista – all black hair and pillar-box red lips, tanned to the colour and texture of leather – waved and shouted 'Coffee?' Robin nodded, held two fingers up, and strolled to the back of the café, where the other girls sat whispering in a patched-up leather booth. 'This is Violet,' she said, pushing me towards them, thumbs pressed firmly into my shoulder blades.

The two girls looked up at me, with a bland curiosity, as I

stumbled, caught myself, and smiled; they said nothing. After a moment, the shorter of the two – a girl with green eyes and pale, almost translucent skin – smiled and waved her cigarette coyly, gesturing me to sit by her side. The two were sharing a pot of tea clearly designed for one, which steamed lazily beside a thick, leather book on the table.

'Queen bitch here is Alex,' said Robin, sliding into the booth beside the other girl and throwing an arm around her, swiftly brushed away. She nodded, coolly, and sat back, weaving her hair into a thick, rope-like braid as she watched me, eyes hooded, almost black.

'And this little cherub—' Robin pinched her own cheek between finger and thumb and squeezed it white. 'This is Grace.' Grace rolled her eyes, passing her cigarette back to Alex, who took it, smoke curling in the air between them. Robin turned to the girls as I wedged myself in next to Grace, who slid closer to the wall, as though to leave a foot of space between us.

The girls smiled at me, dimly, before turning to Robin. 'Did you . . . ?' Alex said, softly.

'Not yet,' she replied. 'But good things come to those who wait, right?'

The waitress set two tall, black coffees down with a clatter, a pool forming around them, rolling down the almost imperceptibly slanted table towards me. She dabbed it with her apron, and I looked up, finding myself greeted by a girl with the same, deep features as the barista, but a good twenty years younger. 'Hey, Dina,' Robin said, the words sing-song, mocking. 'How's it going?'

'Fine,' Dina said, turning away and stalking into a back room behind the bar.

'Religious nut,' Robin said, sliding a coffee towards me. 'I'm surprised she hasn't come at us with the rosary yet.'

'Or a stake,' Alex laughed.

'The power of Christ compels you, etcetera.' Robin's voice drew a swift warning look from the woman at the bar, and the girls went on in a whisper. I sipped the coffee, concealing a wince at the bitter taste, the dry, sickly layer it left on my tongue. This wasn't the first time I'd tried to at least pretend I liked it – I had read enough to know all the people I admired adored it, and took it black – but then, as before, the taste gave way to a hot, fast-moving nausea, heartbeat racing like that of a rabbit in a trap. Still, I clung tight to the cup, feeling the warmth nip at my fingers, and made plans to jettison it the moment the girls were distracted, though the weary-looking plant at the edge of the booth, I soon realized, was plastic. The frayed leather seats, flickering light-bulbs and dusty, sun-bleached paintings had implied that from the outset.

'So what else are you studying?' Grace said, turning to me, Alex and Robin absorbed in some labyrinthine conversation whose thrust I'd long since lost. She peeled open a half-eaten stick of rock, sugary-sweet on her breath.

'English, and Classics,' I said.

She looked me up and down briefly, so quickly I might have imagined it. 'Annabel seemed to like your idea in class, yesterday.' She paused. 'I think she—'

'Hey,' Robin said, leaning in between us. 'This is important.'

Grace leaned back in the chair, a counterbalance. 'What?'

'Blood or cherry?' We stared back. 'Lipstick, dipshits. Jesus. Some help you are.'

Alex elbowed Robin, pulling her bag from under the table. 'I've got to go.'

'But we haven't decided yet,' Robin whined, refusing to move.

'Are you wearing the black dress?' Alex said.

'Yeah.'

'So wear the red. It'll pop,' she replied, smacking her lips. 'Now come on, piss off.'

Robin slid out of the booth and leaned over the table, one leg outstretched behind. Alex kicked her, and she withdrew it, Dina narrowly avoiding a fall. 'Nice to meet you . . . Shit,' Alex laughed. 'I was going to . . . What's your name again?'

'Violet,' Robin answered. 'Her name is Violet.'

'Alright,' Alex said. 'Well, nice to meet you, Violet.'

I nodded, a little burned. She'd forgotten my name. 'You too.'

After she left, the conversation continued, Robin choosing by committee colours for nails, length of lashes, contacts in various colours for a party at her boyfriend's dorm that weekend. Still heady from the caffeine and the cloud of smoke perpetually surrounding our booth (the girls passing a single cigarette between them at all times, Robin's almost-spent lighter seemingly the only one they owned) I opted to make my escape – to quit while it appeared I was ahead.

'See you next week,' the girls said, as though there were no question of my return, and I flushed, grateful at the implication.

I took the long way back, past the beach, where the sea whispered a soothing, steady rhythm, a tenor crooning from the pavilion at the end of the pier. In the streets close to home, lonely people watched families on flickering TVs, curtains illuminated in the same, mocking patterns; the neighbour's dog sniffed at my hand through the fence, before the grizzled old woman who lived there called him in.

'Good evening, Mrs Mitchell!' I shouted, in my best talking-to-the-elderly voice. Her grandson – a squat, apple-cheeked boy with a bowl haircut, a year or so older than I was – sat at the lit window above, white walls papered in posters of dragons and wizards. I looked up at him, and smiled; he pulled the curtain shut as Mrs Mitchell slammed the door without looking back.

Chapter 3

All weekend, I couldn't sleep. I paced the halls, watched reruns of *Murder, She Wrote* with Mum at 3am, the news at six, seven, eight. I scraped the mould off the crusts with a knife and made toast for us both, while I mimed conversations I might have with the girls (assuming they invited me back). I worked the theoretical common ground at which our personalities might intersect, making lists of topics I could raise that might somehow make me seem interesting, or witty, or both. I scrawled opening lines and points of conversation in my diary, before tearing them out, ashamed to see my desperation on the page.

I found a stack of mouldering catalogues by the door, and made a list of clothes I thought might make me more like them, make-up they might wear, so wholly unlike my own. I mimed my mum's voice on the phone while she slept, nervously peeling strips from the wallpaper by the stairs. She didn't notice.

On the Monday, however, there was no sign of the girls at school. I wandered from one class to the next, imagining them around every corner, among the faceless crowds. I walked by the sports fields, hoping to catch sight of Alex, whose name I had seen on the team rosters for both netball and lacrosse; wandered the cavernous halls of the library, looking for Grace; and by the art studios, imagining I might find Robin there. Not, that is, that I would have admitted this, to either myself or the girls I was balefully stalking. I told myself I was exploring, finding my way around.

As I waited outside the English classroom, I saw the quote from Chaucer written in arched letters on the blackboard. I still remember it now: 'How potent is a strong emotion! Sometimes an impression can cut so deep / That people can die of mere imagination.'

'Hey, new girl,' a sing-song voice rang behind me, startling in the silence.

I spun around to find myself watched, warily, by a short – petite, I suppose, is the word – blonde girl, dressed head-to-toe in the school's sports colours. She fingered the tape wrapped around her fingers. She was pretty, in a sleepy way, eyes heavy-lidded, like a doll's. The kind you want to close with your thumb.

'What are you doing?' She looked at me with a half-smile, a mixture of sweetness and suspicion.

'Just . . . Getting my bearings,' I said, twisting my fingers, palms tight and sweating.

'I saw you last week with the weird girls. Not that it's any of my business, but . . . Well, you seem nice. If you want to make friends around here, you might want to avoid getting stuck with them.'

'Why?' I was less surprised at her opinion of the girls – though naturally, I was curious – than the very fact of having been noticed at all. I'd imagined myself invisible, disappearing into the crowd.

'You really want to know?'

I nodded. A soprano began singing halfway down the hall, a little off-key. The girl winced.

'Okay, well,' she said, shifting her backpack from one shoulder to the other. 'You remember Emily Frost?'

I wound the name around, picked at the threads. It had a familiar ring to it, but where I'd heard it, I couldn't say. I shrugged.

'Where'd you go to school again?'

'Kirkwood.'

'So you're from round here. You must've seen it on the news. The one that did a Richey.'

'A what?'

'Richey. Manics Richey. Disappeared. Never seen again. Jesus, do you even read?' Her tone was oddly sweet, gently chiding; I nodded. 'Emily was all over the news last year. She looked like you, except . . . ' She trailed off. The image came back, and I knew what she was going to say. 'Pretty. Prettier.'

'Oh yeah. I remember. But—'

'Right, good.' She grew more animated, stepped towards me. I heard the rustle of tissue paper, smelled the chemical scent of Clearasil and body spray, a chemical musk. 'So she was best friends with Robin, and the four of them did *everything* together. And then they had some kind of fight one day, didn't speak for like a week, and then poof! Gone. Everyone says she killed herself, but they never found the body.

'I mean, clearly there was more to it,' she went on. 'If you even mention her name near them, they just get up and leave.' She lowered her voice. 'I mean, if something like that happened to *my* best friend, I don't think I'd be quite so cool about it, you know?'

I tried to muster a half-smile, a non-committal response. 'Why are you telling me this?' I said, finally.

She shrugged. 'Care in the community, I guess. Do you want to get some lunch? I'm Nicky, by the way.'

In the grim heat of the canteen, I found myself in a cloud of strange associations and artificial smells – coconut, lavender, lemon, all wrong – while girls with avian limbs and immaculate teeth giggled and clucked. The girl beside me had a laugh like a pony's whinny, the dead eyes of a beetle.

They talked quickly, the conversation bouncing easily from one topic to another in long, breathless sentences, all featuring people whose names I didn't know, though I nodded along, trying to keep up. A girl opposite painted her nails, brush dripping slow rolls of indigo blue; another doodled incomprehensible lists in a sticker-covered notebook, and for a moment, I wondered if I might fit in.

And then I saw them. Robin, Grace, and Alex, walking slowly across the grass, just as they had on that first day, the three of them smiling with quiet satisfaction, careless and somehow wild. I saw Robin's hair burning fiery in the light, the moth-bitten chic of her coat; I saw Grace, preternaturally pale, large sunglasses covering the dark circles that seemed always to haunt her eyes; the crisp white of Alex's pressed shirt, the sophisticated, sidelong glance across the Quad.

'Ugh,' Nicky said, her shoulder pressed against mine. 'They're so weird.'

I made a vague murmur of agreement, felt a pang of envy, a bitter ache in my teeth. As I stood to leave – making my excuses, the girls nodding and smiling blankly before resuming their chatter – I felt Nicky squeeze my wrist between bony fingers.

'We're going to the pier later – want to come?'

'I . . . I've got homework.'

Nicky groaned. 'We've *all* got homework. Come on. It'll be fun.'

I felt the sharp edge of her thumbnail in the soft swell of my wrist; a brief flash of irritation, first at her, then at the other girls, for leaving me here.

'Okay, yeah. Maybe. I'll meet you there?' I said, striving for the non-committal. I felt a thud of guilt as she smiled; it dissipated as the girls rounded the corner, and disappeared from sight.

Freed from Nicky's vice-like grip, I did my best to slip away, squeezing between groups of girls who didn't move as I passed (though on purpose, or simply because I'd so quickly disappeared into the invisible mass of average students, I couldn't tell). In the cool air outside, there was no sign of them, the Quad empty but for a few pockets of girls in pairs, sharing secrets. Starlings hopped along the architraves above the open doors, swooping down to tug twitching worms from the dirt.

Two hands pawed at my face from behind, clumsy fingers poking at eyes and cheeks, and I screamed; a cackle echoed across the Quad. As I turned, Robin grinned her lop-sided smile, eyes puppet-wide and gleaming. 'Come with me,' she said, turning on her heels and walking away.

I stood, transfixed. 'I still have classes,' I called after her. She looked back, and I blushed, furiously, catching the eye of two girls, who'd turned to stare at the crack of nerves in my voice. My heart thudded with such force that I wondered if they could hear that, too; I smiled at them, willing them to look away.

'Robin,' I called again, as she loped away, headed towards the long school driveway. She didn't look back; didn't seem to care whether I followed, or not.

And so, without thought – without question, or doubt, or even the briefest flicker of pride – I followed her, down the hill and through the school gates, the Campanile bell sounding a warning behind.

'Come on, just take one. *One.*' Robin's shoulder pressed against mine, in the town's only real fashion store, where pop music hissed through invisible speakers, and girls tripped giggling between changing rooms, making catwalks of the aisles.

'I can't,' I whispered back, looking down at the candied rows of nail polish, names underneath seeming all wrong, the inverse of themselves: Buttercup for a grassy green, Seashell for baby-blue, Moonlight for black.

'It's not difficult,' she whispered. 'I'll show you.' I watched her hands glide above, like a magician practising a sleight-of-hand. She paused, hovering briefly for a moment, plucked a neon yellow from the rack. In a single, swift motion, it disappeared. Even watching, I couldn't tell whether it was in her pocket, or up her sleeve.

'See?' She moved to admire a case of lipsticks, their black cases shining like beetles. I stood, stunned, waiting for a looming security guard to swoop in and drag us away.

Nothing happened. No one came.

I followed Robin to the counter, where she hovered, thoughtfully chewing her lip. 'It's my birthday next week,' she said, pointedly. Her eyes fixed on a red lipstick. 'That'd go so well with my hair, don't you think?'

'I'll buy it for you,' I said. 'I don't mind.' I had twenty pounds in my purse, my weekly allowance – though I also knew Mum's bank details, and that the settlement sat there, largely untouched. It rarely occurred to either of us, it seemed – that we could have things, live differently, somehow. So we went on as we always had, with off-brand canned foods and frozen microwave dinners. For Mum, it was enough.

Robin rolled her eyes. 'Whatever. If you're too scared, then don't.'

'I'm not scared,' I said, uselessly.

'Well then,' she said, turning to examine a baby-pink t-shirt she'd never, ever wear, eyes lowered, watchful.

I put a trembling hand over the counter, picking one, then another, examining each with what I hoped was casual disinterest. The harried sales assistant explained a refund policy to the mother of a screaming nine-year-old; as the assistant turned away, I slipped the lipstick into my palm, and down my sleeve.

A hand at my shoulder, a heavy slap. I flinched.

'Good girl,' Robin said. 'Let's go.'

The Furies

The air in the street outside was a thrilling relief. I gulped, realizing I'd been holding my breath since I'd tucked the lipstick into my jacket. As we walked, she slid the nail polish out and held it between finger and thumb, close to my face. 'Got something for you, too.' I felt a rush of warmth, a sweet thrill at the gift.

I slid the lipstick from my sleeve, and did the same. She took it, clicking open a mirror she pulled from her pocket – an item even I hadn't seen her take – and applied a dark slick to her lips as we walked, shoppers forced to dodge her, tutting as they passed.

'How do I look?' she said, turning to me, pouting.

'Gorgeous,' I laughed. It was true. To me, at least, she did.

She grabbed me by the shoulder and planted an exaggerated, ridiculous kiss on my cheek. 'Now you're gorgeous too,' she said, grinning, the lipstick smudged with the impact, flecks of red on her teeth. I felt I ought to laugh, but couldn't; I was too stunned. I stumbled along beside her, speechless and blind, as she chattered on about classes, homework she refused to do ('on principle,' she said, not explaining what, exactly, the principle was) and girls she hated, their crimes seeming to me like instructions, things I would no longer say or do.

As I look back, it seems ridiculous. And yet, though I have loved, and been loved, in the decades since we met, no infatuation could compare to the outrageous intensity of those first weeks with Robin.

I wanted to know every part of her, and she craved my secrets just the same. We each felt the raw crush of the other's nerve-endings; we shared experiences great and small, sitting under trees dropping red leaves around us, glowing in the autumn sun. Occasionally, I would think of Emily Frost, as we passed the faded posters stuck to lampposts and trees, and the question would gather in my throat – *Is she the reason you like me?* But I'd brush the thought away, press it wilfully into forgetting, and take her interest in me as my own; raise some new topic of conversation, a new intimacy shared.

It seems impossible, now, to imagine an intensity so feverish, such delirium. Perhaps that's a symptom of getting older. One's feelings wear down, no longer sparking so keenly. Still, when I think of Robin, of those early days when our friendship was new and unfamiliar, I feel a swell deep within my chest, an echo of those heady days, when we ducked into a rain-battered chip shop and shared a single cone as we walked along the promenade, laughing at the withered old women and screaming kids, who seemed so stupid, so beneath us, so deserving of our contempt. When we smoked rolled-up cigarettes and stubbed them out in the sand, the detritus of summer – cans, fools' emeralds made from broken bottles – shifting beneath our feet. When we drank sickly-sweet alcopops from glass bottles, breaking the caps on the metal backs of graffitied bus seats. Every breath, every moment, possessed with an illusion of glamour, of filthy decadence, purely because it was ours, we two our own radical world, a star collapsing inwards and bursting, gorgeous, in the dark.

Not, of course, that I was able to imagine this then, still chattering shyly as we walked along the pier, the setting sun turning the sea blood-red. I heard a familiar voice, and turned to see Nicky bounding towards the two of us. Robin let out a groan, and I swatted her arm. 'Shhh,' I hissed, feeling my cheeks redden as Nicky approached, caught in a lie. I'd mentioned her invitation to Robin earlier – this, admittedly, an attempt at making Robin jealous, though it seemed only to have the opposite effect: she had told me I was lucky, blessed to have been rescued, her hatred of Nicky vicious and clear.

And yet, I realized, as Nicky approached, *it was Robin's idea to come here, now.*

'How are you doing?' Nicky said, as she strolled towards us, clutching an enormous stuffed bear (or cat – it was cheaply made, and hard to tell). She saw me staring at it. 'Ben—' she turned and pointed to a tall, tanned boy in a football shirt, lurking several paces behind '—he won it for me. Isn't it cute?'

'If you're into that kind of thing,' Robin muttered.

Nicky ignored her, and turned to me. 'Are you coming to the party on Friday?'

She looked at Robin, who scowled back. 'What party?' I said, at the same time as Robin said 'Yeah, she's coming,' the two of us laughing, awkwardly.

'Awesome,' Nicky said, pretending not to see, though a half-smile passed on her lips, a whisper of a smirk. 'Also,' she said, expression instantly serious, tone conspiratorial, 'I wanted to ask . . . Is Grace okay?'

I felt my stomach drop; glanced at Robin. 'I . . . I haven't seen her. Why?'

'Well, Stacey – you know Stacey, in the lacrosse team? She broke her finger at a match last Friday night. Which is horrendously bad timing, because we need her for the squad when we play . . . ' I felt myself dragged into the long and complex history of the school lacrosse team, and nodded dimly, waiting for her to return to the matter in hand. '*Anyway*,' she said, finally, 'she was at A&E and she said she saw Grace in the waiting room with Alex, looking like she'd been hit by a bus.'

'She's fine,' Robin said. She looked out at the seagulls criss-crossing in the air, diving at unsuspecting tourists clutching fried doughnuts and newsprint-covered chips.

'I don't know . . . Bloody nose, black eye . . . Not that you'd know under all that make-up, mind. It's a shame, really. She's got such a pretty face.'

I shook my head. 'I haven't spoken to her. I didn't know anything had happened.' I turned to Robin. 'Did you?'

'No,' she said, looking down between the broad slats of the pier.

'Well, I thought you might know. Jodie – Jodie with the short hair, the lesbian-looking girl in the upper class – she asked Alex if Grace was okay this morning when she saw her, and Alex said she didn't know what she was talking about. Which is kind of weird, right? I mean, if she was there and all. Which she must've been, because Stacey wouldn't lie about something like that.'

I shrugged, though it seemed, based on Nicky's sideways look, that my attempt at nonchalance was unsuccessful. 'I'll let you know if I hear anything,' I said, at last. This seemed to appease her. Nicky smiled, leaned in to kiss my cheek – an affectation I suspected (though I couldn't be sure) she'd adopted in some sly imitation of Robin, one's lips marking the spot where the other's lipstick had been, before – and bobbed off towards town, boyfriend in tow, leaving the two of us walking silently towards the sea.

Robin spoke, finally, when we reached the railings, looking out into the nothing. 'Her dad's a total psycho.' She clung on, leaned back, and swung there for a moment, before pulling herself back. 'Grace's, I mean. He's why she's always got bruises.'

I turned to face her, a dull sickness rising. 'He hits her?'

'Yeah,' she said.

'Oh,' I said. 'Can't we—'

'She says it's not our business. Like, she won't talk about it. Ever.'

'Oh,' I said again, uselessly. Silence fell, broken only by the clack and chatter of seagulls swooping above, the waves rattling the pier below. 'Where's the party?' I said, at last, desperate to break the silence. I felt bad for Grace, truly; but my thoughts kept wandering back to Nicky's other comment. The party. Robin hadn't said anything, and if Nicky hadn't brought it up, I wasn't sure she would've mentioned it at all.

'Halloween party,' she said. 'My boyfriend's throwing it. You should meet him.' She chewed, thoughtfully, at her finger, biting off a hangnail and spitting it into the water below. 'Lots of boys in his halls, too. You might find one yourself.'

'Halloween isn't for another week.'

'So?'

'I don't have a costume.'

'You won't need one. Wear what you've got on now, and no one'll tell the difference.'

I threw a bottle cap at her, sand rolling back on the wind. I'd never been with a boy, never so much as kissed one. I wasn't entirely sure I wanted to. I thought back to my old school, scrappy, howling boys who'd tug and paw at the girls who let them, who encouraged them, and who told each other elaborate stories of who loved who, and how they'd fucked. It all seemed a lot of work, even if they *had* shown any interest in me (which, of course, they hadn't).

Still, the prospect of a night with Robin, in what I imagined might be the more sophisticated, mature company of university students, was too tempting to refuse. 'Can't wait,' I said, as the last spark of the sunset clipped the edge of the horizon, and the first brush of night air echoed in the wind.

The university was on the far side of town, only a couple of miles from the Kirkwood – and it possessed none of the grandeur of the grounds to which I'd by now become somewhat accustomed (though even now I am not wholly immune to the bloom of evening light behind the Campanile, or the froth of raindrops glowing above the Great Hall's sage and silver dome on a cool spring day). I'd only ever been dimly aware that it existed, and even now never thought of it as a university. It was 'the old poly', or 'the college', to residents of the town, and I had never thought of it in any other terms.

All *béton brut* and gabions, grey crumbling into black, it was impressive, in its own way, and almost a better fit for the town: ugly in a way that seemed to be somehow intentional. Aggressive, even. The tower, indeed, had cut a lonely but ever-present figure in my childhood, the only tower building in the whole town – wide and squat, with gangways connecting its two halves, a ladder leaning on the sky. The leaves hung wincing from the trees, or cracked underfoot, scratching at the pavement; the sky grey and fat with mist, words made visible in the cool night air.

When Robin and I had met, in the dim lights of the bus station, where the shelters rattled in the evening wind, she'd thrown her arms around me in an overblown hug. 'You look amazing,' I said, the words muffled by the crush of her shoulder, the wide, black brim of her witch's hat.

'I know,' she said, pulling away. 'What . . . What are you meant to be?'

I tugged at the back of my coat, the blooming flash of red. 'Red Riding Hood,' I said, blushing; knowing, already, that it was stupid, a childish idea.

She laughed. 'Okay, so, before I say anything else: you are adorable,' she said, the words shot through and veined with sarcasm. 'But this is a grown-up party. You need to look the part.' She pulled me down onto the cold metal seat beside her, and began rooting through her bag, chewing thoughtfully at her smudged, blackened lips.

An old man, stinking of sweat and stale alcohol, paused to stare as she reached for my chin; instructed me to close my eyes, and hold still. I don't know how long he stood there, though the smell of him lingered as I sat, waiting, feeling myself watched. And yet the touch of her, the assurance with which she smoothed foundation into my skin, brushed powder gently into the hollows of my eyes; the way she laughed, a little, when she told me to pout, the feel of breath on my skin as she leaned in to paint my lips . . . *It doesn't matter who sees*, I thought. *I don't care.*

'There,' she said, at last. 'What do you think?'

I opened my eyes, blinking in the light; caught my reflection in the threaded glass of the windows as the bus shuddered in behind. Eyes lined with soft, smudged kohl, made them wider, their expression somehow no longer mine; lips lined fat, a blooming red. A painted shadow in the hollow of my cheeks.

I looked wholly unlike myself, somehow, drawn into a new self by her. And as I blinked once, and again, I felt a shudder of recognition. My features made fuller, more vivid, I looked, now, like the taped-up photos of Emily Frost, pocked and faded by the wind.

'Do you like it?' she said, she, too, watching my reflection in the glass.

'Wow,' I said, unsure what else to say.

She talked, almost without pausing for breath, all the way to the campus, flitting from one topic to another. About her little sister, whose obsession with a certain TV show meant Robin had to listen to it playing through the walls in the middle of the night. About a tattoo she'd been thinking of getting, that she'd drawn 'fifty thousand times' but couldn't get quite right. About a horror movie she'd seen but couldn't remember the name of, though a scene in which a woman had been chopped to pieces had struck her as 'fundamentally unrealistic,' because 'there'd obviously be way more blood.' I wondered about mentioning the accident, the strange absence of blood (in memory, at least) – but I couldn't find the words. I'd told her almost everything, but never that. I didn't want her pity; wasn't sure I could bear to be anything but the girl she thought I was.

At the foot of the tower, voices and music roared from an open window several floors above. Robin grabbed my hand, and we walked through the wooden doors to a dull reception area, a single security guard sitting at a tiny screen, surrounded on all sides by lewd graffiti and defaced postcards. 'Ladies,' he said, with a grunt. 'You students here?'

'You really don't recognize us by now?' Robin said. 'It's me! Robin. Tenth floor.' He shrugged and turned back to his screen, disinterested.

'I can't believe that worked,' I whispered as we stood in the lift, Robin picking at her make-up in a mirror coated with dust and handprints, '*FUCK THE TORIES*' scrawled in lipstick overhead.

'Whatever. One of the boys would've come and rescued us, anyway,' she said, with an overblown wink. I laughed. I had doubts about her boyfriend Andy's capacity for rescue, based on the stories I'd heard from Alex and Grace earlier in the week, but held my tongue.

The lift shuddered to a halt on the eighth floor. 'It only goes this far. Party's on floor ten.' She kicked the door, once; then again. It opened with a groan, and we stepped out into a dull corridor, the air curdling with a lingering smell of damp clothes and spilled beer.

I walked a few feet behind, pausing to examine the lurid posters and photographs stuck to each door. As I looked at one – a poster for Glastonbury Festival, two years earlier, the list of bands in such tiny print I had to lean in to take a look – the door swung open. I stumbled backwards, and Robin swung around, turning back.

In the doorway stood a tall, scraggly student, hair mussed as though he'd been interrupted from sleep, though given the pounding music above, this seemed highly unlikely (though I would eventually learn, through my own undergraduate experience, that it is indeed possible to sleep through anything, if one has enough work to ignore). 'What's this?' he yawned.

'Howdy,' Robin said, not missing a beat. She extended a hand with a half-ironic formality which seemed capable of diffusing even the most fraught situations. 'Robin Adams, pleased to meet you. This is Vivi. We're going to a party – want to come?'

He stood staring blankly at her outstretched hand for a moment, blinking away sleep. 'You're inviting me to a party in the building I live in?'

'Well, it's my boyfriend's party, so I figure technically I'm the hostess. Kind of,' she said. 'That means I get to invite who I like, even if they do live a few floors below and consider themselves above a formal invitation. And even if they don't introduce themselves properly. Like, with a name.'

He glanced at me, for a split second, before turning back to Robin. 'I'm Tom,' he said, with a smile that gave his face an almost wolfish quality, attractive in a way I couldn't place. I felt a flash of envy, in spite of myself, as he finally took Robin's hand.

'Charmed, I'm sure,' she replied, coyly. 'Well, we're going to the party. Come if you want, or don't. Your choice.' She turned and strolled down the corridor, and I followed, looking back briefly to see Tom leaning in the doorway, still dazed by the encounter. He waved; I turned away and rushed to catch Robin, cheeks flushed with shame.

'Bit of a rake, no?' she said, when I reached the tenth floor to find her sitting on the railing, the ten floors below a sheer drop.

'He looked like he needs a shower.'

'They're uni students. They all look like that.' She laughed. 'God, if you don't like him, just wait till you meet Andy.'

On this, she was not mistaken. Andy, I would soon discover, was a skinny, mantis of a man, who – when we finally arrived, after a circuitous conversation with a student sitting red-eyed on the floor outside – was holding court on a single bed in an incongruously large dorm room, filthy dreadlocks clinging to his white, pimpled back in the fetid heat of the room. Even above the music, his voice carried shrilly, surrounded as he was by dazed students passing a succession of thick, glowing joints.

'I'm not saying Ayn Rand isn't problematic,' he said, grandly. 'It's just that some of her ideas weren't entirely without a kernel of truth. It just requires an open mind to see it.' He coughed, a brittle, hacking cough, and Robin sidled up beside him to pat him gently on the back. He pulled her in for a nauseatingly long kiss, pausing for a drag on a joint, breathing the smoke into Robin's open mouth. She turned to the group and, to my horror, pointed to me. 'This is Vivi,' she announced.

'Hi, Vivi,' they replied, as though hypnotized. *Vivi*, I thought, as I waved, awkwardly, and wandered to the makeshift bar in the far corner of the room. *She sounds like fun.* I poured a slug of off-brand cola into what looked to be an unused mug, whose faded university label proudly advertised 'exceptional careers for exceptional students'. The warm liquid stuck in my throat, sharp and cloying.

I watched the mass of students, and wondered if this might be my own future; then, too, what exactly might be said to recommend it. I saw a girl dressed in a sleek Hepburn dress and tiara swaying precariously close to the open window, while a boy, deathly pale and shimmering with fake blood talked at her, staring wide-eyed into the middle distance. A few feet away, two girls – each with hair in luminous colours, turquoise green and Barbie pink, their make-up vivid, clown-like – sat cross-legged on the floor, engaged in a conversation that seemed to be turning sour. The girl facing me seemed to be growing more unsteady with every sip of vodka, taken directly from the by-now half-drained bottle; I counted a further three gulps before she rose, swaying, and stumbled out into the white glare of the hallway. A group of boys in ragged caveman furs stormed across the room, howling wildly, and proceeded to empty a carton of washing powder out of the window, onto some poor victim below. When it hit, they roared louder still, their hoots reminiscent of some monstrous creatures I had seen, once, on a nature programme.

Robin bounded over and poured herself a drink, topping mine up with a large slug of rum as she did so. 'You like?' she said, grinning.

'Yeah, it's cool,' I lied, lifting the mug to my lips. The liquid was hot and searing; a rancid, chemical smell. I lowered the cup without swallowing, relieved to find her attentions elsewhere.

'I love university parties. Not exactly the height of sophis-tication, but it's nice to be around adults for a change.' I searched her face for the irony absent from her voice, and nodded, solemnly, suppressing my own opinions on the matter. 'Listen, I know it's not normally your thing, but . . . Do you want one of these?' She opened her palm, revealing a couple of white pills, their texture dusty, imprinted with a flower.

'If it's an aspirin, then definitely,' I said, drily.

'No pressure. It's just . . . I thought I'd offer, so you don't feel like you're missing out.'

The boys roared again, now hurling bricks of soap and sopping balls of toilet paper out into the street below. The princess returned, tapped her friend on the shoulder, and gave her a weak kiss; the swaying girl still swayed, and the talking boy still talked.

I took the pill from Robin's outstretched palm, and held it, nervously, in my own. I felt Robin wrap her arm around my shoulder with something like tenderness. 'If you don't like it, all you have to do is say you want to go. That's it. If you feel weird, we'll go straight home.' The press of her, the promise, was enough: I swallowed the pill, washing it down with the searing, sour drink.

For the next fifteen minutes, I felt nothing, though I shud-dered at every suggestion of warmth, every heartbeat a portent of doom. I had heard the stories of otherwise well-behaved teenagers who had died a sudden death from their first encounter with drugs, and imagined the cold words of the coroner's report. My heartbeat quickened and slowed, the sense of panic rising and falling as I remembered, somehow, to breathe.

Still nothing, one moment of nothing after another, a nothing hollow with anticipation, until all at once a panoramic, gorgeous fullness burst around me, the air syrupy, the people diaphanous, unreal. I felt suddenly detached, watching the students around me, each with their own unique preoccupations and ideals, and felt a sense of oneness, an appreciation of other subjectivities beyond my own. Potent chemicals and sweat-ravaged debauchery: the source, no doubt, of the open-minded idealism for which students are known.

I turned to Robin, wanting to tell her everything – not only of this moment, but my whole life story, every secret emotion I had ever held in my heart, all the things I couldn't say – only to find her seat now taken by the boy from the eighth floor, whose name I could no longer remember. Had he told us? I wasn't sure.

'How did you get here?' I asked, reaching for the arms of the chair in an attempt to still the roiling room.

'The stairs,' he said, flatly. 'Have you . . . Are you drunk?'

'That sounds like something I am,' I said, the words nonsense, confused. I felt a burning heat in the palms of my hands, and released the chair from my vice-like grip.

'Little more than drunk, judging by those pupils,' he said, leaning in towards me.

I pulled away. 'It's none of your business.'

He winced. 'Ouch.'

'Sorry,' I muttered. I looked for Robin, scanning the room for the red glow of her hair. I saw her, back with Andy, who sat on the floor while she straddled his shoulders from the bed above, leaning over him occasionally for a kiss, her hair falling in strings down his chest, his fingers clutching at them, possessively. I felt sick, overwhelmingly sick, and looked down at the space between my knees, where the lines of the carpet curved and swelled like the roll of the sea.

'Do you want some water or something?' I'd forgotten I was being watched. I turned to him, slowly, feeling my neck and jaw tense, tongue thick in my throat.

'Please.' I felt both brimming with life, and horribly close to death. 'It's so hot,' I said, as he handed me a plastic cup filled with dirty, bruised ice.

'Sip it,' he said, not letting go of the cup. 'Don't gulp it, or you'll throw up.'

'Okay,' I said. The syllables sounded wrong, almost like a sing-song. 'Okay, okay, okay,' I said, impressed by the cadence of the letters. He laughed, took a step back, as though unsure of himself; then paused for a moment, and sat back down, slowly sipping his drink. I felt a swell, another flush of love for the people around me, and, in the moment, this stranger, who had come to me with iced water and kind words. 'Thank you,' I said, with what I hoped was a smile.

'Any time,' he said. 'Would some fresh air help?'

'I'm not . . . I'm not going anywhere near that window.' I heard the words slur a little as I spoke, returning with a perfect echo.

'Oh god, no. You're absolutely not going near any windows, or sharp edges, or anywhere without childproofing.'

'I'm not—'

'I don't mean that,' he said, catching my meaning before I

61

could finish my sentence. 'I just mean you don't need to worry. You can't get in much more trouble than you already are.'

He extended a hand, and pulled me up towards him. Grateful to escape, I stumbled with him into the corridor, where the bright lights and lurid posters swam kaleidoscopic above the stained tan carpets and beaten, grey walls. Stumbling down the stairs, I felt the glow of the fluorescent lights, switching on and off rhythmically as though time had slowed to accommodate their usual invisible flicker.

The words on the posters followed me down the stairs – *Dance Society Meet next week, Mason Hall, 5pm; Basketball Tryouts Tuesday – shorties need not apply!; Kafka's Metamorphosis :: Auditions Monday!!!* Occasionally I felt a rumble of doubt, the same hot sweat rising from the soles of my feet to my chest, but the feeling disappeared as soon as I had identified it, the memory delirious and fleeting.

As we reached the ground floor, the rhythm of the music echoing from above seemed still as loud as it had been in the dorm room. I put my hands over my ears, my head aching; Tom stopped as we rounded the corner, and put my hands back by my sides. 'Act normal,' he whispered, and walked me past the security guard (though the caution was unnecessary, he now absorbed in a tattered paperback with no interest in the activities of the students who occasionally disturbed his reading). I thought of Robin as we left the building. *She'll be fine*, I told myself. And then, a little bitterly, *she said she'd stay with me, and she didn't, so it doesn't matter anyway*.

There is something enchanting about fresh air when

intoxicated; though remaining steady in it is a skill I have yet to master, even now, when the mood of a long night strikes and I wander these old streets, unseen and unheard, after a night at home sipping a rich wine and, on occasion, taking some strange combination of powders and pills. Nowadays, of course, these are more likely to be opiates or sedatives prescribed by my friendly and dutifully sympathetic family doctor; still, that feeling always reminds me of this night, when the air was hazy and alive with a kind of magic.

Outside, the sky had cleared to black. As I looked up, he steered me around the slick of washing powder and soap thrown from the floor above, and we walked in silence towards the lake, around which student halls were arranged. With hindsight, 'lake' is, perhaps, a little too grand: the light of day would reveal it to be little more than a large pond, surrounded by concrete walls on all sides. As we approached, a flock of birds burst into flight, disappearing into the infinite darkness above.

He tucked his hands into his pockets; took them out, as though caught.

'You don't say much, do you?' he said. I felt a sort of pity for him, a painful identification; I didn't know what to do either.

I shrugged. 'What do you want to talk about?'

He said nothing; turned and sat on the graffitied park bench behind. I joined him, wondering what I was doing; why I was so eager to follow this stranger into the dark night.

He leaned forward, elbows resting on his knees. 'How old are you?'

'Seventeen,' I lied, feeling ashamed the moment the word left my lips. What was I trying to achieve?

He turned and looked at me, doubtfully. From the tower, a firework sparked and burst, leaving a yellow trail through the sky. I watched as it spiralled, dwindling down, the casing landing with a splash in the dark water. He drew breath beside me, and paused.

'My girlfriend . . .' he began. I felt a pang of loss at expectations I hadn't realized, or at least admitted, I was harbouring: some midnight kiss, a childish imagining of romance. 'She's at Cambridge.'

I looked at him, unsure if I was imagining the note of apology in his voice. 'How'd you meet?' I said, the words ringing false, cheerful. We were amateurs reading lines, failing to perform.

'The usual. Same school, same friends . . . You know.' I nodded, solemnly, though I, of course, had no idea. 'I think she's probably met someone else, though,' he sighed.

I gave a non-committal murmur, and he continued, though now – the chill of the night gnawing at my skin, the memory of Robin now an ache – I wanted to go back. I waited as he went on – a lack of letters, calls returned late or not at all – and, finally, gave a dramatic shudder. 'I'm cold.'

He said nothing for a moment, as though surprised at the interruption; surprised, it seemed, to find me there at all. He blinked, and stood, and I followed. Occasionally he would pause to examine a discarded beer bottle on the ground or one of the dolls I now noticed had been hung from the sparse branches of the trees, which creaked and groaned in the wind.

Every time I looked back, he smiled, and I mirrored him, unsure how else to respond. It was as though we were playing a game, the rules of which I – in my intoxicated state, at least – felt myself unable to grasp.

'Where the fuck have you been?' Robin hissed as we entered the reception area, where she sat perched on the security guard's desk, he now a little put out, realizing he was no longer of use. She jumped off the desk and moved so close it seemed her breath was mingling with mine. Her pupils were wide and deep, and it looked as though she had been crying, her eyes wet, shards of mascara littered underneath. I saw Nicky, lurking behind, watching with interest; I waved, dimly, and she smiled, disappearing up the stairs.

'She's fine,' Tom said, wearily. 'She just needed some fresh air.'

'Really?' Robin said, her tone arch. She turned to me. 'Fresh air?'

I nodded. I felt oddly ashamed, a swell of guilt rising as I tried to recall my reasons for leaving her behind.

'Wanna go home?' Robin said, after a pause. I felt the world lurch forwards, and another wave of nausea struck me like a punch to the gut.

'Home sounds good.'

'Okay,' Robin said. She turned again to Tom, who was already walking back towards the stairs. 'Thanks for looking after her,' she said, though I thought I heard a note of sarcasm in her voice.

'Any time,' he replied, without looking. His footsteps echoed up the steps as we left the tower, and stepped out once again into the night. The brief moment of warmth in the reception hall served only to heighten the cold outside, which now felt biting and cruel. We walked in silence, down the hill towards the edge of campus, through a dark passage lined with chicken-wire fences and overhanging trees fused into a tangled canopy above.

'I'm sorry for leaving,' I said, a little relieved at the sound of my voice which, for the first time in hours, sounded like my own.

'It's fine,' Robin said, a few paces ahead. We walked a little longer in silence, before she added, 'I had a fight with Andy. I think we're over.'

I felt a rush of relief at this, the implication that perhaps her tears were not on my account, but his. 'I'm sure it's not that bad,' I offered, awkwardly.

'How would you know?' She turned to me, eyes flashing anger.

'I don't, obviously,' I said. 'What I mean is . . . ' I clawed for some non-committal phrase, something to appease her. 'I don't know. Maybe it'll be better in the morning. You probably just need to sleep on it.'

She sighed. 'I don't want to be rude,' she said, slowly. 'But what experience do you have, exactly, that puts you in a position to be doling out relationship advice?' Her eyes were dark in the orange glow of the street lamps, her shadow long and distorted up ahead. I felt my cheeks burn red hot, and, grateful for the cover of night, I looked down at my feet, watching the fabric of my shoes flash and listening to the tap of the pavement as we walked.

The Furies

When we reached the mermaid, Robin leaned in and gave me a stiff peck on the cheek, gripping the hair at the nape of my neck with a clutch that felt just a little tense, her squeeze a little too tight. Without a word, she turned and walked away, her figure casting a long shadow as she disappeared into the night. I walked home in a stunned trance, remembering as I reached my front door that I had told my mum I'd be staying at Robin's (her house a cover for a party expected to go on until dawn). I climbed the stairs and nervously crawled into bed, my mind uselessly grasping for answers as I tumbled into a cold, dreamless sleep.

Chapter 4

Robin chewed her pencil, turning it about in the gap between her teeth with a hollow click. I rose from my seat, ostensibly to sharpen my own pencil. In fact, I was bereft of ideas and looking for something to steal. Annabel's cryptic prompt: 'Destination'. The air was milky, tinged pink, the windows draped in gauze and tulle. A faint smell of slowly rotting flowers mingled with clay and turpentine on the air. Annabel – whose cheekbones pressed up against her wrinkled skin in smooth points, and whose white hair hung down her spine in thick, loose rings – liked to change the studio weekly, following some unspoken theme. Sometimes spartan, white and clean and sometimes moonlit, the sky blocked by starry batiks and luminescent, the effect was one of perpetual change: our ways of seeing challenged, time and again.

Annabel hadn't spoken to me directly for several weeks. Hadn't even looked at me, in fact, though occasionally I'd feel as though I was being watched, sitting in the studio trying to untangle the threads of a lecture, or a prompt. But whenever

I looked at her, she seemed to be absorbed in a book while chewing thoughtfully at a hangnail, or scrawling furiously in a paint-flecked notebook, as though none of us were there at all.

Muddled sketches of airports and cars; pastel beaches and sunbathers, both realist and cartoonish, idealized or grotesque: my fellow students had responded to the prompt as unimaginatively as I had, though with varying degrees of success. Except, that is, for Robin. Hers was a dark, gloomy charcoal sketch, black dust lining her fingers and smudged at her wrists: a wood of trees curving claw-like above a rocky path. Emerging from the light at the end, two figures stood in silhouette, limbs monstrously thin, the backs of their hands barely touching, brushing against one another.

Hers was the only work Annabel would peer at from above, as she made cursory circuits of the class (usually only as the Headmaster passed, his passion for 'active teaching' being taken rather literally, for Annabel, at least). I watched the other girls watch Robin with an envy that disappeared in an instant, a shadow only seen in the corner of the eye, a weakness for Annabel's attentions none of us would willingly admit. But I felt it – the dim awareness of it was its own kind of shame – though when she passed I leaned farther forward, arms wrapped around my work, embarrassed at the childish scratch and scrawl.

Annabel looked up as though about to speak, interrupted by the shuddering bell, the shuffle of students awakened from the silence. 'Complete these for next session and we'll discuss,' she shouted over the noise, 'and try not to be too vapid, if you can possibly manage it!' She paused, and turned to me. 'Violet – a word, if I may.'

I froze. Robin turned to me and grinned, stuffing the drawing carelessly into her bag. She shuffled past, mouthing 'See you later.' I smiled, weakly, my stomach churning with fear.

As the studio emptied, Annabel rifled through a mass of papers, not looking up. I stood, nervously mute, as the plastic clock ticked a full minute above. 'Here we are,' she said at last, handing me a crumpled sheet of paper. 'You wrote this?' I felt a knot of shame, sensing what was coming next. It was a belligerent, thoughtlessly thrown together admissions essay, drafted in the hope my application might be rejected, before I'd been tempted by the photos of ancient archways, the sun blooming behind the Campanile. Though I'd succeeded in impressing Annabel so far – or, at least, had avoided the cold glare of her attention – I'd known, somehow, that it would come back to haunt me.

'"The purpose of art",' she said, reading my words, '"is to horrify the idiots who say they have taste. Taste means nothing. Fuck taste. The idea itself is a relic of a version of history that doesn't apply to me, or anyone not closer to being buried than being born."' She looked up at me, eyebrow sharply raised. 'You wrote this?'

'Yes, Miss,' I said, staring down at the page.

'And you believe it?' I looked up. She stared at me, eyes cold, rolling a silver pen between her fingers.

'I . . . Well, kind of.'

The rolling stopped. 'Kind of?'

'Yes.'

'Yes, kind of, or yes, you mean it?'

'Yes, I mean it,' I said, finally, though in truth I wasn't sure – the words then had seemed a little much, and now, absurd. It was a guess, a leap: grasping for the answer she wanted to hear.

'Good,' she said, softly. 'Very good. Violet, I hold advanced classes for those students I think have promise.' An endless pause; I looked away, unable to hold her stare. 'I'd like to invite you to join our little study group, if you're interested.'

The blinds whipped furiously in the breeze. 'Yes, Miss. I mean, Annabel. Sorry.'

'Good. I'm glad to hear it,' she said, rising from her chair and walking towards the window. 'Though I would ask that you keep this between us. It is strictly invitation only. Off the books, as it were.' She slammed the window shut. 'Do you know Miss Adams?'

'I don't think so.'

'Robin,' she said, turning to me. 'The red-haired girl. I saw you admiring her work. She's very talented.'

I blushed. 'She is.'

'She'll meet you before class and bring you along.' She sat down at the desk and picked up the pen, hand hovering over the page. I stood, waiting for some kind of detail – a time, a day even – but she said nothing. After a moment, she looked up, as though surprised to see me there. 'That's all then, Violet.'

In the corridor outside, the cool, fresh air made the studio seem suddenly stifling, my lungs thick with turpentine and paint, eyes adjusting to the light of day. A short, round-faced girl with a shadow of hair above her lip stood waiting, eyeing me nervously. I looked at her, ashamed for us both, and hurried away, though where to, I wasn't sure.

The soles of my shoes clapped against the marble floor, heart thudding in my chest. I was alone, the place deserted, silent but for the infrared hum of the scanners below. I peered over the rim of the mezzanine that circled the entrance hall, all Doric columns and gold railings, mahogany cases behind housing grinning taxidermied voles, death masks, and candied jewels.

I had been reading some fiendishly dull (yet still to this day widely read) textbook on the history of realist art and – lulled by the numbing warmth of the old radiators and seams of afternoon sunlight that filled the top floor – had fallen asleep at my desk. When I woke, I found a sky-blue paper bird folded on top of my book, a precise, delicate little thing. I unfolded it, gingerly, and stared down at the words. 'Welcome to the club. Campanile, 6 o'clock sharp. Brace yourself. R.' I looked out of the window, and saw the clock's black hands click on – 5:50pm – threw my books into my bag, and ran.

I heard footsteps behind, a mumbled curse. The Dean of Students was balancing a teetering stack of books on one arm as he stumbled across the mezzanine opposite. 'Violet,' he said, catching my eye. 'What on earth are you doing here so late?' His voice echoed across the hall. Loath to shout back (my own voice reedy, thin), I waited until we'd met in the middle, by the stairwell, to answer.

'I was studying, sir. I lost track of time.'

'Evidently.' He chuckled. 'You know, the library closes to students at four, except for around finals.'

'I didn't realize,' I said. 'I'll get out of your way.'

He drew breath, as though about to speak – then paused, resting the books on the ledge. Their spines, leather-bound in different, faded colours, each read of a similar topic: *The Persecution of Witches, a History*; *Demons and Darkness, a Study of the Occult*; *Contemporary Theories of Magick*. I imagined the crash as they fell, willed it a little, to interrupt the conversation I was about to endure.

'Violet,' he began, rocking his neck back and forth. (I imagined his muscles loosening, imagined the words: trapezioid, splenius, levator scapulae . . .) 'If you're having trouble making friends . . . ' He reached a hand for my shoulder, fingers clubbed and nicked with cuts.

'I'm not,' I said, abruptly, stepping back.

His hand hung suspended for a moment; then, seeming to remember himself, he slipped it back into his pocket, fingers toying with something underneath. 'It's just . . . Well, you're here so late. Not that we don't encourage commitment to one's studies, but . . . '

'I'm friends with Robin. And Grace, and Alex,' I said, a slight wobble in my voice that could have related to either the intimation that I was friendless and alone or my frustration at being waylaid. I caught a brief flicker cross his face, a shadow of doubt.

'Well, that's good,' he said at last. 'But do make sure to keep making friends in other groups, too. You don't want to get tied into a clique, now, do you?'

'No, sir,' I lied. I could think of nothing I wanted more.

'Good, good. I'd better be getting on,' he said, smile fixed wide as he slid the books into his arms. 'Help me open this door now, would you?'

I waited until the door closed behind him, and ran down the stairs, catching myself as I tripped once on the third floor, and again on the first. I pushed the heavy main doors open, air bracingly cool, and ran towards the Campanile.

The first bell rang as I stepped under the arch, the noise deafening, vibrating in the air and through the ground beneath my feet. Robin wasn't there.

I opened the little bird in my palm (now mangled, since I'd been unable to put it back together) and read the words again. 6 o'clock sharp. I peered back through the arches, but the Quad was deserted, silent but for the rustle of leaves between each of the bell's long tolls. After a moment, I stepped back into the shadows and looked up into the tower's golden underbelly, then around; following a carved serpent knotted around the grille, I saw it. Another folded note, tucked between the bars. Another bird, this time a deep crimson colour, and more complex than the last. I reached in and plucked it from the grate, and as the last bell fell silent a key fell to the ground with a sharp ring. I scooped it up, and tried the lock.

A crack, a rattle, and the grille slid open, the void black within. I stepped inside, and felt the air begin to sour as the inner door slammed shut, darkness stony and absolute.

'Hello?' I whispered, my voice ringing back. I reached

around, scraped my knuckles on the stone walls, slammed palms mutely on the door behind. Silence crawled into every space, into the cracks between the bricks, the knots in the wooden door. I plugged the keyhole with my finger, gripped the handle tight, and stood until the air stilled, panic settling heavy around me. I took a deep breath. Was this some kind of initiation? Or – I thought, guts turning over and again – was it simply a cruel joke?

And if so . . . how long would she leave me here? An hour? Or all night? I felt my heartbeat quicken further as I turned back into the narrow chamber, finding a recess to my right. I took a step towards it, pawing at my pockets for a lighter with one hand (smoking still an affectation more than a habit, an excuse to lurk where the girls might be) and holding my other arm in front, pressed against the damp, creeping walls. In a ridiculous moment of vanity – pretentious, thinking myself some out-of-century bohemian – I'd bought matches, instead. I struck two out, missing the strip in the darkness, before the third caught and the room burst into a brief, warm light.

'If this were a horror movie, you'd be about to die,' Robin said, breath hot against my cheek.

'You bitch,' I said, my heart thudding, as she bent double, gulping with laughter. 'What was that for?' The match burned out, singeing my fingers, and we stood, again, in the dark. She clicked a switch, and a torch lit the chamber in a bright, full beam.

Seeing me again, she leaned against the wall and resumed her hysterics.

'Sorry,' she said, as I began to laugh too (though perhaps

with relief, rather than any sense of humour about the situation). 'I just couldn't resist.'

'Well, thanks a lot. That's at least a decade taken off the end of my life.'

'See! That's the spirit. I did you a favour. Die young, leave a beautiful corpse, blah blah blah.' She looked me up and down, a split-second glance that made me immediately aware of my body, filling the narrow space. 'Come on. Follow me.' She paused. 'Lift's out of order, so we've got to walk.'

She swung the torch around to reveal a flight of steps leading upwards, some strange language etched on the ceiling and walls in faded, white chalk. Up we went, the darkness warped and flickering behind Robin's silhouette, distorted by the light. After two flights, the floor beneath turned from stone to wood; our footsteps echoed loud and hollow, the occasional board wobbling or creaking underfoot in warning. Robin quickly disappeared ahead, her footsteps heavy above, leaving me feeling my way in the dark. I felt my way through turns in the stone staircase, keeping my balance with the wall; lit another match and looked up to see another five or six floors, the light fleeting in the draught that blew it swiftly out.

'Violet?' Robin's voice rebounded sing-song down each flight, passing me by and continuing into the darkness below.

'Yeah?' I shouted back, taking a moment to steady my breath.

'Come on, fat arse. Pick up the pace a bit.' I winced, ashamed, and duly hurried, grateful that the darkness disguised my blush.

By the time I reached the top, I was giddy and breathless, all too aware of the altitude and my own horrifying lack of balance, the stairs having lost their railings two floors earlier. There was a horrifying void in the centre of the tower, down into the darkness of what I would later realize was the old elevator shaft, a fall into which one would be unlikely to survive.

In my exhaustion I stood for a moment, listening to the hiss and scratch of rats several floors below (and, I would soon discover, the flutter of bats in the belfry above). I steadied myself against the wall – a fortunate move, as the door swung open with a crack, a rush of warm air rushing into the cool stairwell.

'Woman, get a move on,' Robin said, grinning. She extended a hand, and I took it, feeling unsteady with vertigo as the darkness loomed below.

I stepped forward into the wide room, struck by the brightness from within. The moon was streaming silver through the four huge, white clock faces, each of which took up the best part of every wall. I heard my own gasp echo from the walls like a dull chant; above, the bells hummed as a gust of wind brushed by.

It was breathtaking, details clambering one after another: the Victorian chaise longues in faded brocade, piled high with jumbled papers and rolled-up sketches, painting and ink. The marble bird perched on a broad mahogany desk, surrounded by candles and strange, sober little dolls. Even now, decades later, the same trinkets line the walls; with every passing year, still more appear, lost, beautiful things that make the tower their home.

'Hi, Violet,' Grace said, not looking up from the book splayed open in front of her. Alex, sat beside her, gave a half-smile, waiting for me to catch my breath. I walked to the farthest clock face and looked out, shoulders level with the lowest point.

Outside, the campus shone lavish in the falling light of the moon winking above the trees. Beyond, the town glowed dull, and farther still the infinite black of the sea glittered as it met the sky. Several feet below, a raven swooped, disappearing into the darkness of the woodland beyond the school gates.

I turned away, struck with a sudden vertigo as my eyes followed it down, and walked a long, slow circuit of the room. I felt the other girls watching, waiting for me to speak. I picked up one object after another, as though only by touch could I make them real. A rag doll in a dirty gingham dress, eyes gouged, posed grotesquely on a stack of books; a vase of flowers which looked long dead but somehow retained their scent.

A comic mask and an infant's dress, which left my fingers powdery white when I reached out to touch its silk and lace. A winged brass figure, too heavy to lift, though its base was the size of my palm; a blown-glass vase, faded grey and muddy with earth; four deer skulls, antlers broad and piercing, like outstretched hands.

'Make yourself at home, why don't you?' Robin said, finally. She flopped down on the chaise longue, her feet in laddered tights resting on the table, drinking whisky from a bottle she'd tucked inside the lining of her blazer. She held it out to me. 'Want some?'

'No, thanks,' I said, with a weak smile. I'd found the journey up the stairs harrowing enough. The prospect of making my way down while sober seemed impossible, let alone intoxicated.

With a jolt, a mechanism below rattled and shook, the elevator roaring into life. I glanced at Robin, and she shrugged. 'I thought it was broken. Good exercise though, huh?' I felt my cheeks burn, cruelly, and turned back to the shelves, running my fingers along the bruised white face of a porcelain doll.

A click of heels echoed on the flagstones outside. Another broad scrape of the door, a rush of cool air from the stairwell, whistling through the cracks in the brickwork, unsettled by the relentless tick-tick-tick. Annabel stood, tall and imposing in the doorway, two books slung under one arm. She looked at us, one by one, as though appraising each of us in turn; I felt exposed, somehow, as she looked at me, her brow furrowed for an almost imperceptible moment. At last she smiled, though her eyes were still flat and cold. 'So we are five again at last,' she said, softly. 'Tea, anyone?'

'Forgive me, if I may,' she began, lowering herself into an armchair, legs crossed beneath her. 'I would like to go over a couple of things we've already covered for the benefit of our new student. Is that okay with you ladies?' She looked at Robin, Alex, and Grace, who nodded, mutely.

She turned to me, eyes bird-like, black and ringed with tan. 'So, Violet, welcome to our little group.' She smiled, the slightest of gaps between her front teeth, like tombstones in a graveyard; a warmth that seeped through my skin, a doll becoming real. 'How much have the girls told you so far?'

'Nothing. I mean, not yet,' I said, glancing at Robin, who clicked her pen, and began sketching in the margins of her open book.

'Good,' Annabel said. She paused, blowing softly into her

mug before taking a sip, looking at each of us as she did so. 'We meet every Thursday, for two hours, at 6:15pm. You may schedule office hours with me, should you find yourself struggling with the work – but there is to be no mention of this class or discussion of our lessons beyond these four walls. Is that understood?'

I nodded. She smiled, eyes deathly and emotionless. 'I assume you're aware of the history of this school, no?'

I wondered why it was that I kept being asked this by tutors, and why each assumed I had some idea. 'Some of it,' I said, weakly.

'I suppose we should start from the beginning,' she said, placing her drink on the desk, steam rising hot. 'This institution was founded in 1604, by Ms Margaret Boucher. Originally, it had only four students, all orphaned, or taken from parents who could not provide them with the due care they required. The Poor Law made it rather easier for Ms Boucher to do her work, since pauper children were given the opportunity to become apprentices. Naturally a formal girls' school would have been something of a tricky prospect, since there were barely any schools for boys in the area as it was, but Ms Boucher was able to tell interested parties that she was simply offering something of a training academy for these young women, teaching them the arts of good manners, etiquette, and the like.'

She pulled a pin from her hair, and turned it around in her fingers, a thin, white smudge of clay on the edge of her hand. 'The reality, of course, was rather different. Ms Boucher had been something of a scholar, though of course there were few opportunities for a young educated woman to use this knowledge at the time. She loved the Greek and Roman tragedies; adored folk myths, studying them with an almost anthropological eye. She read plays and poetry, devouring whatever she could get her hands on, and regularly journeyed to London to see performances by Shakespeare and Marlowe, and others since forgotten. She spent three months in Italy, touring Florence and Rome, completely alone, purely to see the great works of Michelangelo and the other great Renaissance painters.

'So, as you can imagine, she was hardly inclined to teach her students the importance of correct cutlery placement.' She gave a wry smile; bit her lip, as though catching herself unguarded. 'Soon enough, the school had sixty pupils, then a hundred; mothers would send their daughters here clutching forged notices of their parents' deaths, in the hope that they might have a better life than the one which seemed their fate.'

The clouds above shifted and the moonlight began moving from the east clock face to the north.

'But in 1615, the fashion for witch finding reached the area. Women were dragged from their beds and burned at the stake, or thrown into the sea bound and weighted with stones. Neighbours betrayed one another for the witch finders' gold. So-called moral society ran amok, with endless accusations made in bad faith. Heaven help the woman who is perceived imperfect, or of unusual character . . . So I am sure you can imagine the outcome for Ms Boucher, whose school by this point was a source of envy and bitterness among those who believed women should be seen, and not heard. She was accused of occult magic, of summoning demons from the earth and teaching her pupils the wicked arts of witchcraft, and thus sentenced to death.'

She picked up the mug again, and, finding it cooler, began to drink, the silence thick between us. 'That's awful,' I said, finally, willing her to go on.

'You just wait,' Robin interjected.

Annabel shot her a warning look. 'What we know, however, is that her accusers – for their numerous faults – were not entirely wrong, though naturally, they did not know it. At the time, accusations of witchcraft could be based on seemingly anything. She was simply unlucky. A local farmer said she'd cursed his crops, spirits trailing through the fields, uprooting them from the earth. It was his word against hers, and of course, his won out.

'But Ms Boucher did, in fact, have a rather involved interest in the occult. She knew the myths, the ancient rituals, the Greek mysteries, and Celtic spells, primarily as a scholar – but such knowledge comes with certain temptations. Why simply read about it, when you can experience it for yourself? And so, she had been known, on rare occasions, to attempt these rituals. As she experimented with the arts, her interest became one of almost scientific curiosity. As far as we know, however, before the trial, she had not had much luck.

'The lore, then, goes as follows. The night before her execution, she invited four of her students, all sixteen years old, for a final dinner in the tower. Right here, in fact, in this very room.' I felt an involuntary shudder, and looked at Grace, who offered a weak smile, apparently having experienced the same flicker of the past.

'They ate dinner, sipped wine, talked of their studies. It was as though nothing were out of the ordinary, but that Ms Boucher was to die the next day. And then, at nine o'clock, Ms Boucher performed a ritual, and summoned the Erinyes: the Furies of ancient myth. They stood before the trembling girls, dressed in black sable, tall and regal; their hair writhed with snakes and fire, their fingers dripping blood. In their eyes, it was possible to see the very depths of the human soul, the darkest imaginable desires reflected back into the mind of the observer, irrevocable and sickening.

"'Erinyes," she said, "take these girls' souls in your hands, and help them to protect this place. They will be your conduit, your intention made flesh; they will destroy the corrupt and murder the wicked, oh goddesses, if you will give to them your gifts." And the Erinyes did. The Furies joined hands, and reached for the girls, who reached, trembling, back, trusting their teacher completely– though they were, understandably, terrified of the ghouls that stood before them. If only I could gain the same respect from my students,' she added, with a wry smile. The four of us laughed, a nervous flicker. Alex and Grace exchanged a glance, and Robin stared intently at Annabel, pencil hovering just above the page.

'The next day, she died, burned at the stake in the centre of the Quad, where the wych elm now stands. But as the fire burned, onlookers swore they saw three figures surrounding her, protecting her from the flames. Most of the children had been sequestered in their rooms, so as to avoid the horror taking place on the grounds of their school. You must remember that this was the only home many of them had ever known and Ms Boucher had become their protector in the absence of their own mothers; the one who saved them from their intended fate.

'But the four girls sat here, in the tower, and watched the burning. And they vowed, among themselves, to avenge the evils of men, the force of the Erinyes resting in their souls.' She paused, and leaned slowly forwards, her eyes fixed on mine. She held my gaze until I looked away, and laughed, a soft, low sound. 'That's all myth, of course. But it does make a very good story. And the basic facts are true.'

I looked up. 'Which facts?'

She smiled again, curling her fingers around a black pendant that hung around her neck. 'That a society was founded the night before Ms Boucher's execution. A society which continues to this day, and of which you four, now, are our newest members. I was a member, as was Alex's mother; there are other names you would no doubt recognize, but as we keep each other's secrets, I will not be providing you with a who's who. The information reveals itself naturally, if required.'

'And you do . . . magic.'

Annabel laughed. 'Oh, heavens no. Some of our members do enjoy practising the old rites and rituals for fun, from time to time – but all that is simply our society's mythology, a tale that makes the telling a little more fun.' She folded her hands in her lap, nail imprinting knuckle. 'What we do in this class, however, is discuss the history of the great women of art and literature, the joys of aesthetic experience – things forgotten these days, abandoned in the curriculum. We teach, essentially, the things Ms Boucher would have wanted, out of respect for her knowledge and love of learning.'

A dull pang of disappointment rose in my stomach, and settled. 'Okay,' I said. 'But why us?'

Her eyes were pool-dark. 'Why not you?'

'I . . . I don't know.' I felt the other girls watching, the air suddenly close between us. After a seemingly interminable silence, Annabel shuffled in her seat, and pulled a book from the table beside her.

'Shall we continue where we left off?' she said, turning to the other girls. It was as though I weren't there, and never had been. Robin gave me a sympathetic glance as she spread her book, and Annabel began to read. The clock's black hands clicked onwards. 'So the women had great power,' I scratched aimlessly in my notebook, writing rote, unsure to which text, or to which women, she was referring, 'but it came with quite a cost.'

It was that soft, still hour unique to autumn evenings, when the ember smell of bonfires mixes with the salty breath of the sea, and the leaves stop falling for a moment, as though afraid. Pylons stalked above the fields on tip-toe, the only sound our footsteps crunching leaves into the tarmac, damp from the brief shower that had rattled the clock faces while Annabel watched us leave.

At the foot of the stairs, Robin had lit a cigarette, and passed it to me. We stood under the arches, smoking in silence as we waited for the girls to follow, footsteps echoing faint circles far above. When they emerged at last, I followed the three of them down the long driveway, towards (I assumed) the bus stop. I paused to look at the faded timetable, and Robin turned back, brows arched in confusion.

'Aren't you coming?' she said, glancing at Alex and Grace just behind.

'Where?' I said, feeling a swell of delight. *Stay cool*, I told myself, as though I knew what that meant.

'Church,' she replied, palms upturned like it was obvious.

So we had walked, through the empty fields, under the old bridge; hopped over railway tracks and badger setts underfoot. Into the woods, brambles snagging ankles and exposed wrists, creatures crawling overhead and rustling through the dead leaves. Robin led the way, whistling a song I felt I knew but couldn't place, while Alex and Grace whispered, hands clasped tight.

At the edge of the woods, we came to an abrupt stop. The grass bank led down to the train tracks, wires whipping overhead: the mainline, the route out of town, to London, and onwards to the rest of the world. Beyond the tracks, a fence tied with faded plastic flowers in memory of a name long washed away, and behind that the old church in silhouette against the moon. Robin kicked the grass below, and sat facing the tracks. She looked up, and patted the ground beside her. 'We're early,' she said, as I sat down.

I recognized the bottle of wine she pulled from her bag. It was cheap, and potent, and empty bottles of it lined the kitchen, leaving red rings on the counter that neither my mum nor I ever thought to clean. Robin clicked the screw cap, took a long swig, and passed the bottle behind me to

Grace, who did the same. Alex, too, took a sip, before passing it to me.

'Go on,' she said. 'Drink up.'

'You'll need it,' Robin added.

I took the bottle, feeling the liquid lapping at the sides, the smell rich and coppery. I felt dared, caught out. I took a sip, winced; took another, feeling the warmth paint a line through my chest.

Robin smiled, taking the bottle from me. I felt my cheeks flush hot, a sense of being cocooned, warm hands on my skin. I could see why Mum liked it. 'So . . . Are you in?'

I looked at her. 'In what?'

'The club, idiot,' she said, knuckles brushing my arm. 'Thought ol' Annabel might've scared you away. She'll kill you if she smells weakness.'

'No way,' I said, flushing at the thought. *I'm not weak*, I thought, as though saying it might make it true. 'I'm in.'

The truth was, I wasn't sure *how* I felt. I wasn't sure I believed any of it, though Annabel had told the story with such conviction it seemed impossible that it could be anything but true. *But either way*, I thought, *what's the harm? Being one of them like this is still better than being alone*. And yet, as I said the words, there was a shudder of doubt I couldn't place – what I suppose in hindsight one might call intuition, though in the moment it seemed like fear.

She arched an eyebrow. 'Promise?'

' . . . Really?'

She grinned. 'Go on.'

'I promise.'

A lighter clicked behind me, and the distinctive sweet smell of cannabis ripened the air. She leaned back, took the joint from Alex, and turned back to me. 'You've got so much to learn.'

I laughed. 'Like what?'

She shook her head. 'All in good time,' she said, taking a long, thoughtful inhale. The town glowed a hazy orange in the distance, lights fading, one by one. Grace absent-mindedly played with her hair, searching out split-ends in the dim light; Alex leaned over to catch the wine bottle as a gust of wind toppled it from a precarious position in the grass. 'It's getting cold,' she said, to no one in particular.

There was a rising rumble in the east, and Robin rolled onto her knees. 'About time,' she said. I looked at the sky, waiting for the lightning to flash, but the sky was still. The noise grew louder, a shuddering constant. She grabbed my hand, and pulled me to my feet. 'Ready?'

'What?'

'Get ready.' She looked at me, illuminated by the white light that came from behind, growing brighter with the volume of the roar, unmistakable now: the thunder of an oncoming train. I turned to Alex and Grace, who stood poised beside me, faces blank, staring into the light. My heart began to pound, pulse thudding in my temples; the back of my neck was hot, palms slick with sweat, Robin's nails against my skin. I wondered, briefly, if they were about to push me onto the tracks, the thought vivid, real as a nightmare.

'We can't . . . ' I began, the words drowned out by the train's mechanical roar. I saw dark flashes of memory, fragments of the past. Morbid visions of burned-out eye sockets and fingernails peeled back: the girls pulled me forwards, and we ran, the rush of air pushing us stumbling onto the opposite bank. I turned and saw dead faces through the glass, wearing my wild-eyed grin like a mask.

'See?' Robin said, panting, laughing. 'Feel alive, don't you?'

I nodded, breath still catching in my throat. She passed me the end of the joint, still somehow smouldering, and I took a drag, feeling my heart shuddering beside my lungs; a feeling pleasant, while one is young enough not to picture it at last giving out, with one final, bitter thud. 'Fuck,' I coughed.

Alex laughed. 'Yep.'

When the silence fell again, it was transfigured, a physical presence lingering in the air. I followed the girls through a gap in the fence, careful not to disturb the tattered memorial tied to the post. 'GONE TOO SOON', it said, the face smeared and washed away. They walked between the tombstones and their ink-stain shadows, passing from one row to the next. Grace looked at me, eyes hollow in the dark, and smiled. 'Nearly there.'

At the end of the graveyard, seemingly as far as possible from the church itself, they stopped. A row of squat, overgrown tombstones, crawling with moss, tall grass all but covering the names etched into their faces. Robin took a sip of wine, and splashed a little on the ground below. 'A toast,' she said; the girls smiled, the ghost of a laugh. She turned to me. 'So let's talk about Annabel's story. What did you think of the ending?'

'It was good. I mean, I liked it,' I whispered.

'You can talk normally,' Alex said. 'They can't hear you.'

I cleared my throat. 'Right.'

'A question for you,' Robin said, rocking back and forth. 'Let's say you're Margaret Boucher. Why would you invoke a bunch of ancient underworld revenge demons if you weren't planning on exacting some revenge?'

'I don't—'

'Rhetorical, Violet, rhetorical. Because, duh.' She leaned against the tombstone beside her, tapped it twice. 'Mr Edward Cooke,' she said. 'Claimed Margaret cursed his cows so they wouldn't give milk. Died a month after the burning, gored by his own bull.' She pointed to the next. 'Mrs Elizabeth Moran. Told the witch finder she'd seen Mags worship the Devil. Three months later, a candle from her own, personal altar caught on her dress, and poof!' She motioned with her hands. 'Finger-lickin' good.'

I laughed. 'You're insane.'

'It's all in the death records,' Grace said, softly. 'It's like a massacre.'

'Right,' Robin replied. 'Because that's exactly what it is.'

She pointed to another, and another. A man who'd claimed she'd poisoned the well, drowned; a woman who said she'd given her nightmares, crushed by a falling beam as she slept. We walked the length of the yard, the tombstones placed together, at a distance from the church – their superstitions seeming to confirm the unnaturalness of it.

'But that's not all,' Alex said, as we reached the end of the row. 'All these dead parents left behind daughters. And Elm Hollow – now run by Ms Boucher's second-in-command, who are all busy mourning her loss – takes them in. Trains them to be upstanding young ladies, real pillars of the community.

90

And for the lucky four who get advanced study classes . . . '
She trailed off.

'This is my favourite,' Robin said, brushing moss from the
rim of a cracked tombstone. 'Jane White. Invited Ms Boucher's
lover to stop by for a little supper, if you know what I mean.
Poisoned by a leaf of belladonna in a glass of milk.'

'What's that?'

'Deadly nightshade. You've heard of that, right?'

'Seriously?'

'Seriously.'

A silence fell, for a moment. 'I didn't even know that was
a real thing,' I said, and meant it. I'd always assumed it was
a fictional creation. Like magic. And curses. And vengeful
demon spirits.

'I know. Nor did I. Don't sweat it,' Robin said, rooting
through her pockets for another cigarette. The hiss of burning
tobacco was the only sound. 'Kinda funny that's the thing
you're incredulous about, though, dipshit.'

'Good point,' I said, laughing in spite of myself. She was
right. This was all madness, a fairy tale run riot.

Alex handed me the wine bottle, and I drained the last sip,
sediment blacking my tongue. The girls watched me, a ribbon
of tension hanging between us. I felt my skin chill, gooseflesh
on my arms, a white-hot current down my spine.

'So . . . ' Robin began at last, looking up at the moon. She
looked back at me and smiled – a smile I'd come to know,
the last dark laugh before a dare. 'Remember that promise
you made about being in?' An owl cracked its wings above,
and the four of us flinched at the sound.

'Jesus Christ,' Alex said, laughing. 'That's ominous.'

'It is,' I said. 'Count me in.'

Crows cawed overhead, the morning sky a cruel and vivid white.

I clung desperately to sleep, feeling the cold pinch of sweat and dew on my forehead, the pitiless dry scrape at the back of my throat. My stomach rolled once, then again, and I staggered to my feet, past the steaming embers of the fire we'd made, and into the long grass, retching as quietly as I could.

'What the fuck?' I heard somewhere behind.

'It's fine,' I said, wondering if the force of desperately wanting it to be true might be enough to make it so. 'It's me. I'm alright.' I wiped my lip on my sleeve, winced at the acid smell; rolled my sleeve inward to hide the stain.

Robin snorted, her voice hoarse with smoke. 'Poor Vivi can't hold her drink, huh?'

'Nope,' I said, sitting down beside her with a thud. She was cross-legged, rolling yet another cigarette, fingers fumbling over each other. Grace sat with her arms around her knees, her hair a tangled, black mess. Alex's head rested on her bare shoulder. She rolled an almost empty water bottle towards me, and I drained it in a single gulp. I felt better for a moment, and then much, much worse. I lay down and closed my eyes, sun shining red through the skin.

Memories began to surface, one by one, like bubbles in champagne. Each disappeared before I could catch it; running, falling, laughing. Robin climbing down from the holy font, wiping spit from her lips; putting two fingers in the wine and pressing them to my head, saying something I couldn't recall. A sharp, cold thud, metal through the air. A laugh, first shy, then riotous, a howl, a call to come and see.

'Hey,' Robin said. I opened my eyes with a start. She stood over me, nudging my shoulder with her boot. 'Time to go, Sleeping Beauty.'

I sat up, and groaned as the world tipped forwards. She laughed, and held out a hand. 'No offence, but you look like shit.'

'Thanks.' I brushed the grass from my legs and back, and prayed for a moment of stillness, the trees swaying a little in the distance.

'Hurry up, for fuck's sake!' Alex shouted, already approaching the tunnel. 'I need a shower before class.'

'Oh god,' I said, imagining my mum realizing I was gone, that I'd never made it home. In the months before the accident, I'd begun to 'act out', testing limits by arriving home two or three hours late. I left the question of where I'd been to my parents' imaginations. (Though I'd been reading on the beach, or lurking in the library . . . Still, their assumptions had resulted in both the attention I craved and a gratifying sense of injustice at the fact they would assume the worst.) I'd been 'grounded' each time, a punishment that allowed me to spend more time in my room, alone, uninterrupted. That, I suppose, was the point.

Now, however, I imagined Mum pacing the halls, frantic, growing ever more furious, giving way to terror as the dawn crept in; I imagined the punishment I would receive when, inevitably, I walked home, hung-over and ashen, stinking of smoke. Being grounded, now, when the girls had at last let me in, would be more than I could bear.

Robin kicked my bag upright, and bent to pick it up. 'Seriously, get a move on,' she said, handing it to me and walking away, arms outstretched as she balanced along the silver curve of the rail.

The girls talked without focus all the way home, Robin seemingly determined to fill the silence, until we parted at the mermaid statue staring out to sea. I walked home slowly, stopping to buy mints and a pint of milk (Dad had always had a glass of milk on the rare occasions he was hung-over: usually only New Year's Day), and saw my reflection, gaunt in the windows of empty cars.

I turned my key in the lock, heard voices inside, murmuring. I waited for Mum's slippers pacing down the hall, the relief· and anger on her breath.

And yet, when I entered, there was nothing.

Mum's feet hung from the end of the sofa, room hot with sleep and stale sweat, the voices crackling from the TV. A glass of wine spilled on the floor, glass upturned, cracked. I went to my room, relief at my absence having gone unnoticed curling into something else, some bitter-tasting thing. I shook it off, changed my clothes, and went to school, slamming the door behind me as I left.

Chapter 5

Clutching a steaming coffee (no milk, but three packets of sugar – I was yet to fully accustom myself to the taste), I slid into the booth beside Grace and flicked open a packet of cigarettes I'd purchased en route (Lucky Strikes: Robin's brand), opening them to the girls without a word. Grace shook her head; Robin took two, placing one in her breast pocket for later.

In the weeks since my introduction to Annabel's advanced classes, Alex and Grace had warmed to me considerably, helping me to catch up on the classes I'd missed.

'Nice coat,' Grace said, running a hand through the tattered fur. 'Is it real?'

'I don't think so,' I said, though I wasn't sure; I'd stolen it from Mum's cupboard, shaking off memories of her and my dad in faded photographs, faces rose-lit by snow.

'You know you gotta inhale, right?' Robin said, her face expressionless, blank.

'Sore throat,' I lied, watching as she took a long drag – too long, I suspected, proving a point – and exhaled three rings above.

'Where's Alex?' I asked, finally.

'She's en route. She got back kind of late last night,' Grace said.

'Where from?'

'Some dinner thing. Her mum made her go. "Networking", whatever that means.'

'The life of the hideously wealthy is one of many inconveniences, darling,' Robin added, mocking Alex's low drawl.

'Everyone here's hideously wealthy,' I said, a tinge of bitterness in my voice – a hangover, I suppose, from years of being poor. Robin and Grace looked at each other, then back to me.

'Are you serious?' Robin said. She took a sip of my coffee, and grimaced. 'What have you done to this?'

I stared at the two of them, utterly lost.

'Well, we must be dressed sharper than I realized,' she said, at last. 'We're on scholarships. She's the academic nerd; I'm here on creative skills alone. That's why we're in Annabel's class. Christ,' she said, leaning back and sipping her tea. 'You didn't think I was in there on the strength of my brain, surely? I'm literally teacher's pet. Even *I* don't know why she let me in. I mean, it's not like drawing's going to help her take over the world, or whatever it is she's planning to do.' She looked at me, expectantly.

'I . . . I hadn't really thought about it.' And in some way, it was true: I'd already identified the mark of the scholarship kids. I recognized it – the shyness, the furtive looks – because

I felt it too. Robin and Grace, though – they went about campus with such assured confidence, reflected in the way everyone looked at them . . . They couldn't be on scholarships. They belonged there more than anyone else.

Robin laughed; Grace smiled as she emptied another sachet of sweetener into her mug.

'But Alex isn't on a scholarship?' I said, finally.

'God, no. Her mum's loaded,' Grace said. 'And . . . ' She leaned in towards me. 'She and Annabel go way back. Although,' she added, lowering her voice, 'Alex's mum doesn't know she's in her class. So don't mention it if she's there.'

'Why?' I said.

Grace coughed and nodded almost imperceptibly towards the door; Alex was approaching in dark glasses, heels clicking on the tile.

'I'm so fucking hung-over,' she said, dumping a glossy leather bag on the table and sauntering over to the counter. 'Anyone want anything?'

'Coffee – black as your soul!' Robin called back. Alex raised two fingers in response, and ordered two coffees, both black.

'If her mum *is* home,' Robin whispered, 'she's a big shot, and she knows it. *Total* bitch. Be warned.'

'Anyway,' she said, abruptly, as Alex approached, 'I liked it, but I don't know if you guys would be into it.'

'What are you talking about?' Alex said, sliding in beside me.

'Just some movie.' Robin shrugged. 'Not your thing.'

Grace swiftly changed the subject, and I lit another cigarette,

Robin resting her coffee on a tattered sketchbook, doodling in its margins.

For all the grandeur to which I'd become accustomed on campus, Alex's house still came as something of a surprise. Tucked deep among the canopied streets of what my dad had once referred to as 'Snobbery Avenue', the house sat far back from the road, a curved path leading from the wrought-iron gates to the main building. Across the lawn was a squat cottage Alex called the 'Potting Shed', but which looked to be roughly the size of my house. 'It's for guests,' Grace whispered as we passed. 'Although her dad lived there for a while during the D-I-V-O-R—'

'I can spell, you know!' Alex shouted from up ahead.

'You can? Really?' Robin said, elbowing Alex, who pushed her back – a little forcefully, I thought, though Robin didn't seem to mind. I wondered why anyone would break up when they lived in a house like this. If my mum and I could avoid each other in our cramped, tired little house, it seemed as though you could go days here without knowing anyone else was even there.

The other girls kicked off their boots in the hallway and disappeared into one of the many rooms off to the side. I knelt and began to untie my laces, unnecessarily, looking around at the paintings that hung on the walls: stone busts and sculptures of the sort I'd only ever seen encased in glass. I brushed the tips of my fingers on the bronze arm of a woman whose eyes sparkled green, braced for some alarm to sound, a stern guard to appear.

'Come on, Violet!' Robin shouted, from what by now sounded like several rooms away. I followed the sound of glasses clinking, drawers opening and closing, a stool pulled along a stone floor, and found the girls in a wide, brightly lit kitchen, like something from the magazines Mum used to buy.

'What happened? Get caught by the ghost?' Robin said, patting an empty stool beside her. I sat, palms cool on the marble counter.

Alex snorted. 'Trust me, Dad's not coming back.' She pulled two bottles from a wall criss-crossed with a huge grate. 'Left the wine collection, at least.'

'Ah, *oui, oui,*' Robin said. 'Your finest Chianti, garçon.' She tapped two fingers on my thigh. 'I've always wanted to say that.' I laughed, and she squeezed, her hands tender, nails sharp.

'So is the lady of the house here tonight?' Robin said.

'God, no,' Alex said, rolling her eyes. 'she won't be back for a while. She's in the States, doing some research thing, I think.'

'Swish,' Robin said. 'So we've got the place to ourselves?'

'Yeah,' Alex said. 'The bitch next door is popping by to check on things from time to time, but she's out tonight, so the coast is clear. I know for a fact she steals a bottle of this every time she drops by – so by my logic, the more I drink, the more likely my mom is to notice and can her for it.'

'We'd be honoured to assist in your noble mission, in that case,' Robin said, taking a long gulp, a kiss of red staining her chapped bottom lip.

'Thanks, Robin,' Alex replied, raising her glass. 'You're a true friend.'

'Come on.' Robin grabbed my arm as she stood. 'Let me give you the tour.'

I followed her through the kitchen, to the dining room, all white and gold, with chandeliers that rang lightly as we opened the door. 'Wow,' I said again, unable to contain my envy.

'This is nothing.' Robin pushed a heavy, wooden door and felt around for a light. 'Look at this,' she said, as a row of lamps burst into life. I followed her as she stepped forward into a cavernous room filled floor-to-ceiling with books and sculptures; huge, brightly-coloured paintings hung on each side of a fireplace whose mantelpiece sat just above my eye level. 'This is what they call an *office*,' she said, turning to me. 'Can you even imagine?'

She wandered around the shelves, plucking out objects and turning their faces to the light, examining them as though searching for clues. I did the same, imitating her casual wanderings, as I peered at the broad, breathless brush-strokes of a painting of a woman holding a child high, the two of them screaming with laughter and joy.

'What did you say her mum did?'

'She's some kind of researcher. She wrote a book on the occult a few years ago – real creepy, ghosty stuff. Not that there's any money in that, apparently, but it's not like they need it. Their money is *ancient*,' she said, picking a glass butterfly from its perch and placing it in her palm, where it glittered in the light.

I said nothing, turning to look at the heavy books that lined the shelves. *The Mystic Rituals of Ancient Greece*, read one; *Daemonology*, read another.

'Hey,' Alex said, peering around the door, Robin and I frozen, caught in the act. 'Shall we order a pizza?'

'Oh, Alex, you're not going to make us burnt slop again? Shame.'

'If you don't want any, that's fine,' Alex replied, abruptly.

'I'm just messing with you. Come on, Violet. Let's go make the most of our host's most impeccable hospitality.' Placing the book back on the shelf, I followed Alex and Robin into a dimly lit, cosy lounge, where the fire crackled and hissed as the wind roared outside. Grace sat under a thick, fur blanket, stretched out on an ancient leather sofa, her pale skin given an apricot warmth by the fire's golden glow. I curled into an armchair, resting a stiff cushion on my knees, the room yet to shake off the cold outside.

'More wine?' Alex said, handing me the bottle.

'Thanks,' I said, though I was already feeling the effects of my first glass, the wine potent, my drunkenness syrupy, mellow.

Robin sat on the floor by my knees, her hair falling around my feet. She reached an arm up, without looking back, and I passed her the bottle. She shook it, holding it up to the light. 'Alex! Bring more wine!' she shouted. Grace shot Robin a warning look, and I felt my own cheeks grow hot.

We sat in silence, listening to the rumble of the wind outside, Alex's muffled voice in the kitchen as she ordered food.

'So this project,' Robin said, as Alex returned, tucking herself into the blanket by Grace's side. 'We're meant to be researching what, exactly?'

Alex looked at Grace, who shifted onto her elbow. 'Did you

do *any* of the reading?' she said. 'Any of you?' she added, looking at Alex, who gave a sheepish smile.

'Well, shucks, Grace, I didn't think I'd need to,' Robin said, grinning. 'I knew you'd do it for me.'

Grace sighed, a put-upon sigh that suggested she didn't really mind (secretly, I told myself, she quite enjoyed her role as the responsible one, the girl who saved us all). 'The gist is that Mirandola says there are two types of magic, but one's bad, and the other's good.'

'Like black magic and white magic?' Alex offered.

'Kind of,' she said. 'But this is a high-minded Renaissance philosophical guy, so it's a little more . . . Hang on.' She leaned over the back of the sofa and pulled the book out of her satchel. Her shirt rose up a little, revealing a glimpse of a bruise blooming on her waist. The shock of it chilled me: the remembering. We didn't talk about it, so it wasn't happening: our denial a collusion. And yet, occasionally, in unexpected moments, the truth of it revealed itself – a hideous cruelty, a violence on her skin.

Robin looked up at me; she hadn't noticed. 'Oooh, a bedtime story. Yay.'

'Here it is,' Grace said, having either not heard Robin's comment or chosen to ignore it. '"Magic has two forms, blah blah blah . . . " Ah. "One consists wholly in the operations and powers of demons, and consequently, this appears to me, as God is my witness—"'

'I'll never go hungry again?' Robin said, rolling her eyes.

'Shut up,' Alex snapped, following Grace's fingers, underlining the words as she read.

'"As God is my witness, an execrable and monstrous thing. The other proves, when thoroughly investigated, to be nothing else but the highest realization of natural philosophy."' She looked at us, shyly, and went on. 'He goes on a bit, but *then* he says: "The practitioner of the first always tries to conceal his addiction, because it always rebounds to shame and reproach, while the cultivation of the second, both in antiquity and at almost all periods, has been the source of the highest renown and glory in the field of learning."'

'What a nerd,' Robin scoffed. 'Him, I mean. Not you.'

'So what I think Annabel wants is examples of the second,' Grace went on. 'Which seems kind of easy, since he basically reels them off in here.'

'Great,' Alex said. 'Mum's bound to have loads on that.' The gate buzzed, and she stood up. 'I'll go get the pizza. You guys pick a film.'

'Or . . . ' Robin said, grinning.

'Pick a film,' Alex called back from the hall.

I paused, for a moment, cursing myself for my curiosity, my eagerness to please: finally, I asked the question I knew she was waiting for. 'Or what?'

Robin pointed at the rows of books on the shelves, the endless trinkets and toys. 'Or, we could do something actually fun.'

'I'm tired,' Grace said, glancing nervously at the door. 'I'd rather watch a movie.'

'What, are you scared?'

'No, but—'

The front door slammed shut, and the three of us flinched; the footsteps that thudded down the hall had an urgent rhythm.

'Robin,' Alex said, appearing in the doorway. 'You promised you wouldn't start this again.'

'What are you talking about?' I said, helplessly.

Alex sighed. 'She—'

'She?' Robin said, with mock outrage. There was a glint in her eyes as she winked at me, willing me to play along.

'Last time *Robin* was here,' Alex went on, 'she spent all night going on about doing one of the rituals from Mum's books. And apparently she's going to do it again.'

I looked at Alex; then at Robin, and Grace. 'Like . . . Like Bloody Mary, or something?'

Robin scoffed. 'What are you, twelve?'

'*Exactly* like Bloody Mary,' Alex said. 'A stupid, childish game.'

Robin glanced at me, with a look of despair, and shrugged. I rolled my eyes, the look an imitation of hers, and wondered, as I did it, why I had; hoped, nervously, that the others hadn't seen.

The girls began to argue again, though the tone lightened, their usual chatter resumed. Robin and Grace stood at the cabinet stacked with VHS tapes (concealed behind a wide, painted screen – these apparently not in keeping with the room's elegant decor).

I was a little jealous of the way the girls seemed entirely at home here, intimately aware of the order of things, yet oblivious and accustomed to their luxury. Their sisterly bickering over what to watch ('You always pick that.' 'Because it's good!') made me smile, matching my expressions to theirs as I hovered behind.

In the end, it didn't matter what they chose (though it came down to two Hammer horrors – one zombies, one vampires, neither name of which I can recall). After a slice of pizza (just one, though I was hungry – I'd heard Robin's jibes about a girl at least two dress sizes smaller than me, a fact she seemed braced to raise at any moment) and another glass of wine, I felt myself sliding into a heady daze, eyelids heavy and thick, and leaned back into the enveloping wings of the armchair.

When I woke, wrapped once again in my tattered fur coat, the house was silent, the fire no more than a few dull embers glowing red in the dark. On the TV, a thick white line shuddered down the screen, strobing the room.

I blinked away sleep, and tried to remember where I was, and why I was alone. I stood, blinking, beside a case of herbs, dried crystals and silvery powders. *Arnold Hill, 1969*, a silver plaque read at its base. The glass bottles, no taller than my thumb, were fat and round, cork stoppered and tempting. I plucked one from the bottom shelf. *Water Hemlock (Cicuta maculata)*, it read, in faded, black ink. I put it back, pulled another: *Oleander (Nerium oleander)*. As I placed the bottle back in its slot, my eye caught on a half-filled jar, dried leaves, at the back of the case. I leaned in, plucked it out. *Deadly Nightshade (Atropa belladonna)*. It reminded me of some long-forgotten joke – *a thing Robin would like*, I thought. In a single movement, I slipped it into my pocket.

The floor was bitterly cold on my feet, ice-like and brittle. I walked out of the room, now empty and lifeless, the plush carpet in the hallway a kind relief. I whispered a tentative 'hello?' into the darkness. At the end of the corridor, Robin peered around a doorway. She beckoned, and I followed, rubbing sleep from my eyes.

'What are you . . . ?' I whispered, gripping the door with one hand. I was a little unsteady on my feet; remembered the warm stupor of the wine.

'Looking for something,' she said, matter-of-factly.

'I need some water,' I sighed.

She pointed behind me. 'Third door on the right. Meet me in the "office" when you're done.'

When I returned – after multiple wrong turns, the house winding and cavernous, seeming to grow in the dark – Robin was sat with her feet on the desk, a large book open on her lap.

I sat on the edge of the desk. 'What's this?'

She reached for my glass and took a long sip. 'An execrable and monstrous thing,' she said, grinning. 'Want to help?'

I said nothing.

'Come on,' Robin said, reaching for my sleeve. 'Look at this and then tell me you don't.'

I leaned over the desk chair, aware of my breath shifting strands of her hair. It was an ancient book, the pages painted in vivid colours, edges coated in crisp gold leaf. 'Wow,' I said, running my fingers along the page. I sighed and stood upright. 'What about the others?'

'Trust me, they don't want to be disturbed. *Alone time*, you know.'

I didn't; I hadn't. I thought of Grace's legs thrown over Alex's knees as they sat together on the sofa; the way their hands seemed to touch, lightly, fingers intertwined.

'I . . . Okay, no. I mean, fine. Didn't realize they were—'

'Well, they're not super public about it, I guess. *Anyway*, I want to do this with just you. It's a bonding ritual. For best friends.' She reached for my fingers, pressed them down on the book. 'It's like extra credit, too. Annabel would be *so* proud.'

I picked up a silver snuff-box from the desk, pretending not to care – to be thinking it over, weighing it up. On some level, I knew what she was doing. I was being told what I wanted to hear. And yet, still . . . It didn't matter. I wanted it to be true. That was almost enough. Emily, her shadow lingering over us, Robin's last best friend – my doppelgänger, as Nicky seemed determined to remind me at every opportunity – was a constant presence, to whom I felt myself constantly compared. *Best friends*, Robin had said, eyes wide in the dark, breath hot with wine and anticipation, and I thought, to my shame, *I've won*.

'Fine,' I said, at last.

'I love you.' In a split second, she was up – placing the book on the table and whirling round the shelves, pulling trinkets and candles and gathering them in her arms. 'Bring the book,' she said, and I followed her back to the living room, where the darkness was deep and still.

She sat on the rug, beside the low coffee table, still littered with pizza boxes and empty bottles, the brittle shards of a broken glass glinting as she lit three tall tapers and placed them in the elaborate candelabra she had taken from the office. She opened a wooden box, and placed five stones on the floor, and sprinkled some silvery dust from the tin I'd been examining, carefully outlining the circle.

'Come on,' she said, patting the floor beside her.

I pulled a cushion off the sofa and gingerly lowered myself to the floor, facing Robin, the candles flickering between us.

'So what do we do?'

'Shhhh . . . All will be revealed.' She crossed her legs, opened the book, and flicked through its heavy pages with licked fingers, until she found the page she was looking for. 'Abracadabra,' she said, grinning.

I looked down at the items between us, and inhaled, slowly. The wind picked up, raindrops thudding at the window, and I waited, endlessly. She plopped the book on the floor with a thud, and smiled. 'Okay,' I said. 'So . . . What do we do?'

'Did I not just tell you to shhh?' she said, not looking up. 'I wondered why Annabel talks more slowly when you're around. Now I get it.'

I blushed. I'd seen the girls shuffle in their seats as Annabel went back over things they'd learned before; the way they looked at each other, brief frustrations flickering between them. The way Robin always pulled out her sketchbook and drew, the paper tilted slightly towards Annabel, as though attempting to pull her attentions away.

In those moments, when Annabel was talking to me alone, I felt my nerve endings flicker, the hairs on my arms creep slowly to attention; felt Robin's eyes turn dark, a jealousy simmering in the air.

She cleared her throat, and took my hands in hers. 'Okay, so: close your eyes.'

I closed them, briefly, and opened them again to see her staring at me, smiling. 'I knew you'd do that,' she said. '*Keep* them closed. Don't open them until we're done.'

'Fine,' I sighed. I was still fuzzy from the wine, and felt a mild headache gathering behind my eyes.

She squeezed my fingers tight as she began to read from the book. '"Goddess Hecate, we come to you as your willing daughters, and ask of you your benevolence."' I felt a flush of goosebumps on my arms. A warning crack of thunder echoed outside.

'"Goddess of the moon, we come to you with our hands open and hearts yours, in the golden light of your mother's sky. Goddess of crossroads, we come to you open to the possibilities that you may open to us, the roads we tread not only ours, but yours, and our hearts given over to your immortal power."' She let go of one of my hands and placed it, palm up, on my knee. '"Goddess of darkness, we trust in your light, and ask you to guide us through the depths of night, when the stars fall crumbling at your sides. Goddess of witchcraft, of spells, and sorcery, grant us the knowledge of magic, and the strength of your heart. Goddess, we come to you, your daughters, giving to you our willing blood."'

I felt a sharp pain drive through my palm, and pulled my hand away, opening my eyes. I was bleeding, a thick, red welt drawn down the centre of my palm; I looked at Robin, horrified, as she dragged a thin, gnarled knife down her own palm, and pressed it to mine, squeezing my hand.

'What the hell?' I shouted, trying to pull away.

'Shhhhh,' she whispered. She looked at me, her face serious

for a moment, and then laughed. 'Come on. Like you'd have let me do that if you'd known it was coming.'

'That *hurt*.' She had my hand still in her grip, thick, warm blood pooling between our palms. 'Let go.'

'Wait,' she said, grabbing the dregs of a bottle from the table. She took a sip, and passed it to me. 'Toast our union.'

'No way,' I said, wriggling my hand, surprised at the force of her grip.

'I'm serious, come on,' she said, waving the bottle at me. Realizing it was the only way out, I snatched it, and drained the last of it.

'There,' I said, slamming it down on the table. 'Now let go.' Released from her grip, my palm burned, dripping loud splashes of blood on the floor below. I held it to my mouth to stop the flow, blood salty and warm on my lips.

Robin snorted. 'Your face is an absolute picture.'

I staggered to my feet, woozy from the pain. 'Fuck you,' I said, walking across the tiles, through to the bathroom, my bleeding hand wrapped in my sweatshirt, so as not to drip blood on the creamy carpet. I locked the door, and ran my hand under the tap, an inky red staining the bowl.

'What the hell,' I whispered, staring numbly down at my hand. My heart was pounding, furiously, in my ears, my skin prickling with the shock, and a dim, dizzying nausea seemed to swell from my gut, making me rattle with a sudden sweat. I closed the toilet lid, and sat down, unsteadily, hand still draped over the sink.

I heard a faint knock at the door. 'Are you okay?' Robin whispered. I said nothing, remained still, holding my breath.

Another knock, and another. 'Fuck you, then,' Robin hissed, and padded back down the hall.

There I remained, until the steady drip of blood slowed to a stop. The dizziness was overwhelming, nauseating. I remembered the hiss of tearing skin, and winced, burning with anger. *How could she?* I thought, bitterly turning the ritual over in my mind. *And it didn't even do anything.*

I stared at the blood clotted in black wads but for the bubbles that wept when I moved my fingers. I ran the water once again, flushing the last of the blood down the sink, and looked around, carefully, for spots I might have spilled as I entered the room. My sweatshirt was hard, dried to a crisp, black sheen; but I had avoided making any mess as I entered.

I peeled it off, gingerly drawing my hand through the sleeves, and moved to put it on the toilet lid as I wrapped my hand in tissue paper. On the lid, however, was a thin seam of blood. I stared at it. Grabbing a wad of paper to wipe it up, the realization revealing itself, I became aware of a dampness, a warmth between my legs. I turned to the mirror, and saw a dark circle of blood on the back of my skirt.

I was a 'late bloomer', Mum had reassured me, when I asked why I hadn't yet had my period. 'You're lucky,' she'd said, an answer that failed to satisfy my curiosity. Now I rolled down my tights, and saw a knot of blood, soaking through my underwear, the smell tannin and animal. I rooted through the bathroom cabinet, read the instructions on the tampon box (successful only on the third attempt), rolled my tights into a ball, and stuffed them into the bin.

Finally, I padded back into the living room, the evidence

cleaned away. It looked almost as though nothing had happened but for a half-print of blood on the light switch. I wiped it away with my sleeve, and lay on the sofa, gathering a blanket around me. *It's a coincidence*, I told myself. *It's just a coincidence, that's all.*

Winter

Chapter 6

I sat at the base of the mermaid, the stone as cold as a mortuary slab. I had been early, and now he was late. I watched the Christmas shoppers through misted breath, the air heavy and bristling with life: the first day of the holidays, lights flickering over crowded streets. My palm itched, and I scratched through my dampened glove; finding no relief, I peeled it off, and stared down at the welt, still sticky, clotted black.

In the weeks after the night at Alex's house, I'd grown used to its dull throb, hot and damp with sweat. It had never quite healed, bleeding occasionally on my schoolbooks, or leaving a sticky smudge around coffee cups and wine bottles. Neither Robin nor I had said a word to Alex and Grace, though each glanced at the scars or the prints they left, tight-lipped, refusing to ask. I felt their irritation with us both, like parents annoyed at a misbehaving child.

And in this way, I suppose, the spell had worked. Robin and I were by now inseparable, our own unit. We did everything together, though over the last few days I'd become preoccupied, distracted, a little lost to her.

Because I had met a boy. Or rather, I had met a boy again, and had, on our second meeting, been kissed. The specifics were a little hazy, happening as they had in the early hours, after no small quantity of drink in Andy's room, stolen tinsel littered around the floor. Tom and Andy, it seemed, were now friends, though the two of them barely spoke; it was Robin who drove the conversation, the mood, every movement in the smoke-filled dorm.

When she and Andy threw us out, wanting time alone, Tom and I had stood by the lake in the freezing cold, just as we'd done before (though my memory of the night, still, was blurred, shrouded in the furred glow of intoxication). 'I'd like to take you out some time,' he'd said, and I'd told him I'd like that, too.

Later, remembering that first kiss, I tried to remember whether his spit had tasted different from my own, tried to pinpoint the musky smell of his hair. Tried, too, to pick apart the doubts that followed. Was being kissed a pleasurable sensation, or was I doing it wrong? And why, exactly, was he kissing me?

It doesn't matter, I told myself, blinking the thought away. *I have been kissed*. It was a milestone reached, my first, thrilling entry into adulthood.

When Robin asked, I shrugged, and told her nothing had happened – that I wasn't interested, didn't know what she was talking about. And as we'd left campus for the Christmas break, she'd asked me what my plans were. I'd said I couldn't meet today, the kiss still sugar-sweet in memory, the thrill of remembering biting at my skin; a secret I would think of only when I was in my room, like my sister's box of baby clothes, which Mum kept hidden under the bed. I'd tell Robin tomorrow, when it was done: when we would pore over every detail, and she'd be proud: this, too, another thrill.

'There you are,' Tom said, as though I were the late one. He ran a hand through his hair, a move I was certain I'd seen on TV, and I wondered if it was an affectation; I blushed, caught looking just a moment too long. 'Want to go for a walk?'

'Sure.' I shuffled in line with him, and we walked, him talking, me murmuring in response. He'd been studying hard, he said. I wondered the same mysterious things I wondered about other boys, when one brushed up against me, or sat beside me on the bus.

Did they think the same way I did? Or were boys fundamentally different, wired so they were our opposite? Did they notice the brush of body parts like I did? Did they notice me at all?

'What about you?'

I'd lost myself. 'Sorry – what?'

'How's your school-work going?'

'It's . . . Yeah, it's fine. You know. Boring.'

He looked at me, narrowing his eyes a little. 'You strike me more as someone who's kind of into it.'

'Into what?'

He laughed. 'School-work. I have a suspicion you're playing it cool.'

I shrugged, and looked out to the water, caught in a lie.

'Have you sorted things out with your girlfriend?' I'd been trying to work out how or when to ask; now the words simply spilled out.

'Yes and no, I guess,' he said, eyes cast down at his shoes. 'It's over.'

'Oh,' I said, wincing. 'I'm sorry.' I wasn't sorry, of course. I was relieved.

'It's fine. We both knew it was coming.' There was a note of bitterness in his voice.

I looked at him. 'Shall we get a drink?'

'That sounds like a very good idea. Hang on a sec, though. I need cigarettes.'

He ducked into a dimly lit shop, while I waited outside. I pretended to read the posters tacked to the window, cards advertising services nobody wanted; slips of paper, cats lost, dogs found. Finally, Tom appeared in the doorway, stooping below the frame, though he didn't need to. I thought better than to point that out.

'Supplies, mademoiselle,' Tom said, raising a carrier bag, clinking as he lifted it.

'What's that?'

'Drinks,' he said, without sarcasm. 'You're not old enough to go to the pub, are you?'

I stared at him. 'We could . . . I mean, if you went to the bar.'

'Nah,' he said, grabbing my shoulder and guiding me down the promenade. 'Al fresco is much more fun.'

Through the crowds by the pier, past the flickering signs and sideshow freaks, towards the park, with its grand old bandstand shot through with holes. The shade of the crematorium, thin whirls of smoke above; boats whirring by on the broads at impossible speeds. I'd walked this way hundreds of times and, much as I'd hoped it might be some way transformed, it felt no different today as I walked alongside Tom, talking of his favourite music, the books he adored. I had a vague sense that I was supposed to be impressed, he erudite, knowledgeable, old, and wise – but it seemed as though every observation was one I'd heard before, told better, by someone else. Still, I nodded.

'And Bukowski – I mean, that's a genius. You read *Post Office?*'

'No,' I said, though I'd leafed through a copy once, in a library, and found it dull, self-absorbed.

'What? How? It's the best. The *best.*' He stopped, looked around, and threw his coat down on the grass, sitting squarely on it with a thud. I lowered myself down beside him, gingerly tucking my coat beneath me without taking it off. The grass was damp, my fingers cold.

'Let's try another one,' he said, opening a bottle of cider on the edge of his shoe and handing it to me. '*Slaughterhouse-Five.*'

I shrugged. I'd seen it. I'd read the back. I thought it sounded silly. Boyish. Dull.

'Christ. What are they teaching you up at that girls' school – embroidery?'

'Something like that.' I smiled. I suppose in some instinctive way I knew the role I was supposed to play here. I'd be passionate about his interests, coy about mine (uninteresting, bland, boring); I'd listen intently, hang on every word, respect his expertise. I don't know how I knew this. I suppose every girl does.

But the more he talked, the clearer my own thoughts became, revealing themselves one by one. I didn't want to be here. I was bored. I didn't want to kiss him, though before I'd thought I had, didn't want to entertain his endless thoughts. I sipped my drink, and wondered when I could leave. 'I've got a dinner thing with my parents,' I'd say, parents plural, in line with my resolute dullness.

'It's been fun,' I'd say, and disappear, enigmatic, never to be seen again. His feelings, if a little hurt, would soon recover, and I'd go home, never to make the same mistake again. A wasted afternoon, nothing more.

In fact, two hours later, I would sit in the blue-lit toilet of the bus station, all stinking citrus and vomit tang, flypaper and neon bars. I would wash my hands, sit back down, paw through my skirt, looking for traces, leaves, blood in the seams. The light bleaching everything, I closed my eyes, pulled a crisp leaf from my hair, crushed it between my finger and thumb. This, I realize, makes it sound more dramatic than it actually was. The reality of it, I suppose, was rather more banal, my thoughts reasoned, logical. I couldn't go home like this, and for the first time in a while, I very much wanted to go home.

'What are you doing later?' he had said, leaning back on his elbows. Casual. Relaxed. A little removed.

'I've got a dinner thing,' I replied, looking at my watch. 'Parents. Can't get out of it.'

'I see.'

A silence fell.

'What?' I said, finally.

'Nothing.'

Silence again.

'Okay.'

'Okay what?' He turned with a half-smile, exposing yellowed bottom teeth, greased with tar.

'Okay, it's nothing.'

'Okay.'

' . . . You're kind of an asshole, you know.'

'Thanks a lot.'

'Any time.'

'Except tonight.'

'Except tonight.'

I felt the ground shifting below. I couldn't quite place what was happening, what strange territory we were in. Was this flirting? It felt a little like flirting might, my heart fluttering in my throat; and yet there was something else, a vague guilt I couldn't place. Somehow, I felt I'd let him down. I'd disappointed. I'd failed to be the cool girl I'd suggested I might be. I'd not lived up to expectations.

It should be said, however, that this analysis is the benefit of hindsight. In the moment, it was simply a feeling buried deep in my gut, the knowledge that I'd done something wrong.

'I should probably get going,' I said, finally.

'Okay, then.' He didn't move.

I brushed off the damp leaves and blades of grass sticking to my hands and legs. He looked up at me for a moment, before doing the same, a low sigh as he shook out his jacket.

A frisbee sailed between groups of screaming children, mothers arched over pushchairs, whispering secrets. We walked through the park into the arboretum, no more than a few rows of trees beside a boarded-up construction site, glossy signs advertising a new, doomed hotel. He was talking again, as though nothing had happened, and as I told myself, reasonably, nothing had. I listened, agreeing with more enthusiasm, more grace, more impressed with his ideas than I'd been before, attempting to offset my slight.

'So I was thinking about spending the summer doing some kind of activism. I just don't know what for, yet. Maybe Greenpeace or something.'

'Cool,' I said. 'That'd be amazing.'

He stopped, wrapped an arm around my shoulder, planted a kiss on my head; stayed there a moment, his nose and lips in my hair. I moved, laughing a little as I shrugged him off. He took my hand.

'Come here a minute,' he said.

'I've got to . . . '

He squeezed a little tighter; I followed him, arm stiff, shoulders tight, my whole body caught rigid. *It's fine*, I told myself. Shouting, shaking him off, would be stupid, melodramatic. *It's nothing. It's fine.*

We stopped between the trees, light flickering through the leaves. He looked at me, smiled, and kissed my cheek, breath catching with a yeasty tang. I leaned away a little; he kissed again. *Maybe this is romantic*, I thought. *Maybe I'm just too uptight.* A child ran past, laughing, tugging some growling, rolling toy. We moved a little deeper into the trees, the brush thickening, faded crisp packets and broken bottles crunching underfoot.

'Where are we going?' I asked, still too aware of the hot, damp grip of his hand around mine.

'Shhhh . . . ' he said, smiling. Sometimes, looking back, I imagine some sign, something sinister in that smile, but I really don't think there was. It was just a smile, though I felt my heartbeat quicken, skin flush with fear.

'I've got to—'

'Shhh . . . five minutes,' he said, squeezing my hand again.

We reached a dull clearing by the boards, surrounded by trees; we stopped. He pulled me in, kissed my cheek again, first one, then the other.

'You okay?' he whispered.

'I need to go.'

'Okay,' he said, and wrapped an arm around my waist, the other digging fingers into my shoulder blade, under my back-pack. I felt my knees bend, lowered to the ground, where twigs crackled underfoot.

'I don't . . . '

'Shhh . . . ' he said again, a hush I'll never cease to hear. I could've struggled, perhaps, clawed, fought, bitten, pushed away, shouted, screamed . . . all the things a girl's supposed to do in a situation like this. But I didn't. Duly hushed, I shut up, closed myself off, and didn't say another word.

'Is this okay?' he said, pushing my skirt up to my waist, his other arm pressing my shoulder into the dirt, supporting his weight. I said nothing, closed my eyes; he kissed my forehead in response.

The rest comes to me only in flashes, fragments of memory.

My neck softly nuzzled, a hot breath in my ear, every twig and stone beneath digging into my back. A kiss on each cheekbone, hair pushed away from my eyes, hand spilling dust and dirt. The dank, yellow smell of him, damp, sour sweat. The sharp first stab, a knot rising through me, burst in a moan; another gentle 'Shhh . . .'

Closing my eyes, feeling hands try for tenderness. His face, sweat dripping from his forehead onto my neck, expression contorted, like skull creeping through skin. The ugly, animal shape of us, the shame of what we were. I wondered if this was what I'd wanted, told myself it was, clung to reassuring thoughts that at some point, that day, I'd considered the kiss. Perhaps it was my fault. Maybe I'd wanted too much. Confused things. Confused him.

And then, he was done. Done with a gasp and a sigh, and he slumped forwards, his chin sharp in the curve of my neck. Counting the seconds as they passed, I listened to him breathe. He pulled away, stood, extended a hand to help me up.

I brushed myself off and followed him, silent, as we walked back the way we came; he was still talking, again, as though nothing had happened. And I didn't lead him to believe otherwise. I laughed, nodded, agreed, as we walked back through crowds, towards the bus station, where the light caught in scratches on the plastic shelters, and I sat, waiting to go home.

The university bus pulled in farther down the stand; he looked at it, then looked at me.

'You should get it,' I said. I knew what he was thinking. He should wait. See me off.

'You sure?' he said, turning towards it.

'Yeah, definitely. Mine won't be long.'

'Okay. Cool.' He smiled, leaned in, kissed my cheek; I felt a wave of nausea at his breath. 'I'll see you around.'

'Okay,' I said, and watched him leave. I dug my fingers into my stomach, pressing nails into flesh, and stood, a moment, waiting. Then into the blue-lit toilets, trying to make myself clean; then onto the bus home, conscious of a dampness in my lower back, fingers pulling a knotted stick, releasing blood.

'Hi, Mum,' I said, seeing her standing in the living room, lights off, curtains closed, TV flickering white.

'Hi, sweetheart,' she said, not turning to see me. 'How was your day?'

I thought about it. I ran a hand through my hair, matted thick; shook my hand loose. 'Fine,' I said, smiling even though she wouldn't see, as though that made it less untrue.

'Good,' she said, still rapt in the show.

Upstairs, I stuffed my clothes into a pillowcase, eyes determinedly averted from the stains. I couldn't put them in the laundry basket, for fear of being seen, and yet the look of them – their very presence – sickened me. I tied the pillowcase shut, and stuffed them into the bottom of the cupboard, slamming the door behind.

I ran a bath, scalding hot, and stepped in, feeling my skin burn feet-first, and I lay there, staring at my body, sickened, until night fell and the cold set in.

It's nothing, I told myself, watching a spider crawl across the ceiling, black with mould. *It's fine,* I said, drawing lines with my fingers; the string around wax paper, case around butcher's meat. *It's really no big deal,* I willed as I lowered myself underwater, feeling thunder rolling in above, and was grateful for the storm: the rain began to pelt the window, echoed by my racing, tired heart.

I saw her before she saw me.

She was hunched over a book, her back rounded, shoulders sunk low, as she held a sandwich in one hand and a coffee in the other. It never ceased to amaze me, when I saw Robin on her own, how small and close to invisible she could be but for the shock of her hair and – when she saw you – her wide, snaggle-toothed smile. It was as though the girl I knew was an act, a staged excess of personality which shrank away the moment she was alone, leaving the shell of her behind.

'Hey,' I said, taking a seat in the booth opposite.

She looked up, blinked; became herself again. 'Hey, bitch. What's cooking?'

'Nothing. What are you reading?' I knew. I'd left it in the tower weeks ago for her to find, convinced she'd love it – a lurid history of the Manson murders, nauseating in its details. We'd found a shared obsession with sleazy true-crime stories and pulpy paperbacks. It was exactly the kind of thing she'd like.

'Nothing interesting,' she said, slapping it down on the table, spine cracked, facing upwards: the smile she gave ferocious.

'Rumour has it,' she began, slowly – teasing the words out, one by one. 'Rumour has it that a certain best friend of mine started the festive season with a dirty hookup. With a certain friend of my boyfriend's.'

I felt my cheeks burn hot, a vicious swell of tears.

'Oh my god, it's *true*,' she said, leaning forwards. 'Did you two fuck in the park?'

'I don't know what you're talking about.' My voice shook; cheeks prickled, nausea rising at the memory. Hands, mud, hair snagged and caught.

'You do. Oh my god, you *so* do. Fucking hell. Never had you pegged as that much of a slut.' She laughed, shaking her head. 'I thought that was my bit.'

She waved, and I turned to see Alex strolling through the door, throwing a teasing look at the washed-up musician lurking in the corner. He'd dedicated numerous songs to her over the last three months, all roundly ignored. Still, she liked to toy with him, mixing coquettish glances with an absolute rebuttal of his attentions, at which we would laugh, riotously, between hushed whispers and looks in his direction.

'Don't say anything,' I hissed, pleading with my eyes. 'Please.'

'Hey, slut,' Robin said, her tone light, though her eyes were still fixed on mine. 'How's it hanging?'

Alex launched, enthusiastically, into a tale of some culinary nightmare: a misadventure prompted by Grace's inability to follow a recipe, and which ended – as all Alex's stories tended to – 'So we gave up, and opened a bottle of wine.' It never failed to impress me, the way Alex was so casual about what seemed – to me, at least – to be mature, sophisticated tastes.

She was a year older than the three of us, having spent a year in New York after her GCSEs, interning for a friend of her mother's in some ultra-cool advertising agency. The way she made time for manicures (a habit strange and pointless to the rest of us, with our chipped, bitten nails coated in lurid paint), the fact she could drive, her ability to describe in detail the qualities of different types of wine, at least, as far as we knew, none of us possessing the knowledge to confirm or deny her sweeping statements, all gave her a maturity that we could only imitate, each privately peacocking our stolen quirks in front of our parents and peers.

'Be right back,' Robin said, sliding from the booth. 'Got to see a man about a dog.' She pointed to a man in a lurid, purple tracksuit, thin and pale, from whom I knew she bought powders and pills whenever Andy was indisposed, or out of favour.

Alex and I sat for a moment, watching as she sidled over and struck up what seemed to be a casual conversation, with an ease I could only envy. I looked at Alex – the bitten curve of her lips, swoop of cool brow – and we laughed as she placed a hand on his arm; her mark added another coffee to his order, as we knew he would. With Robin, certain things were inevitable. It was part of her effect.

'Violet,' Alex said, softly. I turned to look at her, her eyes sparkling bright green, ringed with black, her lashes impossibly long. 'I wanted to ask you something,' she said, glancing back over at Robin. 'I don't suppose you know anything about a book going missing from my mom's office, do you?'

I blushed. I didn't know, of course, but I could guess. 'What book?'

'Just one of my mom's weird old ones – it's kind of an antique. Leather-bound, gold edges, expensive-looking . . . It's disappeared, and she's *pissed*. She's threatening to call the police if I don't tell her where it is.'

'The police?'

'I mean, she won't. It's just a threat, I think.'

I sipped my coffee, reaching for an excuse. 'Maybe it was your neighbour,' I said, the words strangled in my throat.

'I doubt it,' she said, leaning back. 'She's too drunk to read most of the time as it is. And anyway, I can't imagine she'd be interested in ancient rituals and occult practices.' She looked down at my palm; instinctively, I balled it into a fist and tucked it under the table.

I laughed, faintly. 'You never know.'

She smiled. 'I have a feeling – don't quote me on this, obviously – but I have a feeling Robin took it. We were talking about it that night at my place, and then, by "complete co-incidence", it was gone the next day.'

'Hmmm.' I couldn't remember talking about it with the others. I thought it was just Robin and me. *You were drunk,* I told myself. *It was probably while you were asleep.*

Silence fell between us. 'Well,' I began, nervously. 'If she says anything about it, I'll let you know. But . . . Well, she doesn't seem like the stealing type, does she?'

Alex snorted. 'So she *does* have it. God, Violet. You're a terrible liar.'

'Ready, bitches?' Robin said, leaning over the table.

Alex smiled at me. 'Ready,' she said, sliding out from the booth and walking towards the door, leaving me trailing, as ever, behind.

Chapter 7

Nicky pointed at the group of girls lingering beside the wych elm. I imagined Ms Boucher, burning as the women around her – the girls, like me – screamed and clasped their hands and begged the pain to stop. The Dean and Headmaster wrangled with fence poles and tape, creating a temporary cordon around the blackened trunk, its branches now split and hanging thanks to a lightning strike during the winter break.

'I'm sure it's a rumour, obviously – you know what this place is like. But I heard she gave Patrick Chase a blow job in the stairwell after the party. Which is weird, because I thought she was kind of a prude.'

I liked Nicky or, at least, still didn't quite understand why the other girls didn't. She seemed nice enough – a gossip, yes, though I'd found this a useful trait in learning the who's who of the rest of the school, a kind of crash course in the secrets shared between my fellow students, who still, for their part, seemed to view me as the 'new girl'.

'But anyway, that's nothing compared to what I heard about Victoria Riley – you know, the girl whose family own the stables? Looks the part – long face, big thighs? Well, Anna said that she'd been seen . . . ' I drifted off, watching the girls whispering, mocking the Headmaster as he wrangled with a pole which bent against the solid earth below.

'And Robin who you hang out with, too—'

'Wait, what?' I said, yoked back to Nicky's chatter by the mention of a familiar name.

'She was there last year, too.'

'Where?'

'In the clinic. Melanie Barker was in there with her.'

'What clinic?'

Nicky narrowed her eyes. 'Were you listening to anything I just said?'

'Sorry, yeah. I mean, I was, but I got distracted. Go back a bit.'

She sighed. 'Okay, so: Melanie Barker – you know, the one who looks like Madonna, except if Madonna was ugly and kind of fat?' She spoke slowly, as though trying to communicate with someone in another language.

'Right,' I said, though I didn't.

'So she's bulimic, although you'd never know it to look at her. And last year she got into buying these diet pills, through a friend of a friend or . . . whatever. Anyway, they were like speed. Sent her completely nuts.' I wondered if Nicky had ever taken speed. Doubtful. She seemed suddenly naive, though I couldn't quite determine whether that was an altogether bad thing, the welt in my palm still hot and crisp.

'Obviously she got busted by her parents, and they sent her off to the Appleyard. It's like the Priory, I guess, except instead of celebrities, it's full of rich kids who drink too much, or, like, steal their mum's Valium, or whatever.'

'Okay.' I fingered the bracelet on my wrist, trying to act uninterested. 'So what's that got to do with Robin?'

'They were there at the same time. Melanie and Robin, I mean. Not that they sit around bonding about it, or anything.'

'What was she in there for?'

She shrugged. 'No idea. Drugs, booze, food, mental problems, whatever – it's like a one-stop-shop for that kind of thing. But apparently one day your buddy lost it. Like, literally, lost it. Started walking down the corridors screaming about how they'd never find Emily Frost, and they'd never find the body, and it was all her fault, blah blah blah. *Anyway* . . . ' She moved on to another story, something involving Melanie, truth or dare, and a wine bottle, the end of which I felt no desire to know.

I looked back towards the wych elm, where the teachers had finished their work. The Dean stepped back, shielding his eyes against the silvery light needling through the branches. The Headmaster said something to the girls, and they laughed. The Dean shook his head, turned, and walked away, hands clenched in tight fists. He saw me looking, released them as though caught; he waved, briefly, and disappeared under the arches, head bowed in thought.

Annabel sat, cross-legged in the winged armchair, while the four of us lounged on sofas, books piled around us, sipping spiced tea and listening. The ancient radiators in the Campanile cracked and wailed like a chorus; the women on the walls looked on. Our study had turned to the archetypes of women, the origins of what Annabel called the 'feminine myth'. I hid behind my book, having fallen too far behind on the reading, it seemed, to catch up. The books I'd opened over the break had sat abandoned and unread, scattered on surfaces among ashtrays and half-drained bottles, both Mum's and my own, the two of us clutching our oblivion like a shield.

Endless stanzas of Greek and Roman literature – supposed to give us a grounding in the figures that dominated the art we were to study – seemed to swim, listlessly, in front of my eyes, their rhythms brittle and awkward.

'Women, though maligned in Athenian society – relegated to a second-class status, alongside outsiders, and slaves – are emboldened and empowered in tragedy,' she said, smiling. 'One need only consider Medea, to whose speech our own leaders have referred time and again, as indicative of our plight. "Most of the time, a woman is full of fear, too weak to defend herself or to bear the sight of steel – but if she happens to be wronged in love, hers is the blood-thirstiest heart of all." She was the ultimate threat: the woman wronged by man, seeking a vengeance that its audience – almost entirely male, remember – would be hard-pressed to argue with.'

Grace nodded. I could see Robin craning, a little, trying to catch my eye.

'I still can't believe you did that, you whore,' she had said as we walked to class, referring once again to my 'dirty hookup', a subject she'd refused to let drop. 'It's going to take me months to recover.'

'Me too,' I had replied, coldly, surprised to see a flicker of recognition pass across her face. But before she could respond, Grace had joined us, and the conversation had drifted elsewhere. Since then, she'd been offering awkward grimaces, apologetic smiles. Still, I couldn't meet her eye.

'What else were men afraid of? Let's look to the tragic form – the home of all their most unimaginable fears. The worst that might happen, performed in front of their very eyes on the stage. Sisterly relationships, so the plays seem to suggest, are fine – Antigone and Ismene, Electra and Chrysothemis – they have affection, warmth for one another, which tragedy seems happy to allow. The choruses, too, were often presented as women, and were, in general, favourably disposed to female characters.

'But unsupervised, private female friendships? Oh no. Women, alone together, without the supervision of men, almost always caused disaster in their households, and the wider community, these freedoms resulting in madness, anger, sexual desire, or jealousy resulting in death. Women are not to be left alone, together, or tragedy will surely follow.'

She tapped the bruised textbook open on her lap. 'Consider the critic who says, and I quote: "Women become tragic figures by men's absence or *mismanagement*",' she said, her voice practically hissing with derision. 'In Sophocles, "Antigone's actions begin after her uncle Creon refuses to bury her brother Polynices. In the *Oresteia*, it is only after her husband has been fighting in Troy for ten years that Clytemnestra takes power in Argos" – murdering him for sacrificing her daughter, among other abuses, I might add.

"And Medea becomes the aggressor when her husband abandons her for a marriage he believes will improve his social standing, leaving her and her children to starve." This,' she said, closing the book and placing it on the table, 'is your primary text, in the study of the Classics. And yet any of us would struggle to find fault with these women's actions, extreme as they are. It is the actions of men that make them vengeful, not through mismanagement or absence, as the text says, but out of cruelty and selfish desire.'

She stood, as she always did when reaching her point, and walked to the window, her back to us. A screwed-up ball of paper landed in my lap; I looked up and saw Robin pointing to it, eyes glinting, willing me to open it.

'You look sad,' it said, her handwriting large and jagged, all but crawling off the page. I thumbed the soft, torn edge of the page, searching for the words.

'Picture a society in which this is the foundational idea: that men's actions are eminently reasonable, while women's are, by their very nature, irrational and wrong. I shouldn't think that's too difficult to imagine, no?'

I picked up my pen, and began to write. 'I am sad,' I wrote at last, and threw the ball back. Annabel turned to us and smiled. The thin, wintry light seemed her colour; she stood, proudly, like the women of whom she spoke. I imagine her now, when I do the same: feeling myself performing, as I suppose she did, too.

'Melanippe, though, says this – though of course, through the words of Euripides, a male playwright: "Men's criticism of women is worthless twanging of a bow-string and evil talk.

Women are better than men, as I will show . . . Consider their role in religion, for that, in my opinion, comes first. We women play the most important part, because women prophesy the will of Zeus in the oracles of Phoebus. And at the holy site of Dodona near the sacred oak, females convey the will of Zeus to inquirers from Greece. As for the sacred rituals of the Fates and the nameless Ones – 'the Erinyes' – all these would not be holy if performed by men, but prosper in women's hands. In this way women have a rightful share in the service of the gods. Why is it, then, that women must have a bad reputation?" She has a point, and makes it well.

'Even with this fragment, however, it seems that women are doomed to two fates. It is our lot to be seen as either unpredictable and irrational mortals, maligned and repressed by the actions of men, or sacred beings, goddesses of a higher realm, among the Fates and the Furies.'

The large hands of the clock faces ticked in unison, reaching five to the hour. Annabel sighed, looked at each of us in turn, and sat back in the armchair, as though exhausted. As though the force of her words had been too much.

'That's all for today, girls,' she said, softly. 'Don't wreak too much havoc before our next class.'

As we reached town, the moon full and bright, streetlights and arcades burning in the darkness, Robin hooked her arm around mine, and we walked to the mermaid in silence.

'They're all bastards,' she had simply said. I rested my head on her shoulder a moment, her hair soft and smoke-sweet. The shift had been wordless, Robin's sudden understanding drawing the colour from her skin, hands trembling, slightly, as we sat together on the bus. As Alex and Grace walked away, she squeezed my hand, tight, and while the black, creeping mass in my gut remained, it seemed a little lighter, its power lessened, shared.

'Can I ask you something?' I said, softly.

She nodded.

'Do you know Melanie Barker?' I hadn't planned to ask – and yet, now, I couldn't help myself. She looked straight ahead, barely reacted at all. After a pause, she turned to me.

'Who?'

'Melanie Barker.' Another pause. 'The one that looks like Madonna, except fat and ugly.'

'No.' The silence weighed heavy between us, filled by the distant cry of gulls above the pier. I took a deep breath, pushed a little more. 'Nicky told me she was in some clinic place. She said you knew each other.'

'And you believe her?' she said, icily.

'I . . . I don't know.'

'Seriously, Violet. Don't believe a word any of those bitches say. They make shit up just to make their boring lives interesting.' She paused. 'I don't know why you talk to her, anyway. Especially as she was the one spreading the rumour about you and . . . '

I blushed furiously. *Who else knows?* I thought, a wave of shame bubbling to the surface. I felt around for a change of subject, a distraction.

'What's up with the others?'

'Who?'

I turned to her, making a face: Who else? At the mermaid, Grace and Alex had left without a word, though Grace had given me a brief, imploring look, willing me to follow. When I'd hesitated, Alex had rolled her eyes while Robin smiled, a flash of what I thought might be victory behind her eyes. I'd picked a side during this split second of indecision, in a fight I didn't quite understand.

She laughed, bitterly. 'Oh, you know.'

'The book?'

She pulled a spool of bubble gum from her jacket and rolled a section around her finger. 'How do you know about that?'

I said nothing, waited for her to go on. She pulled the gum off with her teeth, leaving a red trail where she'd bitten down, white at the nail.

'They were going to burn it,' she said, finally.

'Why?'

'I don't know. But you know who burns books?' She plucked a beetle from her sock, and held it up at eye level. It shook out its wings, preparing to fly; she flicked it, a lazy arc into the sand. 'The Nazis, that's who.'

She said it with such conviction that I laughed. She glared at me. 'What?'

'You can't compare Alex and Grace to the Nazis.'

She turned away, angrily, but I saw the hint of a smile curling the corner of her mouth.

'Vee are zee evil Nazi lesbians, and vee come to burn zee books,' I said, wondering even as I spoke why I was the one appeasing her. Given the circumstances, it seemed a little off.

She snorted, and the tension broke, the air cooling between us. 'You are such an idiot.'

'So where's the book now?' I said, after a pause.

'Not a chance.'

'What?'

'You'll tell Alex,' she said.

'I won't.'

'Sorry, Vivi. Not a risk I'm willing to take.' She grinned. 'Unless you want to . . . you know.'

I said nothing, pretended to examine a scrap of paper stuck to the bottom of my shoe.

'You do – you totally do!' Two girls passing looked in our direction, sensing gossip.

'Shhhh,' I said. 'I do not,' I added, though the words seemed false, even to me.

'Yeah, yeah, yeah.' She grabbed my hand. 'Come on, Vi. Be honest. It'll be fun.'

'Fun like last time?' I said. 'When you stabbed me, you mean?'

'I didn't *stab* you,' she said, laughing. 'It was an expression of friendship, bonding us together forever.'

'I'd have preferred a bracelet.'

'Stick around long enough, I'll get you one of those too, oh yin to my yang,' she said, loosening her hair from a thick knot and shaking it out. 'Look, have a think about it. But just so you know—' She scooped up her bag and slung it over her shoulder. 'I'm going to pick up supplies on Saturday. I'll be here at eleven if you decide you want to . . . have some fun.'

'Supplies for what?' I said after her, but she walked away without a word.

'And so the beautiful Medusa was punished by Poseidon, and transformed into a monstrous thing – a creature who, for her sacrilege, was doomed to turn to stone all those who looked upon her.' I turned the page, rapt. 'Thus, she provides the most fertile subject for da Vinci, Caravaggio, and numerous others throughout the history of art: the glint in her eyes the prey turned predator, and back once again. The woman who escapes her place, and is returned to it: her severed head a warning to us all.'

I ran my fingers across the glossy print, Annabel's words reflecting the lamps in the reception hall, where I'd been called to collect – so I was told – some attendance-related paperwork on which I would forge my mother's signature once again.

'Violet – a word, if I may.' The Dean stood smiling in the office doorway, clubbed fingers wrapped around the door frame like shells: an unwelcome surprise. I'd intercepted the letters sent home, the Elm Hollow crest on the envelope giving their contents away. 'We have some concerns', they would begin, and would end with an invitation to a 'conference', between my mum and the Dean.

One becomes used to pointless meetings as an adult: endless sit-downs and talking-tos, each party going through the motions and walking away unchanged. But then, as seems to be the case for my own students, now, a meeting between parents and teachers seemed the ultimate indignity – a shame I wouldn't shake.

The Dean, meeting my mum, stained sweatshirt over filthy jeans, stinking faintly, would be embarrassment enough. But if Annabel saw her – saw what I was from, and thus what I might become — I shuddered at the thought. I couldn't stand it, the pitching realization, the flush on Annabel's pale cheeks as she turned and walked away. It was an encounter I would do anything to prevent.

I sat on the edge of the old armchair, watching as the Dean settled himself, his fleshy skin visible through his shirt, thin patches of sweat at the seams of his elbows. He smiled, warmly, a practised openness I'd seen before, in the eyes of paramedics, doctors, police: the hollow empathy of people trained to care. There was something unsettling about it. It seemed a little unfair, given the circumstances: before the winter break my grades had been good, though not great. My attendance, admittedly, had been a little haphazard, the temptations of wandering the streets with Robin too much to turn down. Still, it seemed to me I was doing well – or at least, I had been, until recently.

'How are you doing, Violet?'

'Fine, sir,' I said, flatly, peering down at my hands crossed on my lap.

'Good. That's good.' He clicked his tongue three times and leaned forward. 'Violet, I'm a little concerned. I've been looking at your recent grades, and it seems as though you're falling a little short of our expectations.' He paused, waiting for me to meet his eye. 'I know you're used to a rather less conventional teaching method, so I wanted to check in. Are you finding it hard to keep up?'

I felt my pride, bruised, swell in my chest, and looked up. 'No, sir.'

He licked his lip, tongue poking dry, like a cat. 'So you're capable of understanding the work?'

'Yes, sir.' I gave a weak smile, a grimace.

He sighed. 'Then, Violet, if I may ask . . . Is there perhaps something else going on that's preventing you from making the best of your situation?'

I said nothing, staring him in the eye, hoping wilfulness alone might make him drop the subject. He stared back; I felt a chill, a flash of fear I couldn't place. My heart picked up its rhythm, rolling in my chest.

'Sir,' I began, weakly. 'If I'm in trouble . . .'

'You're not in trouble,' he said, leaning back, chair creaking beneath. 'I just wanted us to have a little talk, to see what we can do about getting things moving back in the right direction. I assume you want to go to university?'

'Yes, sir.' This wasn't quite the truth, but nor was it entirely a lie. I'd put little thought into it, though I'd absorbed snippets of conversation from the girls, and from the rest of the school. University, for the students of Elm Hollow, was an inevitability: the goal towards which all of us were to strive. Which made sense, I suppose. For when the end of school came, who in their right mind would choose to stay in the confines of our miserable little town?

'That's good. Very good. But I'll be honest, Violet: the best universities will start opening for applications in October. They'll be looking for a copy of your transcripts and, quite frankly, at the moment you don't have much to show them.'

He sighed, a little roll of flesh pushing over the edge of his belt. 'I know it seems dull, but you need to start planning ahead, and get those grades up, if you're going to apply to any of the top-tier universities. Which, based on your scores before this semester, I believe you'd be more than capable of.'

I felt a sting in my throat, heat rising in my cheeks. He placed a tentative hand on mine, and I looked away. I was angry at myself for crying, especially in front of a teacher – *especially* the Dean, with his penchant for rescue well-known. We'd all heard the stories of how he 'did everything he could' for Emily, how he'd taken a week of personal leave to help with the search. I didn't want to be another charity case. Once the first tear fell, however, more followed, until my shoulders shook with sobs.

He handed me a tissue. 'Violet, it's okay to have a wobble from time to time. Everybody does. You're in a position, now, where you can recover, and nobody has to know.' I felt the hot dampness of a large hand pressed over mine, the calluses rope-like on his palm. I looked up. 'Between you and me, we can come up with a plan to get you back on track in no time.'

I gave a weak shrug, unsure how to respond to this small kindness, afraid I'd cry more if I tried to speak. *Get off me,* I thought, thinking of Tom, loathing the touch of his flesh on mine, the sickening creep of sweat. At last, he let go. I wiped my hand roughly on my skirt.

'So, what can we do?' he said, pretending not to notice, flicking slowly through a thick book of university codes and courses. 'Some of our students take on additional projects to prove how committed they are to their studies. Are you doing any extra-curriculars?'

'No,' I said. He waited. 'Sports aren't really my thing.'

'What about music? Band, perhaps?'

I sighed. 'I can't play anything.'

He leaned back in his chair, tapping his foot against the edge of the desk. 'Well, how about . . . Hmmm.'

'What?'

'Well, I'm working on a book, and I could use a research assistant. It's not a conventional extra-curricular, mind. But I could write you a glowing reference come admissions time – assuming you'd earned it, that is.'

I paused. 'What kind of book?'

'A history of Elm Hollow – or at least, the myths that surround it.' He tapped a pen on the edge of the desk. 'Of course, if it's not of interest, that's fine. I'm sure we can find something else for you to—'

I didn't wait for him to finish. 'No – no. That sounds perfect,' I said, dabbing the crumbling tissue around my eyes.

'Great,' he said. 'We'll meet here on Tuesday evenings – provided your mother won't mind you being late?'

I took my cue to stand. 'She won't notice, I'm sure.'

He narrowed his eyes, briefly, chose to ignore the comment.

'One thing I would ask, Violet,' he said, walking me to the door. 'If you wouldn't mind keeping this between us, I'd be very much obliged.'

'No problem, sir,' I said. He smiled, gums showing, a thread of spit between his lips, and closed the door. I shuddered, shaking off the way he'd looked at me – the gooey, cosy concern, as though he might somehow understand, if I let him simply *try* – and walked away, books thumping, bruising, in my bag.

I found Alex and Grace in the smoking shelter, wrapped in thick coats, bare legs turning shades of blue in the winter air. While I'd been in the office, it had started to rain, great drops slapping on the glass roof as I slid in beside them.

From the moment I said hello, I knew I'd interrupted something, some private conversation of which I was not a part, *unless*, I thought, with ever-present teenage self-absorption, *I was the topic* – the thought immediately chilling, sick. The girls said nothing; Grace smiled, while Alex looked down at her knees, one scraped and bruised from a fall.

'What happened?' I said, pointing to the graze.

'Hockey.' She shrugged. 'The usual. Nicky's a psycho in attack.'

'You look . . . ' Grace began, gently. 'You look kind of tired. Are you okay?'

I wondered, for a moment, whether to tell them what had happened with Tom. To admit that, yes, I'd barely slept, couldn't eat, was on what seemed something like academic probation. They looked at me, warmly.

'I'm fine,' I said, forcing a smile. 'Thank you, though.'

'If you ever . . . Well, you know . . . '

We fell silent again, a fog gathering around the Campanile outside, clinging to the gleaming tower clocks. Grace squinted, before looking at her watch. 'Have you done your Aesthetics homework?'

I grimaced. 'I can't remember what it was. Annabel's going to kill me.'

'You'll be fine,' she said. 'She loves you. Lucky thing.'

'Nah,' I said, though I felt a rush of pleasure at the suggestion, tailed by a knot of shame at the fact that in a couple of hours I'd no doubt disappoint. 'I don't—'

'You can have a look at mine, if you want.'

'Oh. Yeah. Thanks.'

'No problem.'

The silence fell again.

Without Robin – who seemed incapable of allowing a silence, or, more accurately, of allowing one not placed there by design, a dramatic pause for emphasis. I imagined our friendship, the three of us: quiet, calm, and – I supposed, ruefully – pleasantly dull.

'Do you know what Robin's up to?' Alex said, finally. I wondered whether she'd been thinking the same thing.

'What do you mean?'

She laughed. 'If I knew, I wouldn't be asking.' She peeled open a packet of gum, rolling the stick into a careful loop before placing it on the tip of her tongue. Grace leaned in as though about to bite it away; I blushed, then blushed at the blush itself, ashamed to have been caught looking. 'I didn't think you'd tell me, anyway,' Alex said, a kindness, here, in the absence of a comment – I suppose they were used to it, the only couple in school or, at least, the only one to admit it. 'But you really don't know, do you?'

'She doesn't have to tell me everything,' I said, flatly.

'Be nice, though, wouldn't it?' She stuck her tongue out,

white-tipped with gum stretched, veined pink and blue.

Grace thrust a sheet of paper between us, whipping in the breeze. 'Homework.' We stared at her, blankly. 'For Aesthetics. If you want it.' I took the paper, tried to make sense of her tiny, creeping hand. 'And you,' she said, nudging Alex on the shoulder with two fingers, needling what I imagined was a bruise. 'Stop interrogating Violet. If she knew, she'd tell us. Wouldn't you, Vi?'

The truth was, I wasn't sure. But I smiled, brightly, and nodded. 'Yeah. Of course.' I tucked the homework in my bag, carefully, and turned to leave. 'I'll see you in class,' I said, cheerfully; wondered whether they could hear the hollowness in my tone.

The wind howled around the mermaid, and Robin, as usual, was late. I fought to light a cigarette against the breeze, my umbrella tucked under my arm, skin damp through my thin jacket. In the grey drizzle, the town seemed even further removed from the lushness of Elm Hollow, this sad, forgotten seaside town, with its dirty beaches, shards of glass, and plastic bags washed up in the muddy sand.

A seagull landed on the pavement, mere yards away, and looked towards me, eyes dead and yellow. Robin ran towards it, and it flew away, wings beating with soft claps.

'I don't know if you noticed, but I just saved your life,' she said. 'Those things are monsters.' I laughed, and she grinned. 'I'm really glad you came.'

'Yeah,' I said, awkwardly. 'I'm . . . I'm glad too.'

We wandered along the tattered promenade, past children

waving pinwheels and old men eating chips with dirty fingers, the air salty and coarse. We walked by head shops, butchers, and shabby arcades, machines ringing, coins clattering to the sound of whirling, woozy songs; smelled fried doughnuts and the dried-beer tang of boarded-up pubs; down a narrow cobbled street lined with black-and-white buildings, which leaned conspiratorially inwards, creaking with the weight of gravity and decline.

Two men sat silently on a park bench, sharing a quart of whisky straight from the bottle; a mother pleaded with a screaming child to just, for a moment, *just a single second, please stop crying.*

'Here it is,' she said, pausing at a dusty window, a blue, faded door. The wooden sign creaked in the breeze, shaped like a crescent moon. *Lunar Rune,* it read, in curled, peeling letters. 'Come on.' She grabbed my hand, and led me inside.

As the door closed, the bell's chime fading, the suffocating haze of incense, sandalwood and lavender, was overwhelming. From the low beams hung knotted dream-catchers and wind chimes, brought to life by our entrance.

Shelves on every wall were filled with candles, toys, and stones, a faded card by each one explaining its unique mystic qualities. Some hidden speaker hissed with a combination of whale song and monkish chants whose rhythms seemed to rattle my teeth.

'Ladies,' a voice said.

'Holy shit,' Robin said, staring at the figure behind me. I spun around. 'I mean – sorry. Hi, Annabel. Didn't expect to see you here.'

She smiled, dimly. 'I could say the same to you.'

Robin gave her usual smile, and rocked back and forth on her heels. 'What are you shopping for, miss?'

'You know I prefer "Annabel".' She held out her hand, teasing the wick of a long, white taper. 'It's so hard to find candles that last more than a night.' She looked at me as she spoke; then turned to Robin, who stiffened, following her gaze. I felt a brief, momentary thrill at being first; at being seen, for once, before her. 'And what brings you girls here?'

'Just browsing,' Robin said. I wondered if I was imagining the flicker in her voice. She wasn't usually fazed by Annabel, visibly, at least; yet now, in the moment, she seemed unsure, as though forgetting herself. She rocked backwards again, and turned away.

Annabel watched, a slow smile appearing on her face, before turning back to me. 'Well, I shall see you girls on Monday. Enjoy your weekend.'

She turned from us, abruptly, in the way I remembered from my first conversation with her in the art studio. It was impressive, the way she could end a conversation with a simple gesture, making you feel as though you were barely even there. Making you feel, too, a painful desire to be noticed, for her to turn back again and fix you in her sights: to take you in.

We walked the store in silence, listening to the rhythmic clang of the old till, the hushed words and rustle of brown paper bags. Finally, the doorbell rang to signal Annabel had left; Robin laughed.

'So weird seeing teachers out of school, isn't it?'

'Especially in a place like this.' I closed the book I'd been

149

staring blindly down at, thin pages filled with sketches of women dancing, trees pulling at their hair.

'Yeah,' she said. 'Come on.'

From the outside, the shop had looked small, unassuming, but the musty front opened on to a wide chamber filled with books, a mezzanine floor above. I passed shelves dedicated to *Celtic Myth and Folklore*, an entire wall given over to *Lore of Creatures* (broken down into subcategories for *Faeries, Unicorns, Animals,* and *Beasts (General)*.)

In *Norse Gods*, tan leather books were held in place by rearing wolves carved in stone, and a section devoted to *Herbalism* grew thick with ranging plants whose sticky leaves left imprints on the spines of every book.

'Hey,' Robin said, from across the room. I turned, and she beckoned, raising her finger to her lips.

'What?' I whispered.

'Come closer.'

I stepped towards her. 'Closer,' she hissed. I took another step, and she dived towards me, a chalky skull on her fist. I screamed and fell backwards into a stand of flyers, scattering advertisements for healing therapies and crystal magic to the ground.

'Excuse me,' a tall, thin woman said, appearing in the doorway. She glared at the two of us as we tried to contain our laughter.

'Sorry,' Robin said, sheepishly. 'My friend scared herself.'

The woman watched us with narrowed eyes as I scooped up the spilled flyers. 'Mystical Walks of the Pagan Gods', one said; 'Harnessing the Sea: A Workshop' another.

'This is ridiculous,' I whispered, as Robin ran her fingers through a large bowl of beads, the sound roaring like the sea. 'We're not going to find anything here. It's just tourist crap.'

'Oh yeah?' she said. 'What's this, then?' She held up a squat, black candle in a cork-topped glass.

'A candle.'

'Sarcasm doesn't suit you, you know.'

I rolled my eyes. 'Go on, then. What kind of candle?'

'The kind we need.' She passed me the candle, and grabbed another two, the glass clinking as she rolled them together in her hands. 'Might as well stock up. Just in case.'

We paid, the old woman still glaring at us as we did so.

'These aren't toys, you know.'

'We know,' Robin said, with a sarcastic smile. The woman's hand hovered, a moment, before she took the crumpled note; before she could change her mind, we were out in the street, blinking in the silvery light. We walked back the way we came, stumbling as we laughed at the old woman, the strangeness of her old curiosity shop; the types of people who'd shop there, ageing hippies and single women seeking love potions, cursed like woodcut beasts.

Robin sat at the base of the statue and began to roll a joint. In more civilized towns than ours, being so conspicuous in our drug use might have been risky; to us, however, it was nothing, the sweet smell of the joint mingling with the salt of the sea, of burnt driftwood and candy floss. She took a long, lazy drag, and passed it to me.

'Hey, I . . . I got you something,' she said. The uncharacteristic pause made my stomach drop, with the sense that she'd been building up to this, choosing her words carefully. When she didn't go on, I turned to her, raised an eyebrow, and blew smoke in her face. 'Fuck off.' She laughed, her elbow sticking in my rib.

'What is it, then?'

She fumbled in her pockets, one, then another, before rooting deep into her coat. 'A-ha,' she said, finally. With her free hand, she plucked the joint from my lips. She looked up, and exhaled, slowly. 'This is kind of nerdy.'

'No surprise there,' I said, with a gentle nudge.

'I figured it'd suit you, you know.'

'Touché.'

She pulled out a thin, silver chain, another looped through it. On each was a twinkling, silver pendant. She pressed them together, forming a circle. 'See? It's a friendship bracelet. You said you wanted one,' she added, a faint blush on her cheeks that might have been the pinch of the breeze.

I threw my arm around her shoulder. 'You are such a loser.'

'I know,' she said. 'Give me your hand.'

I held out my arm, rolling up my sleeve, and she tied the bracelet around my wrist, carefully. 'Now you do mine,' she said. I tied it, my fingers chilled by the thin, cool chain.

'There you go,' she said, smiling. 'Together forever, and all that.' She held my hand, tight, and we watched the lonely people of the town, and pitied them. Pitied everyone, in fact, who wasn't us.

Chapter 8

She had the frayed edge of my sweater between finger and thumb, twirling it as we listened to Annabel. I tried to concentrate, to listen, but I felt my attention constantly drifting back to her hand, thoughtful, possessive, refusing to let go.

'You no doubt played with toys,' Annabel said, 'created magical stories, imagined whole worlds shared between you and your friends. Play, for children, and the development of the imagination, is a mode of expression, of unity in experience. We learn, as children, to form contracts of agreement, a shared belief in things which, to those on the outside, are creations of the mind, inventions, and fantasies.'

She crossed her legs in the armchair, leaned her elbows on her knees. 'But to the child, this isn't an active process. Everything they imagine is real. I, for instance, believed in fairies – I *saw* them, convinced as Lady Cottington herself, even as she sketched the fairies she would tell her parents she'd pressed. As children, we can believe things at the same time as knowing, as being an active participant in, their creation.'

Robin shuffled a little closer, her hand now touching mine. I leaned over the arm of the chair, pulling myself away.

'You told stories, with these inventions, great, swooping tales of life and death, love and betrayal, of worlds colliding time and again. Stories which had the weight of myth behind them, those grand narratives that underpin all human experience.' She looked up, at each of us in turn. 'But how? How do we know, as children, that the betrayal of a loved one may lead to death and suffering? That the good doctor may save us, with some last-second intervention; that the winged ones come, beautiful and terrifying, exquisite in the shadow of death? That revenge, sometimes, is a right?'

Robin coughed, looked at Alex and Grace, who stared wilfully forward, refusing to acknowledge her point. The fight we'd been having before Annabel hung between us, thick with words unsaid.

'Once again, we are left facing something we cannot explain. It is a glimpse of the eternal, the a priori, the enduring arche-type. For we see, and we believe, and we *know* these fictions, the truths that underpin our whole existence, our human form. They may be games, may only be childish play, but they are the foundations of the stories that teach us – or remind us, depending on how you look at it – how to live our lives.

'And yet,' she said, turning a page in her notebook, words surrounded by thin, swooping sketches, Giacometti figures reading in the margins, 'you are no doubt aware, or, at least, becoming aware, of the slow decay of adulthood. The loosening of the imagination, the dry, straight misery of believing what you see, of trusting only what you can hold in your hands. It seems strange to me, even now, that we see the move into adulthood as something positive, the "growing out of" old ideas, aspiring to lives that are lived on a dull, simple level. Marriage, desk jobs, the rejection of wonder. The march towards death, losing gut knowledge, love of beauty, joy, along the way. The dull, rote processes of meaningless jobs; hollow entertainment over meaningful experience. Filling our waking hours, that we might at last be released into some fitful, dreamless sleep; bland conversations, hour after hour, with no thought behind them, moment by moment creeping ever towards the abyss.'

The birds nesting in the clock tower had stilled their wings, rapt; the wind had dropped, silence falling all around. I thought of all the ones who weren't us, who weren't part of this secret society: who only saw lives as they seemed, and not as they could be.

'For the ancient Greeks, however, lived reality was one shared with the presence of those we might now call the "imagined". For Hesiod, *daimones* walked the earth alongside mortals; in the *Phaedo*, Plato tells us that the souls of the angry dead hovered above tombs and graveyards, lingering in the mortal realm. And in Xenophon's *Cyropaedia*, these same souls track the wicked, taking vengeance where they might.

'These souls – mortals departed – walked side by side with the gods and monsters of the whole Greek cosmological system. Divinities walked the earth, real as one's own skin, and just as tangible. They shared the same space in the mortal realm, all partaking of the same reality, the same physical space. The Greeks were attuned to this, as were almost all cultures before our own, modern space: their imaginations were not curtailed by adulthood, but flourished, allowed to see the world on multiple layers at once, not narrowed by the walls we, now, build around us.

'And then, we wonder why our sense is always of something having been lost. Of a longing, of missing a thing we cannot name. We ask ourselves: "What is missing from my life? What is it I want? What is it that I need?"'

I felt a pinch on my thigh, and slapped Robin's hand away. Annabel looked up, startled at the interruption; when she resumed, I turned to Robin, and mouthed 'fuck off'. She shook her head, pinched me again.

She'd left for Andy's as the sun set, begging me to come along. But the risk of stumbling into Tom was too great. I hadn't seen him since our 'date', and he hadn't called – a fact I knew I ought to find upsetting, but which was only a relief. I'd almost managed to push it to the back of my mind, emerging only in dreams (those same dreams that carried the litany of other things I'd sooner forget – all blood and bone and shattered glass). If I could leave it there, I'd rather do so.

I went home, watched TV, read a book. I smoked a cigarette out of my window, and rolled over onto the bed. In the lull before sleep, I woke up with a jolt, and peeled back the curtain to see a lightning-bolt crack in the glass.

'What the hell?' I hissed at Robin, standing in the grass below, shivering in a t-shirt.

'Let me in,' she mouthed, pointing at the back door.

I crept downstairs, past my mother sleeping on the sofa, her head tipped at an uncomfortable angle on her chest. Slowly, aware of every sound, I peeled open the back door.

Robin breezed inside, her skin ice-cold on mine as she leaned in for a hug. She smelled of cinnamon and wood smoke, and when she pressed her hands to my cheeks I caught an earthy ring of pot; her eyes were red, pupils wide and pitch dark.

'What are you doing here?' I whispered. She pressed a finger to her lips, and pointed upstairs.

I felt a dull, grim shame as we stalked through the house; caught her staring, briefly, at my mother's lonely silhouette, the TV flashing blue behind. I wondered what she thought of the duct tape that held the bannister in place, the damp oozing through the ceiling, down the walls. With each step I shrank a little more, and as I gripped the handle of my bedroom door I wondered if it might be too late to ask her to leave, to forget all that she'd seen.

'Hey,' she said, waving a hand in front of my eyes. 'What are you doing?'

'Nothing,' I whispered, and opened the door.

She wandered around, reaching for objects, touching every-thing she could, while I sat on the bed, watching. She opened the wardrobe door, ran her fingers through the folds of an old, tattered dress; picked up a burning candle, spilling wax on the thin, white sheen of my desk. She picked at the edges of a chest of drawers, revealing the MDF beneath, and leaned in close to see the necklaces hanging on my cracked, dusty mirror.

'Robin,' I said, finally. 'Why are you here? It's late.'

'You know I'm a creature of the night.' She grinned, turning to face me, playing cat's cradle with a shoelace I'd tied into knots months ago, and thrown down beside the bed.

'I'm sure you are. But I'm not. I'm tired.'

'Your light was on.'

'I was about to turn it off.' This was a lie. Since the accident, I'd always slept with the light on, a cloying, childish comfort. I shook off the last of sleep. 'Want a drink?' I said.

She nodded.

'There's probably some wine downstairs,' I said, sliding off the bed. 'Stay here, and don't do anything,' I added. 'If my mum wakes up and finds you're here she'll kill me.'

When I returned, I found Robin picking chunks of black varnish from her nails, reclining up against the headboard. The book – Alex's book – was open on her lap, pages golden in the light.

'What's that for?' I said, pouring the wine into two mismatched mugs. They were the only things I could bring down from my room without arousing suspicion, though the reality was that all the wine glasses we owned were cracked or drying on various surfaces, dusty with sediment.

She turned the book towards me as I sat down beside her. 'Ever heard of poppet magic?' I shook my head, and she tapped two fingers on the page. 'From here,' she said.

'"The Use of Dolls to Cast Spells on a Given Subject," I read aloud. '"The subject of the poppet spell will be at the mercy of the wishes of the witch who casts it, whether that be for protection or revenge."' I ran my fingers over a sketch of a doll, bound with twigs and cloth. 'These spells must be used with extreme caution,' it said beneath. 'Poppet magic is an art not suitable for beginners.'

I looked at Robin. 'What's he done?'

'Who?'

'Andy.'

'Nothing,' she said. 'He's fine, thanks very much.'

'Then . . . what's this about?'

'Nicky,' she said, matter-of-factly.

I sighed, closed the book, and pushed it aside. 'No way.'

'You're protecting *her*?'

'She hasn't done anything,' I said.

'Bullshit.'

'Come on, Robin. This is ridiculous.'

'Don't be a wuss,' she said, grabbing my hand. 'If there's anyone around here who deserves it, it's Nicky. All we're going to do is give her a little touch of the spirits. No big deal.' She pinched my skin between her fingers. 'The magic equivalent of that. That's all.'

I shook her off. 'Fine, fine. Whatever.' As I said the words, I felt sick, a gut feeling that I had made the wrong choice. With Robin, though, there was no going back. 'So what do we do?'

She smiled, teeth bared. 'Got any Barbies?'

'What?'

'Barbie dolls. Or any dolls, really.'

'I'm sixteen, Robin. Fucking hell.'

'I don't mean "Have you played with any Barbie dolls lately?"' she said. 'I mean, are there any Barbie dolls in this house? Hidden in an attic, under the bed . . . Something like that?'

I felt my stomach lurch, sick, as it always did when I thought of my dad and sister. The familiar blue light flash and stink of blood came in a blink. 'Why?' I said, finally.

'So that's a yes?'

159

I sighed. 'My sister's room. She used to play with them.'

Robin rolled off the bed, and moved towards the door. 'Let's go have a look.'

'Wait – wait. Robin, I can't.'

She stared at me, eyes wide, bright. 'Why not?'

'I haven't been in there since she died. Mum wants to leave it as it was.'

'Christ, we'll put it back. It'll only take a second.'

'What do you even want it for?' I said, hearing my voice crack.

'Robin, you can't—'

'Look, look – I'll be right back. I won't touch anything else, I swear.'

'Robin—' I hissed as she disappeared out into the hallway. I threw my head back against the headboard, closed my eyes, felt the anger rise and fall. Minutes passed, endlessly. I willed her to come back, horrified at the thought of having to fetch her, to set foot into my sister's abandoned room, with its Care Bears, fairy lights, pictures of birds tacked to every wall, clipped from a book.

'Hey there, beautiful,' she whispered, poking a blonde doll's head through the crack in the door.

'Robin, get in here,' I hissed.

She closed the door behind her, and sat down on the bed, waving the doll proudly in the air. 'FYI, Violet, this isn't a Barbie. This is Sindy, the cheaper, nastier British version. Kind of a skank. Possibly a crack whore. Which, to be fair, is probably about right for our purposes.' She paused. 'What was your sister's name?'

160

'Anna,' I said; it was the first time I'd said it out loud since she'd died.

'To Anna, then,' she said, raising her mug, a splash of wine rolling over the side. 'Get the candles.'

I reached over beside the bed, the candles we'd bought earlier that day still tucked inside a paper bag. She rooted around in her backpack, pulling out a Swiss Army knife, a length of black ribbon, and a clutch of tiny vials I recognized from the craft shop, packed with dried leaves and powders, labelled in a crisp, green hand. 'Got a bin?' she said, looking around.

'What?'

'A bin.'

I pointed to the wastebasket under the desk, overflowing with paper, nail clippings, cigarette butts, and receipts. She tipped the contents onto the floor and placed the bin beside the bed.

'Did you have to do that?'

'Sorry. Kind of a mess in here already though, right?'

I kicked her with my heel. 'Fuck you.'

She turned, crossing her legs on the bed facing me, the doll lying face down between us, and opened the book again, heavy pages whooshing as they turned. 'Okay, so we're meant to make the doll ourselves, but I figured one of these plastic soulless horror bitches would be more appropriate for Nicky – right?'

I rolled my eyes. 'Right,' I said. 'So what do we do?'

'Imagine Nicky's here, in the form of this doll.' She plucked three stalks of thistle out of a jar, jerking her finger back and sucking it as one caught her with a barb. She pressed them

161

to the doll's chest, and handed it to me. 'You hold her still, and I'll do the tying.'

I held the Sindy out in front of me, trying to keep her steady as Robin slowly wound the ribbon around the doll. 'Poppet, we see you for what you are, and who you represent,' she whispered, looking down at the doll. 'Vivi,' she said, looking at me. 'We've both got to say it. Repeat after me.' She cleared her throat, and began again. 'Poppet, we see you . . . '

I echoed each line in a whisper as she tied the ribbon tight around the doll's arms and neck, and flicked open the corkscrew from the Swiss Army knife. 'What are you . . . ' I began.

'Shhhh,' she said. She placed the corkscrew on the doll's lips, and began to turn, the plastic breaking with a soft pop. 'Keep your secrets, poppet; keep them close. Let our will be your fate.' She looked at me, and I took the corkscrew, pulling at the handle as I spoke, a ragged void torn horribly in the doll's face, eyes still bright and smiling.

'We curse you, poppet, for what you have done, and bind you from the things you are yet to do. Let the Furies take your breath, and the Fates cut your thread.' I stared at her. This sounded more serious than 'just a pinch'. She snipped the ribbon, and the doll landed in the bin with a clatter. 'Hold your breath,' she said.

'What?'

'Hold your breath.' She popped the lid off a thin, glass bottle and poured a glutinous, black substance into the bin, turning the doll's hair snake-like, the tear in her face making her the Medusa, screaming back. Even with my breath held, I caught the chemical smell in the back of my throat, bittersweet like petrol, nail polish, cough medicine. The match sparked, and I realized what she was about to do.

'Don't—' I said, as she dropped it from high above, the bin's contents bursting into vivid, red flames, the black smoke monstrous, stink of plastic and burning hair.

I threw open the window, and Robin held the bin out into the rain, wincing as the steam swelled around her arms. When she finally pulled it in, her hands were singed red, skin peeling back. 'Fuck,' she muttered, dropping the bin to the floor. I kicked it upright, the plastic burning my toe. 'I guess that's why they say to do it outside,' she said, drily.

'And that's why you're meant to make it out of . . . anything but Sindy,' I said. We looked at each other, and down into the bin, where the doll's torn face had melted into a rictus smile, arms bent and hair melted into a solid, stinking mask. Our eyes met again, and we laughed. It was a giggle at first, descending into a riot, laughing until our ribs ached and our jaws grew tight.

When we finally gained something like control (punctuated with the occasional snort, a hiccup, a giggle) she peeled the doll from the base of the bin and held it upside down, between two fingers. 'I'll put this back,' she said, and disappeared into the hallway.

I lay back, heard the door click, felt her lie beside me, fingers intertwined. I turned to face her, and she looked away, a half-smile on her face. 'I'm knackered,' she said, voice barely more than a whisper, as she began to fall asleep, the hollows in her neck rising to meet bone. 'That was too funny.'

We fell asleep on the bed holding hands, our bracelets

resting beside one another as we slept. When I woke up, she was gone, an origami bird propped on the pillow beside me. I unfolded it, fingers smudging the still-wet ink. 'See you in class. Love you.'

I sat up, still smiling, the curtains flapping in the breeze. It was a day I'd want to keep, a memory fixed in amber. I reached for my diary, the words – the story of our perfect, thrilling day – already arranging themselves in my mind.

On the side table, I felt empty glasses, crush of ash and stone, abandoned papers, and used-up pens – but no diary. I peered behind the table, between it and the bed; in the drawers, and under the feet. I turned everything upside down, tearing at the pieces, mess scattered and thrown. I retraced my steps, memories, every moment since I'd seen it last.

But still, it wasn't there.

When I arrived at the tower the following day, I found the girls staring at me, wide-eyed. I walked across to the table, where the three of them sat huddled around a book; felt a shudder of realization as I recognized the torn pages and smudged ink.

My diary.

My secrets: now theirs.

I remembered what I'd written, the words I'd meant to tear out and throw away: the horror of what had happened with Tom scratched into the page while it was still raw, though it had faded with each passing day. Now, knowing they'd seen it – knowing they'd read the words, known the vivid burn of shame – I felt violated, once again.

I looked at Alex and Grace, listened to Annabel, picked up the thread.

'Perhaps,' she said, 'it might be better to live our lives in pursuit of those things that unite both worlds: the real, and the imaginary. Perhaps we should see ourselves drawn not to the future, not towards what I imagine, to you, seem like impossible boredoms, repetitions, and tiny deaths, but to the magic of our own, unique pasts. And the past we share with those who came before, for whom lived experience was the pursuit of those things that make our hearts beat a little faster in our chests, and fill our lives with a little more magic, our souls vibrating with the thrill of identification.'

She closed the book, looked at each of us in turn. 'Perhaps we should exercise our minds, follow our beliefs, and our wills just the same. Maybe that's just living. Or maybe it's the path to the sublime.'

The bell rang, and she looked around as though surprised. 'Well,' she said, 'I suppose that's all for today. And if you could work out whatever's going on between you before our next class, I'd be very much obliged.'

Only when the elevator began its mechanical roar did any of us speak, and then all at once. Alex and I turned to Robin, each shouting about our respective stolen books. Grace stared down at the pages, inky fingers tinged blue-black; Robin, apparently delighted to be at the centre of it all, sat in Annabel's chair with a half-smile.

We were interrupted by the bells above, and fell silent, glaring at each other as the chimes rang overhead, the birds fluttering in response. When they stopped, Robin sat up, elbows on her knees. 'Can we all just chill out? Just for a minute?'

Alex and Grace stared at her, Alex passing a fleeting glance at me as I sat down. I blushed, caught sitting on command, and considered standing up again.

'Remember when Annabel did that class on revenge?' Robin said, grandly, though with a look in her eye that suggested she was more nervous than she'd admit, unsure of her approach, like someone walking a little too close to a sheer drop. The slight crack in her bravado stilled me, and I blinked, reminding myself why I was angry – but the full force of my earlier fury failed to quite materialize as it had moments before.

'Robin—' Alex began.

'And she said,' Robin went on, one hand raised, 'women owe it to each other to seek revenge for those wronged?' She looked at Grace, for a moment, and then to me. 'That it's, like, a right?'

'A need,' Grace said. 'She said it was the foundation of sisterhood, I think.'

'Exactly,' Robin said, beaming. 'So when an opportunity for revenge presents itself, we owe it to the sisterhood to take it – don't we?'

Alex turned to me. 'This is a really bad idea,' she said, softening her tone. 'It's too dangerous.' Behind her, Robin pulled faces, mimicking her concern. 'There are other books, with other spells, but—'

'But this one actually *works*,' Robin said. 'Which is exactly the point.'

I looked at her, then at Alex, then Robin again.

'What does it say?' I said, finally. Alex groaned, pushed back her chair, and walked over to the east window, looking down at the Quad below.

'The Furies may be invoked in order to restore order and reclaim power from those who abuse it. In summoning these goddesses, one asks divine justice to do its work in the mortal realm, to counter the sins of evil men.'

'And?' Alex said, turning back to face us. 'What else does it say there, Robin?'

Robin scowled. 'These rites must only be performed when the situation truly demands it, and even then should remain in the hands of experienced practitioners only.' She paused. 'It says that about basically everything, though. And anyway, we've got experience.'

'You've what?' Alex glared at Robin and sighed. 'You know what? I don't want to know.' She sat down beside me. 'Violet, what happened to you sounds horrible, and he absolutely shouldn't have done it . . . But don't let her talk you into this. It's a stupid idea.'

I bristled at her tone, exhaled slowly through my teeth. 'Patronizing bitch,' I'd called her, secretly, after one too many sugar-sweet vodka drinks. I saw a flicker of a smile pass Robin's face and wondered if she was thinking of that same night; thinking, too, that Alex had all but assured this kind of reaction, an urge to prove her wrong. Robin threw her arm around me before I spoke, and I flinched, pulled away.

'No,' I said. 'No. Forget it.'

Robin stared at me, tendons twitching, corded, in her neck. 'What do you—'

'Just drop it, Robin. I don't want to.'

I slammed the door behind me as I left, the girls silent, my heartbeat pounding in my ears. I paused a moment, half-expecting to be called after, followed, perhaps. But as the elevator rattled up, they didn't move.

Instead, they remained silent, as though waiting for me to leave.

I read the words over and over, trying to ignore the relentless tap of his pen against the page. The soporific warmth, smell of dust burning on the radiator (dead skin, I thought, charred flesh). I chewed my lip, scraped off the crisp, chapped skin, and smeared it, blood-red, on the page.

Outside, the reception gate rattled shut, locked with one click, then another. Mrs Coxon's heels rapped a fading rhythm down the hall, and disappeared, the main doors closing behind her. I'd come to resent that sound, the last movement, the deathly click: it seemed that, during our evening sessions together, the Dean and I were the only people – the only living things, in fact – left on campus.

He stopped a moment, and looked up. 'How are you getting on?'

'Fine,' I said, a slight petulance in my voice. I turned back to the notebook I'd been poring through, the Dean's handwriting so small as to have been incomprehensible during my first weeks of work, though by now – to my strange satisfaction – I'd become fairly accustomed to the loped scrawl, all capitals and crossings-out. My task was rote copying, moving scrawled entries onto index cards I'd occasionally find pinned in strange configurations on the wall.

Occasionally I'd come across a name I recognized – from the mossy tombstones we'd stood beside on that first night, or scratched in the margins of books I'd pawed through in the tower, waiting for Annabel's class to start, their meanings unclear, the links to the passages they sat beside oblique and seemingly random.

'I've heard quite a few sighs,' he said, smiling. 'Are you sure you're . . . ?'

I sat, for a moment, watching him; a little uncomfortable at the way his eyes peered into mine, as though he knew something, anticipating the moment of reveal. 'It's just,' I said, looking away, 'what's this story got to do with anything?'

I knew, of course, what it was – recognized the name: Jane White, Ms Boucher, the belladonna in the milk. And yet his notes told nothing of her death – only that she'd lived in the town during the trials, and had died, mysteriously, mere weeks before Boucher had burned. It was pointless work, a waste of both of our time.

He glanced out at the Quad, the evening light silvery, buildings clipped by a low mist. All week, fog had clung to the buildings, the last gasp of winter. The campus was barely visible but for the squares of light glowing patchwork in the mist; the golden faces of the clock tower, the Campanile's four moons. I'd avoided Robin and the girls, though they continued to watch me, their pitiful looks serving only to make the shame deepen and twist in my gut.

'I suppose this *is* a little dry,' he said, thoughtfully. He turned back to me, and smiled; rose, heavily, from his seat. 'Come on. Let's go for a walk.'

I stared at him, chest tightening at the words, the voice, the echo of Tom. 'It's fine, sir,' I said, softly. 'I'm sorry. I'm just . . . ' I trailed off, fear reaching my throat, an icy grip.

'Violet?' he said, after a moment.

'I . . . ' I felt my voice tremble, tried again for a distraction. 'I had a fight. With my friends.'

He sat down, slowly. 'Which friends?'

'Robin, and Alex, and Grace,' I said, a little stab of shame as I named each in turn. I was telling tales, being childish. They'd never forgive me if they knew.

'Hmmm . . . ' He folded his arms, jacket straining a little at the seams. Since Tom, I'd been newly aware of the size of boys, the strength of them; the Dean, now, seemed to loom large, broad-shouldered, capable of . . . I closed my eyes for a moment, the thought spiralling beyond grasp.

'You know,' he said, softly. 'Usually I'd suggest you try to resolve it. It doesn't do to have arguments lingering.' He clicked his tongue, thoughtfully. 'But in this case, I'll admit, I'm not sure.'

I looked up; stared at him, a flicker of anger, flame pinched between finger and thumb.

'When you're your age,' he went on, 'it can seem like friendships are the most important thing in the world. But sometimes that makes us blind to the fact they're not good for us.' A lamplight fizzed in the Quad, the office light shuddering in response. 'I know it seems impossible,' he said, smile benevolent, imagining himself sage. 'But sometimes it's better to have no friends than bad ones.'

I felt a sting, sharp and hot, in my chest. The cruelty of

the implication. *Without them,* I thought, *what friends do I have?* There was Nicky, I supposed, but our friendship was hollow, superficial. It was patronizing, what he'd said, but – to my shame – not untrue. Without them, I was alone. I remembered the longing I'd felt, before, when I'd imagined myself among them – and yet now I was, I was throwing it away. And for what? Because Robin wanted to get revenge on the boy who'd made me—

'Violet,' the Dean said, reaching a hand for mine; he bit his lip, a gesture I'd seen countless times, a tic. I flinched, heart thudding, viciously, and stood, stumbling back towards the door.

'Don't,' I said, tears choking me, drowning. 'Don't come near me.'

He stood, stunned, by the desk; raised both palms, slowly, before bending to pick up my bag and coat from the floor. He stepped forward, handed them to me, and reached for the door handle, inches from my hip.

There, he paused, the moment interminable. The smoke in his hair, tang of aftershave, cloying with sweat.

'Violet,' he said, again. I closed my eyes, tears catching on my lashes, and felt the breath of him, too close, too much.

He pulled the door open, and I ran, silently, into the welcoming night.

'I've changed my mind,' I said, breathlessly, the words spilling out. 'We need to do it. We need to make him . . . '

I heard a door close, muting the chatter from inside Robin's house: the first time I'd dialled her number. Before, I would have grasped at details, hoping to catch some thread of her, the banal secrets of the home life she rarely mentioned but for the occasional eye roll or groan.

'Are you sure?' she said, softly; a strange nervousness to her, a glimmer of something resembling fear.

I paused. 'Don't you want to?'

'Mum!' she called; I flinched, pulled the phone from my ear. 'Put the extension down. It's just Grace.' There was a soft click between us, a heavy silence. 'No offence. She just knows Grace, you know.'

I murmured something in response, my determination deflated by the interruption.

'If you mean it,' she said, her voice a low whisper, 'I'm in. But you'll need to persuade the others. They'll do it, but only if they think it's for you.'

In the living room, Mum rolled up from the sofa, shuffling towards the kitchen, hands gripping surfaces which shook and rattled with the impact. I looked down at my hands, the bruises and cuts faded, now, to nothing; heard Robin's breath in the receiver.

'Okay,' I said, the word seeming to lighten me, a relief. 'Let's do it.'

Chapter 9

My memories of the cove were framed in the sticky sweetness of childhood, playing among the ruins of the old brickworks, hiding among the tiny caves that appeared in the cracks on the dusty cliffs that surrounded the hidden bay. Sea water lapped at the honeycombed buildings shot with beeswax light, dripping through windows of what might once have been a fairy-tale castle, all spires and chimneys – the old brickworks.

I imagined myself a lost princess, peering through gaps, plucking hermit crabs and starfish from the algae-covered walls. After my sister was born, we never went back, the path leading down to it impossible to negotiate with a pushchair. By the time she could walk, it was known more for its appeal to drop-outs and hippies camping to watch the sunrise (based on a calendar of which few residents of the town could keep track) and misguided teenagers looking to score pot.

Or maybe I was just old enough to see it for what it was.

Either way, I hadn't ventured down the narrow path, through the elm trees that sprung from the cliff above, in several years, and certainly never in the dark. Indeed, I haven't been since, though the memory of the night still appears in view, clear and full-coloured, as though etched in my mind: a night I suppose I will never forget. The old spire groaned in the wind, fallen bricks lay scattered, haphazard, at its feet, and gulls drifted high above, circling like vultures. Underfoot, sand scratched on stone, while crabs skittered ahead, foxes hissing and yowling among the ruins.

In the farthest dome, I saw a light flicker through an empty window. Voices echoed across the cove, caught on the wind; over the mound boys whooped and howled, and on the cliff above two old men sat, dirt seeping into their clothes, unconcerned as the rain began to spit and wind stir. Peering through one of the arches, I saw the girls (dressed all in black, as was I, on Robin's instruction) pottering around a red fire in the centre of the room, which crackled and spat softly between them.

Around the fire were piled mounds of flowers and shrubs, pulled from the earth: blue-tinged sea holly, horned poppies and sea kale, bittersweet and viper's bugloss. Other trinkets gathered, too: candles of varying shapes and sizes, glass beads, bottles shaped by the sea. And around the fire, four gold torches, rippled with engravings, and four matching knives blade-down in the earth.

'Vivi,' Robin said, turning to me with a wide grin, hair burning in the light. 'There you are.'

'We said eight-thirty, right?' I said, glancing at my watch.

'We couldn't wait.' She shrugged. 'Thought we'd come and get set up before it got too dark.'

I smiled, dimly. It seemed unlikely that Alex and Grace were in any rush to begin. Alex having insisted she wouldn't go along with it right up until the end of the week, when she'd said 'See you tomorrow' with a meaningful look. All drama, Robin had said, matter-of-factly. She knew Alex wouldn't be able to resist, no matter how much she protested.

There was a flutter, an echo of something in the corner; a ripple in the shadows. I turned to see Grace clicking the bars of a tattered birdcage, greening with rust. 'What's that?' I said, walking over to see. I heard claws, the faint ring of the bars beneath; she lifted it, carefully, to the light. It was a pigeon, wings slick and silvery, a greenish grey beneath.

'It was the only one we could catch,' Grace said, a smile forming in shadow. 'Turns out we're not much for hunting. Alex kept running away every time it got close.'

Robin snorted; Alex shook her head, blushing. 'I just don't like birds. They're just like . . . ' She gave an involuntary shudder. 'They carry diseases. It's gross.'

I stared at it, eyes black and amber, ringed with gold. Grace pushed the cage towards me, palm holding the gate shut tight. 'You look after it for a while. Make sure it doesn't get away.'

I sat down beside it, the bird flapping restlessly each time the fire crackled; the heat, I suppose, was glaring, flames licking at wingtips and tail. The last time I'd been this close to a bird – by choice, at least – I'd been crouching in the corner of the living room as Dad shooed at a sparrow that had fallen down the chimney, Anna and I giggling and squealing with delight.

When he caught it, at last, he held it close, let us stroke it;

the silky wings and downy neck a thrill, a life contained in Dad's wide palms. I tried to recount the story back to the girls, but in the telling it seemed stupid – a trite, childish thing. I saw Alex and Grace exchange a look, a glance I couldn't read; they turned back to me with the same weak smile.

'Okay then, bitches,' Robin said, standing grandly by the fire, arms outstretched like a preacher. 'Let's do this.' She sat by the fire, and the three of us joined her, each beside a torch and a blade; Alex and Grace by her sides, and I opposite. Through the flames, she seemed already like some penny arcade Medusa, smoke and sparks surrounding her face when the wind washed through.

The rain, now, beat down on the roof with such force it seemed not like raindrops, but like the sea itself, waves of roaring breath. She opened a bottle of red wine with a pop, and poured a little into the flames, which burst orange, spitting rust into the sand. 'For the goddesses we bring to bear.' She took a sip from the bottle and passed it on; spat her gum into the sand. Alex passed the wine to me, and I took a sip, sweet and bitter rolling on my tongue.

'I hope you've all done the required reading,' Robin said, in an eerily accurate imitation of Annabel. I nodded, thinking of the damp photocopies Robin had handed each of us as we left Annabel's last class. *The Fates and the Furies*, it read, Bouguereau's painting of Orestes' torment in faded black beneath.

One section in particular stuck in my mind: 'Once summoned, the Furies cannot be sent back, only leave of their own accord. To summon them without due reason, therefore, is to risk a life of torture, the deepest suffering of the human soul. They are court, jury, executioner, and their judgments will be entirely their own.'

I brushed it off, thought of Tom; thought of the sharp stab in my gut, shoulder on stone, his sweat on my skin. *Due reason*, I thought, and read on.

'Let's begin, then,' Robin said, rubbing her hands together and pressing them close to the fire. 'Have you got the . . . ?'

I nodded, handed her the skirt and underwear I'd worn that day, still stained, dried in the shapes they'd taken in the well of my wardrobe. She took them, gently, and placed them by her side. Slowly, she leaned her torch towards the fire; the kerosene smell caught on the air in the split second before it burst into flames, and the three of us did the same, standing up around the fire, dizzy with expectation. The bird rustled, a high-pitched coo. I leaned my foot against the door of the cage, feeling the feathers brush my ankles as it tried to escape.

'Repeat after me.' She coughed, and raised her torch high above her head with one arm. I saw the knife's blade gleam in her other hand, and bent to pick mine up as she closed her eyes and took a deep, slow breath. I will never forget my friends' faces as we waited, nervously, for her to exhale. Grace's eyes, usually cast downwards, thoughtful and shy, were wide with fear; Alex's mouth was slightly open, transfixed.

'We stand before you, Furies,' Robin said, her voice low, ragged with smoke. 'We ask you to share with us your secrets, your knowledge, your power. We come to you as your humble servants, and accept your judgment, should you choose it.' We repeated the words, my voice unfamiliar, as though coming from somewhere outside of my chest, a foot or two behind.

A breath of wind blew through the arches, swirling the fire's hot breath around and out.

I felt goosebumps prickle on my forearms, and closed my eyes as the cold settled on my skin. We raised our torches higher. 'Furies, we summon you from the underworld, and ask you to join us in our mortal realm.' There was a deafening crack from the flames, a log sparking shards of light, pouring gold dust into the sand; the bird began to coo, now, a steady rhythm, growing faster and more frantic with each breath.

Robin opened her eyes, and stared at me. Grace took the torch from my hands.

'Get the bird,' she whispered.

I glanced at Alex. 'It's got fleas.'

'Jesus, Vi, come on. Don't be a wuss.'

'But—'

'Ugh,' she said, rolling her eyes. 'Come on. You're ruining it.'

I crouched down beside the cage, reaching a tentative hand through the bars. The red hiss of a scratch across my palm; I pulled back, muttered a complaint too low for them to hear. The fire seemed to pick up, a warm swell behind. I reached in again, clutching the bird from above, wings first. It wriggled, legs kicking as I scooped it up and pulled it to my chest, bones writhing underneath, like another hand in mine.

'We bring to you this sacrifice,' Robin said, 'that you might see our intentions are true.' Her smile wide, she nodded at me, and I felt the knife's warm presence in my hand, damp with sweat. The realization felt more like remembering something I'd always known, some shock of the repressed.

'I can't,' I said, voice catching in my throat.

'You have to,' she said, flatly. I looked at the girls; Alex smiled, a glint in her eyes that made me wonder if this was a test – one I would no doubt fail.

The bird squirmed, and settled, as though it knew. 'It's just a pigeon,' I said.

'Violet,' Alex said, her voice sharp. 'You said yourself, it's got fleas. It's gross. Lift it up, and aim for the throat. It's the fastest way.' I stared at Alex, her eyes gold in the light, flickering with fire, her skin damp with sweat. I closed my eyes, breathed in, and raised the bird high, feeling it writhe in my hand.

'Look up, so you make a clean cut,' Robin said. 'You'll hurt it otherwise.'

I stared up at the bird, claws running circles in the air. Drew breath, sighed; drew breath again. I took aim, the knife reflecting spectral on the walls, and closed my eyes. *You should look*, I thought, and I did. I pushed the knife up and in, and dragged the blade across its neck, surprised at the ease with which it tore hide and flesh, catching as it reached bone. Blood spilled hot tracks down my arms, into my eyes, down my neck and chest. I remember thinking it strange that such a little thing could hold so much.

I waited to feel horror, but it never came. No revulsion, no fear; none of the things I had expected to feel as the body stilled and grew heavy. Instead, I felt alive, heart and chest filled hot with light. The body shuddered once more, grew still, turned cold, my arm turning stiff and sticky with blood.

'We present this sacrifice to you, Furies, as we present

ourselves, agents of your will. We pray that you might reveal to us your mysteries, and help us correct those wrongs done to us, and others of our order. We present to you our souls, on the Fates' golden thread, and beg for your grace.' Alex took the body from my arms, hanging by the feet; she dragged her knife down the bird's torn breast, and passed it to Robin, who did the same. Grace was last. She whispered something as she threw the little body into the fire, and stepped back as it turned black, silver, gold once again.

'Look,' Robin said, pointing to the arches of the dome. I turned, and saw a white figure lurking in each, long fingers braced around the frame. Behind, the sea lapped black on the sand, stars connected in a silvery web above. In a blink, they were gone, and I fell into the sand, never realizing I'd left the ground.

I woke up at home, in my own bed, hair still damp and crisp with salt water, clothes still stuck to my skin.

Memories returned like shades, flashes: a cry, cold hands held tight around my jaw. A low howl, like some monstrous beast, echoed from within the cove. An ambulance slowing as I walked by the wheels of an upturned car spinning in the air, the wreck a bright distraction on a busy, crowded street. The glossy spider's web on the window shield; the winking glitter in the glass, red, orange, green. I smelled blood, the same warm blood of the little bird, who writhed as I cut its throat.

I rolled over, and went back to sleep, dreaming of night.

Chapter 10

One reads *Macbeth* and thinks of the washing of hands as a metaphor for guilt. In reality, however, it's rather closer to the truth than the casual reader might expect. Even when the colour fades and there's nothing left visible to the naked eye, there's a stickiness, a stiffness to the skin, like clay drying into your hands, exposing every line, getting into every crack. One might wonder how it was that Shakespeare knew.

I spent the weekend wringing my hands, slathering them with moisturizer stolen from the local pharmacist on some long-forgotten afternoon. It's all I remember but for the brief appearance of my mother at my bedroom door, asking if I wanted tea or juice. I rolled over, said nothing. I was heartsick, trapped in feverish dreams of stags and dogs, of blood and sand and silver fire.

When I finally mustered the energy to shower, I saw two thin lines down my shoulder blades, bruised blue, and had a memory of wings I could not recall in any more detail than the image, black perhaps, feathers possibly wilting. I neither thought of my friends, nor of what we'd done, but passed from one fractured, delirious state to another, all one and the same.

And then, at last, I came to. It felt like falling, a vertiginous drop from one state to another, and I was restored.

'Who can tell me the conventions of the revenge play?' Professor Malcolm looked around the room, each of us averting our eyes. He'd long since ceased to expect answers to be volunteered by me; had, indeed, taken to emitting a low sigh whenever he handed back my essays, with increasingly dire notes scrawled in seeping, red ink.

'Not your best,' he'd written, earlier in the term. 'Disappointing,' at the start of the next. Now he'd stopped writing anything at all but for the circled grade at the top of each essay. Even now, when our paths cross on campus, there's an almost invisible shake of the head, a tension in the set of his jaw: his disappointment ill concealed.

He sighed. 'Thank you for your valuable contribution. It's good to see you've all done the reading.' He turned to the blackboard and wrote the words in chalk, the crack of each letter ringing in my ears.

'MURDER,' he wrote, first. My eyes flickered to the empty seat beside me, Robin absent from class; behind, Nicky clicked her gum, turning the pages of her textbook with glazed eyes.

'MADNESS,' Professor Malcolm wrote below.

I felt a faint shudder of relief as Nicky sensed me looking, and smiled – benign, as though looking through me, a stranger passing by. She was fine, despite the poppet – and whatever had passed between the girls and me before the weekend was just the same. A temporary madness, a folie à deux – no more.

Still, I wondered – turning back to the board where 'GHOST OF VICTIM URGES REVENGE' had appeared, the letters sloping downward and falling away – it had certainly seemed real, in the moment. And ever since, the feeling – a sharp, cold ache that settled in the pit of my stomach, knotted tendrils reaching into my chest – that we had done something very wrong. Some monstrous and terrible thing.

I ached to see the girls, to ask them if they'd felt it too – the shadow of the past emerging from the darkness, bony claws in the spaces between our ribs. The sense of eyes watching, fanged grins in the pooling dark – was it possible we could have imagined such a thing, simply because we wanted it to be true?

'"Vengeance is in my heart,"' Professor Malcolm read, '"death in my hand. Blood and revenge are hammering in my head."' Nicky coughed, motes of dust lingering in the light between us; the Campanile ravens left shadows as they burst into flight.

Finally, I found Alex and Grace sitting cross-legged on the wall outside the Arts building. Grace's head rested on Alex's shoulder, eyes closed as though sleeping, the whispering movement of her lips the only sign she was awake. I walked over, still a little weak, aware of every tendon and vein in my calves as I walked, and sat down beside them.

'Hi,' I said.

Alex muttered a dim hello; Grace sat up and smiled. 'Feeling better?'

'Yeah,' I said. 'Well, kind of.' I changed the subject, a little raw from the experience. 'Where's Robin?'

'I haven't seen her,' Grace said, looking out at the students gathered in front of the library, pointing at the diggers rolling across the Quad with a strange fascination.

They were to tear down the trees during the spring break, despite much protest from the student body. I'd signed a petition, knowing that it would be pointless. The Headmaster was set on his grand green space, and no amount of student protest would change that. He had taken the lightning strike that charred the wych elm to be something of a sign, or an easy excuse to begin clearing the Quad, tearing down the trees whose branches had provided centuries of comfort and shade to Elm Hollow students.

Grace pulled an apple from her bag, and took a bite, juice rolling down her chin. I remembered the bird's blood tracing the same path, the taste of it, the warmth; I blinked away the thought.

We sat in silence, watching the sun stream through the buildings, light buttery with dust. Finally, Robin appeared, shambolic as ever, loping towards us with her backpack slung low at her side. 'There you are,' she said, pinching my arm as she sat.

'Here I am,' I said, weakly.

'I've got news,' she said, leaning across me to take a bite from Grace's apple. She chewed, leaned forward, and spat a mound onto the path below. 'Still can't eat. Christ.'

'You're sick?' I asked.

'As a dog. Haven't been able to swallow for days.'

'What's your news?' Grace said, leaning forward.

'Okay, so: I went to Andy's yesterday, and everyone's wearing black and wailing because – drum roll please . . . '

The three of us stared at her. I knew where this was going. A wave of hot, sticky nausea washed over me; I looked down at my knees. A memory (not a memory, really, so much as a haunting, a single image of an upturned tyre spinning in glass) flickered into my vision, and I asked a question, though I knew what the answer would be. 'What happened?'

'There was an accident. Tragic, really.' She looked at me, and winked, almost too brief to catch. 'Flipped his car on the high road in the early hours. Rumour has it the paramedics found body parts all over the road. A real Humpty-Dumpty type situation.'

There was a silence, none of us quite sure how to react. It wasn't possible. We couldn't have done it. It *had* to be a coincidence.

And yet, I thought, the eyes of the girls aflame with the same combination of hope and fear that I felt, long fingers wrapped around my heart – *what if it wasn't?* What if – through the power of our will, the Furies' rightful vengeance, we'd killed him; the little bird's blood his, sticking clay-like to my skin?

It couldn't be true.

Finally, Alex laughed, a hand at her throat. 'You're sick, Robin.'

She lit a cigarette. 'I know. It's why you keep me around.'

She turned sideways, and put her head in my lap, feet on the wall, and blew smoke in perfect circles into the air.

We sat like this, silent, absorbed in our thoughts – bonded by them – until the clock tower rang ten. In a single movement, Grace and Alex jumped down from the wall, dusted themselves off, and headed in their separate directions to the next class. Robin and I remained, watched them leave without a word. The lavender and lemon in the air seemed stifling and thick; my lungs too shallow, throat closed and tight. I gripped the wall with both hands; Robin curled a finger through the gap and squeezed, tight. *It's not possible,* I thought. *It's a coincidence.* But still the memory remained, like a shadow caught in a still pool. The shards of glass reflecting the ambulance's blue light. The orange glow of street lamps. The black pools glinting on the tarmac, growing smaller as I walked slowly away. I'd been there; I was sure of it.

I felt a sob rise in my chest, felt sick. At least we were in this together. Looked upwards to the sky, watching the white clouds split blue. I took a breath, sighed . . . and laughed. A bark of a laugh, really, almost inhuman. Robin looked up at me, mouth open, for a moment; coughed on her cigarette, and sat up, gasping for breath. We laughed into the faces of students who passed, laughed until it hurt, until our throats were dry, the air too thin to grasp. We laughed, tears rolling down our cheeks, and hugged, and felt nothing but joy, and I was so grateful, so lucky to have a friend who truly understood.

Spring

Chapter 11

'"Midway upon the journey of our life I found myself within a forest dark, for the straightforward pathway had been lost",' Professor Malcolm said, his arms outstretched like some poor ham actor.

'I'm sure many of us in this room can appreciate this sentiment, whether at the midway point of our lives or otherwise.' A few students offered ironic laughs; Robin raised an eyebrow sharply, and rolled her eyes. I, for my part, stared numbly into the shoulders of the student in front of me, trying to wake up, to blink away another excruciating hangover.

Clouds of silver smoke rising languid from an ashtray in a dank café; the tempered crack of milky tablets from plastic slides; a bird's tangled corpse, the prickle of sticky bone and beak as Robin crushed it under a heavy boot. My heart, thundering frantic as I slumped over the edge of the bed, watching peeling posters shudder at the corner of my vision; the perpetual feeling of being watched, the thin rip of paper as I pulled them down, faces torn and jagged.

Little children watching, scared, as the four of us rocked on the swings, hands cold on chain, in an empty playground, before the storm began. Running, screaming, through the rain, manic and alive with violent breath.

My hands bruised black with hair dye, Robin's, then mine; grazed knees, white shreds of skin in the dirt; warm water and cheap wine, straight from the bottle. Nausea. Vomit, marbled with spit, the cool relief of the toilet bowl. Aching bones. Last night's mascara, in fragments on my cheek. Even now, my memories of the spring break are thus, clouded in the low haze of intoxication.

It says something of our shared state that I, in truth, remember those two weeks only in brief, momentary flashes, detached from their source, uprooted and carried on a breeze.

'You look like shit,' Robin hissed, and slid a tiny, rolled-up ball of cling film across the desk. 'Take one of these. It'll make you feel better.'

'What is it?' I whispered, though of course I knew.

'Pick-me-up,' she said, face deadly serious, a web of tiredness under her eyes too. Clearly it wasn't enough to counteract the effects of the previous night. With a sigh, she placed a palm over the wrap.

'If you're not going to take them, at least cover them up,' she said, eyes now a little fierce, their pupils round and glassy. I shook my head, and the pills disappeared in a single, deft movement. I felt abashed, shrinking a little into my chair as Robin turned abruptly to face the front of the class.

I looked out at the burning red-brick buildings, the cluster of sparrows swooping at crumbs in the grass while the campus lay empty, all students still at home, or trapped in class, and the workmen clearing trees having briefly stopped, air mercifully silent. In the spring sunlight, the stony faces of the figures that peered down from the buildings seemed possessed of a new clarity: it was impossible, walking through the Quad, not to imagine oneself watched by disapproving faces, the cool judgment of the dead.

'*The Divine Comedy*, then, represents the journey of the soul towards God, and was an influence not only on Blake, but on Shakespeare, Milton, Eliot, and Beckett, not to mention contemporary writers and artists working today,' he went on, his voice flat and toneless. 'It is the *Inferno*, however, that has most powerfully captured the artistic imagination – primarily thanks to its recognition of sin in its innumerable forms, and Dante's visionary evocation of his many circles of Hell. As Ciardi's introduction explains, Dante's *Inferno* represents the realm of those who have rejected spiritual values by yielding to bestial appetites or violence, or by perverting their human intellect to fraud or malice against their fellow men. It appeals to the voyeur in all of us – the "what-if" that underpins the temptation of sin, and the schadenfreude inherent in the punishment of others for those crimes we, too, might choose to commit.'

He paused and looked around the room, aware, perhaps, that for the first time he had captured the attention of every member of the class. He lowered his voice to little more than a whisper. '"*Lasciate ogne speranza, voi ch'intrate*", the sign says, above the gates of Hell. "Abandon all hope, ye who enter here." A powerful statement, though one the reader finds strangely enticing – the screams of the eternally damned drawing us in, despite our compulsion to turn our eyes away.

'This may be why the *Inferno* has remained such a touchstone of our culture, centuries after its composition. Because who among us can honestly say – or, rather, will be able to honestly say, as we lie on our deathbeds and await our own judgments – that the myriad temptations of lust, of greed, of treachery and violence have not found their way into our own lives? And who among us will be able to resist?'

Every one of us seemed for a moment to look inwards, our doubts and guilty moments revealed to us, for a split second, at least. A flutter of tension passed over the class. Professor Malcolm, undone by the pressure, burst into a hacking, smoke-inflected cough, and the spell was broken. Made uncomfortable by the connection, that brief moment of shared intimacy, students shifted in their chairs and flicked lazily through their notes, searching for nothing but escape.

There was a soft knock on the door. The class looked up as one as the Dean peered through; they looked back down at their desks, uninterested. 'Sorry to disturb,' he said, his face serious, expressionless. He waved, catching my eye as he did so. 'I need to borrow one of your students, if you don't mind.' I winced at the prospect of finding myself singled out in front of the class; caught, too, beside Robin, both of us bloodshot and pale.

The professor shrugged and turned back to the board. 'Robin,' the Dean said. 'May I borrow you?'

She looked at me, briefly, a sideways glance; I looked at the Dean, who placed both hands in his pockets and leaned back against the door, his face expressionless as he watched her gather her things. 'Yes, sir,' she said, following him out of the class. A silence fell, for a moment, until the Professor scrawled 'You were not formed to live like brutes, but to follow virtue and knowledge', tall on the blackboard, and resumed his usual, miserable drone.

There was no indication that anything was wrong but for the line of buses parked behind the school, drivers smoking out front, sour-faced at being called in to work in the middle of the day.

The campus was crowded, all students let out of classes at once, gathering in clusters around the boards that closed off most of the Quad, some whispering, others shouting and laughing, voices high on the wind.

Rain began to spit, and we were steered onto buses, heading into the town, where our parents were to meet us. My parent, of course, didn't; she now phobic of the ringing phone, tucked away safely in a drawer, still connected and occasionally ringing, but always ignored.

I looked around for Robin, for Alex and Grace, elated at an afternoon without classes, not least because I hadn't done the reading – didn't know, for that matter, what the assigned text even was. Finding myself alone, however, I jumped on the bus and took a seat beside a girl whose name I didn't know, and who picked nervously at her nails and refused to meet my eye all the way into the town.

It was only the next day that I found out what had happened, and only then in slivers, gossip caught between radio broadcasts and conversations overheard in the streets.

In the process of cutting down the wych elm, a workman had driven his chainsaw into the trunk, horrified to find the innards of the tree dripping darkly through the cut. Not sap, though it had the same thick, coagulated texture, the same glassy sheen. But the colour was unmistakable. He had crossed himself, and walked away as the first seam of blood rivered over roots and seeped, blackening, into the grass.

Another followed; the tree bled again. He winced, but continued his work, shards of red-tipped bark flying into the mud, upturned like tombstones.

A supervisor passed, and stopped, peering at the seam of blood dripping slowly down the bark of the tree, creeping into rivets, marking the cracks. He steadied himself as he walked a circuit of the tree, resisting the urge to mutter a prayer beneath his breath. Found a crack in the wood, and another, and another; stuck trembling fingers into the gaps, and pulled. The bark came away in a single block, and beneath, the crumpled body of Emily Frost bent double, peering out through empty eyes, maggots writhing in their place.

When the last bus left campus, the police poured in, each choking, sickened by the rotting sweetness in the air. Some said the pulse of creatures below the skin made it look as though her heart might still be beating; the blood, too, suggested she hadn't been there long, though at autopsy this was proven to be incorrect, an anomaly nobody could quite explain. The coroner would conclude she'd been there several months, packed in before the onset of rigor mortis made her too stiff to fit. The claw-mark furrows found later led some to speculate she'd been put there, in fact, before she was quite dead.

In the weeks after that night at the cove, a new closeness had settled between the four of us. With the coming of spring, life creeping slowly back and filling the campus with gorgeous, blooming colour, it seemed all possibility and potential was ours, limited only by imagination. We thought, with the reckless, foolhardy faith of adolescence, that our friendship was impenetrable, a permanent, lasting thing.

I'd even felt bold enough to raise the subject of Emily, as Robin and I lay together in bed, each waiting for the other to fall asleep. 'I just wish they'd find her,' she'd said. 'So we can all move on.'

Now, at last, she'd been found. And I felt sick with envy, sick that they had been reunited: our friendship splintered by her return.

Chapter 12

The spring break was extended by a week, school closing after Emily's body was found, no doubt to prevent hysteria, to give us time to mourn. The town was filled with us, the student body exiled into cafés, lingering on the beach, eating ice creams and ducking gulls as they swooped.

Most students treated it as a holiday, though the drama thickened the air with whispers. Everyone laughed at the warnings given, as instructed by the letter mailed to each of our parents: not to talk to strange men, to be mindful of the dangers of dark alleys and low mist, never to go anywhere alone.

But I was alone.

Robin, Alex, and Grace disappeared, none of them home, or, at least, none of them answering my numerous calls. I had stilted conversations with each of their parents, except Alex's, whose phone simply rang endlessly, for five, six minutes at a time. I was told each of them was 'out', though their parents didn't know, or, as I became increasingly convinced, chose not to tell me, where.

Emily's face was inescapable, and I felt myself addicted, buying newspapers and sneaking downstairs to watch the TV news whenever my mother was asleep. I stared at the pages, or into the screen, like Narcissus at his pond, while devastated friends talked of her kindness and beauty.

Nicky made several appearances, offering wide-eyed anecdotes about her friendship with Emily, though from what I could gather they'd never really got along – but who could begrudge her the attention? Reporters, too, spoke of Emily as a good girl, a kind girl, a *sweet* girl: all the things I had at some point supposed I could be. I wondered: If it were me, would they say the same? And if so, was she ever good, kind, sweet at all?

Those of us left behind whispered amongst ourselves, a chorus led by Nicky, who called daily – I picking up the phone breathless, waiting for the others. She told of hushed calls overheard on extension lines, of theories muttered by mothers after a third or fourth nightcap, daughters listening overhead, poised at the top of the stairs.

There were suggestions of some accident: tree climbing gone somehow wrong, a fall straight into the belly of the tree, covered over by the leaves and left to rot. Nicky shook her head. 'You wouldn't find Emily Frost climbing a tree. Her nails were always *perfect.*' A deranged father, a mother too terrified to speak, though their faces, flickering through the static of our TV screens, seemed genuine, eyes hollowed out with loss.

Ever more outlandish suggestions appeared, gathering strength with every whisper. A pentagram etched into the wood; a letter stuffed down her throat, ink too blurred to read, rotted away by spit and stomach acid. Ms Boucher's name came up, from time to time – 'a witch,' they said, rolling their eyes and speaking of curses, laughing at the suggestion. We learned things we hadn't realized we were too young to know, though we responded to them with a studied indifference: how police might test for DNA, spit and semen in intimate places; the cruel flash of luminal, purple shadows of lividity and finger marks on pale arms.

Reporters plucked out song lyrics and video games, wilfully misreading signifiers and contorting them into lurid inducements to steal, fuck, and kill, and, thus, in a situation in which no one knew much beyond the facts, it still seemed to us that the adults knew nothing at all. We cringed for them, a black, wretched humour that soothed the horror of the crime.

When school reopened at last, a shrine to Emily appeared in the middle of the Quad, where all building work had ceased; beneath the half-cut wych elm (wrapped in black with a shroud around the trunk and body now removed) flowers and photographs appeared, candles left to singe the fur of supermarket-bought teddy bears and handwritten notes. A memorial service was planned, all music classes cancelled, replaced by endless rehearsals in the Great Hall, from which chamber music and the choir's sullen singing echoed in the air outside.

Stares stalked me down corridors, whispers silenced as I entered every room. I knew what they wanted: to know where the girls had gone. But when I told them, they didn't believe I didn't know.

*

'Violet!' the Dean said, as I entered, his tone grimly cheerful; too much, as usual. Since the night we'd discussed the girls, he'd been overly pleasant. He'd chosen not to mention what followed, a kindness I was grateful for, though the fact of it still lingered in the air between us.

The rest of the faculty, by contrast, had turned sombre, remote. Annabel had cancelled our extra classes entirely, a good thing, I supposed, since I was currently her only student, and Professor Malcolm had delivered a lecture on grief so unbearably dull that it made each of us consider our dearly departed the lucky ones.

The Dean, however, had remained cheery – a necessity, I imagined, given his role as the school's main counsellor, though additional, temporary ones had been brought in to assist with the process. The vast majority of students used these, taking every opportunity to drop this fact into conversation – turning grieving into a competitive sport.

'How's my favourite student?' he said, leaning back in his chair. A tall, grey-eyed girl sat on the desk, blonde hair in a high ponytail, feet on the chair below; she smiled, dimly, as our eyes met.

'Fine, thanks,' I said. He looked back at her, warmly, an intimate smile. 'Do you want me to come back later?'

'Oh no, no need,' he said, slapping a hand on her knee. She flinched. 'Violet, this is my daughter, Sophie. She's joining our fine institution next year,' he said, adding a rough pat on the back. She burned red hot with shame; I gave a sympathetic smile, though I still felt a strange envy at daughters embarrassed by their fathers, a desire to shake them, to offer them some kind of trade.

'Oh really?' I said, feigning interest. 'Where are you now?'

'I've been studying in the States,' she said, a gloss of pride in her tone, a coolness rehearsed. 'But my mum's moving to Beijing, so it's there or back here again.'

'Oh.' I looked around, hopelessly, for a reason to leave. On the rare occasions my students, now, see us – teachers – as beings capable of failed relationships and personal affairs, it seems they fall apart; in the moment, my reaction was much the same.

He placed his hand on Sophie's shoulder. 'Maybe you girls will end up being friends, hmm?' She and I both knew, instinctively, that this would never happen – she was tall, sophisticated, beautiful; I very much the opposite.

We were from different circles; would pass in corridors without so much as a glance, as though this conversation had never taken place. I see it now, among the girls I teach: the oil-and-water separation of types, hard to define and yet instinctively known. It's a power one learns as a girl, and never forgets: the ability to place one's peers in their hierarchy with little more than a glance. Impressive, I suppose, in its own, cruel way.

She slid off the desk, ran her hands down the back of her skirt. *Too short*, I thought. 'Well, I'm going to go get my stuff. See you in September, Dad,' she added, picking up her coat.

He stood, pulled her back, and placed a kiss on her head. 'I'll miss you,' he said. I avoided Sophie's eyes, each of us mortified for the other. She shook him off, and headed for the door.

'Feed Poppet before you go!' he added, shouting after her as she disappeared, the click of her heels echoing in the hallway outside. He turned to me. 'The cat,' he said, smiling. 'So – where were we?'

It seemed the Dean was further still from finding any link between them; the names I knew were mingled among those I didn't, and seemed to have no link to our society, or its past.

It gave me a cool sense of satisfaction, knowing my secrets were the ones he sought. Sometimes I made my own little amendments to the cards as I copied them out, usually further obscuring them from his research, though occasionally – for reasons I can barely explain but for the fact it seemed like a kind of tease, a showing off I imagined he'd never see – I'd add tiny details that were, in fact, true, a filling in of missing things that meant nothing to anyone but us.

I didn't tell the girls any of this, of course – though some-times I would toy with the idea, usually after Alex had made some coldly patronizing remark, or Robin had joked about a secret I'd never know, apparently out of spite – a way of reminding me that their friendship would always have existed without me: fundamentally and forever an outsider, no matter how close I got. I could have shown them all I knew – but to do so would be to give up my secret link, the only thing about Elm Hollow that was mine, and mine alone.

The task of writing up, then, became a way of brushing fingers up against the past and finding life still there: my secret, my own living history. But today I couldn't concentrate. The text swam on the page, words incomprehensible, crawling black; I blinked, but couldn't focus, or make sense of the creeping letters. Nothing made sense.

'Everything okay?' the Dean said. I turned, and saw him watching, chair rolled close to mine; felt a shiver as I wondered how long he'd been there.

'Yes, sir,' I said, weakly.

He rolled a little farther forward. I wondered how he'd got the trickle scar that arched beside his eye; caught the outline of pockmarks in the hollow of his cheek. 'Violet,' he said, softly. 'You look like you've got something on your mind.'

I looked down, ashamed to be caught. 'I'm fine, sir.'

'Is it about Emily Frost?' he said, fingers squeezing the arm of the chair. I felt myself grow hot, cheeks flushed; knew he would take that as a yes. And in a way, it was, as all things seemed to be: everything, always, about Emily Frost. I was jealous of a dead girl. Again.

'I think the whole school has been rather shaken by it,' he said. 'I know you didn't know her, but still . . . It's okay to be upset. For your friends, if nothing else.'

'Honestly?' I said, softly.

He looked hopeful, relieved I was at last opening up – imagining, perhaps, that we might talk openly again, me laughing politely at his stories, ludicrous, and inaccurate, as they were. 'Go on.'

'I really couldn't care less.' The words fell, almost of their own accord; the endless tap of his pen stopped, and he leaned back, slowly.

I turned away, though I felt his eyes still fixed on my back, and began writing again. He looked at me a little longer, drew breath as though about to speak, and stopped. The silence seemed to swell, to fill the space; I felt my cheeks burning, blinked away tears. Finally – after what seemed like several minutes – I heard the chair roll thick across the carpet, a sigh; a flick of paper, and the scratch of his pen at last.

I stared down at the page, furious with myself, my inability to keep my thoughts inside. For it was true: I *didn't* care that she was dead; if anything, some part of me felt something like relief. She wasn't coming back, as I'd feared, to usurp my place in the group. *Or at least,* I thought, bitterly, *she's not going to do so alive.* And yet, still, the discovery of the body had made them leave me behind, a third wheel to their grief; just as Mum had done after Dad died, they'd pulled away from me in favour of the dead, the ones whose memory was more vivid than my living presence.

I knew I was being childish; cringed as the thoughts passed (still do, in fact, as I write them here). I was ashamed, too, that I'd shown the Dean this silliness, the strange and pointless envy I felt for the dead girl dripping in my tone. I wondered what he was thinking, as we sat in brittle silence. Before, he'd paused from his work from time to time, to show me some strange engraving, or read a passage he found particularly illuminating, chuckling at the curious deaths and imagined spells with an almost childlike glee.

He'd listened as I ventured my own ideas, attention that I relished, in spite of myself; I felt heard, a flash of the potential I might have had, had I devoted my energy to my studies, rather than the attentions of Robin and the girls. Now I'd lost that, too.

The clock tower gave its low chime, and struck nine, long rings. The Dean turned heavily from his position, hunched over an open book, and looked at me. 'How on earth did it get so late?' he said, thumb pressed against temple, turning. 'How are you getting home?'

I had wondered that myself, having missed the last bus an hour ago. The car park was empty, my fellow students having long since left.

'I . . . I figured I'd walk,' I said.

He raised an eyebrow, tapped his fingers once on the desk. 'Don't you live in town?'

I nodded. He turned, glancing out at the Quad, finger and thumb rubbing, slowly, at his chin.

'No, no,' he said at last. 'I can't let you do that.' He rose heavily from his chair. 'Not given everything with . . . ' He trailed off. 'Give me five minutes. I'll give you a lift.'

'You don't have to—' I began, voice strained and thin. I hadn't been in a car since the accident; had strategically avoided doing so, choosing the boxy safety of the bus to the intimate danger of a car, so easily crushed under wheels.

'I won't hear a word otherwise,' he said, gathering his notes and stuffing them haphazardly into his bag. 'I should've let you go sooner. It's entirely my fault.' He rifled through the chaos of his desk, glancing back at me occasionally as I stood in the doorway, watching. It seemed, when he looked, as though he were about to speak, some thought lingering unsaid. But each time he caught my eye, he pulled back, looked nervously away.

We walked out of the building in silence, a ribbon of tension between us. His was the last car on campus, and I climbed into the passenger seat, kicking coffee cups and crisp wrappers aside as I did so. The back seat was piled high with an array of abandoned items, details of a life; books and boxes filled with papers mingled with rucksacks and camping equipment, a winter coat and a hiking pole.

'Sorry,' he said. 'Not all that organized, I'll admit.'

The car wheezed into life, and as the headlights flickered I blinked, eyes adjusting to the beams. Figures floated in my vision, white shards falling through the light, the grass crawling in the breeze. He tinkered with the radio, and a song whistled through the tinny speakers; he flicked from one station to another, murmuring under his breath.

'I like this one,' I said, finally, desperate to get the journey over with.

'You like this?' He chuckled, offering a smile for the first time since I'd told him how I really felt about Emily. 'I didn't know Barry Manilow was back in fashion.' He put the car in gear, and reversed out, slowly. 'I must be hip again.'

I gave a stage laugh, overwrought. 'Very hip, sir.'

We drove in quiet company, the speakers rattling as we ran over bumps in the country roads, through the darkness to the town. Occasionally he would ask how my studies were going, which classes I liked, and so on; I responded to each with a noncommittal but positive answer, a smile, a balm. I tried to keep my hands from reaching for the wheel, a nervous tic, and begged my heart to still with silent sighs and deep breaths.

As we reached the town, street lamps gave way to the bright

lights of the promenade, with its shabby arcades, Golden Ticket, Caesar's Palace, Lucky Strike all burning bright.

'You know, Violet,' he said, slowly, eyes still fixed on the road. 'I do worry, sometimes. I know you've been through rather a lot, and . . . ' He paused, choosing his words carefully. 'I sometimes wonder if it might be good for you to open up a little bit more. To someone you can trust.'

I stared silently out of the window and tried not to listen, focusing instead on the people outside. A couple walked by holding hands, his eyes cast down, watching her feet; an elderly woman with matted hair in a filthy coat swayed, eyeing them with suspicion. A group of girls only a few years older than me tottered in vertiginous heels and neon skirts, stumbling from one bar to the next; and cross-legged on the sea wall, wiping her nose on her sleeve, was Robin, staring glassy-eyed at the crowd. I placed a hand on the door handle, squeezed it tight. It was locked.

'It's just not healthy to keep things pent up,' the Dean said, staring forwards, chewing thoughtfully at a thumbnail. 'It's okay to be angry, or sad, but you shouldn't feel like you have to deal with those feelings alone—' I grabbed my bag, pulled the lock as the car stopped, and jumped out, the Dean's voice drowned out by the blare of a car heading towards me, driver growling a complaint as he passed. I ran breathless, back to the promenade, but she was gone.

I sat in the spot where she'd been, as though I might somehow be able to follow her thoughts; and when the night grew cold and the casinos dimmed their lights, I walked home, footsteps heavy on the cracked pavements.

'There you are.' I spun around, caught paces from home by a hand that reached from between the trees.

'Oh my god,' I hissed. 'I've been looking everywhere for you.'

Robin gave a smile, the usual high-watt grin a little diminished, her eyes a little bloodshot, raw with recent tears. 'It's been a pretty shitty week.'

'I'm sorry about Emily,' I offered.

'Don't be. We all know she was . . . ' She trailed off.

I turned to look at my house, the living room still flashing with the TV light. 'Do you . . . Do you want to come in?'

'Is that okay?'

'Yeah, just . . . ' I glanced around again. 'I'll need to distract Mum. Make sure she doesn't see you.'

I let myself in, leaving the door a little open behind. My shoes sighing on the carpet, I peered round the corner, into the kitchen, where a dinner plate sat covered in silver foil, glittering in the light; in the living room, I saw her head turn. *Of all the times for you to be awake*, I thought, jaw set tight.

'Where have you been?' she said, her voice still thick with sleep. She rolled herself up from the sofa and walked – a kind of apelike walk, the stagger of one whose sadness is too heavy to bear – into the kitchen. I hadn't seen her in weeks – at least, not in anything but dim light. I prayed Robin wouldn't see her, her eyes yellowing and cracked with blood, skin blue-white and translucent, like curdled milk.

She placed a cold hand on my arm, and I flinched. 'Sweetheart . . . What are you doing to yourself?'

'Nothing, Mum. I'm fine.'

'Something's wrong,' she said. 'Honey . . . Are you taking drugs?' I looked behind her, catching Robin's eye for a split second as she passed. 'It's just . . . You've lost such a lot of weight. And you look so pale.'

'I'm just tired, Mum. I'm working really hard.' I tried to breathe, to stay calm, but an itch of irritation grew in my chest. 'I can't believe you're accusing me of being on drugs.'

'I'm not accusing you of anything,' she said, a nervous crack in her voice.

'I can't believe you're acting like *I'm* the one with the problem. You're such a hypocrite,' I said, my voice low, calm. 'When was the last time you left the house? Fuck – when was the last time you wore anything that wasn't pyjamas? It's embarrassing. *You're* embarrassing.'

She stared at me, wide-eyed with hurt. 'Violet . . . ' she began, stepping back.

'No, Mum. You don't get to pick a fight with me about who's got their life together. I know what I'm doing. I'm in control. But you're a mess. I'm not listening to you.' I pushed past her, and she said nothing as I climbed the stairs; as I closed the door to my room I heard a sob, a moan ill concealed, and I felt nothing.

'Are you on drugs, honey?' Robin said as I closed the door. 'Do you need help, sweetheart? Honey boo? Babycakes?'

With a halfhearted laugh, I threw my bag on the floor. I followed her gaze around the room, the same look as before, examining pieces of the skin I'd long shed. The same faded bedspread, prickled with age. Same posters torn from magazines, blu-tacked to cover the lily-print wallpaper, indigo on dusky pink. Same catalogues, books I'd read once, then again, piled beside the peeling chest of drawers, open, spilling over with clothes I'd never wear. Not now. I wasn't that girl any more, hated the idea that she might think I was.

'So what happened?' I said, sitting on the bed and kicking off my shoes. I poked a hole in my tights, making ever-wider circles around the point. When the nylon snapped, I carried on, nail scraping at skin.

She stretched her legs out across mine, toes pointed, calves softening as she relaxed. 'We've been back and forth between the police station and her parents' house all week. It's been fucking awful.'

I put my palm on a seam of stiff hairs by her ankle, rubbed two fingers around in a figure of eight. 'Missed a spot,' I said, willing her on, resisting the urge to ask her why she hadn't thought to call.

'We were the last to see her, you know? So they think we know something.'

I looked at her. 'Do you?' Silence. 'Know something, I mean.'

She stared at me for a moment, chewing her lip. 'I need a cigarette,' she said, rolling over to crack open the window with one hand, rooting through her pockets with the other. 'Got a light?'

'In my bag,' I said, pointing to the pile beside the door. She climbed off the bed and crouched down, digging around among the mass of coats and shoes.

'Aww,' she said, turning to me with a grin. 'Did Mummy make you a packed lunch?'

'What?'

She held a stained lunchbox high overhead, a half-eaten salad sweating inside. 'Very appetizing.'

I shuffled forward on the bed. 'That's not mine.'

'Whatever, Violet. I mean, it's totally fucking lame, but you don't have to lie about it.'

'I'm serious,' I said, plucking the box from her hands. 'This isn't mine.' I crouched down beside her. 'That's not my bag.'

'Then whose is it?' she said, her tone sceptical.

'I think it's the Dean's.'

'How the . . . What?'

'He gave me a lift,' I began, the words trailing away. I turned it over, tipped the contents on the floor. It looked like my bag – a dull, brown satchel with faded brass clips – but the leather was soft to the touch, unlike the stiff, fake pleather of my own. Inside were papers, miscellaneous: essays half-marked, post-its folded over, caught. Pens in red and green; nasal spray, tissues, a foil of aspirin, half-spent. A notebook, and a tape cassette, half-wound.

'Bingo,' Robin said, plucking the tape from the pile. 'Let's see what he's into. I bet it's *terrible*.'

The rewind whirred; I opened the notebook, perched on the edge of my bed, feet tapping the air, alive with curiosity. Instantly, I slammed it shut. *Was that . . . ?* I looked at Robin, who was absorbed in the whirring tape, and peeled open the notebook again. A newspaper cover, folded inside. 'Our Darling Emily,' the headline read. 'Her Killer Must Be Found.'

'Ready?' Robin said. I nodded, and she clicked play, staring down at the rolling tape.

Minutes of rustling passed. We sat in silence, glancing at each other, then back at the tape player.

'It's blank,' I said.

'Shhhh,' she replied.

'Emily,' the Dean's voice boomed from the stereo. We froze, stared at each other. 'Right on time.'

'Hi, sir,' a girl's voice said. Clipped. A little huskier than my own, her tone deeper, more resonant. Of course.

'You know you can call me Matthew,' he replied. There was another rustle, the sound of fingers brushing the mike. 'How's my favourite student?' I shuddered, the words familiar, known, directed at me. Robin looked up, eyes flashing dark, as they had on the night of the rite – I felt my breath sharp in my chest, felt myself accompanied, a flight, a memory of horror – then back at the tape.

'Fine, thank you,' Emily's voice said, the tone hollow – a shade of something I couldn't place.

'Good, good. Glad to hear it.' A cough. Nervous. 'So, have you had a chance to consider what we discussed?'

A silence, long and still. I looked at Robin, goosebumps on the white flesh of her neck and arms. 'Robin . . . ' I said. She mouthed something that looked like 'Don't', though to me or to Emily I didn't know.

'I can't do it, sir,' Emily said, at last. 'I mean . . . I don't want to.'

I heard the dull rattle of the reception gate closing, recognized the time – 6pm, the familiar sound that signalled the beginning of our research sessions. The Dean coughed again, cleared his throat. 'Might I ask what's changed your mind?'

'It's just . . . It's inappropriate.' Another silence. 'And to be honest, I don't think it's fair of you to ask.' I thought I heard the click of Mrs Coxon's footsteps in the hall outside, but couldn't be sure. Perhaps I simply knew the routine so well, knew his tone, the cosy chatter he'd employed with me.

'Oh, Emily. That's such a shame. I was hoping—'

The microphone brushed again, and then nothing. Absolute silence, a reel of empty tape. The two of us sat, staring, as the tape wound through, and ended with a deadly click.

Robin – hands shaking, skin porcelain-white – flicked the tape to the other side, and found it blank, rewound both sides, and played them again. She picked up a half-empty glass, raised it to her lips, but didn't drink. I recognized the gesture, the logic behind it – to hide a trembling lip, swallow away tears.

I reached out a hand, and she flinched, as though burned. 'He was—' she began. She looked at me, eyes helpless, willing me to understand.

'He was . . . What?' I whispered, though I thought I knew.

She looked away, at the stereo; then back at me. 'Stupid bitch,' she said. 'Stupid, stupid bitch.'

I gripped the edge of the bed, and closed my eyes. *I hate you*, I thought; and then thought, too, *Perhaps she's right.*

Chapter 13

I glanced across at Robin's sketch, copied from a page torn from an old medical textbook, a head rolled slightly back. I'd always liked anatomical words, medical terms – or at least, I'd loved them since I'd sat in the hospital, listening to the medical staff whispering them to one another determinedly, as though the terms themselves could provide a cure – and this one was filled with the best of them. I pinned them down, one by one: subclavian, laryngeal, brachial plexus. Jugular. Carotid. Dissect. Her sketchbook was filled with these drawings ('good practice,' she said) but missing their labels. I listed the words in my diary, as though filling in the gaps.

'Where are they?'

She looked up, tucked a strand of hair behind her ear. 'They'll be here.'

I took another sip of coffee, long cold. Poured the contents in the grass, crushed the polystyrene cup, and threw it into the tracks. In the distance, a train rolled towards us with a steady thunder. Robin went on sketching, and I watched as it passed, one empty carriage after another, windows gold in the dim light.

She'd been unusually quiet since we'd found the tape, her silence bristling, an almost-physical presence (*as though Emily had inserted herself between us*, I thought, jealously). I played with a cat's cradle I'd found abandoned on the beach; wound it around my fingers until the feeling had stopped, and I felt the electric throb and twitch of nerves when the blood rushed back.

There was a rustle of branches, and a snap of twigs underfoot. Alex and Grace emerged from the woods, sitting on either side of us without a word. We looked out at the town in the distance, lights turning the sky the colour of poison; Alex cleared her throat, and glanced across me at Robin, still absorbed in her sketch.

'What happened?' she said, finally. Robin didn't react, though her pencil scratched a little harder on the page. Alex looked at me, a brief flash of irritation on her face.

'We found a tape,' I said. 'Of the Dean. He was talking to Emily, asking her to do something.'

Alex arched her brow. 'Like what?'

'I don't know. She wouldn't do it. She said whatever it was, "was inappropriate".'

Alex looked at Grace. 'That's all it says?'

'The tape stops after that. There's nothing else on either side.'

The girls fell silent, looking out on to the tracks. Alex put her knuckle between her teeth and bit down, leaving pointed rings in flesh. I'd seen her do this, deep in thought, and every time I winced.

'How did you get it?' she said, watching a hawk swoop above the churchyard. 'The tape. Where was it?'

'He was giving her a lift home,' Robin said, without looking up. 'In his car.'

Alex glanced at Grace again, her eyes narrowed.

'I was on campus late,' I said. 'I didn't want—'

'Why?' Alex said. There was a biting tone to her voice that made me blush. I'd heard her use it on the girls who stared at us, or lurked on nearby tables, hoping to catch some sliver of gossip. I felt myself shrink, just as I'd seen them do. 'Why were you there so late?'

'I've been doing a research project with him. As an extra-curricular. I . . . I needed a reference.'

'For what?'

'For uni.'

She scoffed. 'And you didn't think Annabel's would be enough? A recommendation from her can get you in pretty much anywhere you want.'

'I didn't . . . I didn't know that.'

Alex sighed, muttered something under her breath. She looked out into the field, as though steeling herself to be calm. 'So what are you researching?' she said, at last.

I dug my nails into my palm. 'Does it matter?'

'I don't know – does it?'

Robin's pencil snapped against the page. 'Christ, Alex,' she spat. 'This is hardly the point. Emily was scared. Scared of *him.* That's why we're here. Not because Violet's a fucking nerd.'

'I just don't understand why she's . . .' Alex groaned through gritted teeth. 'Fine. Forget it.'

Grace looked at me, lashes low and heavy. 'How sure are you?'

'Completely, 100% sure,' Robin said, before I could answer. She lit a cigarette and the air briefly lit with a sulphur tang; she took a drag and handed it to me.

'Should we . . . Should we call the police?' I ventured, nervously.

Alex snorted, and plucked the cigarette from my fingers as I raised it to my lips. 'No,' she said, flatly. 'I don't think that would do any good.'

'Why not?'

'Does he say, "I'm going to kill you, Emily Frost"?'

'No, bu—'

'Then they'll dismiss it. Look at us,' she said, with a pointed glance at me, then Robin. 'They'll just think we're trying to cause trouble. They already think we're up to something, no thanks to you.'

Robin flinched. 'What's that supposed to mean?'

'I just think maybe swanning around with pupils like saucers while you're meant to be grieving your best friend is—'

'*Meant* to be?'

'You know what I mean.'

'No, Alex, I don't. Please enlighten me.' Robin's hands were shaking; I reached over and squeezed her fingers.

Alex sighed, catching my eye briefly before turning to Grace, who shook her head. 'Forget it,' she said, finally. 'I'm sorry. I'm just really . . . I'm tired.'

The hawk finally caught something, swooping into the graveyard with a sudden, sharp drop; it rose again, clutching what looked like a rat, tail curling as the body writhed, whipping through the black air.

'What are we going to do?' I said, helplessly. I think we all knew; though perhaps it's hindsight that makes me want to imagine that, for a brief moment, we shared the same thought. That there was only one thing we *could* do.

The girls looked at each other, and sighed. Grace shook her head, lowered her eyes. Robin began to sketch again, and we sat in silence, waiting for the sun to rise.

For the rest of the week, I skipped school, intercepting messages from the Dean on the answering machine until I cut the tape, his voice unsettling in his 'concerns about your welfare' and 'urgent' need to see me. I waited for nightfall, when Robin would appear at my window, pebbles splintering the already-cracked glass, each time a little disappointed as it stayed intact.

She brought with her a variety of 'borrowed things', her compulsion to steal apparently multiplied by the fact of Emily's death – tattered issues of *Vogue* stolen from Alex, faces lopped out with sewing shears; a heady bundle of dried sage, bound in purple string. A silver watch, source unknown; an ancient book of matches, Marilyn Monroe pouting on the front.

And yet she hadn't succeeded in getting what we needed: a hair, a fingernail, some piece of him to help us perform the rite. She'd been to his office, feigning tears (she laughed about this as she told me; a nervous response, I supposed). But there was nothing: she'd even kicked over the contents of his bin in the hope of finding a used tissue, all to no avail.

To make matters worse, perhaps as a result of my confinement, I'd begun to have second thoughts. I listened to the tape, endlessly whirring back, the words seared into my mind: I heard frustration in Emily's words, and a wavering. But what I couldn't hear was fear, the 'terror' Robin had caught in Emily's tone. *You didn't know her*, I told myself. *You wouldn't know what she'd sound like scared.* But still I listened, again and again, as though it might reveal itself on the fifteenth listen, or the twentieth.

This, too, was compounded by my own doubts about the Dean. He'd seemed so utterly, almost irritatingly nice. I thought about the news reports, the absolute horror of Emily's death, the violence of it unfolding in increments, details slipped into interviews and statements from newsreaders and police. Fifteen stab wounds, they'd said. A broken wrist, squeezed so hard the bones snapped. Cuts to her throat, clawed in – most likely while she was still alive. Could he really be capable of a thing like that?

But then, too, the way he'd reached for my hand, and squeezed; the tap on the shoulder when he might have said my name. The way he lingered, a little, as he said it, as though thinking it over, attaching to it some meaning I couldn't quite grasp. It wouldn't be the first time I'd been fooled by male intentions; indeed, it wasn't the last. Perhaps I was too naive, too inexperienced, to know man from beast. Perhaps the girls were right.

Robin sat on my bed, eyes watchful, occasionally disappearing into herself mid-sentence, rattling a stick of rock along her teeth and laughing as the sound made me shudder. 'You're such a wuss,' she said, grinning.

'Fuck off,' I said, lying back on the bed and closing my eyes.

She leaned over, elbows bending the mattress; I could smell the strawberry flavour on her breath. 'Are you scared of doing it again?'

'Doing what?' I knew, of course, what she meant; wanted a moment to gauge the right response. I opened my eyes, saw hers bright and unwavering above.

'The rite,' she said. 'Duh.'

'No,' I said, coolly.

'Well, I am.'

'Seriously?'

'Yeah,' she sighed, rolling onto her back. 'I still don't think I'm totally over the last one.'

'That was ages ago.' It was my turn to sit, to lean over her. She held the rock in the air, and I took it.

'I know. But still . . . ' She trailed off. I knew what she meant, though pride stopped me from saying so. It was the inescapable guilt, the feeling – no matter how vehemently you told yourself it was all in your mind, the product of an overactive imagination – of being watched. The hand on the shoulder, the claw to the rib. Once summoned, the Furies – or, at least, the idea of them, their elongated shadows – were more difficult to send away.

'Are you sure we ought to . . . ?' I said, softly.

'Yeah,' she replied, feeling for the light beside the bed. She flicked it off, and I lay back, still clutching the rock, sticky with spit.

I closed my eyes, lids aching with sleep. I felt her arm soften against mine. She always slept like that – flat on her back, with an almost vampiric stillness. Sometimes, when I woke up beside her, I'd hold my palm a few millimetres above her mouth, feeling for breath. When I couldn't feel it, I'd rest my hand, just for a moment, relieved to find her skin still warm. When she drew breath, I pulled away, pretending to sleep, holding my own breath still – a little pinch of irritation catching at my throat as she fell immediately back to sleep, my concern for her not reflected back.

She took a deep breath, as though about to speak; a heavy knock broke the silence, ringing through the house. I sat upright, heart thrumming, dull ache in my throat. Imagined police, the frog-eyed woman who'd asked again and again if I remembered what happened that day in my dad's car, if I could help them see; pictured her face, disappointed, uncovering proof of our plans. 'You're a survivor,' she'd said, squeezing my wrist. 'You're a brave, sweet girl.'

I turned to Robin, who shrugged. 'Go see,' she whispered. I stepped into the hallway and down the stairs, Mum staring blankly into the rolling light of the VCR. 'I'll get it,' I said, though she didn't react. I wondered if she'd heard the knock at all.

Through the riddled pane of glass, I could see a broad shadow. I stepped towards it through the dark, squinting. It knocked again, and I flinched, gripping the sideboard with both hands. I heard a shuffling above, and saw Robin emerge at the top of the stairs, peering through the wooden bars.

'Violet?' I recognized the voice immediately. It was the Dean, his voice weary and dull. 'Mrs Taylor?' I glanced at Robin, who ran a hand down her throat. 'I'm worried about you,' he said. 'We haven't seen you in days. I just want to check you're okay.' I felt a flash of nerves, a pang of doubt. How could he have murdered Emily Frost? This shy, awkward, lumbering man – could he really be a killer?

But why come over this late? I thought, nervously. *There's no good reason to come have this conversation in the middle of the night.*

He leaned forward, peered through the glass, breath misting the pane with a cloud of silver. Finally, after what felt like minutes, he turned and walked away. I climbed the stairs, limbs dragging as though weighed down with stones, and closed the bedroom door. Robin sat cross-legged on the bed, skin pale and damp with sweat. 'That was close,' she said, a half-laugh breaking as she spoke.

I pulled out the desk chair and sat, elbows on knees; ran my hands through my hair, chipped nails catching tangles. 'Do you . . . ' I began, looking up. 'Do you really think he did it?'

She narrowed her eyes. 'Don't you?'

'I . . . I don't know.'

She sighed, leaned back against the headboard. 'Alex said you'd chicken out.'

'I'm not—'

'And she said you'd defend him.'

'Robin—'

She looked up, her glare vicious. 'No. Violet, it's his fault

221

she's dead. We can't just . . . ' Head in hands, nails clawing brow; a shudder. 'We can't let him get away with it.'

I closed my eyes. There was a hollowness to the scene, the words taken straight from a film – all crimes and revenge, knives and claws and screams. It seemed altogether unreal, a hallucination. Was it really possible he could have killed her? I thought back to the tape: the rattle of the reception grate, the knowledge that the two of them were alone. The night I'd been alone with him in his office; the look in his eyes when he saw my fear, his power reflected back. 'Fine,' I said. 'Fine. We won't.'

I flicked off the light and rolled into bed. Outside, a car rattled into life, headlights streaming fingers through the room, Robin's hands gripping my arm tight as she slept.

As the sun rose, turning the room silvery, she rolled over, cold hands against the exposed strip of flesh across my stomach. 'Are you coming to Nicky's party?'

' . . . You hate Nicky.'

She grinned. 'All the more reason to go.' She tapped her nose, conspiratorially.

'But what about the Dean? What about—'

'Drop it, Violet.'

I closed my eyes, still half-asleep, opened them abruptly as she pressed her elbow into my hip. I winced as she looked down at the skin, the nub of bone that had only appeared in the last few weeks; she smiled, rubbed the spot with her thumb, and I relented. 'When is it?'

'Tonight.'

'I'm not supposed to be leaving the house,' I said: a pout, my quarantine having been, after all, Robin's idea.

She snorted. 'You think the Dean's going to be at Nicky's house party? Get real.'

'Then why are we going?'

I stretched, back arching; felt myself watched, her eyes creeping over me. 'Alright,' I said, after a pause. It seemed the thinner I got, the more approving her looks, pointing out the shadow of bones, gaps between thighs and ribs. It had seemed to me – of course – that I looked even more like Emily now than I had before; but, too, saw the girls in magazines, and saw that she was right, we women, turning deathly, pretty as mannequins.

She grinned, and rolled out of bed, peeling a tie from her hair and shaking it out. She turned to me as she assembled herself, ready to leave, shirt smoothed flat, tie edged halfway up, earrings popped in. 'By the way,' she said, pulling a file from her bag and throwing it on the bed. 'Annabel said just because you're sick doesn't mean you get to skip the reading.' I blushed, imagining Annabel knew, somehow, what we were doing – knew too that I wasn't sick, though I'd spent the last three days at home, watching daytime TV and—

'You're welcome,' Robin said, interrupting my thoughts.

'Sorry.'

She gave a half-smile I couldn't read; in the split second I'd forgotten her, she'd disappeared to me. 'Right,' she said, slinging her backpack over her shoulder. 'I'm outta here. Later?'

'Yeah,' I said, rolling up to sit. 'Let me check the coast is clear.'

She rolled her eyes. 'It's fine. A tenner says your Mum's unconscious.' She gave a brief wave and slipped out of the door before I could retort, a little burned by her words – a sudden protectiveness, a guilt for being so cruel, Robin's words a reflection of my own. I remained still until the front door slammed shut, my window rattling a little, and leapt up to shout after her. But when I looked outside, she was running; seconds later, she was out of sight.

I slumped back onto the bed, knees to my chest, the dust hanging in the air, held captive by the sunlight. The file sat unopened at my feet; I prodded it with my toes, as though expecting it to burst into flame. I heard the TV flicker into life downstairs, Mum presumably having woken at the slamming of the door; winced again at Robin's cruelty. I pulled the file towards me, and opened it, gingerly.

Pinned to the topmost sheet was a folded piece of paper, pinned together with a clip. I peeled it open and saw Annabel's distinctive script. 'This may be of interest,' it said, simply. 'Please ensure you read it.' Underneath, a caricature, added by Robin (the strokes undoubtedly hers, sharp scratches of ink). I felt a flash of anger at the fact she'd read the note intended only for me and spoiled it – imagined her hands sticky and childish, grasping. I turned it over, searching for some other sign – a get well message, perhaps, or an inducement to come back soon – but found nothing. Outside, a child laughed as a car sped by, stopped, abruptly, before driving on. I turned back to my work.

'In 1484, Heinrich Kramer made one of the earliest attempts at prosecuting women accused of witchcraft,' the paper began.

'He was quickly dismissed by the local bishop as "senile and crazy", and was expelled from the city of Innsbruck. By way of revenge, he wrote the *Malleus Maleficarum*, a text which would go on to become the most influential book on witchcraft in the Western world and would result in the murder of thousands of women across Europe and beyond.' I read on, the essay a detailed history of the trials that followed; the spread, infection of minds with ideas of folk magic and petty slights. I pictured Margaret Boucher, swallowed by flames, and felt a bitter rush of anger, the murder brutal and cruel.

'The damage one man can do,' the paper ended. 'The bitterness of the bruised ego, the cold-blooded wrath of a man scorned: the repercussions impossible to overstate. One can only hope that, as a culture, we have left such things behind, and yet–'

I turned the page, rapt, but found it blank. 'You should draw your own conclusions,' Annabel had said, once, leaning forwards in the tattered chair. 'You should apply these lessons to your own lives and think – always – for yourselves.'

I had expected Nicky's house to possess the same grandeur and ancient richness as Alex's, a kind of understated, assured wealth. The reality, however, was quite different, the house white and gleaming, surrounded by sweeping lawns and silver birch, walls of panelled glass streaming bright across the stone-flagged terrace, pool glistening in the red evening light as people swam. 'New money,' Robin said, bitterly, and I wondered, again, what she thought of my house, what she thought of me. I shook it off, as Nicky bounded across the lawn.

'Too cold to swim, surely?' Robin said, coldly.

Nicky flashed a bright smile, doll eyes ringed with smudged mascara. 'Not at all. I'm glad you could make it.' She turned to me. 'Are you feeling better?'

I nodded. 'Much better.'

'Mr Holmsworth was asking after you today,' she said; I hoped she hadn't noticed how Robin and I both bristled at the mention of the Dean's name, vivid, sharp. 'He's nice, isn't he?'

'Yeah,' I said, after a pause. Robin, regaining herself, grabbed my arm. 'Have you seen Alex and Grace?'

Nicky pointed to the house. 'They're inside somewhere. Help yourselves to drinks – Nathan's bartending.'

'Your boyfriend?' I said, as Robin began to pull away, her fingers tight around my wrist.

'Oh god, no.' Nicky laughed. 'Brother.' I smiled in response and gave an apologetic shrug as Robin dragged me towards the house; Nicky's smile a little shadowed, hollowed by the slight.

The music echoed across the lawn, Robin singing along in a low growl: the words 'doused in mud, soaked in bleach', ringing in my mind. Inside, girls sat knotted together on sofas, drinking from plastic cups and picking at the snacks artfully placed in bowls that read 'Party!' in felt-pen lettering.

'Some party,' Robin said, as we joined Alex and Grace on a sofa, bare legs sticking to the clear plastic laid to protect the white cushions beneath.

Alex gave a weak smile; in the bright lights, the hollows under her eyes were a bluish-grey. I looked at Grace, who was chewing her fingernail and watching as the girls outside jumped into the pool, another attempting (and failing) to capture the moment on film, the camera flashing at the moment the girls hit the water.

'Are you okay?' I said, nervously. I hadn't spoken to the girls since the night at the tracks; had assumed our spat had been forgotten, though it seemed, now, that I was wrong.

Robin stood, abruptly, looking down at me. 'I'm going to find this bartender.' She waited, a moment, as though expecting me to follow; when I didn't, she spun and walked away, knocking a plastic cup to the floor with her elbow as she passed.

I looked at Alex and Grace again. 'Look, if it's about the fight—'

'It's not,' Alex said, flatly. 'Not everything is about you, you know.'

Grace placed a hand on Alex's knee. 'Alex, don't.'

'I didn't mean—' I began, silenced as Grace turned to me and gave an apologetic smile. 'Oh my god,' I said, cringing as she looked away. A stain of blue-black shadowed her jaw and neck, a patch of newborn-pink skin shining sickeningly at the edge of her hairline. She'd foregone the artful make-up she normally used to cover it – knowing, I supposed, that it wouldn't disguise this. 'What happened?'

'Guess,' Alex said, glancing at Grace through hooded eyes. She reached out for her, wiped a tear away with her thumb. 'It's nothing,' Grace added, turning to me.

'It's—' I breathed a long sigh, choosing my words carefully. 'It's not—'

'So, guess what?' Robin said, climbing over the back of the

sofa and landing between us with a thud. 'Nicky's brother's hot.' We stared at her, the interruption bracing. 'I know,' she added. 'You'd think he'd be all bug-eyed like her, but he's not.'

'Robin,' I said, softly.

She handed me a sloshing cup, the sticky liquid inside spilling over my fingers. 'I'm going to see if he wants one of these.' She rooted in her pocket and pulled out a plastic bag of dusty pills. 'Want one?' she added, waving it at the three of us. Alex and Grace shook their heads; I opened my palm, and she placed one in the centre, closing each of my fingers one by one. 'Enjoy,' she said, planting a kiss on my closed fist.

I felt the girls watching me as I swallowed it, the sickly drink chasing the pill in a hot swell that radiated through my chest. When I looked, they glanced away, as though caught, and for a moment we were silent.

'You can't let him keep doing this,' I said, finally.

'Violet,' Alex began, a warning tone in her voice.

'We should do something. Call the police—'

Grace raised a hand, and I stopped. 'We're not going to—'

'But Grace, Jesus—'

'No,' she said, the flicker of a sob in her voice. 'No. Please, Violet. Just drop it.' She looked at me, eyes meeting mine; saw the question I wanted to ask.

I folded my arms, but felt childish; unfolded them, feeling the faint warmth of the alcohol and the pill seeping under my skin. I felt Alex squeeze my shoulder, the briefest of touches; flushed, ashamed of my reaction. 'I'm sorry,' I said, turning to Grace again.

Grace shrugged. 'Don't be. It's fine.'

It's not, I thought, but smiled, aching with Grace's pain as she smiled back. The music changed to a loud, thumping hip-hop track I'd heard before, a hit with the girls at my old school and, it appeared, those at Elm Hollow, who jumped up from their seats, squealing with delight as they bounced and shook to the rhythm. It seemed so easy, being them – there was a lightness in the way they moved that extended to everything about them. The way they laughed, bounced off one another as they sang along to the words; the way they wandered around Elm Hollow, unaffected by the ghosts that lurked in the portraits and busts that lined the halls. Even now, in the aftermath of Emily Frost – after a brief school-wide period of mourning, itself seeming somehow shallow, a thing performed but not felt – here they were, dancing, giggling, as though nothing could possibly be anything other than perfect.

I realize, now, that this was as illusory as most of the things I thought I knew, back then; that teenage girls, in the main, are all racked with the ache of womanhood, the sudden real-ization that squandered youth is fleeting, and will be much sought after, too late. The strange attentions of boys, and men; the vivid pains of seeing oneself, that sad illumination – I know it, and see it in my girls, now. And yet, as the music pounded – as Grace shuffled in her seat and winced; as a girl motioned to Alex at a rapped phrase as though it referred to her, and glared at her when she didn't react; as I felt the sudden rush of the pill kick in, and was sickened by it – it seemed as though we, among our peers, were the only ones singled out for such misery.

'Can I ask you something?' I said, turning to Alex. My eyes seemed a little behind my movements, the swell of the high turning everything liquid and bright, vivid in a way that seemed grotesque.

She looked at me, eyes narrowed. 'Depends on what it is.'

I paused; chose my words carefully, though I knew there was no subtle way to ask the question that had been on my mind and now, in my intoxication, swallowed me whole. I took a deep breath. 'Do you really think the – he – killed Emily?'

Alex raised a finger to her lips. 'Shhh. Not here.'

'Please, Alex. I know Robin thinks it, but . . . Do you?'

She looked at Grace, who nodded, slowly. 'I think it's the most likely explanation.'

'But . . . He's so nice. Why . . . Why would he?'

Alex leaned towards me, I noticed her eyes still pink-lined from crying. 'I think—'

A scream erupted from the far side of the house; Robin cannoned through the dancing girls, drinks spilling on the carpet, the crowd watching wide-eyed as she grabbed both of my arms and pulled me up. I stumbled, shin cracking against the coffee table, its glass surface shuddering at the impact. 'Robin, what the—'

'We've got to go,' she said, tugging at my wrist; I flinched, her grip Chinese-burn tight.

'No, Robin, what the—'

She turned to me, and stared for a moment, her pupils pool-dark and wide. 'We have to go,' she said again.

'Not until you—'

'How dare you?' Nicky screamed, rounding the corner. 'How fucking dare you?'

Robin spun around, loosening her grip. 'Excuse me?'

'Stay away from him,' she said, voice trembling. A boy appeared behind her, tall and reedy, but with the same wide eyes and blonde hair as Nicky. *Nathan*, I thought, half-smiling at the root of Nicky's anger – Robin caught, no doubt, straddling the boy, just to prove she could. As he stepped into the brightness of the living room, however, I saw a red welt blooming on his neck; two jagged half-moons, seeping blood.

'This bitch,' he said, reaching a hand for his neck; trembling as he pulled it away, the blood pooling in the lines of his palm. 'She's insane.'

Nicky glanced at him, a high-pitched gasp as she saw the blood. She looked back at Robin, open-mouthed. 'What is wrong with you?'

Robin laughed. 'Look, it's not my fault if he likes it like—'

'I never asked you to—' he began, Nicky flinching at the response. She glared at him.

'She's probably got some sort of disease, too. You should get yourself tested.'

He drew breath, as though about to retort, but seemed to think better of it. 'You should leave,' he said, finally, the crack in his voice relieving him of any authority.

Robin turned to me, and reached for my hand, still burning from the pull. I looked at Grace and Alex, who stood, slowly, and followed us out, past the pool and through the birch trees, the music bringing everything back to life once again.

I said nothing, waiting for the inevitable: for Alex's bitter remark, for Robin's spark of self-defence, Grace and I silent as they fought. We'd pick our sides, apologetic glances shared between us as we did so, and stalk off into the night – Grace to Alex's house, Robin to mine. And then, things would return to normal, these moods and petty arguments washed away with the tide.

And yet, as we walked, shadows lengthened by the streetlights, the sound of foxes screeching and nipping in the dark, neither Alex, nor any of the other girls, said a word. Robin tugged at my jacket, possessive fingers crawling into pockets for my cigarettes. I swatted her away, as she pouted; chastened, I pulled the cigarettes from my bag and handed them to her, declining when she offered them to me.

'We can't carry on like this, you know,' she said, the embers vibrating as she spoke. She turned back to the girls, their eyes fixed on the ground. 'I mean, you might be able to live with what he did, but I can't. She was our best friend.'

Alex's head snapped up, her mouth open: I waited for her to retort. She drew breath; sighed, shook her head.

Robin's tone was belligerent, exasperated. 'We have to do something. We can't just—'

'Robin,' Alex said, flatly. 'I'm not disagreeing with you. You're right.' She glanced at Grace, who nodded, solemnly. 'We should go to the police. Give them what we have. They can investigate.'

Robin laughed, coldly. 'Like they did with Grace's dad, you mean? Because that worked out *really* well last time.' A bitter silence fell, for a moment; Alex's mouth opened and closed, stunned, searching desperately for a response. 'Besides,' Robin went on, 'he deserves worse than anything they could do. He murdered Emily. Nothing's going to bring her back.' She didn't look at me, seemed almost to be avoiding my eyes. I remember noticing that before she spoke, briefly, in the same way one feels the tremor before the quake: knowing, then, that the words she'd say next were about to hurt..

'And nobody will ever replace her,' she said, flatly.

The words held in the air like a sting, a barb in my heart. A truth spoken that I already half knew, suspected, but brought to life in vivid colour with those six words.

I felt the other girls' eyes on me, a flicker of doubt, or nervousness; set my expression, mask-like, the blankness itself no doubt a sign of the hurt. She'd excuse it, if I raised it – the words masked with indifference, righteous anger, the white-hot heat of the moment – and yet, while I didn't know what the Dean had or hadn't done, I no longer cared. All I felt was the violent sting of rejection, the bitter sweat pooling on my skin.

'Alright,' I said, finally. 'Fine. Don't go to the police. But what do you want us to do about it?' I knew, of course, what her answer would be. And I hated myself for being led to it; for being so weak – so desperate for her approval.

She said nothing, though her hand brushed against mine as she continued down a winding side street, pausing in front of a house with a garden overrun with weeds, grass knee-high and ragged next to the eerie neatness of the rest of the street.

'For Emily,' she said, her voice little more than a whisper. 'We'll do it for her.'

For Emily, I thought, with a pang of envy, though it felt,

233

in the moment, like grief – not for her, but for my friends, their shared sadness, and for me. If I disappeared – if something happened to me – would they care this much? Or would I be forgotten – a passing entertainment, a mere shadow of the friend they truly loved?

I looked at Robin, who gave a long, low sigh through her teeth, and remembered what she – what they – had done for me. The Furies, the four of us, taking revenge. The things that we could do, the power we possessed, the stories we told ourselves of dreams, snakes, and beating wings and claws that split the air; the way Robin, in our moments of doubt, would pull the four of us together with the force of her belief, words electric and vivid with righteous fury at men, at injustice, and brutal power.

I nodded, reached for Robin's hand as she'd reached for mine, under the mermaid, when I'd told her the truth about Tom. 'For Emily,' I said, softly; in my mind, the words *for them.*

And so, five days later, we retraced our steps through the bland suburban streets, sky huge over the absolute flatness of it all, laughing and talking beneath the air's steady hum. I remember it, that thrilling lightness: the nerves, anticipation, and fear coursing through our blood.

'Welcome to hell,' Robin said, as we passed through miles of boxy houses, shingle and white plastic fronts like rotting teeth, dusty garage doors, crazy paving, names that didn't suit: Lavender Cottage, the Old Barn, Honeysuckle House.

I'd asked Robin how she'd found the Dean's address. She

had feigned a sprained wrist, waiting until the school nurse's back was turned to slip into Reception and finger through his personnel file. I wondered whether I had ever had a choice in the path that led me here, or whether Robin had anticipated my every response, as we'd stood outside his house, just days earlier. I felt ashamed of myself, for being so easy to predict – reliable, and reliably dull.

She stopped at the same garden overrun with weeds, worse in the daylight. I followed the girls down the narrow gap between the houses, through an unlocked metal gate.

Out back was a bird bath, stained white with shit, an upturned watering can, a tired and broken fence. On a washing line that whined with the wind, a set of gardening gloves hung alone, fingers twitching as starlings perched watching on the wires.

Robin ran her fingers around the edges of the plant pots, tipping them with her feet until she found a key. Was it luck, I wondered, or had she known it would be there, able to predict the Dean's actions, as she had my own?

Inside was much the same as out. Curtains closed against the sunlight, carpets worn thin, grey linoleum floors muddy with grease; a damp mat mouldering in the bathroom. A stuffed Bagpuss toy on a bed in a room filled with posters torn from magazines, a 'Keep Out' sign scrawled on the door above a photo: daddy and daughter, smiling by the sea. Another brief flash of envy, blinked away.

'When do you think he'll be back?' Grace said, peering through the door as I stood, staring at the mundane pieces of Sophie's life. It had seemed so glamorous – London, New

York, Beijing – but now, my fingers tracing necklaces hanging from a headless doll, I felt nothing but pity for her. For her life, so much like mine. *Maybe we're doing her a favour*, I thought, faintly. *Maybe she doesn't want to come back.*

'Not for a while, I guess,' I said, turning to leave. I felt caught, somehow, as Grace looked at me through hooded eyes, her skin blue-white in the dim light. We both flinched as a laugh erupted from downstairs, tearing a crack in the silence.

'Shhh,' we both hissed, finding Robin bent double, gripping the edge of a chair, while Alex sat on the sofa, her hand covering her mouth.

'Sorry,' Robin said, shoulders shaking with laughter.

I felt a flush of irritation at them – at Robin, her flippant cruelty, her childishness. 'Can we just take something and get out?' I hissed, looking to Grace for support.

She offered an apologetic smile, before reaching for the object in the girls' hands, the source of their laughter. 'What is it?'

The thought set off a ripple of giggles between the girls again. Alex handed Grace a photo, and the two of us peered at it through the dim light. It was like the 'magic eye' paintings that seemed to be everywhere at the time (but which I could never make out, much to my frustration). The lines shifted, and a crowd of people began to appear, teenagers not much older than us. At the centre of the picture stood the Dean – unmistakably him, the same wide, dark eyes, same round, fat cheeks – in heavy make-up, pale-faced with red lips, his hair a black, tangled mess.

'He looks ridiculous,' Grace said, voice taut with suppressed laughter.

I nodded, saying nothing. There were others in the photo, figures I didn't recognize, all with faux-Bowie lightning bolts, shards of glitter, tall, back-combed hair. Boys and girls, laughing, without a care in the world. Just like us.

A shadow of red in the back of the photo caught my eye. I took it from Grace, and walked to the window, opening the curtain a little, a shaft of sunlight blazing in. I looked closer. Curls, a smile half-concealed, one black eye behind a boy's raised arm. 'Hey,' I said, gesturing to Grace, the others still snickering in the corner. 'Is this Annabel?'

'Oh my god,' she said. She turned it over, looked again. 'That's so weird.'

Robin, rooting through a cabinet of dusty spirit bottles and faded books, turned and looked at us. 'What's weird?'

'Annabel. Look,' Grace said. 'They must be, what – university students?'

'I didn't know they were friends,' I said.

Robin snorted. 'Have you seen the way they look at each other? She practically bares her teeth. We're probably doing *her* a favour getting rid of him, too.'

The words seemed to hang in the air a moment and burst. It was the first time any of us had referred to what we intended to do in anything but the most euphemistic of terms.

'I'm going to find a hairbrush,' I said, after a moment, hoping the girls wouldn't notice the thin band of sweat forming on my forehead, grateful to the darkness for disguising the whiteness I felt in my skin, the chill of it; the nauseating thrill.

'Don't be long,' Alex said, glancing at the ticking clock on the mantelpiece, an hour, still, behind.

I stepped out into the windowless hall, feeling my way to the stairs. My fingers touched the flocked wallpaper, ringed with damp, and coats hung lifeless, smelling faintly of wood smoke and dank, dried sweat. My fingers caught on a door handle, and I wondered briefly about prints, evidence, proof we'd been here. I blinked the thoughts away (*Too late*, I told myself, nervously) and peered inside.

I felt around for a light switch, and the room burst into a blazing light. A bulb swung uncovered from the ceiling, slick with dust. Not a bathroom, as I'd hoped, but the garage, turned into what looked like a makeshift study. Among the petrol cans and scattered tools, a desk covered in papers, with a typewriter in the middle, paper still clipped upright. I scanned the rest of the room: suitcase, golf clubs, broken bookshelves; fetid hanging baskets, waxy blue blocks of rat poison, an empty cage.

I stepped inside and closed the door. Silent but for the hum of the breeze at the garage door, and cold, the sweat pinching now at my skin. I wiped my palms on my shirt, and plucked a piece of paper from the desk.

'Dear Mr Holmsworth,' the letter began. 'Thank you for your submission titled *The Witches of Elm Hollow: Myths and Murders, 1604–1984*. While your proposal is an interesting one, the content seems to me rather too academic for a mainstream audience. I appreciate you taking the time to submit, however, and wish you luck in finding a suitable publisher for your book.'

I turned it over, found another. 'While your research offers an interesting premise, it seems to me unlikely to be taken seriously among the research community – perhaps it might make for a better novel than a monograph?' And another: 'One cannot help but feel that the last "mystery" being over a decade old diminishes the relevance of this submission. With this investigation closed long since (with no signs of reopening), it does feel rather like an (admittedly understandable) personal cause, which would struggle to find an audience in the current, somewhat saturated, market.'

Another ripple of laughter echoed from the living room, abruptly hushed. I put the letters back, carefully, roughly as I'd found them, and picked up the heavier stack that sat beside the typewriter, scrawled upon with notes in the Dean's hand-writing, his distinctive green ink.

A car purred to a stop outside and sputtered out. I froze. Was that his car? It couldn't be; he wasn't due home for an hour, at least. Classes hadn't finished yet. He should be at school.

I slammed my hand against the light switch and pressed my back against the door, still clutching the papers in my trembling hands. Slowly, I sat down on the floor, a move more automatic than considered, as though I could make myself so small that I'd disappear. I'd done this often, as a child, lurking in corners of the house, my parents pretending not to see me, curled small between bookcases and table legs. Anna learning to walk had brought this to an end; she'd been incapable of seeing me without squealing my name, or wriggling free from whichever adult she was with to wrap tiny fingers around my hands and tug at my hair.

The front door opened, the click of locks thunderous in the silence, the slam a death; the hall light switched on, a seam splitting the pitch black of the garage. The pages in front of me glowed white, text smudged by nervous hands: *The Witches of Elm Hollow: A History of Murders from Margaret Boucher to Emily Frost.*

The footsteps grew closer and paused. Shoes thumped, one, then another, on the other side of the wall. A rustle of jackets as he hung up his coat. My heart, pounding, willing him to walk away, thinking of the girls in the living room opposite. *Go upstairs,* I willed him, as though I could push him away with my thoughts. *Go upstairs, and we'll leave, and you'll never know we were here.*

It's possible the silence wasn't as long as it seemed. It's possible, too, that it was longer. I remember – or, at least, I think I remember – holding my breath for the duration of it, though in memory doing so for so long seems impossible. Still, in that moment, it seemed endless. I felt sick, gripped with sweat and fear. I stared down at the page in my hands. 'The things these girls are capable of are almost impossible to comprehend . . . ' it said, the words swimming, floating above the page.

I thought I heard a lighter step; a rustle beyond the door as the Dean turned around. 'That they would murder one of their own,' I read, before my neck snapped back against the door, a thud and crack breaking on the other side. 'I may be ridiculed for the suggestion,' it said, as the cold sound of steel breaking flesh tore through the air; a moan followed, indecipherable, neither male, nor female, nor recognizably human at all.

'I write this, now, with no small conviction – though no

proof – that they will kill again. That they may, indeed, have already done so.' I felt a sticky warmth gathering beneath me, a seam of blood, black in the darkness, seeping in under the door, which rattled as a hand beat against it, each thud a little weaker than the last.

'And yet no one would believe me if I told them. A centuries-long pattern of deaths, at the hands of those too young and innocent for any rational authority to suspect.'

Alex's laugh tore through the silence, shook me from my position, frozen, on the garage floor. I stood, wiping a bloody palm on my jeans, cursing at the telltale stain.

'Violet?' Robin said, softly. 'Where are you?'

'I'm in here,' I hissed back, a flicker of nerves in my voice. 'In the garage.' I stuffed the papers into a box on the shelf beside the door, and turned the handle, a slow click.

The Dean's hand dropped through the gap with a thud, and I lurched back, gripping the shelves to steady myself, unable to pull my eyes away from the fingers ringed with blackening blood. I remembered the bird, the night of the rite: remembered being surprised that such a little thing could contain so much blood. Now, on the other side of the door, a grown man: a river, I imagined, an ocean. I stood frozen, for a moment, and closed my eyes, as though by not seeing, I could make it go away.

The door creaked open a little more, my breath growing shallow with fear, heart thudding in my chest. 'Violet,' Robin said, again. 'It's okay. Come out.'

It's okay? I thought, clawing for breath, fingers white around the steel bars of the shelves. I looked around, searching for some way out that wouldn't force me to face the body, the horror of what they'd – we'd – done; but the garage door had no inner handle, accessible only from outside. I grabbed a Stanley knife – blade rusted, half-blunt with age – and slipped it into my pocket. I wouldn't use it, I knew that much – but its presence was a small yet desperately needed comfort.

Don't look down, I told myself, as I stepped towards the door. If I could just look away, I wouldn't have to face it: wouldn't be trailed by the memory as I slept, greeted by the dead eyes on waking. But the sight of the girls, standing opposite, staring wild-eyed and slick with blood, was an image equal in horror – their hair in dank, dripping strands, clothes shining adamantine, glossy black. Robin looked smaller than ever, drowned and wretched. Only Grace looked at me, with a glance almost apologetic, for a moment; a lick of blood rolled down from her brow to her eye, and she wiped it, coolly, with her sleeve. Behind, the spray tore a streak across the walls, seeping into the flocked wallpaper in seashell shapes.

Alex looked up, as though only now realizing I was there. She frowned. 'I thought you were in the bathroom.'

'I heard him coming . . . So I hid. But then the door . . . ' I gestured to the body, still not looking down. I couldn't; couldn't face the thing I thought I knew, now. That the girls hadn't wanted to kill him because he'd killed Emily Frost. They'd killed him because he knew that they had.

'Is he dead?' I said, uselessly; I knew he was (of *course* he was), but the words slipped out before I could catch them.

'I think so.' She looked at me, the pause hanging heavy

between us. 'He came for us. Fuck.' She gave a slow, thin sigh through her teeth. 'What a psycho.'

There wasn't time, I thought. *He didn't know you were there.*

'He would've killed us,' she said, still staring at me. 'We could've died.'

The silence swelled; I realized their eyes were on me, all of them. Saw the blade of the knife shaking slightly in Alex's hand, the light skittering on the wall. They were waiting for me to speak, to say something: but the words simply weren't there.

Alex looked at Robin, then back at me. 'Can you check his pulse?' she said, eyes flashing in the dim light, the barest glint of a smile.

I felt my stomach roll over, chest tighten. I couldn't look at him. Couldn't bring myself to see what they'd done. 'I . . . I can't,' I stuttered, the shame, even then, a sickness.

'Go on,' she said, with a bitter laugh 'I mean, really, it's the least you can do.'

I knew what she was doing; what the three of them were doing, now, as I looked to Robin for support, and she looked away, avoiding my eye. They were making me complicit. (Though as I write this, now, I realize that I already was, most likely – in the eyes of the law – party to a murder, premeditated and cold. That I'd imagined his death might come about in a different way – through occult spells, ancient magic – would, to any reasonable jury, be immaterial in determining my guilt.)

I closed my eyes, steeled myself, drew breath. One thing at a time seemed the only way, the cruel fact of the body too much to take in at once.

Eyes still open, wide with shock, blood rolling upwards from neck, to ear, to matted hair. A wound so deep as to be black inside, a rictus grin, bloodstained teeth and chapped lips. Arms raised in a defensive pose, scattered with bloody seams. The carpet turning black, a tannin, urine smell. I was embarrassed for him, being seen like this. I wondered if his last thoughts had been of fear, or whether there'd been a flicker of shame at this final indignity.

I reached gingerly for his wrist, the absurdity of the situation rising, adrift. Except for a primary-school class on the human body, I'd never felt a pulse for proof of life. Even then, it was only my own – and so disgusted was I at the mechanical pump at my wrist that I'd held my breath and willed it to stop, horrified to find it only thudding louder in my ears. I spent the night awake, listening, feeling my insides beat against my skin.

As my fingers touched his wrist (still warm, something I remember being surprised at, though only a few minutes had passed) a clatter from the kitchen broke through the silence. Grace pitched backwards, gripping the doorframe; Robin stared at me, eyes somehow pleading, while Alex remained perfectly still. There was a soft thud, a rustling. A high-pitched miaow.

'Poppet,' I said, as a fat, round-faced cat loped in. (*Pets* do *look like their owners*, I thought, bitterly.) He circled Alex's feet, then Grace's, in search of affection, apparently uninterested in the body on the hallway floor.

Robin laughed, nervously. 'I think I just had a heart attack.'
Alex shot her a look. 'Shhh.'
'He's dead,' I said – choking, almost, on the words, too loud,

too real, the crush of flesh still on my fingertips. (I still feel it now, sometimes, the memory making it impossible for me to eat meat without wincing. A small inconvenience, I suppose, but one no one ever mentions in romanticized accounts of murder – that vegetarian food is largely tasteless, and dry.)

'Alex,' I said, after a moment. 'What do we do now?'

She looked at Grace. 'I . . . I don't know.'

'What do you mean you don't know?' I said, my voice shrill, arched.

'I don't *know*,' she said, meeting my eyes with a cold glare. 'Just . . . Just shut up a minute and let me think.'

I looked to Robin, who shrugged and glanced down at the body. The horror I'd seen in her eyes moments before had faded and their usual light, although faint, was unmistakably creeping back. I followed her stare, and it was true: it seemed the longer we stood around it, the more faint the sense of horror became. Poppet sauntered over, tentatively licked at the pool of blood; finding it appealing, he continued, the scratch of his tongue the only sound. Disgust rose, then faded again.

'We could make it look like an accident,' Grace said, wiping at a smudged fingerprint on the doorframe with her sleeve. 'A fire, maybe?' The three of us stared at her, blankly. She shrugged. 'Alright, fine. You think of something, then.'

We stood, silent, looking at each other, all searching for a better idea.

'Okay,' Alex said, finally. 'Grace is right.' She pointed into the living room. 'There's a fireplace in there. We'll start it, and make it look like it got out of hand.'

Poppet's eyes flashed, as though catching a shadow. The smell of the body, the dampness underfoot, rose as the air grew thin, humid and tense. I shook my head. Alex turned, followed by Grace. Robin was standing still behind them, skin a deathly white.

I willed her to follow the girls – to leave me alone, just for a moment, so I could take the Dean's book from the garage and stuff it into my bag. Had I imagined the words, misread them somehow? Or was he telling the truth – that the girls had killed Emily Frost themselves, all the while performing their grief to teachers, parents . . . to me?

'Come on,' Robin said, turning to leave. I hesitated, for a moment, and she looked back at me. 'It's going to be okay,' she said, reaching for my hand. 'Don't freak out. It's fine.'

Tentatively stepping over the body (watched warily by Poppet, who trailed after us, several feet behind), I followed her into the dark room. She looked back, and I met her eye for a split second before I realized what she was checking: that the body hadn't moved, clinging desperately to life. Made nervous by the thought, I did the same, struck by the uncanny stillness, the broad-shouldered body bereft of life and blood.

Alex and Grace were hunched by the fireplace, whispers undercut by the tearing of papers being ripped from books. Robin reached into the cabinet and handed me a whisky bottle, gummy with age. 'Not much here,' she said, turning to Alex.

I saw my chance. 'I think I saw a petrol can in the garage.'

'No way,' Alex said. 'If they find petrol on anything, it won't look like an accident.' She paused. 'The oven's gas, right?'

We worked silently, seagulls yowling overhead, Poppet

perched on the sofa, a listless paw draped off to one side. Twice, I ranged towards the hallway door, thoughts of the Dean's words rising over and over in my mind. Each time, however, I felt myself watched, and wound back.

Alex wiped her hands on her jeans, dried blood dusting around her. 'I suppose we'd better change,' she said, with a grim laugh.

'He's got a daughter,' I said. 'Her room's upstairs. The first door.'

Alex looked at Robin, a split-second glance. They knew something was wrong, but not what. 'Can you go and get us some clothes?' she said, sweetly. 'You're the only one who's got clean shoes.'

You could take yours off, I thought, bitterly, but said nothing; I turned back into the hallway, feeling their eyes on me as I passed the body, glancing down so as not to step in the black pool around it. My arms and legs felt weighted, leaden, as I climbed the stairs, not touching the bannister (though I'd touched it before, I was certain – when the murder we'd planned had been one that wouldn't leave prints). I felt sick, every cell trembling at the top of the stairs. I sat on the edge of Sophie's bed, pressing my forehead to my knees. *It's impossible*, I told myself. *They wouldn't kill Emily. She was Robin's best friend.*

And then – possessively at first, trailed by a creeping dread: *I'm Robin's best friend.*

And, desperately as I wanted to believe that they'd never hurt her – couldn't possibly have killed their friend, no matter what – the body in the hallway, the girls' bloodstained hands, *my* bloodstained hands, served as both rebuttal and rebuke.

It doesn't matter if it's true or not, I thought, straightening up, hands digging into the edge of the bed. Another body, another death – another murder, more real than the others, the proof seeping into our skin and becoming part of us. Us, as a unit, whole.

Unless, I thought, *they kill me too.*

'What the hell are you doing up there?' Robin hissed, from the foot of the stairs.

'Coming!' I shouted back, abruptly hushed. Poppet – finally realizing something was amiss – began to miaow, a steady, plaintive sound, followed by a thud, a screech, and a hiss. As I entered the living room, I saw him crouched in a corner, tail swinging hypnotically back and forth, watching the girls with wide, yellow eyes.

Alex saw me looking and laughed. 'If you're about to give a lecture on animal cruelty . . . '

'I'm not,' I said, handing her a pile of clothes and unzipping my jeans. I slid into a pair of tracksuit bottoms, buttons cold against my calves, the fabric straining at my thighs; Sophie was at least one, maybe two sizes smaller than I was, and tall.

Robin grinned, watching me struggle. 'Nice poppers.'

'Fuck off,' I said, blushing.

While the others changed, rinsing blood down the kitchen sink and whispering words I strained to hear, I stood at the window, peering through a penny-width gap. It was getting dark, the sky blazing red and gold. My heart tumbled in my chest, every sound making me flinch; a car passed, and I stepped back, stumbling into the dining table. A glass tipped over the edge and smashed on the edge of the chair.

'Jesus, Vi,' Robin said, peering nervously around the door-frame. 'Are you trying to kill me?' She threw me a lighter. I held it, staring down at the neon-pink case. 'You ready?'

I stared at her. 'You want me to . . . '

'It's only fair,' she said, seemingly without malice: simply the childlike confidence in the value of fairness between friends. I heard the click of the gas, the back door opening beyond.

'Come on,' she said, stepping towards me. 'You can do this.'

'I can't,' I said, weakly.

'We'll do it together.' She pulled a strip of crumpled news-paper from the fireplace and held it towards me.

'Robin, I—'

'Come *on*, Vi,' she said. 'It's the only way, now.'

I thought of the papers in the garage: the story of them, of us, the history we shared – shared now, all of us, having spilled blood together. She squeezed my shoulder, fingers still damp and soap-sweet. 'Come on, babycakes,' she said, one last time. 'Teamwork,' she added, with a sideways grin.

I clicked the lighter, a scratch of flint, a spark; it went out. She laughed, and I laughed too, in spite of it all – in spite of the body behind us, watching us with glassy eyes.

I shook the lighter, clicked again; it lit, the paper bursting gold with sparks. She threw it into the fireplace, and we stepped into the cooling air, closing the door on our secrets as we disappeared into the light.

Chapter 14

Annabel stepped away from the easel she had propped in the centre of the room. Arms folded, she looked at each of us in turn, while we stared at the facsimile of the painting, brush-strokes flattened on the glossy print. The rolled-up sleeves, the arched spurts of blood, drops splitting mid-air; the vivid chiaroscuro, murder by night . . . It was all so familiar, an image burned into each of our minds.

'*Judith Slaying Holofernes*,' Annabel said, finally. 'By Artemisia Gentileschi. A woman painter, depicting a woman murdering a man. A scene that the four of you will no doubt recognize.'

My stomach dropped; I willed myself not to look across at the other girls, though the question hung heavy between us, unspoken: *Does she know?* The air barbed with the thought, the image coming to life before us, the memory monstrous; for a moment, I smelled the tannin smudge of blood, felt my hands sticky with it. Wondered if this was what guilt really felt like.

She lowered herself slowly into her chair, a sharp breath through the nose, closing her eyes. 'Or, at least, you should. If you haven't started your final project by now, you're too late.'

Robin sighed, almost inaudibly; my heart rattled against my ribcage, seeming to beat louder still.

'Some speculate,' Annabel went on, 'that Artemisia – this Italian master, a woman far ahead of her time – has a link to our school's founder. Indeed, Ms Boucher spent six months in Florence before her death, and was known to the gallerists and patrons of the arts in the city – so it is highly unlikely that their paths did not cross. To what extent, however, we can only speculate. It may be simply another of the tales that have been passed down through our little society.' She coughed, looked at Grace, and smiled; I watched as Grace smiled back, impassive, showing no sign of the horror I imagined she, too, felt. 'Some say she inspired Shakespeare as he wrote "the Scottish play": not, as her murderers might have claimed, in his portrait of the devil women who taunt Macbeth and Banquo on the heath, but Lady Macbeth herself, the driving force behind all action.

'But I digress,' she said, turning back to the painting. 'This painting, according to some critics, is the direct embodiment of Artemisia's desire for revenge. The victim of rape, betrayed by a dear friend, Artemisia – again, according to many of those who seek to impose a narrative upon her – painted the slaying of Holofernes as a response to those feelings of fury that ran through her in the aftermath.'

She slid the painting aside, revealing another, similar scene.

'This, by Caravaggio, depicts the same murder: the death of Holofernes at the hands of Judith. And yet,' she said, pointing a bony finger at the woman, 'see the softness of her arms? The expression of confusion on her face, the self-doubt?' She shook her head. 'Caravaggio fails to recognize the bravery—' she paused, searching for the right word. '—the force of will required for a woman – the "weaker" sex, outmatched, physically, at least – to commit such an act. Whereas in Artemisia's painting, we see it clearly, and whole. The sheer size of Holofernes' fist as he claws at her maidservant, the determined, wilful expression on Judith's face, the delicacy of the cameo she wears flecked with blood, her fingers tearing at hair . . . Artemisia understands the strength – both physical and emotional – required for a woman to take her revenge on man.'

She looked at Robin, for a moment, then at me. I felt exposed by the look, turning back to the painting, as though she could read the night in my eyes. 'See also the difference between the maidservants in these two paintings. For Caravaggio, the maid is the old crone, watching on as her much younger mistress commits the act. Whereas for Artemisia, the women work together, their forces combined to defeat the man. One almost imagines them plotting, together, the half-smile passing between them as they crept into Holofernes' tent, their glances exchanged as he slipped into a drunken, stinking stupor.'

She slid the painting back, covering the Caravaggio again. 'Artemisia, in other words, makes the slaying of Holofernes about not merely the man – the victim of murderous women, that most terrifying of archetypes – but, in equal measure, the brutal power of female friendship, of those secrets women share between themselves, in those moments men are too blind to see.'

I felt Robin's arm brush against mine in the chair as she shifted; the hot bristle of the hairs risen, gooseflesh prickling beneath, just as it had after the murder, when we'd run through the suburbs, our footsteps slapping on the pavement. It wasn't long before smoke began to rise in black plumes above the houses; a crack ruptured the quiet night, chased by sirens shooting by. The air was bonfire sweet for a while, until the sour burnt-plastic smell drowned it out.

As the house crumbled, the tension between us began to dissipate. They'd killed him, yes, but I'd lit the match that burned the house – and with it, the Dean's theory about the girls. About all of us. All of it was gone, destroyed, done, and outside the tomb of the house it seemed absurd that I'd ever believed it. Or at least, that I'd thought it mattered.

We sat by the promenade, laughing, spitting, making ourselves seen. Robin and I walked into a gift shop, rattling rainbow rows of rock and spilling jars of sand on the floor, daring the owner to throw us out, our alibi secured: he wouldn't soon forget we were there. I wondered if the old man could sense what we had done, as he watched us warily, afraid to ask us to leave. He said nothing as Robin took a souvenir lighter from the rack and slipped it in her pocket; said nothing, too, as I dropped a pound coin on the desk, hoping she wouldn't see.

We knew – of course we knew – that things might go wrong from here. We might not get away with it. The body (the body, now, not the Dean, no longer, in our minds, a person) might be recovered before the flames ate it up, found with that macabre tear across the neck. (*Jugular, carotid, subclavian,* I thought, the words a soothing rhythm.) They might find fingerprints, oily smudges of boot marks on carpet, stray hairs, and spit; a neighbour might've seen us as we slipped through the gate and ran, in the minutes before the flames began to lick at the windows.

We knew, too, that the haze of guilt would descend, soon enough. And yet, in the moment, whether the result of some vibrant adrenaline surge, or the knowledge that it couldn't last, there was a romance to it. It's why the words, now, seem melodramatic, too overwrought. I've toyed with numerous ways to say it, all trite and cliché. But the plain fact is this: in the face of murder, all life seems thrilling, all chaos and potential. It's a high, a buzz, a decadent light – and for a little while, it didn't matter what anyone said, or thought. Only the electric sense of life, and the power we had to take it. The power we had to kill.

At the base of the mermaid, Alex threw an arm around my shoulder, squeezed thin fingers around my bare arm. 'I'm sorry for being a bitch in there,' she whispered, her breath hot in my ear. 'I think I was freaking out a bit. You know?'

I nodded. I knew. She looked at me, waiting for a response. 'Yeah, me too,' I said. 'It was pretty intense.'

Robin leaned forward. 'That's an understatement.'

I laughed. 'I just can't believe we . . . I can't believe we did it.'

'I know,' Robin said, picking at a piece of dried gum and

throwing it to the gulls. 'Just goes to show,' she added, in a pitch-perfect imitation of the Dean, at once chilling and absurd, 'you never know what you're capable of until you try.'

Annabel leaned back in her chair, as she so often did at the end of class, as though the effort had proven too much; or, it seemed, today, the clench of fear still tight around our hearts, that she simply wanted to be alone – to no longer have to look at us, the disappointment a shadow behind her eyes. *But she doesn't know,* I told myself. *No one does.* And it was true: for now, at least, campus was just as it always was, the Dean's absence as yet apparently unlinked to the house fire in the suburbs. I'd read the story on the cover of the local paper as I bought cigarettes, the newsagent glaring at me as I put it back without paying: nothing to suggest a body had been recovered. It couldn't have, yet, given the fact it burned through the night, a glow visible from my window as I tried, unsuccessfully, to sleep. I willed the hours on, the seconds seeming stuck miles apart; as though time had stopped, the night now fixed in place.

'I'll expect your essays by the end of next week,' she said, closing her eyes and tilting her head back a little, revealing the hollow at the base of her neck. 'Two thousand words, minimum, ladies. I expect great things.'

Nobody said a word until we reached the middle of the Quad, the grass sugar-coated with daisies, sky robin's-egg blue; the brightness saturated, thick. We sat beside the wych elm, where the faded cards and waterlogged teddy bears, the dead flowers left for Emily, afforded us a kind of privacy; students passed at a distance, watching the girls (and me, ever the third wheel) take a moment to pay their respects to their lost friend.

Alex leaned forward, looking over at me. 'You okay?'

'Fine,' I said, a brief stab of displeasure at being singled out. 'You?'

She said nothing. Robin tugged at a handful of grass, pulling up roots, and began to thread them together. 'I don't think anyone knows yet,' she said, seemingly to no one.

'When did you say you saw him?'

'Who?'

Alex sighed. 'Who do you think?'

Robin looked at her blankly. 'When we . . . '

'Jesus Christ,' Alex said. 'Sometimes you are just . . . ' She trailed off, gathered herself. 'You said he turned up at Violet's house. When was that?'

'A couple of days before.'

'*Which* day before?'

Robin looked across at me, and shrugged. 'Tuesday,' I said. 'I'm sure it was Tuesday.'

'What time?'

'What?'

'What time was he there?'

I stared at her. 'I don't know. Eleven? Eleven-thirty, maybe?'

'You don't know exactly?'

'Fuck, Alex, I wasn't taking notes. Does it matter?'

'It might.'

I looked at Robin. 'It was probably closer to eleven-thirty,' she said, though I couldn't tell whether she believed that, or whether she simply wanted Alex to move on.

We sat in silence a while, in the wych elm's black shadow, and watched students pass between classes, the birds flitting from one building to another.

'There we go,' Alex said, finally, gesturing to the main building, where Mrs Goldsmith, the music teacher, jowls cleft and twitching like a guinea pig's, stood in hushed conversation with a woman whose name I didn't know. She took a long drag from a cigarette, flouting the rule that smoking was prohibited except in specifically designated areas, and brushed a tear from her cheek with a sleeve.

I looked away, ashamed (though for her or me I wasn't sure – within minutes, this would be all over campus, a sign of distinct weakness), and caught Nicky's eye across the Quad. She didn't approach, until Alex – to my surprise – called her name, and rose to her feet. When she reached us, Alex enveloped her in a hug, from which Nicky seemingly couldn't extricate herself.

Robin and I looked over at Grace, whose expression suggested she had as little idea what Alex was doing as we did. Her shoulders shook, Nicky peering wide-eyed over them, offering the occasional weak pat on Alex's back, an attempt at comfort through her confusion.

Finally, Alex pulled away, still squeezing Nicky's arms tight as she let her go. 'I just . . . ' she began, voice trembling. 'I don't think I ever thanked you for . . . for this.' She gestured at the faded photo of Emily pinned to the tree, the dead flowers shaped in her name. 'I heard you arranged it, and . . . Well, it just means a lot. Emily would've loved it.' I felt Robin tense a little at this suggestion; rested my hand softly on hers. I wasn't sure what, exactly, Alex was doing – but Robin arguing this point, I imagined, wasn't part of the plan. I knew, too, that Nicky hadn't arranged the shrine. As far as I knew, that was the work of the choral society, appealing, I assumed, to their sense of drama – the visual accompaniment to the Requiem Mass they'd been rehearsing all semester, in memoriam. This did not, however, stop Nicky from taking the credit as offered.

'It's the least I – we – could do,' she said, smiling beatifically. 'I mean, she and I weren't really friends, but I wanted you guys to have something to . . . you know. Remember her by.'

'It really means a lot,' Alex said. 'Especially when . . . ' She paused, turned to look at the three of us, still sitting on the grass below. 'Especially when we don't know who we can trust. You've been such a good friend, and we've been so mean. I'm sorry.'

Nicky glanced at Robin, and at me. I smiled, hoping to counteract the scowl I could feel burning from Robin, without having to look. Fortunately, Nicky's interest was elsewhere. 'Who can't you trust?' she said, looking back at Alex, who lowered her eyes.

'I shouldn't have said anything.'

'Alex,' Nicky said, in the whispered tone I knew – I recognized it from when the girls disappeared before, leaving me alone (a memory that came to me now with an almost visceral flinch, *You're not one of them* tearing a streak through my mind) – 'it's okay. You can talk to me about anything. Nighthawks for life, right?' She tapped the school crest on her sports bag, and Alex smiled, eyes still ringed with tears.

'The thing is,' she said, '—and please, whatever you do,

don't tell anyone you heard this from me . . . My mom would kill me if she knew.'

'I won't,' Nicky said, a little too quickly, Alex's words still lingering half-said. 'You know I'd never do that.' And for what it was worth, this part was true: wherever she could, Nicky would erase her sources, not through any instinctive pseudo-journalistic integrity, but simply because she preferred to *be* the source, shaking her head and smiling sweetly when asked.

'Well . . . ' Alex turned to the three of us – still dumbstruck – and lowered her voice. 'You know Mr Holmsworth – the Dean?' The very mention of his name flashed the image of the body once again through my mind; I felt myself grow pale, and looked away.

Nicky leaned in a little more, the down of her cheek white in the midday sun. 'Yeah?'

'A few nights ago, he was . . . Well, drunk. Really drunk. And my mom heard from someone – I don't know who, someone in the bar, I guess – that he was saying things. Weird things.'

Nicky's eyes were saucer-wide – as, I suppose, were ours. *What is she doing?* I thought, nervously. I wondered how much of this she was making up as she went along, a sensation akin to watching someone walk a tightrope without a net. 'Like what?'

'Things . . . ' Alex sighed, shook her head. 'Things about Emily. About what happened to her. Things that made whoever heard it think he might have had something to do with it.'

'Oh my god,' Nicky said.

'I know. Mom said they should go to the police, but . . . I don't know. I don't think they have. Not yet, anyway.'

'Why not?'

She shrugged. 'He's the Dean of Students. *Here*. There's no way anyone's going to throw an accusation like that at him without being sure. I mean . . . Imagine what the parents would do – they'd *lose* it.'

Nicky nodded, solemnly. I'd seen her mum once before – a bird-like, sharp-bobbed woman who'd parked her Land Rover outside the school entrance earlier in the year, refusing to leave until the Headmaster met with her to discuss an article in the school newsletter which made passing reference to an Elm Hollow alumna who'd had some minor success with a now-touring rock band. 'You think this is aspirational?' she'd screeched, voice ringing down the corridor, through the walls of the Headmaster's office. 'This is not in line with the supposed values of this school, and certainly not what I am paying you to encourage in these girls. Not at *all.*'

'The thing is,' Alex went on, 'he was saying he wanted to . . . well, kill himself. That he didn't deserve to live. And honestly, if he *did* have something to do with what happened to Emily, I hope he does. I hope it *hurts.*'

Grace – seeming finally to recover herself from the confusion the three of us had shared throughout – rolled up and reached for Alex's hand, pulling her into a hug, Alex sobbing with such melodrama I felt a grim smile begin to tug at my lips. I put a hand over my mouth and looked away, hoping to appear overcome with emotion at the horror of Alex's tale.

'Anyone,' Nicky began, the inflection in her voice almost that of a politician offering platitudes in a trying time (I almost saw her, thirty years hence, in a crisp suit, manicured hands gripping the sides of a lectern), 'anyone in your position would feel the same. You poor, poor thing.'

Alex didn't respond; a silence fell for a moment, Nicky examining each of us in turn. Only Robin didn't appear to be playing along; she continued to stare blankly at the memorial, the plastic bouquets crackling in the low breeze.

'Well, look,' Nicky said, finally. 'You know if you ever need to talk to anyone, you can talk to me.'

Alex turned and smiled. 'Thanks, honey.' ('*Honey?*' I thought. *Where did that come from?*) 'Just . . . Please don't tell anyone you heard it from me, okay?'

Nicky smiled; this was tacit agreement from Alex that she could tell whoever she wanted the content of our talk, if not the source. 'Of course, sweetie.' She leaned in and gave Alex a peck on the cheek, Alex stiffening as she did so.

We were silent, again, until she disappeared. 'Do you really think that'll work?' Grace said, as we watched the small gathering of teachers now sharing Mrs Goldsmith's packet of menthols, huddled in nervous conversation.

'I have no idea,' Alex said, softly. 'I guess we'll soon find out.'

'It seems unimaginable that we should find ourselves gathered once again, mourning yet another tragic loss in our community,' the Headmaster said, pacing the wooden stage at the end of the Great Hall, between the stone plaques and tombs, death peering in on all sides. The altar loomed behind, cross gleaming in the sun like an insult. Though there were weekly assemblies scheduled for the student body as a whole, Robin and I rarely attended: on Friday mornings, they were a tempting period to skip. *And yet*, I thought, gazing up at the grand chandeliers; the faded frescoes on the ceiling, framed with gold; the stained-glass windows, with their ornate histories in ruby, and emerald, and sapphire – *it was such a pretty place to sit, and think.*

A ripple of tuts ran through the audience, starting with the lacrosse team and rolling outwards to the rest of the gathered students, while teachers (who would, under normal circumstances, have plucked out offenders and publicly chastised them for their rudeness) averted their eyes, staring numbly down at their feet, pretending not to hear.

Nicky had proven herself more efficient than even Alex had imagined. Within hours, letters of protest had appeared at the Headmaster's door, first from students, and then, the next morning, from parents. She'd remained true to her word, however: nobody knew from whom the rumour had originated, only that we all believed it to be true. We'd been gathered, it seemed, for an ostensible assembly of mourning for the Dean, a chance for us to 'share how we felt', or – as we well knew – for the Headmaster to quell the 'hysteria' he'd claimed had possessed us, according to a conversation overheard from the girls' toilets, whose pipes echoed the contents of confidential conversations to the girls always listening in.

'But if they're all saying it,' the Chemistry professor had replied, tentatively, 'doesn't that suggest that maybe . . . '

And they *were* all saying it. Everyone (except the four of us, of course) had their own version of the same story. The way he'd reached for a hand or, worse, a knee when some inconsolable girl sat sobbing at his desk; the way he'd offered compliments to girls who thought themselves ugly; the times he'd told them that they shouldn't listen to the cruel words of boys, and that soon enough they'd find a man who understood and appreciated them . . . It was all meant well, at the time – I knew that now, of course – but in the cold light of suspicion, every kindness became a threat; a goodness made sinister.

That they believed it – the lie, *our* lie – only served to heighten Robin's conviction that we were somehow protected, supported in our actions, by the Furies we'd invoked months before. 'It's in line with their philosophy,' she'd said, as the four of us walked through campus, the buildings burning fire red in the spring light.

'Shhh,' Alex had hissed. I caught a glance, a flicker, as she looked at Grace; a new shadow of worry, her usual assuredness shaken by Robin's flippant, needling tone.

I, too, had doubts about Robin's conviction – though the shadow of the Furies still woke me in the night, a vicious tug from the base of my spine, a sickness in my gut, the smell of rotting flesh. It seemed, sometimes, as though Robin were baiting me, willing me to say out loud what we'd done; a vicarious thrill, I supposed, though her eyes seemed occasionally deadened, without their usual spark, her voice coming from behind a mask.

But for my doubts, the idea was a comfort, her feverish

belief somehow infectious. For the horror of what we'd done – the stopping of a beating heart, spilling of innocent blood, which still, to this day, stalks my dreams – was a thing so unimaginably awful that to place it in the realm of the fantastic, to will it into fiction, seemed to lessen its impact, momentarily, at least. *Maybe she's right*, I had thought – or, rather, willed, a silent prayer – as she'd opened her textbook at Baudry's *Charlotte Corday* and hissed 'She's one of us,' while Annabel stood mere feet away. I'd felt my cheeks burn a furious blush, and saw Annabel smile; felt a rush of relief that she hadn't heard.

'We may never know,' the Headmaster went on, 'why or how such a tragic accident could befall one of our own—'

A wail rose from the back of the hall, where one of the senior girls – a girl whose name I didn't know, but whose greenish-blue hair and nose piercing I'd admired, from a distance – stood and glared at the Headmaster, her voice echoing through the crowd. 'We know!' she howled. Behind her, Annabel sat, arms folded, impassive under the stone angels' watch, the only teacher not staring intently at the floor. The only one who smiled, for a split second, when the girl added, 'He killed Emma Frost!'

I caught Robin's eye, the slightest of glances; she was deathly pale (a hangover, I assumed, though since the night of the murder it seemed all four of us were occasionally stricken by the memory, our blood draining rapidly away at the thought). The Headmaster cleared his throat, a warning; but the faculty remained silent, seated around the edges of the hall. 'We don't know anything to suggest—'

'We do! We all know what he did!' another girl shouted, the first emboldened by the support. 'He's a murderer.'

'Sit *down*,' he said, but the note of weariness in his voice seemed only to rouse more students to their feet. He turned to the choirmaster, who began the requiem, but the choir were all but drowned out by the chants of the girls around us – 'Murderer! Murderer!' – building in both volume and speed, the whole student body on their feet.

Except, that is, for us. I couldn't say whether it was the word itself, the brutal rhythm of it screamed by our peers, or whether it was the realization that we'd started something which had now sprawled, horribly out of control, becoming something larger and more unimaginably cruel than we could have possibly imagined. It might simply have been the finality of it: the empty chair, the mournful mass. I closed my eyes, willed the shaking from my hands.

Robin coughed into her sleeve. I glanced at her, nervously. She reached for my hand and squeezed it tight, arm shaking with the force of it. *Is she crying?* I thought, as she leaned forward, burying her face in her hands. It couldn't be. *Don't,* I willed her, *not now.* Only after a moment did I catch the spark of a smile under her blazer's bruised sleeve, teeth burrowed into her hand in an attempt to stop the laughter. As the choir sang, she doubled down, shoulders shaking.

She can't be, I thought. *It's not funny. It's not.*

Feeling eyes on the two of us, I leaned over, arm across her shoulder in something I hoped looked like comfort, and pinched her arm, tight. 'What are you doing?' I hissed. She turned a little towards me, her face contorted, wracked with the effort of controlling laughter that refused to be contained. Her hair stuck to my lips; I peeled it off, knowing this would make her laugh more; and when it did, in spite of everything, I laughed too, pressing my face into her shoulder.

I turned to the girls, who stared straight ahead, an expression of horror on their faces that would have almost certainly given them away, were it not for the saving fact of Emily, their grief something the other students imagined there instead, a mask imposed upon us – a relief. All of us, together – Robin and I laughing, violent and grotesque; Alex and Grace wracked with a bitter, tragic chill – were protected from what we'd done. Immune, in this moment at least, from the consequences of the crime, the punishment. Murder, now, a joke.

When the assembly finished at last (the requiem abandoned, the Headmaster's words drowned out and long forgotten), we followed our fellow students out into the Quad, hanging our heads as we passed Annabel, who looked over our heads at the clusters of girls huddled, sharing stories of the Dean's 'odd' behaviour, the 'inappropriate' things he'd said. She wrapped a gossamer-light shawl around herself, and watched, no doubt taking in the aesthetics of the scene.

Alex and Grace joined the two of us still laughing (though quietly, imagining ourselves unseen) on the grass, damp and glistening with spray (the caretakers had seized the rare opportunity when the whole school was called in to water the parched, dry grass).

'Urgh,' Robin groaned, wiping a slick of mud across her bag. 'Fucking idiots.'

'What was going on in there?' Alex said, glaring at Robin.

'Were you—' She lowered her voice to a whisper. 'Were you laughing?'

'Sorry,' I said, grinning. 'It was just—'

'You're just like Emily, you know that?' Alex spat.

I felt my cheeks turn hot, a flash of anger, first – then, with a shudder, a flicker of fear. 'What?'

'No matter what stupid fucking thing she does – no matter *what* – you stick up for her.' She tore a blade of grass into pieces, dropping them to the ground. 'It's pathetic.'

'Fuck you, Alex,' Robin said, stiffly. 'Just because she's got a sense of humour—'

'A sense of humour that's going to get us arrested.'

'Oh, calm the fuck down. No one even noticed,' Robin said, though her eyes darted around, pupils wide and black.

Alex looked at Grace. 'We noticed. It was pretty hard not to, frankly.'

'Fine. Fine. No fun, ever again. Got it.'

'That's not what I—'

'You know what, Alex?' Robin said, rolling heavily onto her feet. 'Fuck you.'

'Oh, real smart. Real *eloquent!*' Alex shouted, as Robin turned and walked away.

I stared after her for a moment, stunned, before turning back to the girls.

'Great. Nicely done, Alex,' I said, rising to stand, the world unsticking itself for a moment, a laconic vertigo rippling the edges of my vision.

'She's out of control,' Alex said, coldly. 'You need to make her—'

'*I* don't need to do anything,' I spat. 'Maybe *you* need to stop being so . . . ' I felt around for the words, the right thing to do, though nothing came. I was exhausted, suddenly, the weight of it all sudden and cruel; and I staggered after Robin as she disappeared between the blocks, realizing only too late that the girls hadn't asked me to come back.

We sat in stolen deck chairs on the terrace, the chill of the early evening seeping through our skin. We'd been at Robin's house all afternoon, her parents holidaying somewhere – 'some McFun forced-corporate-entertainment camp,' she'd said, before changing the subject – drinking recklessly, working our way slowly through the bottles in their drinks cabinet, water spilling on the floor as we replaced each stolen sip.

She handed me a skin of white powder, and I took it, recklessly, as though it might erase the images still lingering in my mind; the raw bodily smell I kept catching as I moved, though from where it came I didn't know. I'd showered since, though I hadn't washed my hair; the thought of blood matted into the black dye sent a shudder, now, down my spine – not entirely unpleasant, a vivid thrill coiled in the risk.

She stood; rocked back and forth, the record player crackling from inside as she sang along, the words slurring into each other. 'Jesus died for somebody's sins, but not mine,' she sang, clicking her jaw after every phrase. I did the same, an automatic response. I'd been gnawing the inside of my cheek, the flesh raw and ragged, tasting of blood; the yawn offered a respite, albeit a brief one.

'Jesus died for somebody's sins, but not mine,' she sang

again, rocking back on her heels, stumbling back into the glass doors, her drink a lurid splash across the window. 'Fuck,' she muttered, turning to survey the mess.

'Sit down,' I said. 'You're making me dizzy.'

'No,' she said, gripping the back of the chair. 'You're making *me* dizzy.'

I groaned. 'You're not making any sense.'

'It's like seeing double, with you,' she slurred, digging her fingers into a bowl of glass beads and throwing them in the air, wincing as they fell. I covered my face with my arms, the beads hitting the floor like gunshots. 'Like you're you, but you're also her. I don't know why.'

I'd been trying to find a way back to our argument with the girls since we'd left campus. 'You're just like Emily,' Alex had said, the words burrowing deeper each time I remembered: Emily was dead. And if the Dean was right, the girls had killed her. But each time I returned to the subject (which so dazed me that my thoughts seemed to circle around it, like water in a drain) Robin glared at me, and – as though trying to spite me – swallowed another pill (palm pressed to mouth as though holding in a secret), or drank so intently from the wine bottle that I had to wrench it from her hands, promising not to ask again.

The music gained speed; I sat up, the wooden slats pinching my thighs. 'What?'

'Oh, she was so good,' she sang, spinning around. 'Oh, she was so fine.'

'What are you talking about?' I said, catching the slur in my voice. 'Who do you mean?'

She went on dancing, eyes closed, face turned upwards to the moonlight. Against the blazing garden fence, the pieces of her blurred, disembodied white, becoming Bacon's lurid triptych. Under her chin, jutting out with bared teeth, I spotted a dried smudge of something, a half-print shadow that was probably ink, or eye shadow. Still, I couldn't look at it; couldn't look at her, knowing, in this moment, she was thinking of Emily, the girl she'd killed: the girl who looked like me, but wasn't. It seemed like everyone always was. 'I've got to pee,' I said, stumbling to my feet, wrap still in hand, and wandered inside, leaving the patio doors wide open behind me.

I drank in the details of her family, of her, found in trinkets. By the stairs, a framed newspaper clipping of Robin at eight years old, her drawing chosen for the council's 'Safety First' initiative; a cracked clay mug in the sink, 'Mummy' painted across the front. ('My sister's,' she said, catching me looking. 'You think I'd make something that ugly?') It was all utterly unlike I'd imagined: her room littered with fairy lights, torn posters on the wall, a king-size bed with deep-pink sheets. It seemed too homely, too *nice*, to be Robin's. 'Mum's a clean freak.' She'd shrugged, hanging her blazer in a white wardrobe etched with lilies.

I stopped at a wall of shelves, filled with ornaments and photo frames (Robin and Emily, as children, a tease: with a squint, I could pretend they were us, friends all our lives); antique teapots and crystal glasses; a wooden box with an embroidered lid, a teddy bear crosshatched into the top. I peeled open the lid and looked inside, examining passport photos and orphaned keys as though they might hold her secrets.

'Let's go out,' she said, grabbing the backs of my arms. I jumped; dropped the lid down, and spun around. 'I need some fresh air. And,' she added, grinning, 'the fair's in town. I *love* the fair.'

I groaned. 'I *hate* the fair. And I'm tired.'

'Oh my god, you're slurring. Barely even—' She paused, burped, shook her head. 'Barely even making words. You need it too. Come on. Dance it off.' She pulled me up off the bed, her hands cold and damp with sweat, while the song went on, faster and faster, until I felt my heart begin to shudder, sickly.

'*You're right*,' I said, over-articulating each word, teeth cracking the *t*. 'See? Not slurring.' I lost my balance; steadying myself, pressed my back against the door, coat handle bruising my shoulder blade. 'Let's . . . Let's go out.'

I was grateful for the sobering cool as we walked, the darkness curling around us, though the sky still glowed a deep, low blue, the trees in silhouette shadowless against the night. I pulled a peony from a hedge and squeezed it as we walked towards the glow of the town, the petals turning to flesh as we walked through the fair. Children screamed, the faint *pop-pop* of toy guns fired at rubber ducks, watched over by dead-eyed Felixes and grinning Tasmanian Devils. Occasionally the Haunted House would erupt with a Vincent Price laugh, one cracked skeletal arm raised up to the sky as *Thriller* played on an endless loop.

'You know what they call this?' Robin said, turning to me. She held out a stick of candy-floss, lurid pink and furry on my lips.

'Thanks,' I said, pushing it away. 'Call what?'

'This, right now.'

'What?'

'The witching hour.' She turned to me, and winked.

I laughed. 'How very apt.'

'Hey, ladies – you wanna ride this?' a voice called, words lingering in the air.

Robin turned, and I followed her gaze. Between the burger van and ticket truck, a tall, thin man stood clutching three bottles of beer, swaying a little with the effort of standing still and pointing at his groin. I tried to make out the writing on his t-shirt – a slogan, the print cracked and faded – as a group of boys in gas masks ran between us, jumping the railing at the dodgems and hijacking the cars. 'Ignore him,' I said, walking on.

She stood, frozen, staring back. 'Robin,' I hissed. 'Come *on*.'

She looked at me, briefly, and then grinned – that too-familiar grin, white hot with suggestion. 'Nah,' she said. 'Come on. I've got an idea.' She rubbed her hands together like a cartoon villain, as Vincent Price cackled again. I snorted, the candy-floss sweetness catching in my throat.

She walked over, and I followed, a few steps behind. I looked again at the shirt, his eyes following mine; he brushed at it as though rubbing an invisible stain, beer splashing from the open bottles as he did so.

'Hey there, mister,' Robin said, her voice sweet, coy; young. 'Who are those beers for?'

He smiled – overconfident, one chipped tooth revealing itself. 'People old enough to drink.'

272

'Great,' she said, reaching for the bottles. He raised them high in the air, mockingly. She turned back to me. 'Well, this one's clearly all talk.'

'Typical,' I said, playing along, hoping he didn't hear the nervous catch in my voice. 'Let's go.'

He lowered the beers, licking at a spot on his hand. 'You can have them,' he said. 'But then you owe me.'

'Pfffft.' Robin rolled her eyes. 'Not interested. Thanks.' She began walking away, lit gold by the Ferris wheel glowing behind. The rolling lights seemed to be moving a little too fast, dizzyingly bright. I closed my eyes.

'I'm just teasing,' he said, quickly. 'God. Don't like to play, do you?'

'Are you kidding? I *love* games.' She took two bottles in a single snatch, and handed one to me. 'Wanna ride the big wheel?'

He looked at me, neither of us completely sure who she was speaking to. 'You do it,' I said, taking a sip from the bottle – lukewarm, his thumbprint on the rim. The very thought of being off the ground made my stomach roll up into my chest. 'I need a break.'

She grabbed his arm. 'Alright. Take me . . . What's your name?'

'Mike,' he said. She snorted, and he blushed. 'What?'

'Nothing. Come on.'

They stumbled up the metal steps, footsteps seeming to echo through my teeth. I sat on the bottom step, only to be brushed away by a park attendant; walked across to the Wurlitzer, and leaned against the side, feeling the ride's steady rumble behind me. I closed my eyes, and waited for the nausea to pass. I fumbled in my pockets for the wrap I'd had earlier, but it was gone – no doubt stolen back by Robin's creeping hands.

When I opened my eyes, they were high in the air, her legs pressed up against his in the yellow car, swinging playfully back and forth. She was saying something, her face animated – playing her most utterly charming self. By the time they reached the ground, the two of them were arm in arm, whispering and giggling (he possessed an oddly high-pitched laugh, like a child's).

She gestured to me to follow, and I felt a twinge of envy, a little tug in my chest – as I always did, whenever anyone who wasn't Alex or Grace captured Robin's attention (and even, sometimes, when they did – though I wouldn't admit this at the time). I'd come to blame – superstitiously, I suppose, or merely as an excuse – the bonding spell, the scar in my palm that still shone silver-white that occasionally wrenched me from sleep with a sharp, vivid pain, which disappeared the moment I opened my eyes. *It's why I want it to be just us*, I told myself. *Because we're one person when we're alone.* In hindsight, however, beyond the white-hot flush of youthful jealousy, I suppose it was just that. Still, at the time, I felt it, the frustration coiling heavy in my chest as I followed them from one stall to the next.

'I'm going to go,' I said, as he missed his third throw on the coconut shy. I'd hoped to sound cool, nonchalant – but as I heard myself speak, the tone was that of a petulant child left out of some playground game.

She spun around. 'What?'

'I'm going. I'm not just going to be your third wheel while you cheat on Andy.'

She raised an eyebrow. 'You hate Andy.'

'Yeah, but still . . . I'm tired. I want to go.'

'No, you don't. You just need a second wind. And *anyway*, a)—' she raised one finger '—me and Andy are over.'

'For real this time?'

'Wow. Thanks for the sympathy.'

'I just mean—'

She hissed, raised another finger. 'And *b)*,' she said, with a quick glance over her shoulder, a playful smile at Mike, who was purchasing three more tokens for the game, determined to win her a toy. 'You don't *really* think I'm going to sleep with him, do you?'

'Well, you're acting like you're going to.'

'After what he said? Fuck that.'

'What did he say?'

She rolled her eyes. '"Hey, ladies,"' she said, in a low, nasal voice. '"Wanna ride my dick?"'

'I told you to ignore him,' I said, rolling my eyes. 'You were the one that wanted to . . . '

'Wanted to what?'

I shrugged. 'Give him what he wanted.'

'You seriously think that's what I'm doing?' She groaned. A passing child pointed and laughed, and she made a face at him, pulling her bottom lip with her fingers, revealing gums burning red, receding from teeth. 'Christ, Violet,' she said, as his mother pulled him stumbling away. 'How thick are you?'

'Well, what are you—'

'Wait and see. Just . . . ' She wrapped her palms around my wrists, threading her index finger under my bracelet. 'Please stay? Pretty please?'

I knew I would. Still, I pretended to waver, looking over her shoulder at Mike, who was trying to persuade the stall attendant to let him buy a toy outright. 'Fine,' I said, at last. 'But if you start making out, I'm leaving.'

She leaned in, kissed me on the cheek. 'Deal. Now let's get this idiot out of here before he hurts himself.' She turned to him. 'Are you trying to *cheat*?' she said, playfully, every phrase sharpened to a point. 'What a fucking *loser*.'

She hooked her arm through his, and leaned in, her hair brushing his shoulders, a move I knew well. I'd been on the receiving end of it many times, as she wheedled some class prep out of me, or tried to persuade me to come and do something stupid and irresponsible. It always worked. It was working now. 'Let's go back to your house,' she said, looking up at him.

'Why?' he said, pulling away a little.

'Because I don't want to spend all night surrounded by screaming kids.'

He stopped, raised an eyebrow; wobbled a little in place. 'How old are you?'

'Old enough to know better.'

I laughed, in spite of myself, at the line – ridiculous, overblown, like something from a bad film – a laugh that made the two of them turn to me, briefly, as though surprised to find me there. 'Come on,' I said, feeling my cheeks turn pink. 'Let's go.'

He stared at me a moment, then looked back at Robin, eyes glassy in the light. 'Okay,' he said, finally, and the two of them began walking ahead, footsteps out of rhythm, stumbling a little as they tried to keep a single pace.

I rooted numbly through my pockets, wondering if Robin might have dropped a wrap or something in there. (She was always without a coat, except in the coldest weather, when she'd be wrapped in tattered fur, patchy with overuse, using my pockets to store the things too small for her bag, or too big to be tucked inside her bra. Sometimes, in the mornings, I'd wake up with pieces of her in there – little trinkets, treasures dusty with sand, pieces of paper folded into angular creatures. She'd never asked for any of them back, and so my dresser drawer was filled with them, a piecemeal gallery of half-remembered nights.)

Tonight, however, there was nothing. Each step out of the vivid bloom of the fair seemed to pull me a little further down, my eyes seeming to burrow deeper into my skull as the darkness drew in. 'How far is it?' I asked, softly; either they didn't hear, or they chose not to respond.

By the time we reached his flat (in a weather-beaten concrete block, stairwells reeking and slippery underfoot), the two of them seemed a world unto themselves, his hands occasionally moving from her shoulder to the small of her back and below. She didn't push him away, but feigned a stumble, his arm reset around her neck; I cringed each time their dance began again.

He unlocked a dark-green door, paint chipped and peeling, and held it open for the two of us. When I lingered, he shrugged

277

and followed Robin inside, while I waited, counting the seconds, willing away the looming sickness. I'd collapsed into a lull that made the air crackle uncomfortably at my skin, waves of goosebumps rising and falling with each step – that bleak hour when one wonders why on earth it all seemed so appealing and you vow (on the lives of second-tier friends and relatives, just in case) to never again so much as consider drink, drugs, or any other vice. The ascetic life, or a transfer to either nunnery or prison, seems – for a little while – an alluring idea.

Robin's head peered around the doorway. 'Come *on*,' she hissed, reaching for my hand, pulling me in, the crushed black wings of her eyeliner crumbling at the points.

I remember the musty, fetid smell of damp; the green-painted walls, dull, Formica countertops; the brown corduroy sofa, battered and stained; the dirty lino floors that squeaked underfoot. A skateboard, propped by the door, under a pile of scuffed shoes and tattered trainers. Dim streetlight orange oozing through the windows, draped with yellowing blinds.

'Nice place, huh?' Robin whispered, turning to me.

'Lovely,' I said. 'Can we go now?'

She looked around, casting eyes up and down. 'Hey, Mike . . . Got any booze?'

He slumped on the sofa, and pointed to the top of the fridge, where several half-empty bottles sat, sticky with dust. Robin took my hand, and we stood, rifling through the bottles. 'Peach fucking schnapps?' she said, turning to him. 'You gay or something?' He clicked the remote, the room flickering as the PlayStation whooshed to life, music crackling from the TV as he picked up a controller and began to play.

'Nerd,' she whispered to me.

'I think we should leave,' I hissed back.

'I think *you* should relax.' She pulled out a tiny bag of powder, a yellow face grinning on the front, and poured it onto the glass chopping board, splitting the parts with a steady knife click. I looked around and spotted a grubby bottle of vodka on a high shelf. I climbed onto the counter, grease sticking to my knees and palms, and handed it down to Robin.

'That's more like it,' she said. She clicked the cap, and took a sip, grimacing as she swallowed; handed the bottle to me, shaking her head. 'Salud,' she said, as I tipped my head back, the lukewarm vodka burning the cut-apart ridges of my mouth. I winced; closed my eyes tight, seeing stars, and leaned against the sink, bending backwards slowly, feeling every vertebra crack.

Music began to hiss from the stereo, overlapping with the roar of cars and horns coming from the TV. She spun the wheel, and the volume rocketed, rattling the plates and cutlery reeking in the sink. I stepped away, dizzy, the rhythm still thudding between my fingernails, and flopped down beside Mike on the sofa. He didn't notice, too absorbed in the fizzing lights of the game.

Robin sat on his other side, the board on her lap, scratching out white lines on the surface. She nudged him, once, then again with more force; the car skidded off the road and he groaned, set down the controller as she handed him the board. 'What's this?' he said.

'Party fuel.' Her eyes flickered to me, then back to him. 'Go on,' she said, rolling a note between her fingers. 'Or are you scared?'

He snatched the note, rolled it a little tighter. In the glass, I saw his features turn mask-like, exaggerated, as he leaned over, adjusted himself, and took a phlegmy, sickening snort. He shook his head, eyes closed, and passed the board to me, before Robin pulled it away. 'She doesn't want any of this.'

'Fuck off,' I said, reaching for the board. 'Give it to me.'

She stood, eyes narrowed, and placed the board on the floor, a cloud of powder swelling with the impact. 'Violet, listen to me. You need to sit this one out.' She turned to him. 'So what do you do?'

I don't recall his answer; had already lost interest (more accurately, I was never interested – though I suppose had he said something vaguely interesting I might have paid more attention). I plucked the vodka from the table, and took another sip, rolling it around my tongue, my anger petulant, childish. Slowly, I shuffled forward. *She can't tell me what to do*, I thought, bitterly.

As I rose to stand, he gripped my wrist tight, thumb pressed between bones. 'What the—' I began, wrenching my arm away. He didn't loosen his grip. For a split second, I felt the crush of branches underneath, the hands pressed against my shoulders, collarbone straining beneath; blinked back to the moment, and turned to him, my free hand peeling his fingers away. His eyes bloodshot, pupils like pinpricks, he swallowed, shook his head, and coughed. I pulled again, and he let go, leaning back into the well of the chair and closing his eyes.

I looked at Robin, then back at him, as a single streak of blood rolled from his nose to his chin.

I looked at her again, her mouth open, tongue set between teeth. 'Robin . . . What the hell did you just do?'

I suppose there are moments, best (or at least most commonly) experienced in the heady years of adolescence, when a girl decides who – or what – she is going to be.

Girls who chase boys, who twirl their hair and walk through clouds of chain-store perfume, learning their allure. Girls who like books, who revel in their solitude, and lonely girls who don't; girls who eat, and girls who don't. Girls with piercings, tattoos, scars. Angry girls, who bare their teeth and scratch at their arms. Unironic boy-band pink-clad girls, who scream and wail and *live* in every breath. Girls who read *Vogue* and spend their Saturdays with jealous hands on clothes their allowances won't afford. Girls who long to be mothers, and their own mothers who long for their youth. Art girls. Science girls. Girls who'll make it out alive. Girls who won't.

And then, there are the invisible girls: the ones nobody thinks to be afraid of. The girls who hide in plain sight, flirting and giggling; girls for whom sugar and spice is a mask. Girls who spark matches and spill battery acid on skin. Girls for whom the rules do not apply.

I reached for Robin's arm. 'Is he . . . ?'

'I don't think so.'

'You don't *think*—'

'Hang on.' She leaned over, placed a hand flat against his chest. I felt my breath still for a moment as we waited; almost imperceptibly, her hand rose and fell, and she pulled it away. 'He's fine,' she said, wiping her hand on her skirt.

'He doesn't look fine,' I said, watching the beads of sweat forming, one by one, on his forehead, his skin a chalky white. 'What was that?'

'I don't know. I found it at Andy's.' She snorted, turned to me with a grin. 'Told you you didn't want any.'

'Are you seriously laughing right now? He might be—'

She glared at me. 'Chill out, Violet. You're being weird.'

'*I'm* being weird?' She parroted the words back in a high-pitched voice, fingers like puppets in the air. My head ached, my skin ablaze, hot with fury.

'Robin, please,' I said, the words thin, forced (sounding for all the world like her imitation of me, much to my frustration). 'I don't think we should be here. We should call an ambulance, and then we should go.'

'They think it's okay to treat us like shit,' she said, as though continuing some thought I'd missed. 'They're all the fucking same.'

'He didn't *do* anything.'

'Are you kidding? He's got, what—' She leaned in towards his face, pointing at the sallow spaces under his eyes, the cracks in his damp skin. 'Ten years on us? And you can't tell me he didn't know that, because he *asked*.'

'And you said old enough!'

'Like he didn't know better,' she said, rolling her eyes. 'Like he couldn't have said, "You know what, actually, I'm a grown man, and I'm going to take responsibility for my actions, apologize, and walk away from this situation I got myself into." Please.'

'Oh, because you're *such* a great example of taking

responsibility for your actions.' I felt my stomach drop, the words thoughtless, torn from bitter roots.

She flinched. 'Excuse me?'

The CD caught and skipped, a brittle beat; I heard footsteps outside, the two of us frozen as a figure in silhouette passed outside. She stared at me, the tendons in her neck braced, flickering as she leaned over and stopped the disc. 'Not taking responsibility for what?' she said, after a moment.

I looked down at the floor, a scuff mark black in the tile. 'Forget it.'

'Tell me what you meant, Violet.'

'No.' I heard my own voice, petulant, like a child facing a furious parent; closed my eyes as she stepped towards me, fists clenched tight, knuckles pressing through flesh. She sighed, the tension seeming to ease from her and into the air, prickling my skin.

'Come on,' she said, quietly. She reached out and placed her thumb on the white scar in my palm, nail catching in the nook. 'Please, Violet. Tell me what's wrong.'

I sighed, not looking up. 'When we were at the Dean's house . . . I found something. In the garage.'

She said nothing, though her hand seemed to tighten, just a little, around mine. I went on. 'He'd been writing about . . . Well, about you. And Alex, and Grace. And he said . . . '

I trailed off, nervously; looked up. 'Spit it out,' she said, her voice cold, eyes flashing golden in the street-lamp glow.

'He said you killed her. The three of you. Because she was going to tell him about the society.'

She took a long, shuddering inhale, the pause seeming to

go on for minutes as I waited for her to speak. A siren howled in the distance, the gulls cackling overhead. 'That's what you think?' she said, softly. 'You really believe that?'

I said nothing, willing her to tell me I was wrong. This, the simple act of denial – a laugh, maybe, a giggle – this might have been enough to make me doubt myself. We stared at each other, the room thick with dead air.

'Wow,' she said. 'Wow. Okay.' She took a step back, then forward; looked over my shoulder to the kitchen. I watched as she passed, heard the drawers slide open, one by one, trying to find the words to fix it – to fix us. The look in her eyes, the way her breath caught as I said the words, made me doubt them; made me question how, in fact, I'd ever believed them in the first place.

'Robin,' I said, 'I'm sorry. I didn't . . . '

The noise stopped. 'It's fine,' she said, appearing in the doorway. She was clutching a black-handled knife, its blade reflecting the streetlight glow, silver and gold. I froze. She smiled, and walked past me, her shoulder brushing mine.

Silhouetted in the light, she kneeled on top of Mike, carefully, settling herself on his lap. It seemed rehearsed, somehow; a little too much, like playacting, macabre and unreal. She turned to me. 'You really think I murdered my best friend?'

The word hung in the air a moment, the absence of euphemism clotting and heady. *Murder,* I thought. It was the first time any of us had said the word aloud.

'I don't . . . ' I began, weakly.

She looked down at Mike, then back at me. 'You honestly believe that I wanted that to happen? You think I'm that shitty a friend?'

'I didn't say you wanted to. I don't know what happened. Nor did he. I didn't . . . '

'You didn't what?'

'I didn't read that far.'

She stared at me, blankly. 'How much was there?'

'A whole book. It was all there. Everything from the ones who killed Margaret, right through to . . . '

She took a deep breath, collecting herself. 'You're right. You don't know what happened. You don't know anything.'

'Then *tell* me.'

'If you've been thinking that this whole time,' she said, wiping the knife against her thigh, 'why are you friends with me now?' There was a note of the little girl in her voice, a hurt that made my chest tighten with guilt.

'Robin, I really didn't mean . . . '

'Is it because you're stuck with me? Because you think I'll what – tell on you for being there when we killed him?'

'It's not—'

'Because if you want out, I won't tell. You can just go. I won't tell anyone.'

'No,' I said, my voice shaking. 'It's not that, at all. I want to be your friend. I *am* your friend.'

'Or is it that you like it?' She paused. 'Maybe you want it to be true, because it'd make your sad, pathetic life a little bit interesting.' As she said the word again, she pressed the flat of the blade against his neck, the skin turning white around the edges. 'Maybe that's it,' she said, thoughtfully. 'That's why we're friends. Maybe this is what *you* want.'

'Robin, please . . . I don't. Please . . . Please don't.'

And yet, despite the words of protest, the hissing, cringing prissiness of my voice, still some part of me knew she was right. I wanted her to do it, wanted to see what came next. I wanted to see the insides of his throat, the rhythmic spurt of blood in little firework plumes; the wide-eyed horror, the absolute stillness.

I knew it was illogical. I knew it was *wrong*. And yet there's a thrill to it – a kind of killer's high, I suppose, a distant cousin of that touted by runners and lovers yet to be disillusioned – which I'd been experiencing since the night at the Dean's house. Textures too brittle, colours too bright, every sea breeze perfumed with some audacious, sweet-blossom smell . . . There was a kind of gorgeous, blooming immensity to it all.

Put like this, of course, it seems like madness. I know that. I'm ashamed to admit it, of course. But in the moment, when all was potential, it was a longing experienced at gut level.

'Robin,' I said, at last. 'Let's just go. Please.'

She turned to me. 'Go search the place. Look for anything worth having.'

'What?' I said.

'Go look around. Look under the mattress, or whatever. See if he's got any cash hidden away.'

'You're not—'

'Violet, for fuck's sake. Get on with it.' In the dim light, her skin glowed with sweat, burning hot. I sighed – an exaggerated, over-the-top sigh – and began my reluctant search of the bedroom, gripping surfaces to steady myself.

I flicked the light switch, and found a sad, boxy room. The bed was unmade, the smell of unwashed sheets tart and over-whelming; three posters hung faded on the walls, two of women in various states of undress, one of some speeding car, the mountains blurred behind. On the side table, a stack of pornographic magazines sat beside a mystery novel, splayed half-read, spine cracked; a lamp with no bulb sat, abandoned, by the bed, beneath an ornamental sword. I opened the ward-robe, where rows of identical, faintly creased suits hung alongside cheap sports jackets and faded polo shirts, and rooted around in the back. I found a stack of videotapes, old football matches scrawled on the labels; a broken Walkman, crushed cover; shoe boxes, filled with old playing cards. I put them back.

Under the bed, too, I found nothing but junk – a sad, dejected collection of lost things, the secret possessions of a boy who couldn't grow up – and under the mattress, I found only more pornography, pictures of girls who looked younger than me. I dropped the mattress down, disgusted, and went back into the living room.

Robin was still straddled over him, knife poised, her face close to his, skin almost touching. 'He doesn't have anything,' I said, sitting on the arm of the chair beside them.

'He's got something,' she said, turning to me with a half-smile.

'What?' I looked around, briefly, my eyes drawn back to Robin, her hair down her shoulders like spilled ink.

She pressed the edge of the blade slowly into his skin, as though daring it to split; I held my breath, the warm froth of anticipation rising, my skin tingling, bones tightened, muscles free. She leaned in and whispered something in his ear. I felt my legs unsteady, my arms ache with the need to reach out, touch; a tug of envy, indulgent and bitter.

'A hard-on,' she snorted. 'Fucking men.'

Outside, the street lamps flickered, a split-second break in the light; I heard footsteps, a laughing woman screeching as she passed. *Do it*, I thought, a voice I hadn't realized I possessed. *Do it, Robin. I dare you.*

'You want a go?' she said, finally.

'What?'

'If you think *I'm* a murderer, and you still want to be *my* friend, maybe you've got a touch of the ol' bloodlust yourself – hmmm?' She shifted a little, flexing her toes to loosen a cramp, and climbed down, pirouetting off his lap, knife still shining in her hand. She wiped it, roughly, on her skirt, and held it towards me, blade first. 'Go on.'

'I can't.'

'Yeah, you can. It's easy.'

I looked down at the knife, the air electric with the threat. *Take it*, I told myself. *Take it so you're safe.*

'Atta girl.' She grinned. The handle was damp, plasticky, toylike. It seemed impossible that it could do anything; a kitchen knife, blunted with use. She tipped her head towards the body, the faint rise and fall of his chest. 'Go on.'

This, I suppose, is the point at which I could've said no. Could have told Robin I wouldn't (a bold, brave refusal) or couldn't (nervous, afraid; much closer to the truth). But the frisson of the previous moment still rang in my bones, a dull ache – a what-if. *After all*, I thought, *he's a pervert. He brought us here, even though he has to know we're* . . . I stopped. *Just girls*, I'd thought. Just girls.

I stepped towards him, heart thudding, froglike. I steadied myself on the arm of the chair, my head still aching, eyes dry and chalky, and settled. Climbed astride him, lowered myself around the weird, comical stiffness, that sad, useless, male thing; giggled, Robin's laugh an echo in response. I squeezed the knife's warm handle, rubber soft against fingertips, and lifted it, imitating Robin. Pressed the blade against his neck, to the side of his Adam's apple, the skin turning white at the point. *I could do this*, I thought, a cool and gorgeous thrill. *It's so easy.*

'You can do this,' Robin echoed, catching the thought. 'It's easy.'

I looked down at his face, blood and mucus pooling, fat bubbles on his lip; the shadow of a beard poking through, blackening pores. Eyes flickering underneath closed lids, a tremor. I pressed the knife harder, a tiny knot of blood rolling down the blade, leisurely, thick.

What was it that compelled me in that moment? As I look back, now, still I wonder: Was it the fear of discovery, the pursuit of oblivion? Was it power, the violence of my – our – potential? Or was it the shadow of Emily Frost, eyes hollowed black, looming over us – Robin's perfect friend, the beautiful, tragic victim?

The ringing phone shot through the silence, and I pitched

back, jumping upright in an instant. 'Fuck,' I said, turning to Robin, who bent double, elbows skyward, gripping her stomach.

'Oh my god,' she said, without looking up. She breathed slowly through her teeth, a hiss. 'I thought you were actually going to do it.'

'I was,' I said, a little hurt. 'I was just about to—'

She rose up, and I caught a flash of something in her eye I barely recognized; hadn't seen, before, in Robin. A glimmer of something burning out. Was it fear? Was she scared of what I'd do?

'Robin,' I said, nervously. 'I was—'

She stepped forward, took the knife from me again, Mike's jeans smeared quickly with his own blood. 'Let's go,' she said, dropping the knife with a clatter into the sink.

I ran the tap until it disappeared beneath the water (imagining washing away prints, though – I supposed, turning back for a moment to watch the slow rise and fall of his chest – we hadn't committed a crime. Not much of one, anyway). And then, we left, closing the door behind us with a soft click and running down the concrete steps, through the silent streets. Back, always back into the night.

Chapter 15

'*Ruinenlust*,' Annabel said, tapping two fingers in the dust. 'The beauty in ruins; the bliss found only in decay.'

I looked at Robin, her eyes fixed on the pencil in her hand, trembling. She pressed it onto the page, the lead crumbling with the sheer force of her, willing herself still. I nudged her, gently, but she ignored me – didn't seem, in fact, to notice I was there.

Alex, too, was watching Robin through narrowed eyes. She reached out a hand, and pulled the pencil from Robin's grip, turning to face Annabel with a grim, determined expression. Outside, the sky was white-blue and blinding; I pressed my fingers to my temple, a dull ache ringing in my ears.

After we'd left the flat, we'd wandered the streets, the lamps flickering; Robin had dropped another pill on my tongue, pulling me towards her by the collar of my coat.

'What are you doing?' I said, feeling her fingers creep from shoulder to neck, nails leaving imprints in the hollows. She'd pressed down, a little, for the briefest of moments, thumbs sharp and hot against my windpipe, and for a split second I'd wondered if this was what Emily had felt, in her last moments: that crush of love and hate, the cruel and rotten bliss of friendship.

She leaned in, slowly, I stood perfectly still; a little light-headed, my pulse quickening against her thumb, afraid to pull away. She brushed chapped lips at my cheeks, breath hot and damp, and let go; walked away, stumbling towards the closed pier.

Annabel pulled the blinds with a sharp tug. 'What is it about collapse that inspires in us so sweet a nostalgia? Why are we drawn, so irresistibly, to what we most fear?'

I'd left, then, brought sharply and cruelly to myself; the tang of sweat (the boy's, Robin's, mine, all mingling on my skin), the acid burning in my throat, nauseating. Halfway, I turned back, the guilt brief and consuming, but when I reached the pier she was gone, the tide roaring at my feet. I wondered if she'd jumped or fallen; felt ashamed at wondering if that might be a relief.

'The bricks of these very buildings are susceptible to destruction. It might be immediate, whether through forces natural or man-made: the storm, the flood, the bomb. But it might, instead, be gradual, a slow process of decay that may already have begun. The rot in invisible beams, the wearing away of cement, the stone floors beneath worn down by your feet, and mine, and the feet of those who trod these paths before us.'

She paused, glancing briefly at the four of us; brushed a strand of hair from her face, revealing skin cracked like frozen leaves. Grace smiled, as though to distract from Robin, who'd lowered her head to the desk, eyes staring blankly at the page below. I saw Nicky peer over, brow arched, a slight smile on her face.

'It seems to me that the experience of *Ruinenlust*, then, is a form of haunting. As we walk through ruins, the shadows of the dead stroll along beside us, their surroundings gleaming anew. One wonders if they, too, imagine us – if they simply cannot help themselves, aware as we are that all these structures, these so-called solid foundations, legacies left in stone, are simply ephemeral, and fleeting.

'And with that revelation – the revelation of ruin, of entropy, of endless decay – we are left to ask . . . What remains?'

She sat, slowly, on the edge of the desk. 'Diderot, I believe, puts it best, when he says: "Everything comes to nothing, everything perishes, everything passes, only the world remains, only time endures."'

The class watched her as one, the room still, breath held in our throats, waiting. She looked up, briefly; blinked, as though remembering herself. 'That's all, ladies. Essays due next week.'

She stood, stooping to glance at the Campanile beneath the blinds, and left, the class slowly coming to life as the door closed behind her. Nicky glanced at Robin again, then at me; she mouthed 'Is she okay?' It was an exaggerated gesture, too much; the few girls who hadn't noticed Robin's behaviour looked over, eyes narrowed as they watched.

'She's fine,' Alex said, coldly.

'Are you sure?' Nicky stepped towards the four of us, a look of false concern on her face. 'I mean – should we call the nurse? She looks awful.'

Robin turned to face Nicky, eyes wide and bloodshot. 'You know, your brother's a shitty—'

'Robin, leave it.' The force of Alex's words, the shock of her tone, made Robin flinch; she gave Nicky a sweet smile, and leaned onto her elbows, face in her palms.

'Hey, Nicky,' I said, desperately. 'Can we . . . Can we talk?'

She smiled. 'Sure. Now?'

I nodded, and we stepped outside, the girls watching me with suspicion. I didn't have a plan; simply wanted to distract Nicky, for a moment. To pull Robin from her glare.

'What's up?' she said, sweetly. 'You look kind of tired.'

'I'm fine. I just . . . Do you know what the reading was for English? I didn't get it down.'

She stared at me, blankly. I blushed, the lie hanging in the air between us. 'You couldn't have asked me that in there?' she said, finally.

I shrugged. 'You know what they're like.'

'I . . . ' She rolled her eyes. 'Whatever. I get it. It's Kafka. The one about the bug.'

As she turned to walk away, she paused, as though about to speak. I waited, willing her not to ask anything, to require me to think. She glanced at me, briefly, and walked away, footsteps cracking on the stone hall floors.

I slipped back into the studio, where Grace and Alex stood on either side of Robin, whispering between themselves. 'What's *wrong* with her?' Alex said, as I closed the door with a click.

'It's just a hangover,' I said; the words hollow, unreal. 'We went to the fair, and . . . '

Alex looked at me, blankly. 'It doesn't look like a hangover.'
'It's a really bad one.'

She sighed. 'We're . . . Well, we're worried.'

Robin sat up, slowly, a smile spreading on her face. 'We're worried,' she echoed, coldly. 'You're so thoughtful, Alex. Thanks so much.' She stood, gripping the desk for balance, and slid her notes into her bag. 'Come on, Vivi.'

I looked at her, nervously. There was a coldness in her eyes, a dark, brittle glare; the trembling of her hands continued, a violent, cruel thing. She caught me looking; gripped the frayed sleeves of her blazer, fingers turning white at the nails.

'Do you think . . . ' Grace began. She looked at Alex, who nodded. 'Do you think you should maybe get some help again?'

Robin's mouth fell open, a little, stunned; the four of us still, trapped like the stone figures held in despair, the instant of their greatest pain. She looked at me for support. I closed my eyes, searching for something I could say – some way to tell her I loved her, desperately, and yet the girls were right. The bluish shadows beneath her eyes, the sweat pooling in the hollow of her collarbones, the breath visible in the strings of her throat, her decay, the threat of her doing, or saying, something to reveal what we'd done, was all too much to bear.

I saw, too, her vacant expression in my own, caught in the split second before I'd look away from the glare of my reflection; wondered if, perhaps, her so-called sickness were treated, my own might be soothed, too.

Or at least, this is how I justified it to myself at the time. I wonder, now, whether some shameful part of me – some rotting, blackened spot – knew that, while I'd never leave her of my own accord, her forced removal might provide my way out: my escape from the horrors that our friendship had made.

'I don't . . . ' I began, weakly. I looked at her, watched the shiver of goosebumps on her skin, the flame in her eyes. 'I don't know what to say. Maybe they're right.'

She stepped back, the words a physical thing, and looked down at the floor. I glanced at Alex and Grace, who looked back helplessly. Her shoulders rose and fell with her breath, and she looked up, eyes livid. 'I cannot *believe* you. You absolute bitch.'

'I'm not saying—'

'Do you *know* what she tried to do last night?' She pointed a trembling finger at me, Grace and Alex staring, open-mouthed. 'Of course. Of *course.*'

I shook my head, feeling a sob swell in my chest, the hot stab of it. 'Don't, Robin.'

'She thinks we murdered Emily.'

A sharp intake of breath. 'What?' Alex whispered, softly.

'She thinks we murdered her, and—' She laughed, a cruel bark. 'She thinks that's so, so cool. So cool, in fact, that she nearly killed a guy, last night, just to prove she's one of us.'

'No, I didn't— I—' I stumbled, the situation spiralling, lost to me.

'Why would you—' Alex began.

'You don't understand. I didn't—'

'Don't lie, Violet,' Robin spat. 'You're pathetic at it.'

I stared at her, stunned. 'I'm not lying. I—'

'Yes, you are.' She stepped towards me, her breath hot, ammoniac; I felt the cut on my hand begin to bleed, my own nails clawing deep. 'You're a liar,' she said. 'A filthy, ugly, slutty liar, and—'

'Robin, stop. Stop.' Grace put a hand on her shoulder, and she wheeled around, knocking Grace backwards.

'And *you*—' Robin wiped her hand on her shirt, a bloody stain on white. '*You* act like you're so innocent and sweet, just because Daddy's a—'

I heard the glass shatter before I realized what had happened, the movement so fast I wondered if she'd done it with the sheer force of her anger. Robin turned and looked at the broken window, Alex's hand still raised and trembling.

The four of us stood in silence, the realization a piercing, bitter horror. The devouring, fanged cruelties; the Furies, the girls we'd become.

The door opened with a creak, and we turned, caught. Annabel looked at us, blankly, and sighed. 'Girls,' she said, coldly. 'You should go home.'

I looked at Alex and Grace, expecting them to say something – an apology, an excuse – but they stared down at the floor, Alex's fists still clenched tight.

'Go,' Annabel said, finally. 'All of you. Go home and get some sleep. You are excused.'

I sat at the foot of the stairs, the TV too loud in the living room: an advert for some children's toy whirring. I caught my mum's thought in the air as it passed: It was a thing Anna would've liked. Would've clung to, selfishly, shoulders braced and tiny arms flecked with marks as she hid it out of view – as though by looking at it, we were stealing it away.

The phone was still in the drawer. I pulled it out, rested it on my knees at the foot of the stairs; dialled Robin's number, picked at the wallpaper as it rang, and rang, and rang, almost hypnotic in its steady rhythm. I closed my eyes, rested my head against the wall. 'The person you have dialled cannot be reached at this time,' a clipped voice said, abruptly. I clicked redial, waited again. 'The person you have dialled cannot be reached at this time.'

I clicked redial again, and it rang: four, five rings. And then, a muffled click. A silence. The cold whirr of the dial tone. I dialled again, entering the numbers carefully, whispering them aloud as I pressed each key. It didn't ring. Just a steady *beep, beep, beep.* There was someone there – and they'd cut me off. I swallowed, throat raw, jaw stiff and cracking. Robin's phone had caller ID.

I heard Mum move in the living room and rolled heavily back to my feet. I didn't want to talk – not to her. Not now. I took the phone, unspooling the cord behind me as I dragged it up the stairs, as far as it would reach. *She'll call back,* I told myself, stumbling back to bed, door open just a crack, so I could hear. *She'll call back, soon. She has to.*

But the phone didn't ring.

The next day, I made weak tea in a dirty cup, and drank it in bed, where I sat cross-legged, surrounded by books, whose glossy prints swam in front of my vision, lush greens and blues, bodies naked and fat and joyous. I could barely remember what the coursework project was: simply that I'd checked these books out, weeks earlier, in an attempt at 'research'.

The phone rang. I jumped up, and ran to the top of the stairs, answering with a breathless, 'Hello?'

'Good morning! Is that Miss Violet Taylor?' a voice said, cheerfully.

'Yes,' I replied, feeling my heart stop, a moment, and snap back into some offbeat rhythm. I didn't know who it was, but it wasn't her. Wasn't them.

'I'm Daniel Mitchell, from the *Evening News*,' he said. 'I was wondering if you had a minute for a quick chat.'

I froze. 'What about?'

'You're a student at Elm Hollow, aren't you?'

'Yes,' I said, flatly, steeling my voice.

'Good. It's a great school, isn't it?'

I didn't reply. He went on. 'I'm told you were receiving some "one-on-one" tuition from Mr Holmsworth – the Dean of Students, who recently passed away?'

I flinched. Who had given him my name? And why?

'I thought you might be able to answer a few questions for me. If you're not too busy, that is?'

It could have been anyone, I supposed, one of Nicky's friends, caught up in the excitement, alighting on my name as a way to differentiate herself or the others – a sliver of gossip so minute as to have been overlooked, attention instead squarely on the others.

But it could, too, have been one of them: Alex, perhaps, trying to deflect some roving eye onto me. *Why?* I thought, nervously. *What would that achieve?*

'Miss Taylor?' the voice said again, distracting me from my thoughts.

'What do you want to know?'

'Well,' he said, clearing his throat. 'I'd be curious to know whether you felt like he was acting in any way strangely in the run-up to his death. Any suspicious behaviour, anything like that?'

'I don't . . . I don't know.'

'You were reasonably close, weren't you?'

'What?'

'You must have had quite a close working relationship to . . . Well, for him to drive you home late at night. You must have felt you could trust him. And he you,' he added, his tone bright, despite what seemed like a sliver of implication in it, which cut cold through my skin.

'Who told you that?'

'I'm afraid I can't say. Can't reveal my sources, you know.'

I thought of Alex's reaction when Robin had told her about the ride: the accusation, the threat in her tone. Who else could have known? Who else would it be?

'They're lying,' I said, coldly.

'Is that so?' he said, as though the question were rhetorical, a theory needing thought. 'It really doesn't matter if you did – get a lift with him, I mean. You're not in any trouble. If anything, I'm trying to work out if your other teachers should have . . . Well, should have known.'

'Known what?'

'That there might well have been some kind of . . . ' He clicked his tongue, thoughtfully. 'Some kind of predator on your school campus.' I wondered if his way of speaking – the mid-sentence pause, the repetition – was a tic, or an odd journalistic technique, delivered for effect.

'I know you've been through rather a lot already, Miss Taylor,' he went on, filling the silence. 'I imagine you're still reeling from the loss of your father – an accident, was it?' I felt the floor shudder underfoot, gripped the bannister for support. 'And to lose your little sister at the same time – awful. Really awful. So I can't imagine how you must be feeling about this near miss. And Violet – may I call you Violet?'

'No.'

'Okay then. Miss Taylor it is. But you know, it's okay to be scared. Anyone would—'

'I'm not scared,' I said, flatly.

'Excuse me?'

'I'm not scared. Not of him.' I paused (my own dramatic pause, now – I wondered if it was catching, this strange inflection). 'I'm scared of other people, yes,' I said, the words seeming to gather their own momentum, beyond my control. 'But I was never scared of him. You're being lied to, sir. By whoever told you what you think you know. If I were you, I'd go back and talk to them.'

I hung up, the phone hitting the receiver with a clatter, hands shaking. *What was that about?* I thought, with a creeping horror. *What are they doing now?*

I peered through the window of Robin's front room, saw my reflection peering back, threw a handful of gravel at her window, as she'd done so many times at mine. After the call,

I'd dialled her number over and over again, with no response. I'd tried Grace, too; then Alex. Feverish with panic, my thoughts crushed into one another like waves against the docks, fear rolling in, chased away by sheer force of will, the rushing, endless chant: *They wouldn't tell. They wouldn't.*

But the will hadn't been enough. I'd staggered down the stairs, thrown my bag over my shoulder, and walked, knees shaking and calves wracked with every step. It was mid-afternoon, and the coffee shop was almost empty, Dina perched behind the counter with a book. 'Have you seen them?' I asked, breathlessly. She stared at me, coldly, and shook her head. 'Not all week.' She shrugged. 'Long may it continue.'

I walked the pier, the mildewing creep of evening clotting in the air. The mermaid, too, was surrounded by kids who seemed younger, unfathomably younger, than us (though, I supposed, it couldn't have been by much. I simply felt older, ground down by experience: burned out and shucked away). The gates to Alex's house were locked, the buzzer hissing unanswered, lights off inside, and Grace's house looked empty from the street, though I was too afraid to knock.

Robin's, then, was the last place I tried.

'*Excuse* me,' a voice said, the front door opening with a crack. 'You might have rung the bell.' I recognized Robin's mum from the photos I'd seen in the hall: homely, in a way I'd always wished my own mum could be; giving the impression of one whose hugs would be soft, reassuring. She looked me up and down with something resembling disgust, and I felt suddenly, briefly ashamed; aware of myself, shadowed with exhaustion.

'Mrs Adams?' I said, offering a wide, apologetic smile. 'I'm sorry. I didn't think anyone was home.'

She stared at me, saying nothing.

'I was looking for Robin?' I said, my cadence rising, as it so often did in front of adults. (I'd been corrected, often, at my old school for doing just this – yet at Elm Hollow nobody seemed to mind. Our teachers' minds, I supposed, were on loftier ideals – leaving such things among the pitifully minor concerns of the public-school teacher whose aspirations have long dried up.)

'And you are?' she said, crossing her arms across her broad chest, a button in the centre about to burst.

'Violet Taylor. Nice to . . . nice to meet you,' I said, nervously.

'Ah,' she said. 'So you're the famous Violet.'

I nodded, a little swell of pride blooming in my chest. 'Yes, Miss.'

'I'm sorry, Violet,' she said, stepping back towards the door. 'Robin isn't home. And I'd appreciate it if you didn't call again.'

'What?'

'I don't want you in my home. I don't want you anywhere near my daughter.' She slammed the door shut, and I stepped forward, too late, the glass panel shaking with the force of her on the other side.

I knocked, once, then again; slammed my palms against the door. 'Mrs *Adams!*' I shouted, a crack in my voice. 'Robin?'

The door swung open again, and I stepped back, caught by surprise. A man stood in the doorway, Mrs Adams lurking just behind, the expression on her face one of satisfaction, of victory. The man looked down at me with eyes I recognized: Robin's.

'Who are you?' I said, belligerently.

He laughed, the same mocking scoff I'd heard from Robin, endlessly. 'You should go, Violet.'

'Who *are* you?' I asked, again, the realization creeping, tendrils black and cruel. 'Where is she?'

'I'm her father,' he said, his voice calm, flat. Patronizing.

I remembered our first conversation, first moment of closeness: 'Hey! My dad's dead, too,' she'd said, and I'd apologized for bringing it up. It was impossible. She wouldn't.

'Her *step*father?'

He raised his brow; I felt the briefest flicker of satisfaction, noting his surprise. 'No. Her father. Now please,' he said. 'It is time for you to leave.'

He closed the door again, and I beat my hands against it, furiously. I caught myself, suddenly, pressed against the door; felt ashamed of the violence of it. Turned around, walked across the lawn, crushing flowers in their carefully laid beds as I stepped into the street. I looked up at the windows, a mobile of paper birds hanging Technicolor in Robin's, the notes we'd passed hung with invisible threads. 'Robin!' I called, throat scratching with old smoke and sickness; the curtains below twitched, Mrs Adams' shadow darkening the door.

'What was *that* about?' a voice said as I stepped back into the street.

'Jesus Christ, Nicky,' I said. 'What are you doing? Are you . . . Are you following me?'

She snorted. 'No. God, no. I'm sure you're super interesting and all, but . . . No. My boyfriend lives just up there.' She gestured up the hill, towards the townhouses that overlooked the rest of the town. 'But seriously – what have you done to piss *her* off?' she added, undeterred.

'I have no idea,' I said, walking away, Nicky tripping along just behind.

'I always thought her mum was kind of nice. Unlike *her*,' she added, pointedly.

'Oh yeah – she seems it.'

'She's a teacher. She was at my primary school, but I wasn't in her class, although Johanna was, and *she* always said . . . '

I stopped listening. *What just happened?* I thought, still burning hot with anger. *And where is she if she's not at home?* My thoughts seemed to trail one another into the dark, as I tried to piece together what had happened, Nicky still chattering endlessly beside me. *Maybe she's at the clinic again*, I thought, though I didn't believe it; relived instead the way Alex and Grace had stared, open-mouthed, when Robin had told them what we'd done. What *I'd* done. *They wouldn't tell anyone about that*, I thought, as my mind volleyed back: *Would they?*

'Come on, Violet. It's going to be *so* fun.'

I swatted Nicky away. 'I hate those guys.'

'Which guys?' She straightened a little as we passed a shop window, flicked out her hair, two thick strands stuck sweating between her shoulders. A car beeped as it passed; she flattened her skirt against her legs and giggled, a clumsy imitation Monroe.

'All of them. They're gross.'

She rolled her eyes. 'If you like girls, you can just say it, you know.'

'I don't like girls.'

'Alright, alright,' she said, smiling. 'Just . . . Well, I don't think they're gross. They're just boys. But it's going to be *such* a good party. Everyone's going to be there.' She paused. 'Well, almost everyone.'

I sighed, knowing I was being teased, knowing she was about to tell me something she knew I'd want to know. I didn't want to give her the satisfaction, and yet . . . 'What do you mean?' I said, at last.

She shrugged. 'Maybe you know more about it than I do already. They're *your* friends, after all.'

'What?'

'Well, Verity Farron said she saw the police at Alex's house yesterday morning. She and Grace haven't been at school since.'

It was as though the world had stopped; the street pulled back with a sickening lurch. 'What?'

'Yeah,' she said. 'So weird.' She paused. 'Anyway, are you coming or not?'

'Where?'

She nudged my shoulder with a fist. 'The party.' She rolled her eyes. 'Duh, Violet. You are so scatty. I don't know how you get from one moment to the next.'

I took a deep breath, steadied myself. 'Nah,' I said. 'I'm not in the mood.'

'Spoilsport.'

'Whatever.' I pointed to the street we'd just passed. 'Doesn't your boyfriend live up there?'

'I was just keeping you company,' she said, smiling. 'But I can take a hint. I'll see you around, Vivi.' She reached up and kissed my cheek, gently; I didn't move, couldn't. *Violet,* I thought, stiffly. *Only Robin calls me Vivi.*

That night, I dialled her number three times, four; no answer. On the fifth, it didn't ring. I pictured Mrs Adams pulling the cord from the wall, pulled taut between fat fingers, skin carved white with bleach. 'Bitch,' I said, staring into the receiver. 'You absolute bitch,' I said, again.

I knew I wasn't helping matters; wondered if it was a kind of harassment, this constant calling. Whether she'd call the police, if the girls hadn't called them already. If they hadn't told them what we'd done – the three of them, stories matched to counter everything I could possibly say, making the murder mine, and mine alone.

I sat on the floor, pinching the skin on my stomach between finger and thumb, missing the comfort of who I'd been before: childish, soft, all puppy fat and soft joints. I didn't recognize myself now, the rounds of my knees turned sharp and squared off; bony feet and hands, mechanics and pulse beat visible through skin. How I'd let myself become this person I didn't know – it was a process that seemed as easy as falling, absorbed with thoughts of the girls, of being one of them: of skipped meals and neat drinks and moments passed forgetting.

And all, it seemed, for nothing. I'd given all of myself away, both soul and flesh. All I could do was wait.

I shuffled downstairs, made a cup of tea (the milk sour, bags sticky with damp), and sat on the sofa next to Mum, who eyed me nervously, as though afraid of what new cruelty I might inflict upon her. I reached for the remote, and flicked through channels aimlessly, looking for some mindless distraction. The air was thick with sour breath and rotting food, a plate upturned on the side-table, chips in mayonnaise turned translucent, sticky with decay. I bit my lip; tasted blood, the bitter acid in my throat.

Mum reached gingerly for my foot, and squeezed, and for a moment I wanted to tell her everything: to confess it all, and start again. I wanted to bury my forehead in her bony shoulders, let her run her fingers through my hair; wanted her to hold me, as she'd done before, and tell me I was a sweetheart. *Her* sweetheart.

But, I thought, pressing the buttons harder, the rubber imprinting ridges on my thumb, *it's too late for that. She couldn't help, even if she wanted to.* The screen burned bright with early morning kids' TV, characters burbling mindlessly, and I blinked away tears, feeling hopelessly, terrifyingly adult. I pulled my foot away; dropped the remote beside her, and went back upstairs, slamming the door behind me with a crack.

I tapped at the studio door, gently. 'Hello?' Annabel called from inside, a note of irritation in her voice. I peered through the crack, and she beckoned, with her usual cool smile. 'Violet,' she said, simply, as I stood beside the desk.

I fingered the hem of my skirt, nervously. I hadn't expected her to be here; didn't know, now, what I'd intended to say.

She laid down her pen, slowly, and stared at me. 'What can I do for you?'

'I . . . ' I began, nervously. 'I was wondering if you'd seen the others. If you . . . If you knew where they were?'

She gave a half-smile, pity mingling with what I guessed was irritation. 'I'm not here to assist with your social calendar, Violet,' she said, though without viciousness. I wondered what she knew, whether the girls had told her what they'd planned.

'I know,' I said. 'I'm really sorry. It's just . . . They're not home, and they're not answering the phone, and I don't know where else to—'

She raised a hand, and I stopped, feeling my heart thudding in my chest, cheeks hot with shame. 'Violet, I can't tell you anything they're not telling you themselves.'

She does know something, I thought. 'But—'

'Vi-o-let,' she said, again; each time she said my name it grew a little more clipped, as though saying every letter individually. 'Let's not be childish, now. You're a woman. You're better than this.'

I looked down at my hands, the chipped black of my nails, skin dried out by the sea. When I looked up again, she'd returned to her study, and I left, eyes stinging with tears.

In the corridor, bodies pressed up against one another, slick with sweat, clothes dank with spilled beer and reeking of smoke. Conflicting rhythms thudded like heartbeats; a strobe flickered from a room at the end of the hall, flash rebounding from cracked mirrors pressed into disco balls tacked to the ceiling above.

'Violet?' Manicured fingers gripped my arm, nails silver and pink; Nicky pulled me squealing into an angular, bony hug. 'You came!'

I smiled, loosened her grip. 'Couldn't resist.' Over her shoulder, a broad, sunburned boy in rugby colours pointed at the two of us, muttering something to a taller, bucktoothed teammate. They leered, and I glared back, eyes cold; felt my skin flush hot as they laughed, hate crawling fingers from rib to rib. 'Fuck you,' I mouthed; they laughed harder still.

'Have you seen Robin?' I said, when Nicky finally pulled away, the sweet scent of her perfume metallic, coppery on my lips.

'God, isn't this party amazing?' she said, as though she hadn't heard me. Perhaps she hadn't; the thrum of beats and constant yowls and yelps seemed to get into everything, drowning out my thoughts. 'I can't wait to live on my own.'

'You're not exactly alone in a place like this,' I said, watching a girl stumble through the corridor in pyjamas, clutching a steaming mug, dodging boys tackling each other into walls.

'What?'

'Nothing. Have you seen—'

'Fuck, I am so, so stoned. *So* stoned. And high, too. Can you be stoned and high in different ways at the same time, do you think?'

'Probably,' I said, peeling a ribbon of silly string from her shoulder, stuck with sweat. 'Listen, Nicky—'

'Yeah?' she said, eyes wide, rolling a little farther back in their sockets, even more doll-like than usual.

'Forget it,' I said.

'Are you looking for Robin?'

'Yes,' I said. 'Have you seen her?'

'I thought you were. You never come anywhere when I invite you.'

'Nicky—'

'It's fine; I get it. Whatever.'

I sighed, forced a smile, jaw tightening with the effort. 'I'm here because you invited me. I promise.' I paused, watched her steady herself. 'I'm here to see you. I was only wondering if you'd seen her around.'

'She's probably with Andy.' She rolled her eyes. 'He's so gross. What does she see in him anyway?'

'I have no idea—'

'I wondered the same thing with Emily, too. White guys with dreadlocks are just—'

'Wait, what?'

'Huh?'

'You mentioned Emily Frost.'

I stared at her; her eyes widened even more, mouth opening into a perfect little *o*.

'You don't *know*?'

'Know what?' I said, flatly.

'He was Emily's boyfriend when she died. I mean, only for about a week, but *still* – when she disappeared, he and Robin got together, like, immediately.' She bit her lip. 'The official story is, like, bonding over their grief or something. But . . . Well, it was kind of slutty on Robin's part.'

I stared at her. 'Just hers?'

'Well, god, no – I'm just as much of a feminist as the next

girl, obviously, so yeah, gross for him too. But, you know . . .
It was kind of weird. I heard—' She paused, looking around
for a moment, an almost comical nervousness in her eyes. 'I'd
heard she had a thing for him *way* before he and Emily got
together. Like, literally, months before.'

I thumbed a black scab on my elbow, picking it off; felt an
urge to stick dirty fingers in the wound and let it spoil. 'Weird,'
I said, finally.

'So weird.' She swayed a little; the broad-shouldered boy
pulled her from behind, arms wrapped around her waist. She
squealed, giggling, and let him pull her into another room,
waving at me as she disappeared. I saw the other boy watching
me, sneering in a way I supposed was intended to be seductive,
or cool; I turned, coldly, and continued down the corridor,
towards the flashing lights.

Compared to the stifling heat of the corridor, Andy's room
was cold, the windows open wide, swinging in the breeze.
Smoke drifted lazily above the group of students draped across
the camp bed and propped on chairs, beanbags, and blankets
scattered on the floor; the air was thick with tobacco and a
sour, boyish smell, damp and unwashed. I looked for Robin,
sitting among them, but the only girls in the room were two
with matching, bright-pink hair in the far corner, absorbed in
their own, intense conversation.

I sat among the gathered group, catching Andy's eye for a
moment; felt a brief, nervous thrill as he paused, mid-sentence,
and watched me sit down. I needed him to notice me: to tell
me where she was. I looked away, sidelong, at one of the other

boys; pursed my lips a little, in imitation of Emily – the photos
I'd seen in Robin's house, never quite meeting the camera's
gaze (though always, one felt, aware of herself being watched.
The will of the figure on the other side of the lens).

'The thing about losing a friend, like I have, in a tragic
way, one you don't see coming,' Andy said, taking a long swig
from a dented can, Adam's apple ticking steadily with the
gulp, 'is that it gives you real insight into what it means to be
alive. A deeper understanding of what's important in life.'

A boy beside me nudged my elbow, and smiled. 'He means
sex,' he said, licking his lips. I stared at him, wordlessly,
watched the grin fade. 'Bitch,' he said, rising heavily from the
floor, brushing my shoulder roughly as he walked away.

Andy went on, undeterred. 'I'm not saying I didn't think
about this stuff before – I've always leaned kind of heavily
towards, you know, deep thinking. The important stuff. Even
though it's hard. But seeing a guy like that – a real good guy,
one of the best – cut down in the prime of his life like that?
I mean . . . It's fucked up. Fucked.'

A few of those gathered nodded sagely, while the others
stared vacantly at whatever luminous glow had gathered just
behind their eyes; one, hoodie pulled up around his
red-blotched face, raised a bottle of some tropical spirit high
in the air. 'To Tom,' he slurred, and the others raised their
glasses in response. Only Andy didn't drink to this, staring,
jaw hanging slack, at me. I stared back, my heart thudding at
the mention of Tom's name.

The floor thundered; the room overrun, suddenly, by
the rugby team, Nicky raised high on shoulders, squealing,

313

slapping hands with another girl, whose single shoe dropped to the floor and skidded across the carpet. She lost her balance, arms wheeling, and grabbed a handful of fairy lights pinned to the wall, the whole thread crackling down and pitching the room into darkness. 'Hey, dickhead!' one of the boys howled, stumbling over me towards Andy, 'got any weed?'

Andy remained still, staring up at him, dead eyes peering through the darkness. 'Get out of my room,' he said, coldly.

'Not until you hook us up,' the boy said, grinning; one tooth missing, I noticed, eyes adjusting to the dark. He had a fat lower lip, the upper merging straight into his nose, like a snout; tiny, red eyes, like pinpricks in wet skin. The kind of boy who made himself apelike, 'character' supposedly counteracting his hideousness. And somehow, it seemed to work; he licked his lips and grimaced at a girl behind, who giggled, hysterically, back.

'Get out of my fucking room,' Andy said, again. A ribbon of tension hung in the air; people began standing, sensing what was coming.

Nicky grabbed my shoulder from above as she stood. 'Let's get out of here.'

I looked up. 'Nah,' I said. 'I'm fine.' I felt a strange thrill, a sharpening of teeth; let go of Nicky's hand as the guy stumbled back, gurgling some incomprehensible call. I looked back as the other boy punched Andy with a solid, meaty thwack; laughed as Andy lunged forwards and bit him, hard, in the upper arm. The boys howled and roared, and people stumbled out of the room, into the corridor outside, the walls shaking with the footsteps as they ran.

I stepped backwards, into the corner, and stood, watching the boys fight. It was strange and somehow sad, the way they lunged at each other, all sinew and flesh; beast-like. *At least when girls hurt each other, we're clever about it,* I thought, grimly.

It was inevitable: the lumbering one won, through strength alone, though – to Andy's credit – he fought back with claws and teeth. Still, when it was over, the boy stumbled into the bedside table, wheezing like a boar, and dragged its contents out. Finding what he was looking for, he disappeared out into the corridor, to riotous cheers: a hero's welcome. Andy lay on the bed, not moving; I wondered if he knew I was there.

Slowly, he raised himself up onto an elbow; groaned, and lay back down.

'You're alive, then?' I said. He flinched, craning his neck to look.

'Oh,' he said, neck rolling back. 'It's you.'

I stepped forwards, flicked on the light. He hissed; I flicked it off again. 'Want a tissue or something?' I said. 'A plaster, maybe? An ambulance?'

'Fuck off,' he groaned. 'I'm fine.'

I leaned over the bed; his face was slick with blood, one eye swollen fat, pulsing blue. 'You don't look fine.'

'I'm *fine.*'

'Okay then. Have you seen Robin?'

'Ahhh,' he said. 'That's why you're here. I should've guessed. Not to offer comfort in this,' he rolled up to sitting, steadying himself, hands gripping the mattress, 'my time of need.'

'I offered. You said no.'

'I didn't realize you were offering *that*.'

I retched. 'Trust me. I wasn't. But I can get you a glass of water if you want?'

'One thing leads to another, with things like that . . . So, yeah, if you don't mind.'

I rinsed a cup in the sink, cloudy water spitting from the tap.

'Thanks,' he said, spitting into it; a thick glob of blood spiralling, strands splitting apart.

'So . . . have you seen her?'

He shrugged. 'Not for a couple of days. Maybe three. I don't know.'

'She said you'd broken up.'

'Yeah?' he said, voice tart with disinterest. 'I can't say I'm surprised. She's been kind of a cunt lately.' He leaned over, groaning as he reached under the bed to reveal a tray, scattered with grinders, papers, and discarded bags.

I felt a prickle of hatred. *How dare you*, I thought, a reflex of disgust. *How dare you call her that?* I blushed, remembering myself. 'Yeah,' I said, finally. 'She really has.'

'Ooof.' He laughed, pinching strands of tobacco between fingers. 'I was joking. But you sound like you really mean it.'

I rolled my eyes. 'Whatever.'

'She's told me all about you, you know,' he said, eyes on me as he licked the paper, slowly. 'I know *all* your secrets.'

There was something about his manner that set my teeth on edge (a turn of phrase I only understood at that moment): the patronizing attitude of a public schoolboy (one which many don't grow out of, a smugness and superiority they see as their right, a distinctly male trait). I could see him, dread-locked and pale now, decades hence, some shark-toothed hedge fund manager, with a 'creative' bent, stalked by the pang of nostalgia for his university days, 'changed' by a year spent 'helping' communities in some third-world country. You know the type. I've seen him at art shows, buying pornographic paintings with no comprehension of their meaning; I've over-heard him explaining his 'collection' to birdlike, glass-eyed women in galleries, before taking them out to dinner, where he will order their meal for them, and talk endlessly, drearily, of himself.

'I doubt that,' I said.

'You look good, by the way,' he said, smoke thickening the air with every word. 'You lose some weight?'

It took a moment to realize the thrust of his conversation, the leering threat in his tone. I stared at him, blankly.

'Can't take a compliment, huh?'

'Give me a smoke,' I said, willing for a distraction.

'I don't think you realize quite how manipulative she is,' he said, as though catching my thought. 'She just uses people. She used Emily. She's used me. And – judging by the way you're looking at me now – she's just about done using you, too.'

'What?'

'"Ooh, Violet,"' he said, his voice reedy in imitation, '"she's totally in love with me. It's pathetic."'

'She didn't say that.'

'Oh, trust me, she did. What's the phrase? "With friends like that . . ."' He began rolling another joint; the one I held was hardly touched. I kept it, the smoke scratching at my still-raw throat. *She wouldn't,* I thought, though I knew it wasn't true: of course she would. It was the way she talked about everyone else – the way she talked about them, to me. I could hear the sting in her voice as she said it, aloof, above it all.

She doesn't care about me, I thought. *She made me think she did, and now she's left me. They all have. They've left me to take the blame for the things they've done.*

I tucked my legs underneath me at the far end of the bed; Andy leaned back against the wall, lit a smoke. We stared at each other for a while, the two of us left behind. 'I hate you,' I said, staring at him.

He took a long drag, thoughtfully; scratched at his beard, wincing as fingers reached the growing bruise. 'Doesn't make it any less true, though, does it?' He winked. 'It's just you and me now, kid.'

I looked at the closed door, and thought of Tom, his hands on me. The memory made the hairs on my arms bristle, a hot sweat crawl down my neck. And then, I thought of Robin, and wondered how she could love a boy like this. I thought of her, and how hurt she'd be by his cruel, flippant tone; and then, how hurt *I* was, by what she'd done to me. 'Sex, love, revenge, and death,' she'd said, as we rode the elevator to the tower, after that first night in the graveyard. 'That's what all these classes are about. They're all the same.'

'Andy,' I said, after a moment.

He didn't open his eyes; head back, skull showing through. 'Mmm-hmm?'

I leaned forwards, rolling onto my knees. He opened one eye (might have opened both, I suppose, though the swelling made it impossible to tell) and smiled, and I hated him with such violence that my bones ached. But in that moment, I hated Robin still more.

I held my breath, looking down at his greasy skin, his filthy hair; the bloody nose, cracked lip. The pulsing vein at his temple, rivering over his skull. I leaned in, and I kissed him, his breath yeast-stale and clotted with smoke. He pushed his tongue between my teeth, groping, possessive little prods, and I moaned, lowering myself onto his lap. *I hate you*, I thought, as he pressed dirty thumbs into my skin, nails black and dry inside me; I swallowed down my nausea, and clawed at his back, feeling cysts split under my fingers. He cried out in pain, and I moaned back, pretended to enjoy myself: performed a great, groaning, filthy show.

When it was done – when he was done – I wiped myself down with a crisp, mouldering t-shirt I found by the side of the bed, and pulled my jeans up my thighs, arms aching with the effort. I felt ruined, and gut sick; overwhelmed with the absence of pleasure in this stupid victory, dirtied by a betrayal I might never shake off.

'I've got to go,' I said. He rolled over, his nakedness shameless and nauseating, the protruding bones and mottled skin of a corpse. He murmured a goodbye, and closed his eyes, a smear of blood dripping into his pillow.

In the corridor outside, I caught Nicky's eye, over the shoulder of some broad-shouldered, bullish sports player. I saw her eyes widen, following me down the hall; swung my hips side to side as I passed, so she'd know just what I'd done.

I walked through the empty streets, the sun lingering low over the trees, shadows elongated in the afternoon light; my arms burned hot, limbs sticky under my skirt – the whole town possessed by a soporific heat. It was airless, as though encased in amber. Doughy men lay cadaverous in the sun, turning pink, moving only to raise cans to gaping, toothless mouths, the air stinking of hot tarmac and blackened meat. My sunglasses were heart-shaped, lips sticky-sweet with gloss. It had been three days since the party, and I still hadn't heard from the girls.

It was only when she was a few feet away that I realized it was her: this skinny, peroxide-haired thing, skin mottled with the beginnings of a burn. 'Come on,' Robin said, grabbing my arm and spinning me round as she passed.

'What the fuck—'

'Just fucking come, will you?'

I followed as she ran through the streets, jumping over cracks, passing the oddly comforting graffiti that hung above the railway bridge: 'Everything will be OK'. In the shade, she stopped and leaned against the wall, tendons in her neck fluttering as she ran fingers through a tangled mass of hair.

I slowed down, stopped, chest pounding. 'What's going on?' I said, once I'd caught my breath.

She folded her arms around herself as though cold. The bridge rattled overhead, a rolling, syncopated thunder echoing for what seemed like forever, disappearing in an instant. We stood in silence, staring at each other.

'What did you do to your hair?'

She stared at me, eyebrow raised. 'Seriously? That's your big question right now?'

I shrugged. 'It looks nice.'

'Thanks.' She felt around in her pockets, digging out a stick of gum. She tore it in two, offered me a dusty piece.

'Where . . . Where have you been?' I said, at last.

She rolled her eyes. 'Literally as grounded as it is possible for a person to be. No thanks to you, dickhead.'

'What did I do?'

She handed me a wrap, powdery white and crushed. I recognized it instantly: the one I'd lost at the fair. 'Look familiar?'

I stared at her, blankly. 'Where did you get that?'

'Mum found it. In her trinket box.' She snorted. 'At least when I go through your family's stuff, I don't leave proof.'

'Oh my god,' I said. 'What happened?'

'Don't worry. I didn't tell her it was yours. Not that she believed me, but . . . Well, whatever. I'm in endless, irrevocable shit. So, thanks, Vivi.'

I blushed. 'Fuck,' I said. 'I am *so* sorry.' I thought of Andy; shuddered at the thought of him, instinctively. And then, of Nicky. Of what I'd done, and what she knew.

Robin shrugged. 'It's fine. Although I've been calling you all day. Have you spoken to Alex?'

'No?'

'Seriously – where the fuck have you *been*?'

'I've been sick,' I said, weakly. 'I had, like . . . The flu, or something.'

'Yuck,' she said, stepping back, making a cross with two fingers. 'Don't give it to me.'

'I'm over it, now. But what's wrong with Alex?'

'She's fine. But Grace's dad went mental. Or rather, *more* mental. She's only just got out of the hospital.'

'Oh my god.'

'Yeah. She's living at Alex's for now. Going over to see her is the only reason my mum's let me out.' She looked around, as though imagining herself being watched. 'Are you okay?' she said. 'You look kinda freaked out.'

'I – no,' I said. 'I'm fine.' I steadied myself, one breath at a time. 'Can I come?'

'Duh. I've been looking for you everywhere. Come on.' She grabbed my arm, and we walked into the sunlight. She rubbed the gooseflesh on my arm, gently; but still, a chill ran heady through my blood.

The house was deathly quiet, the air thick and musty; I smelled rotting food, a wisp of smoke. 'How long has your mum been away?' I asked Alex, as I walked into the kitchen.

'A few weeks,' she said, sliding takeaway boxes and bottles into a black plastic bag, while Robin tinkered with the old record player, the three of us jumping as it burst into sudden, lively song. I knew the voice, the song: Nina Simone. Mum's favourite, back when she used to sing along to the radio, dancing with Anna in her arms. I started running the taps, ostensibly to wash the dishes piled on every surface. (Though in truth I was simply looking for some task with which to occupy myself, to escape the need for conversation. For what could I say? What could any of us say, now?) 'Leave it,' Alex said, turning abruptly to me. 'She won't be back for a while.'

Chastened, I went into the lounge, light seeping through the closed curtains, examining the heavy books and brass sculptures, masks and trinkets that lined the walls. Once-unfamiliar names now stood out, remembered: histories of great women, goddesses and mortals; tales of haggard witches and high priestesses immortalized in dusky bronze; skulls, pieces of animals dried and dead. I picked up my favourites, one by one: the baby, pierced with iron bolts; the painting of Dagol, a howling beast; a set of teeth, filed to bitter points. A porcelain hand, lined in black ink, offering futures without guarantees.

We sat in the same formation as we had that first night at Alex's house, when all was possibility, our friendship a light, gorgeous thing. Now, though, as my friends talked, and laughed, and sipped the sweet champagne Alex had found in the basement ('Dad's favourite,' she'd said, waving two bottles in each hand), I felt weighted down by the force of it. The things we'd done together – the things *I* had done to them – all, now, a mess, a web from which I couldn't extricate myself.

It had all seemed like games, before, when we'd stood in the cove, giggling as we summoned beasts we didn't quite believe in (or, more accurately, we didn't believe in our power to invoke). But we'd fallen so far since then, and I, now, was the worst. I'd believed myself betrayed and betrayed them in return. And now there was no way back.

'I can't believe you didn't mention it before,' Robin was saying, as I dragged myself back to the conversation.

Alex reached across Grace for the bottle, placing a gentle hand on her arm as she did so, whispering something I couldn't catch. Her make-up clotted thick around a bruise we all pretended not to see. 'It's all been arranged over the last couple of days. And anyway, I'm sure you two have plans, don't you?'

'I'm not pissed because I want an invite – although, also, fuck you,' Robin said. She took a long sip of her drink, caught my eye. 'But don't you think it'll look suspicious?'

Alex looked at Robin, an exaggerated confusion on her face. 'What do you mean?'

'I mean disappearing this soon after . . . You know.'

She laughed. 'Oh, shit, of course – taking a holiday. In summer. The classic actions of a homicidal maniac. I'm *so* glad you thought of that.' She took a sip of her drink, and sighed. 'Anyway, nobody's looking at us. The police found the tape in his office, so that part's covered, and . . . '

'Where are you going?' I said, dazed and heady with the champagne. The three of them turned to me as though they'd forgotten I was there.

'Europe,' Alex said, flatly. 'Mum's doing a research trip, and she's got a sofa going spare, so . . . She said we could go along.'

Robin mimicked her, 'Europe. Jolly fucking good.'

'She asked! What did you want us to do? Say no? Stay here with you being all—'

'You know what, Alex, go fuck yourself. I don't—'

I looked at Grace, who gave a long, shallow sigh. 'Guys. Can we just . . . Can we relax a bit?'

Alex gave a conciliatory smile, looked over at me for support. 'It's only six weeks,' she said. 'We'll be back in no time. And then it'll be September, and we'll actually have to . . . Well, pass.' I flushed, thinking of my grades, which had slipped ever further in the end-of-year exams. I'd been given special dispensation, of course – the Dean's perceived mark, an imagined victim (though I didn't have to say this to anyone; the idea seemed to come from those around me, their fears left unsaid). But if I wanted to leave next year, I'd have to work to catch up.

'She's right,' I said, Robin rolling her eyes in response. I stood up, wanting to move on – not just from the conversation, but the house, the town, the mess we were in. If they wanted to leave, I couldn't blame them. I felt the impulse, just the same. 'Let's chill out. I'll get more wine,' I said, stepping out into the corridor, feeling the thump of my heart, heavy and aching in my chest.

In the kitchen, I closed my eyes, for a moment, and imagined myself free; pressed my fingernails into scarred palm, and returned, smiling, the wine swilling blood-like into each upheld glass.

Chapter 16

In spite of all that came after, the last day of the academic year still fills me with a strange joy, a melancholy somehow bittersweet. It's in the corridors charged with excitement and anticipation, the leavers' class on the brink of adulthood, adventures sprawling in front of them. That prickle of sadness, the first bloom of nostalgia; the air saturated with carefully chosen pop songs streaming through the speakers that line the halls as students leave campus for the penultimate time – home, to change for the Summer Ball.

Perhaps as a distraction from the ever-present shadow of the Dean, and the rumours that hung heavy over Elm Hollow as the term came to a close, the student body was for the first time allowed to vote on the ball's theme, with sections of the organizing committee campaigning across campus with decadent visuals and props. A stilt walker stalked the Quad shouting 'Carnival!' while a group of girls in bodices (handed blankets by disapproving teachers before every class) campaigned for Moulin Rouge; flapper girls danced to Gatsby jazz, while a small minority campaigned enthusiastically for the Gothic, dressed in black, grinning fanged in a lonely corner of the cafeteria. More than once, the sight of these rounding a corner had made my heart lurch, sick; I'd laugh, grimly, after the split-second thrust of horror, the figures unseen remaining infinitely more horrifying.

When the vote came, however, only a small group of students voted, and each for their own themes. The deciding vote came down to an even split between Masquerade and, simply, 'White'. The Headmaster, exhausted by the year and with (he felt – the student body inclined to disagree) more pressing matters on his mind, told the girls to work it out between themselves. Thus we ended up with the merging of the two: a White Masquerade ball.

It seems ridiculous, now, that something so childish could assume such importance – one cannot help, as an adult, but cringe a little in the telling – but, raised on high-school movies of prom queens and kings, of kisses under blooming lights, of music and dancing and the all-pervading nostalgia of adolescence, none of us were entirely immune. Even we had obsessed over masks and dresses – a respite, I suppose, from the horror that seemed to surround us. That seemed, sometimes, to come from within.

Annabel, in keeping with the theme, had returned to the subject of tragedy for our final class of the year: theatrical masks leering dead-eyed, hung from lamps and propped on books, strung from roof beams, swinging with the brush of bird and bat wings above. She paced the room, a white powder print on her bare arm, nails brittle white: I wondered what she'd been making before class, what plaster of Paris creation she'd been moulding out of view.

'It is the enduring tale of the jealous,' she said, pointing to the books spread on the table between us, 'the living force of envy itself. A deadly sin, come to bear on the family of Adam and Eve, whose Original Sin – our mother's sin, the female weakness – casts its shadow on our culture even now, like something primitive: teeth bared in anger, the shadowed cast of a jawline in a hollow stare. "I will be a restless wanderer on the earth," Cain says. And in the Tuileries, the stone Cain walks torn with his head in his hands; in Glasgow's Botanic Gardens, he sits forever in a sculpture named *Cain: My Punishment Is Greater Than I Can Bear*.

'So says the Bible, and all that follows: envy, the sin against one's own, the root of all evils.' She looked at each of us in turn, Robin craned forward, as though leaning into her glow. 'Still, like all things, the ancients did it better. No: ancient *women* did it better. The Christian painters of the Renaissance fixated on the tales of men, their revenge noble, powerful, dripping with meaning. And yet no man can outdo Medea – to whom I always seem destined to return,' she said, smiling, 'in the art of revenge. She is the spectre that haunts the very image of masculinity, the one who took a bloody blade to the patriarchy itself. She was the only survivor, walking from Athens wearing the blood of her children and – in my imagining, at least – laughing. Laughing, because the worst was done, and she was made divine.

'Is this motherhood?' she said, and for a moment, our eyes met. 'Medea, who in the *Metamorphoses* visits Hecate, the witch goddess, and in Euripides embodies her: she drives into the heart of herself, and emerges changed, the inevitable result of illumination, shadow.' She sighed. 'Turning oneself inside out, through screaming pain and fear and horror, is – to many ancient Greeks, at the very least – the pathway into mother-hood. For Medea, though, it is the way out. And so she becomes eternal, wearing the blood of her children in her hair.'

She leaned her elbows on the back of a chair, and a silence fell between us, we four students and our teacher, whose every word meant so much to us (indeed, I still shudder at the memory, the flicker of the eternal that she seemed to be able to conjure with her words). 'The fact of tragedy, then, is this: we're doomed to hurt the ones we love, faults amplified from fleeting thought to heinous crime. The deadly sins are just that – our furies turning fate, which in turn begets fury at our fallen condition: each the shadow of the other. And above it all, the light of the moon: the goddesses watch on – Hecate, and her kin, Medea.'

The bells rang above, and outside cheers echoed from the main building; the four of us sat, still, in silence, a thrill lingering in the air. Annabel smiled, and we stood to be given a brief hug, Annabel's fingers seeming to take root around our bare arms in the moment she held us. It seemed like a goodbye, though – as we told each other, after Annabel had left – it was only for the summer. How little, then, we knew. How things would change in the coming hours, these brief moments of joy irretrievably, impossibly lost.

While the first students began to arrive back on campus, the decorators now departed from the Great Hall, the four of us sat in the clock tower, mercifully cool in the dry summer heat. Below, theatrical masks hung between the trees, their eyes lit by fairy lights, sky turning coppery behind. Every one of the buildings around the Quad seemed to glow, the light from the grand arched windows streaming spotlights on the grass. There was, it seemed, a magic to it, a sweetness I hadn't caught in months – summer flowers, I supposed, though I hoped, still, that perhaps we'd been released from the horror of all that had come before.

'Such a pretty evening,' Grace said, joining me at the window. She handed me a glass of wine, Robin at last having finally broken into the cabinet (after several months of trying, hairpins and paperclips littered around it on the floor).

An unspoken truce had settled between us, for the night, at least. All week, four white dresses (handmade by Grace, after a style she'd found in one of the magazines) had hung from the book-cases Alex used as end-tables on either side of her bed. They were simple, elegant, plain – unlike the glittering monstrosities girls showed each other on furtive Polaroids, all hoops and corsets, hideous in their decadence. I smoothed the soft fabric against my skin, joined the other girls.

'Oh my god, listen to this one,' Robin said, leafing through a yearbook. '"When it rains look for rainbows. When it's dark look for stars."'

Alex groaned. 'That is horrendous.'

'And—' Robin snorted. '*And*— "I'll be waiting, everlasting, like the sun." Isn't that from a song?'

'Wait – wasn't yours?' I said, sitting down beside her. Alex snickered. 'From a song, I mean.'

'Yeah, but a *good* song. Imagine wanting your high-school

experience to be immortalized by the words of the great poet Sporty Spice.'

'I'm pretty sure they don't write their songs,' Alex said, taking the book from Robin. 'Anyway, the quotes aren't the best part. I love the "Remember Me" pages. "I'd most like to be remembered for . . ."' she said, in a pitch-perfect beauty queen voice.

'"Murdering a teacher in his own home,"' Robin laughed. 'Probably wouldn't get past the editorial—'

She stopped, mid-sentence. Alex and Grace stared past us, ashen-faced and open-mouthed. I turned, following their gaze; the door to the little kitchen slightly ajar. 'Did you just . . .' Grace said, looking at Alex. 'Did you hear something?'

Alex nodded. Robin looked around at the door, then at me. 'You're being paranoid,' she said, though the words seemed hollow, as though she didn't believe them herself. 'There's nothing there.'

'I didn't hear anything,' I added, nervously. 'Maybe it was a bird.'

'Or a bat,' Robin said.

'Shhhh.' Alex stood, slowly, and walked towards the door, Grace two steps behind. She placed a hand on the door, and flung it back, the brass hitting the bookshelves, a porcelain doll falling to the floor with a crack. 'What the *hell*—'

'I'm sorry— I'm really, I didn't mean—' Nicky stood in the little kitchen, her back pressed against the far wall, already dressed for the ball.

Alex looked at Robin, eyes flashing with anger. She turned back to Nicky. 'How did you get up here?'

'I didn't—' she began, voice trembling.

'Nicky, how did you—'

'The door . . . the door wasn't locked this afternoon. I was just looking—'

'For what?'

Nicky sighed; closed her eyes for a moment, her composure settling. 'For whatever you guys were doing up here. I know you've been coming up here all year.'

'You nosey bitch,' Robin said. 'I fucking *knew* you were—'

'Robin,' Alex said, coldly. 'Calm down.' She turned to Nicky. 'Have you been listening?'

Nicky shook her head. 'I couldn't hear anything.' Alex and Grace exchanged a look.

'Seriously,' she added. 'I was just waiting for you to leave so I could go.'

'She's lying,' Robin said. 'Of course she heard—'

'*Robin*,' Alex said, again. 'Shut up, would you? Just for once?'

Robin rolled her eyes and stalked over to the east face, bristling. I looked at Nicky, her cheeks flushed red, sweat lingering in the well of her collarbones. 'You should go,' I said, quietly, sensing my opportunity. If I was kind, she might not tell Robin what she'd seen; one secret traded for another. 'If Annabel finds you up here, she'll . . . '

'Fine,' Nicky said, grabbing her mask – white feathers, diamonds, a silvery ribbon tie – and heading towards the door. 'The ball's starting soon, anyway.' She gave a conciliatory smile. 'I'll see you there?'

I walked with her to the door. 'Yeah, we'll be there soon.'

We stood in silence as the elevator rolled down; until the metal grate creaked shut, echoing from the bottom of the stairwell. I closed the door.

'She heard us,' I said.

Alex looked at me. 'Are you sure?'

I nodded. 'There's no way she'd have left like that if she didn't already know something.'

'Fuck,' Alex said, slamming both hands on the desk. 'Fuck, fuck, fuck.'

'Maybe she won't say anything,' Grace said, the words almost a question.

'She wouldn't have anything *to* say if Robin hadn't—' Alex spat.

Robin spun around, glaring. 'Oh, fuck off, Alex. It's always my fault, isn't it?'

'Well, you had to go and bring up the Dean. You and your stupid—'

'How was I supposed to know she was hiding in the fucking cupboard? I thought it was just us!'

'Even if it was, it's not fucking funny. You always—'

'Guys,' I said, my heart thudding in my chest. 'Please. This isn't going to help anything.'

'She's right,' Grace said. 'We should get down there. See what she's doing.'

'And then what?' Robin said, voice trembling a little. She steadied herself. 'We can't let her . . . We can't let her tell.'

'No, we can't,' Alex said, sitting down on the sofa. She looked at Robin. 'Where's the book?'

'Alex—' I said. 'We . . . '

'Where is it?' she said again.

Robin stood, walked over to the desk, and crouched down. She reached up into the hollow under the table, and the book fell to the floor with a thud.

Alex looked at me. 'It's been here all this time?'

I shrugged. 'I didn't know.'

'So what do we do?' Robin said, opening the book wide on the desk. As she flicked through the pages, light reflected from the gold leaf, casting sharp beams along the walls.

'We tried this before,' I said, searching for objections. 'It didn't work.'

'You must've done it wrong,' Alex said. 'Most of these rites need four, anyway.'

'But she's not – I mean, we can't—'

'Violet, look. I know you like her – I know you think she's your "friend",' she said, making scare quotes in the air. 'But this is dangerous. She knows what we did – you said so yourself.'

'I know, but—'

'And anyway, who left the gate unlocked? I haven't been up here all day – have you, Grace?'

Grace shook her head; Robin did the same.

I blanched. I'd been up, briefly, between classes, to fetch a textbook. 'Annabel might have . . . ' I began, the words trailing away. Annabel was so cautious about getting caught. She'd never leave the gate unlocked. There was no denying it. This was all my fault. I sat down, steadying myself, while the girls gathered around the book, whispering hushed suggestions and reading passages aloud.

'That one,' Alex said, at last. 'That's it. Let's get the stuff.'

Robin grabbed a lighter from the kitchen, while Grace pulled four red tapered candles from a drawer, handing one to me as she passed. 'Come on,' she said, squeezing my hand. 'It'll be okay.'

I stood at the table, where our masks sat, antlers intertwined. They'd sat on the shelves all year, as though ornamental; but when Robin pulled one down as a joke, a long, white ribbon unwound from behind. The other three were the same, old masks stolen from another time, their long, sharp faces cracked and cold. Only Alex had objected to our wearing them to the ball, only to be swiftly outvoted by the three of us. 'We'll be like Flidais,' Grace had said. 'The goddess of the woods. Ruler of wild beasts.'

'Sounds about right.' Robin had laughed, the mask slipping as she tied the ribbon through her hair. 'Beasts, demons, witches – and us.'

Each of us stood, now, at the table's edge, the book open in front of Alex, who lit a wreath of dried flowers and dropped it into a glass bowl in the centre. Robin lit her candle, and the three of us leaned in to steal the flame. I saw the hairs on her arm stand up, and felt mine rise to meet them. *I don't want to do this*, I told myself, though I felt a dull ache, a quiet longing awakening in the pit of my stomach.

'Ready?' Alex said, looking at each of us in turn.

I nodded, feeling a drop of wax begin to roll down the candle, bracing for the burn as it reached my hand.

She took a deep breath, and closed her eyes. 'Goddess, hear us. We four offer our spirits to you this summer night. We come to you with our souls open, our hearts cool and clear.' The wreath began to crackle, the smell tranquilizing, bitter-sweet. 'We ask of you to help us keep your secrets, and our own, by silencing the one who would speak them.'

I looked at Robin, who stared down into the candle's flame; felt the red wax crawl across my thumb, oozing heat.

'We thank you, goddess, for your Furies and their work, and send them to—' She stopped, coughed, the wreath smoking black.

Her eyes flickered to the doorway, where Annabel stood, staring at the masks on the desk, the steaming bowl. She closed her eyes, as though summoning patience. 'Do *not* tell me you're doing what I think you're doing.'

'We're not—'

She raised a hand. 'Robin, don't. Don't. Put those candles out.' She shook her head. 'I thought better of you girls; I really did.'

'But Annabel,' Grace ventured, nervously. 'Nicky found out. She came up here.'

Annabel stared at her, eyes cold and dark. 'So you decided to do *this*? I cannot *imagine* why you'd think . . . '

'Not just about the room,' Alex said, her voice strained, the words seeming caught in her throat. 'She . . . She found out what we did. To . . . To the Dean.'

She knows? I thought, glancing at Alex; felt a flicker of envy at imagined conversations spark, then disappear, as I looked at her eyes. They were desperate and hopeful, willing Annabel to acknowledge the things we had done. To say that she'd known all along; that she understood.

Annabel closed her eyes again, as though choosing her words. Drew breath, stopped herself; took another slow, deep breath. The usual rush of wind against the clock faces, the rustle of ravens and bats high above, all seemed to hush, waiting for her to speak: an endless, aching silence, the truth of what we'd done lingering cruelly in the air.

She sighed. 'You know what, girls? Just go.'

'But—' Robin began.

'I don't want to hear another word out of any of you. Go on. Get out.'

We crossed the Quad in silence, crushing blossom underfoot, our masks leaving sleek, black shadows in the grass. Robin brushed her hand against mine, and we walked with the backs of them touching, gently, towards the Great Hall. The sky was bruised with the sunset, the fields beyond yellow as though to spite the coming dark; our campus was as picturesque as it had ever been. We passed the wych elm, Emily's portrait still smiling from among the faded cards and trinkets, her candles lit for the very last time. Over the summer, we'd been informed in our final assembly, the tree would be pulled down at last. We were to pay our respects before we left.

Girls dressed in white lingered outside the hall, posing for photos, brushing sweat from their foreheads and cheeks with sticky powders. Boys too – drafted in from the nearest school and given stern warnings about appropriate behaviour on the Elm Hollow campus – looked wide-eyed at the school grounds, and then, at us, as we passed without looking back.

There were gasps as we walked through Reception, conversations turning hushed and icy as we walked by. Never had I experienced such pleasure at being the centre of attention – the centre of all things, it felt, as I took Robin's hand and we opened the doors to the ballroom, entering two by two. The ceiling of the dome was lit with creamy spotlights shining up to the arches, and pendant lamps swaying gently in the air's breath; great sheets of organza hung from wall to wall, and the statues of angels and demons looked down upon us as the gathered students seemed at once to turn, for a moment, and stare. We walked slowly through the room, to the edge of the hall, and stood, watching as the dance resumed, feeling the rhythmic rumble of footsteps and the slow pulse of the bass in our teeth.

The band began to play a slow song, grimly sentimental – *I'll love you, love you, I will love you* seemingly the full extent of the lyrics, repeated ad nauseam – and we watched as students paired off, rocking gently with the beat.

'This is so cheesy,' Robin said, her voice muffled through the mask.

'It's not that bad.' I looked at the swirling blur of students dancing in the centre of the room, under the white hangings, brushing up billows of dry ice and dust in low clouds. On the ceiling, the frescoes were given a new lease of life, heightened by the transformation of the room. The painting of the Moirai, a somewhat dubious pastiche of the panels that line the Sistine Chapel, now seemed alive with beauty, cleansed of the faults that leapt out in daylight. I saw Clotho's thread in gold leaf, connecting with the gilded edges that separated each of the panels, binding all of their tales together; Lachesis examined the thread, her eyes narrowed in concentration as she stooped to read the viewer's fate, and Atropos stood with her shears raised high, prepared to cut the thin thread of life, right above our heads.

'Do you see her anywhere?' Grace whispered, lifting her mask to get a better look as she searched for Nicky among the crowd. I shook my head.

Robin hooked her arm around mine. 'Come on – I need some punch.'

'I think I need something stronger than that,' I said, my voice echoing inside the mask.

We walked the edges of the ballroom, followed by Grace and Alex, who leaned into one another, absorbed in their own, private conversation. 'Do you really think she'll tell?' Robin said, eyes flickering under the skull's thin seams.

'I don't know,' I said. 'If we could talk to her – maybe tell her it was a joke—'

She snorted. 'Funny joke, huh?'

'Hilarious,' I said. 'But everyone knows your sense of humour is way off, so . . . '

She slapped my arm with the back of her hand, nails leaving a scratch. 'At least I *have* a sense of humour.'

I rolled my eyes, realized she couldn't see. 'Whatever,' I said, reaching for the sticky ladle resting up against the punch bowl and filling two cups.

She took one, and raised it in a toast, sliding her mask back with her free hand. 'Let's hope this is spiked.'

'Here's hoping,' I said, taking a sip, the drink sickly sweet and warm.

Alex stepped forward, holding her mask. 'We're going to go,' she said, coldly.

'We just got here.' Robin handed her a cup. 'Have a drink at least.'

'No,' Alex said, pushing it away. 'I'm fine. Thanks.'

'Alex, come on,' I said, looking at Grace for support. 'Don't let Nicky—'

A scream erupted from the dance floor, and we turned, the teachers stepping dutifully forward. 'Put me down!' Melanie Barker squealed, writhing in the arms of a boy whose tux was stained punch pink. 'Put me down, now!'

I turned back to the girls. 'Please don't go. Just stay a bit longer. Please.'

'You guys stay,' Grace said, with a weak smile. 'Have fun. We've got to be up early tomorrow, anyway. We wouldn't be much fun even if we stuck around.'

'Fine,' Robin said. 'Go. Whatever.'

I looked at Alex and Grace apologetically; we shared an awkward hug, Grace wincing as I caught a bruise blossoming at the nape of her neck. 'Have a great summer,' she said, squeezing my hands tight in hers. 'We'll miss you.'

They parted the crowd as they left, masks back on, antlers reaching out towards the ceiling above. I nudged Robin, gently. 'Come on. Let's have some fun.'

She sighed. 'I guess if we're going to prison tomorrow, we ought to make the most of it.'

'That's the spirit.'

And so, in spite of everything – the terrible music, the stares of our fellow students; in spite of Nicky, and all she knew (or didn't know, I told myself, as though saying it might make it true); in spite of Annabel, Alex, and Grace – we danced. We danced on tiptoe, as though we might catch the music with our bare hands, spiralling out of control, not caring a damn about the bitter stares of the girls we pushed out of our way. We danced until our feet ached, and the air was thick with sweat, and the lights went up. We danced a little more, while the students streamed onto the steps outside, lighting lanterns that floated into the dark, sparkling through the glass centre of the dome.

'Girls,' Professor Malcolm said. 'It's time to go.'

'But I'm not ready to leave,' Robin whined.

He smiled. 'Go on. Off you trot. I'll see you both next year.'

'I don't want to go,' Robin said, again, as she sat with a thud on the steps. The buses were lined up outside, students teetering towards them, stumbling in heels, faces wet with tears that seemed too much, an excess of drama.

'Me neither,' I said. 'Not with them, anyway.'

'We could go to the tower.' She leaned back onto her elbows. 'Hide out there for the summer.'

I looked down at her, lit by the headlights of the first bus to leave. 'There's wine in the tower.' I shuddered, the sweat drying cold against my bare arms. 'And my coat.'

'You, my friend,' she said, reaching for my hand, 'are a genius.' I pulled her up, and we walked towards the tower, lurking in the shadows as the buses drove away. When darkness finally fell, the moon was erasing itself; the air cool and crisp with cut grass, hissing with bugs. We walked arm in arm, silent but for the click of our shoes on stone.

'I can't believe you need a coat,' she said, unlocking the grate and slipping inside. 'It's a gorgeous night.'

'It goes with my outfit.'

She rolled her eyes. 'Whatever. Wuss.'

I opened the door to the tower room, bowing as Robin passed. She stopped dead, looked back at me with something like horror. I followed her eyes, surveying the mess. An empty wine bottle without a glass, the muddy scrape of a heel on the edge of the desk; papers scattered all about, furiously strewn, as though some storm had blown in through the clock face and turned the room around; all chaos and disorder. I walked past notes and pictures, torn from their books; I saw a thin vein of ink dripping slowly off the desk, onto the tan leather seat of the chair. The singed edges of a letter, by a stack of burnt-out matches. I picked up the page, damp with a smear of lighter fluid, and wondered why the flame hadn't caught; wondered still more at the absence of text.

'What the hell . . . ' I said, finally. 'What happened?'

'I don't know.' She picked up a cracked spyglass and held it up to the light. 'It's fucking creepy, though. Let's get the wine and go.'

She ducked into the kitchen, and I grabbed my fur coat, still slung over the back of the chair, where it'd been since one morning in spring, when I'd dropped it there and left it, always meaning to take it home.

'Ready?' she said, clutching three bottles of wine. She handed one to me. 'Let's go.'

We lay in silence, staring at the stars. Down the hill, the last caretaker's car roared into life and passed slowly down the driveway, the whirr of the night chasing after it: crickets, birds, the whisper of the wind in the trees, the roar of the sea whistling in the distance. Beside me, Robin's lighter made its familiar whoosh, and the tip of a joint glowed in the darkness, gold as jewellery, red as blood. She took a long drag and passed it to me, our fingers touching a moment as I took it from her hands.

'That thing got pockets?' she said, turning to me.

'Yep.'

She handed me the bag, filter papers, and lighter. 'You're on supply duty, then.'

I felt the familiar, syrupy warmth, the comforting cocoon sensation, skin feverish and combustible. 'Do you really think—'

'Shhh,' she said, shifting closer to me, her head resting on my shoulder. 'No thinking for a minute.'

I plucked a blonde hair from my lip. 'I'm sure you didn't moult this much before.'

'I know. It's gross.'

The wind picked up, the rustle of the trees brittle and cool. I looked away, shielding my eyes from the salty air.

'So what are we going to do?' I said, at last. 'We can't stay here forever.'

She sat up, her body leaving a hollow of herself, a thin frame in the crushed grass. A fox screeched in the distance, birds bursting from the trees. 'We should run away,' she said, turning to face me, eyes sparkling in the moonlight.

'Oh, sure, yeah,' I said. 'That'll be easy.'

She narrowed her eyes. 'I'm serious. You've got money, right?'

'What?'

'I mean, you're loaded, aren't you?'

'Not loaded,' I said, nervously. 'I mean, I only get an allowance.'

'Yeah, but your mum wouldn't notice if . . . You know.' She shivered, looked away.

I saw my chance to change the subject. 'Are you cold?'

'Fuck off. I'm fine.'

I laughed, shrugged off my coat. 'Here. You have it for a bit. I'm warm now.'

She took it without a word, slipping it over her shoulders.

'"Thank you, Violet",' I said.

'Thank you, Violet,' she mimicked back, clicking the cap off a bottle of wine. 'Want some?'

I shook my head. 'Do you really think we should run away?'

She turned to me. 'Unless you've got a better idea. I mean, Nicky's going to tell someone what we did – if she hasn't already. And Annabel hates us, so that's—'

'She doesn't hate us.'

'Did you see the way she looked at us? I'd be surprised if she doesn't try to get us kicked out next year.' She took a sip of wine, dug the bottle into the grass. 'I've never seen her that angry. Ever.'

'She'll get over it.'

Robin shrugged. 'And you know Alex and Grace aren't coming back. Not if the shit hits the fan.'

'They will.'

'They won't. They're probably cancelling their return tickets as we speak.'

I reached for the wine. 'Alright, fine,' I said. 'Fine. We can go wherever you want. How about Paris?' She rolled her eyes. 'I'm serious. Bring your guitar. We'll form a travelling band, except I can't sing. But I'll hold out the hat for people to throw pennies in.'

Robin laughed. '*La Vie Bohème*,' she said. 'We'll get discovered on the streets by the owner of some backstreet jazz club. You'll learn the sax and we'll take up residence in a glamorous little apartment upstairs.'

'Done.' I didn't believe it; nor, I think, did she. It was play-acting, fantasy, childish games. In the light of day, we'd find a way out. But right now, in the moonlight, the grass growing dewy and sweet-smelling, make-believe would be enough to sustain us.

'Come on,' she said, standing up, legs all tendon and bone beneath her dress. I reached a hand towards her, and brushed at the dead grass that stuck to her legs, leaving crosses in her skin. 'Let's make the most of this dump before we go.'

She ran towards the playground, moonlight dripping through the swings' thick chains, and I followed, and we laughed at the world as we spun circles through the pitch-dark night. Behind, the clock faces turned dark, and time, to us, was lost.

Summer

Chapter 17

Owl wings cracked above like a gunshot, worms rolling in the earth beneath me, shifting roots. I opened my eyes, and the moon swelled, wet with dew, stars scattered like ashes in the peach-flesh morning sky. My head ached. I put my cold, wet palms to my face, smelled sweat, felt my jaw ice-cold and hopelessly clenched. The night came back in smudged memories, a shallow blur – dusty pills, spitting phrases from half-remembered spells as a summer storm gathered and drenched us.

I reached an arm to one side, feeling for Robin, finding only grass. The world rocked, turned liquid as I sat up and called her name. 'Robin?' I said, voice cracked, throat rattling with smoke and spit. I coughed, spat metallic in the grass, crushed a daisy with my fingers, called again. 'Robin?'

The first splinter of sun split above the trees, the sky split, too, by the fading stream of a jet; birds chirped and clicked above the school buildings, bricks crisp and cool in the slanted morning light. I stood, slowly, staggering up, my bones straw, muscles holding water, and turned around to see the figure swinging gently on the breeze, hands gripping chains, ankles crossed above the tarmac, a white, discarded shoe, toenails painted turquoise green.

'Robin,' I said. 'Robin?' Funny, now, how many times I said her name, perhaps the only word I spoke that day, would've spoken forever: *Robin, Robin, Robin.* I walked towards her, cartilage crackling, calves thick with pin-pricks, dew licking at my ankles. My jacket crumpled, discarded on the ground; I picked it up, and laid it on my knees as I sat on the swing beside her.

'Robin,' I said, her head turned a little away, eyelids low, lashes sleek with dew.

'Robin,' I said, a hand on her arm, finding it cold, doll-plastic, down velvet under palm. I squeezed, pinched her, slapped bare skin, burrowed fingers into thigh, nails leaving dunes.

'Robin,' I said, again, the last time, my words useless, her name dried out, abandoned. I stepped back, leaned in once again, grabbed her shoulders, knelt at her feet, plucked the burned end of a joint from beneath a shard of broken glass, and knew what I had done.

I put my hand in my jacket pocket, glass biting at my fingers, and squeezed it tight into my fist, drawing blood. I looked up at Robin's white face, lips chapped, blue pooling in the flesh, the grey shadows carving cheeks, and pulled out the fragments of the nightshade jar, one by one, the clear bag torn through. I felt the leaves mingling, sticking to my bleeding hand, and knew that I had killed her, poison pinched between her fingers, rolled in paper, burned red in the black night.

There were many things I could have done, but didn't. I could have called an ambulance, parents, police. I could have called Alex, or Grace, or Annabel, and begged them to help. I could have confessed, told the truth of what happened, the lurid truth of the girl on the swing.

But I did none of these things.

I sat at her feet, watching, willing her to breathe.

I stood, muttered her name, willed again, clawed at the details of her. The powder-blue blush beneath her fingernails. The albumen sheen of her eyes. The cool, damp recess of her mouth, tongue still soft, the scrape of teeth on probing thumb.

I wondered when they'd find her, and how, and the thought of her slumped, fallen back into the grass as her body softened, seemed sickly, grotesque, wrong. I unhooked the clasp of her bracelet and wrapped it around the left chain, where her hand gripped a little less tight; I unhooked my own, and tied it to the right, and begged her to stay, just as she was, as beautiful as she'd ever want to be.

And then, after all this, I went home. Took the same shuddering bus, walked the same streets; smoked a cigarette under the mermaid, bought another pack from the corner shop. Waved to Mrs Mitchell, with her little, barking dog; walked away as she slammed the door. Went inside, made a cup of tea, passed Mum, sighing in her sleep; climbed the stairs, clicked the door, locked it shut.

I lay in bed, staring up at the ceiling, seeing her in the shadows as I blinked, trying to keep from closing my eyes, when she would open hers, pupils rolled back, lost to skull. What would follow seemed inevitable: the shock of the news, the TV's endless scroll; the knock at the door, policemen asking questions to which they well knew the answers. I was the last person in her company. Where had I been at this hour, that hour? What time had I left her? Was she alive or dead?

They would test her blood, and find the nightshade that still rolled in the cracks of my pockets, burning my skin as I brushed it with fingertips, a vicious sting under each nail. They would ask me where I'd found it, or figure it out themselves after speaking to Alex, who would tell them (of course she would tell them) that it had been stolen, pulled from the deck while she slept. Robin and I were the only suspects, and I the last alive: a tale that told itself.

I saw this, saw it clearly and whole, fate's golden thread, and did nothing. Watched the clock tick, watched as day unfolded its colours, gold, red, grey, blue, black, until the inevitable knock at my door finally came.

'Violet?' my mum said, knocking softly, turning the handle, finding it locked. 'Can I talk to you?'

'I'm sleeping,' I said, heart swallowed, sick.

'Just for a minute. You can go back to sleep right after.'

I reached over and unlocked the door. She looked older, now, skin cracked and sallow, as though the flow of her tears had worn rivulets into her skin.

'Darling, there's something on the news I think you should see.'

I closed my eyes, held my breath in my throat. I knew what

was happening, though I still hoped she might not have seen the link. Had I ever told her about Robin? Had I mentioned her name? Or did she think I'd be interested purely because it was a girl from my school, on the grounds of the school itself?

'Come on,' she said, hand skeletal on my arm, her veins blue ribbons under gristled skin. 'It's hard to explain.'

I willed my hands not to shake, the nausea to fade, praying for a moment of relief I knew I did not deserve; sat in Dad's abandoned chair, and gripped my knees as she flicked the channel back to the news. I looked past the TV, at the chipped MDF stand built back to front, the duct tape peeling, gathering dust. I drew breath, and focused.

'*SECOND MURDER IN QUIET SEASIDE TOWN*,' the banner read, as a doll-faced woman mouthed silently into the screen, the studio bright and blue behind her. My heart paced wildly, that old, sickly thrill: I was transfixed. Would I see her there, on the screen? Would they show what I had done?

The camera cut to men in white suits, climbing from a police van, poring through hedges, crouched low on the ground; it showed stock footage of the town, brighter than reality, perfect as the postcards sold by the sea.

'We now go live to the scene,' a voice said, loudly, as the volume clicked back on. I closed my eyes.

'Violet,' my mother said, and I opened them, clenching fists. On the screen, the front door of Grace's house, window smashed; policeman walking down the steps, ashen, horror ill concealed. I leaned over my knees, felt my throat clench as though gripped, vice-tight.

Dressed in black, eyes wide with excitement, hair smooth, shining, unreal, the reporter spoke directly to the camera, eyes fixed on me. 'The victim was found with fatal injuries at home this morning. Neighbours called the police complaining of what was described as dogs howling from inside the house, disturbing the peace on this quiet, suburban street.'

I turned away. 'She's not . . .' I began, words failing. Grace's bruises, smudges under powder. All of us knew that things could get worse. *Would* get worse. And yet it was easier, more tactful, we told ourselves, to ignore them. To give her privacy. To let her deal with it in her own way. We were all, in this way, complicit.

'Police described the scene inside the house as "disturbing",' the reporter went on, 'the victim having been dismembered in what appears to be one of the most gruesome murders ever to happen in this town, which is known more for its history of—' She paused, looked aside; the camera cut to a pale, middle-aged officer, his skin slick with sweat, a faint grey tinge to his skin.

He cleared his throat. Flashes popped; microphones bobbed below. 'This morning, at around five o'clock a.m., we were called to this location to investigate what appeared to be a domestic disturbance. Officers were dispatched and on entering the property were shocked to discover this gruesome crime, which will no doubt strike at the heart of our peaceful community.' He tapped his forehead with a handkerchief, grey with wear. 'We urge residents in the area to remain calm. We will be doing everything in our power to apprehend the killer, and will be investigating all lines of inquiry.'

He took a deep breath, a slight shudder in his chest. 'We can now confirm the victim is one Martin Holloway, aged 55, the homeowner at this property . . .'

I leaned back, swallowed a hot sting of vomit. Closed my eyes again, felt the edge of the cushion bury into the base of my skull, tried to make sense of the words.

'Though of course we cannot confirm this at this early stage in our investigation, this does appear to have been some kind of ritual killing. We are concerned at this point in time for the whereabouts of Mr Holloway's daughter, Grace, aged seventeen, who has not been seen since last night. We have not ruled out the possibility of abduction, and will not do so until we have confirmed Miss Holloway is safe. Grace, if you are watching this, please make contact with local police as soon as you can.'

I knew she hadn't been kidnapped. Of course she hadn't.

'They'd never get away with it,' she'd said, in hushed conversation with Alex, thinking me asleep. 'They would, if they picked the right moment,' Alex had replied, as though imagining themselves characters in a play, cast in some absurd scenario. And, as it would turn out, they did. As, to my shame, did I.

It was another twenty-four hours until they found Robin. She was still sitting on the swing, hair now damp with dew, fingers stiffened tight around the chains. The caretaker, returning for a misplaced set of keys, found her as he drove into the school, at the top of the hill; had he not come back, she might have stayed there all summer, swaying in the breeze as her skin peeled back, flesh sunk, bones cracked. I often wonder, even now: Would I have saved her that indignity, at least? One might like to think so, but in truth, it seems unlikely.

The phone rang, still placed at the top of the stairs. I let it ring, until I couldn't stand the noise; picked up, spat a 'What?' into the receiver.

'Violet Taylor?' the voice said. The reporter from before.

'What?' I said again.

'It's Daniel Mitchell, from the *Evening News*. We've spoken before. I was wondering if I could talk to you about your friend – Miss Adams?'

I felt a flicker of recognition, some memory come to life. The voice connected with eyes peering through a white window, posters on the wall. 'What did you say your name was?'

'Daniel Mitchell. From the *Evening*—'

'Wait – Danny Mitchell? As in, Danny Mitchell who lives next door?'

He stuttered, caught. 'My grandma lives next door to you, I believe. I don't live there any more.'

'You *believe*? What the fuck are you doing, Danny?'

'I'm a reporter. At the *Evening*—'

'The *Evening News*, yeah, I know. But Christ, aren't you, like, twelve?'

'I'm eighteen. It's . . . it's an internship.'

I laughed, coldly, realizing my mistake. Of course he'd known about my dad. He'd lived next door the whole time. 'Jesus, Danny.'

'Daniel,' he said, coldly. 'They've said if it goes well they'll keep me on.'

'Well, good luck. Don't call me again.' I slammed the phone down, pulled the cord from the wall; went back to bed, restless and burning.

The media frenzy escalated, reaching a pitch; I saw the sketch of her silhouette, photos of her face in every newspaper, her gap-toothed smile on the evening news, unavoidable. 'Tragic Loss of a Young Scholar', one headline read. 'Second Death at Exclusive Girls' School', another. 'Mystery Surrounds the Girl on the Swing', another still, and I sat, awaiting my fate.

But the police, stunned by the impact of not one but two mysterious deaths, in addition to the still-unsolved murder of Emily Frost, did only the most basic investigation into what had killed Robin. Inadequately trained and unused to such pressures, this was as much as they were equipped to handle. They sent for basic toxicology tests, Robin's returning with the presence of drugs found, though in non-lethal amounts. Non-lethal, but enough: enough for the media narrative surrounding her death to twist, just a little, to a tale of doomed youth. No longer was she a promising, talented student, an artist with the world at her feet. Now she was a so-called 'wild child', not wholly committed to her work – Nicky's face peering sadly from the television, telling the world of the ways she'd tried to save her friend, to make her get help, to 'find another path'. Robin, tragic Robin: a preventable death, a lesson learned.

'Robin Adams, student at the prestigious Elm Hollow Academy, was known to be involved in the use and supply of certain recreational drugs, despite her friends' and family's repeated efforts to keep her on the straight and narrow.' This became her lede, an introduction that gave the police reason to shrug it off, to go through the motions and confirm their simple explanation for her death. They stood in front of flashing cameras, insisted they would investigate every possibility, made grand statements for newscasters visiting from London and beyond. But when the interest dissipated, as it always does, their 'tireless' work stopped, and her death was ruled misadventure, cause unknown. I suppose in this respect, at least, they were right.

They focused instead on the Holloway murder, making ominous statements, suggesting some depraved cult murderer roaming the streets. But this they revised, too, when it transpired Mr Holloway was often involved in bar fights, and owed a not-insignificant sum of money to creditors across the town. His death, then, became explainable; Grace's disappearance not a kidnapping, but a flight. She had run from the horrors of her own home (Nicky and her cohorts once again confirming lewd details of hospital visits and bruised wrists), choosing the safety of anonymity over the broken love of a bad father. Alex's mother spoke on her behalf, and confirmed police had taken no action on numerous occasions, including the day when we'd seen them at the house, and let our madness do the rest. She refused to let anyone speak to the girls directly; helped them disappear, escape the media frenzy, the mess that they had made.

But I knew. Knew every detail before it was released (local police pathetically gossipy, sloppy with details, leaking ever more sickening details to the local press, wild with delight).

He'd been stabbed, repeatedly, in the chest and neck, as he lay asleep on the sofa. First cut to the jugular, familiar from Robin's sketchbook, annotated in a girlish hand. I saw Alex holding the knife high, decisively, the force of the cut brutal, spurting thick. Recognized it, saw his wide-eyed fear. This time, though, they'd gone a step further. The page we'd glossed over fearfully in the book: the sacrificial rite.

He'd been dragged, writhing, to the floor (the blood sprayed and spread across the tiles confirming that the first blow was not fatal, at least at first), bound at the wrists and feet. I saw Grace, trembling as she saw the hands that had beaten her so many times now tied with piano wire, wearing through the skin; saw Alex's smile, a comfort, a reassurance, that old familiar look they seemed to share.

'Torture,' the papers described it: Flesh burned with scalding water, needle-thin lacerations in the blisters, cut deep. Fingers severed, one by one, wadded with bathroom towels, to stem the blood and prolong the pain. Skin nicked and peeled away, Grace's delicate hands flaying, flesh under fingernails. They'd known exactly what to do.

Not that I said a word. For who would I tell? Who would believe me? Two teenage girls, murdering a fat, lumbering bastard of a man? Unimaginable. Unreal. Some things simply cannot be believed. Even when you know they're true.

Autumn

Chapter 18

The rain beats at the boards of the pier, and I stand, elbows damp against the icy railing. Down into the green-blue water, mossy steps disappear into oblivion below; farther out, the boats bob restlessly in the wind. It's early enough for me to be alone; a Sunday, the church bells ringing over the rise, the faint cut of dead fish carving the air, darkly.

There are ghosts everywhere, in this town, little end of the earth I can never leave. I'm older, now, but still, by all accounts, young; skin still lineless and faint-pored, hands still warm and soft, though my nails are bitten down to reddening tips, blackened with ink and dirt. I fantasize, on these mornings, of walking down those steps, finding the point at which the darkness swells and the world above disappears: like Persephone walking willingly under, at once towards and away from the things that she loves, though she, like all of us, knows better.

But – as with all that's come before – I fall short. I cannot; Eliot's eternal footman snickers, and I am, indeed, afraid.

And in the room the women come and go, talking of Michelangelo.

I spit and turn and walk away.

When autumn came, bringing with it the smell of decay and sickness in the air, I went back to Elm Hollow; back to where I'd left her, alone, watching two sunrises before she was found. I sat on a grassy ridge, the wych elm's roots having left tails in the dirt, creeping across from one side of the Quad to the other. The Headmaster could never have envisioned it clawing so deep, taking so much of the earth along with it; the tearing up had split the grounds like a carcass, carved crosswise and around. The clock faces, too, remained dark, and for his efforts, and those of the janitorial staff, nobody seemed able to open the door at the foot of the Campanile. I sipped a coffee, smoked; saw two legs standing beside me, followed them up. Nicky.

'Hi,' she said, unsmiling.

'Hi,' I said, the same.

She lowered herself down beside me, pressing her heels into the dirt. 'Sorry about Robin.' I stared at her, blankly. 'No, really,' she said. 'She was . . . She was cool.'

'I'm sure she'd appreciate that.'

We sat in strained silence a while, watching as the groundsmen pressed saplings into the earth, the leaves falling from the old trees behind them.

'You didn't tell,' I said, at last. 'After the ball. You didn't tell anyone about us.'

She looked at me, eyes cold. 'I did,' she said. 'But they didn't believe me. They said I was crying wolf.' There was a note of hurt in this last phrase, though she tried not to show it, and I – a kindness I supposed she deserved, after everything – didn't acknowledge the crack in her tone.

'Who did you tell?'

'Ms Goldsmith. She took me to the Head's office.' She sighed. 'I missed the ball.'

I knew, then, I wouldn't find Annabel. I imagined a kind of trade, a sacrifice. 'We can't be having rumours like this,' he'd say, pig eyes misty with satisfaction, moustache twitching as he finally forced her out. 'I'm afraid I can't condone these extra classes. No more of this, next year.' She'd nod, no doubt, her silence more penetrating than words; I saw her gathering her things, a flurry of wrath in the tower, and leaving Elm Hollow, without pausing to look back.

'Sorry,' I said, numbly.

She said nothing; looked up at the tower, clock faces dark and unlit. I wondered if she'd tried the door, as I had; found the locks changed, as I had, too. 'I'm sorry too,' she said, faintly. 'I didn't mean for any of this to happen.'

I looked at her, sunlight tearing white through the blocks behind. 'What do you mean?'

'It was my fault. What happened with Emily. I wanted her spot in the Advanced Class. My mum was in it, the same year Alex's mum was – and Annabel, too. She said if I didn't get in, I'd never "achieve my potential".' She rolled her eyes. 'So I asked Annabel, but she said there wasn't room.'

I stared at her, trying to piece the fragments together. 'Nicky, what are you—'

'So I went up to my mum's attic, and I found the book.

The book of rites. And . . . Well, I did one. And it worked. Emily disappeared, so there was room in the society. But then you . . . ' She sighed; twisted her skirt between finger and thumb. 'Whatever. Judging by what happened I was probably better off out of it.'

'What . . . What one did you do?'

'A poppet spell. With a little doll. I buried it under the wych elm.' She paused, looked at the space where the tree had been, and sighed. 'It's probably gone now.' She climbed to her feet, brushing dirt from the backs of her legs. 'Anyway, I guess we're kind of in the same boat. So . . . I'm sorry. I hope it gets easier.'

I said nothing as she walked away, tripping across the Quad, the sunlight bright and clear, leaves red and gold in the light. The new students gathered in shy groups, separating themselves into clusters that would soon fracture and split, as we had done; would merge into new groups, new friendships, new betrayals. I never imagined a year could be so long.

And then, more years, each a little longer than the last.

I finished my studies at the local university, shadows of Tom and Andy climbing up the walls, on the rare occasions I could be coaxed into attending a party in the old dorm tower. Qualified, sent an application to Elm Hollow, offered to work for free if there wasn't an opening. *Did* work for free, for two years, until a position finally opened. Worked, taught, attended parent-teacher meetings, felt jealous of them all. Became the Dean of Students. Saw his body, sometimes, slumped lifeless against this door, every door that stuck.

But his was not the only ghost. I heard Robin's voice everywhere, saw her in the spaces between, loping along beside new students, new lives. I read chemistry textbooks, clawed through dull papers on toxicity, history books listing infamous poisonings; now, with the internet ubiquitous, I search every night for new publications with even the briefest reference to nightshade, and its harmful effects. Because the horror of nightshade is in the purging effects, and the quantity Robin had taken – smoked, not consumed – seemed too little to have caused her death. Her heart had simply stopped, with no other side effects. She had died, impossibly, perfect.

Eventually, I persuaded myself – as one does, in adulthood, when the imagination fades, and life is lived only according to what's real – that perhaps it hadn't been as I'd thought. I couldn't shake off the Dean's murder; that much was true – but I'd got away with it (as far as one can be said to 'get away with' such a thing, the nightmares and shadows never quite disappearing from view). This much could be left in the past. And the rest – could it be coincidence? A trick of fate, perhaps, that Tom had died the night we'd performed the rite; Robin's heart, for her part, worn down by excess and simply giving out – a tragedy, yes, but one I couldn't have done anything to prevent. Even Nicky's story, now, of the poppet spell on Emily Frost, seemed a kind of delusion. I'd seen Nicky since, a mother herself: a major player in some internet business I didn't understand. She couldn't have done such a thing. It was impossible, childish: absurd.

Funny, how adulthood allows lies like this to become real:

an all-but-gymnastic feat of thinking. But it's easier, is it not, to believe?

As I sat in my office – the Dean's office, still, in my mind – I looked out at the fresh-cut grass, where students sat laughing, texting, reading in the light. A knock at the door; the school secretary peered through the crack, the same wary expression as ever. She'd never quite forgiven me, though for what I wasn't sure – some rudeness, when I was a student, perhaps; a look, a sigh, a groan. 'Phone call,' she said, abruptly.

'Put it through,' I said.

'Transfer system is down,' she replied, half-turned to walk away. 'You can take it in the main office, if you want.'

I stepped into the glassy office, archaic printer scratching and whirring in the background, a fan rattling by my side. 'Hello?' I said, clutching the receiver close.

It was a call I'd been expecting for some time. My mother was dead. A fall down the stairs, a broken neck. I was surprised only at the way she'd gone, having braced myself for the likely possibility of some long, painful death: cirrhosis of the liver, a cancer, perhaps, fast-moving if she was lucky. I met with the lawyer two days later – a squat, bald man, single frayed thread on his sleeve irritating me, somehow, throughout our conversation – and he handed over the keys to the house, which I'd left after finishing school and, aside from the occasional polite but brief visits, never returned to.

It was a ghost house, now, Mum having spent the last two decades living among the shored-up ruins of her married life, never touching the objects left by my father, my sister, or – I was oddly touched to discover – by me.

I sat a while in my old room, staring at the posters fading yellow, the wallpaper peeling, a black smudge of damp across the corner, mould crawling out. Neon bracelets on a ceramic arm; coursework abandoned as I left for university. Robin's note: 'See you in class. Love you.' A photo of the four of us, the Polaroid curling, stained by sunlight. Alex's lips on Grace's forehead, Robin's hand in mine, the two of us laughing, wildly alive.

I flicked the light off, closed the door behind me, imagined them gone. Black bin liners in the kitchen, all memories destroyed.

I peered into my mother's room, briefly – a mess, predictably, loose bottles scattered, clothes crumpled on the floor, the smell of bedsheets unchanged for months, if not years, a tang in the air. In the hall, a framed family photo, the four of us laughing, wearing sombreros in front of a ride at some long-closed theme park. My sister, eyes shut tight against the bright sunlight, clutching a lollipop in the shape of Mickey Mouse. *Her room*, I thought. *I'm going to have to empty her room.*

I stood by the door for several minutes before I entered, checking my phone compulsively, as though expecting a call (though I couldn't remember the last time my phone had rung; my only alerts ever emails alerting me to publications I'd set keywords for – 'Elm Hollow murder', 'nightshade toxicity', and other fragments never solved).

The smell was overwhelming, a sickening, filthy rot, like a pond sick with decay. I retched, ran to the window, and opened it wide, gasping for air; leaned out, breathing heavily, until the air thinned. Dust covered every surface, everything pink under grey. I'd teased her about it, the day she died. *Pink is for babies*, I'd said, as we climbed into the car, the last words she'd hear me say.

Beside the bed, the source of the smell: the algae-covered ruins of a fish tank. I remembered them, though their names had long escaped me. One gold, one black; the diligence with which she'd fed them, day in, day out, and watched my dad clean the tank with eyes wide, protective. She'd collected endless trinkets, some of which stood dry beside it, leaving room for the fish: a roundabout, a slide, a cottage, windows lit yellow, a comforting glow.

I leaned in, peering through the grey water, thick with decay, smelling of death. The water moved, a little, what lay beneath obscured at first, then clear. In the water, perched on the playground swing, sat Sindy, her hair peeling away, still white blonde under green rot. I stepped back from the tank, feeling a thread stick to my palm: a hair, caught on the rim of the tank, red-tipped with dye, twenty years later. Robin's hair, caught on the doll; I imagined her leaving it behind, a smile on her face as she dropped the doll into the water, imagining Nicky submerged: drowned in daylight.

Sweat pooled on the back of my neck, in the cracks of my palms; I threw up, hot and sour, in the bin beside the bed.

After the pier, I return to Elm Hollow, my choice made at last.

I remove the stone at the foot of the Campanile, and take the tower key, just as Robin taught me to. As the lift's out of use, I climb the stairs, slowly, cursing my weak joints, the weight I gained after she died, and have been gaining every year since; my body turning back into my own, its softness a comfort. I push the door, and find it undisturbed but for the creep of nature. The carpet matted with eggshells, nest pieces, dust, black with shit. Two decades' worth of filth, of creatures taking over, burrowing into books, leaving damp trails across the furniture. The air rattling with crawling things, wings fluttering above.

I've seen Annabel since, her name attached to various boarding schools in Switzerland, France, and Rome, though she's as invisible as it's possible to be in a world now almost entirely online: her faculty photograph is always the same, the arches of Elm Hollow looming above. I imagine her, now, the same as she always was; wonder whether she's aged, as I have. Feels older, as I do.

I've seen the girls, too, though they'd curse me for it. Both wearing pseudonyms that don't quite fit, Alex now a lawyer, Grace a writer, recognizable in pictures I've found online, their eyes still just the same. Neither called or wrote, though I imagine they watch me too, from a distance. I wonder if they feel the same weary ring in their chests when they see my face; the same sadness of what we might have been, or done.

I think of them as I sweep the floors, scrub dust from the clock faces; clear the tower of its sickly-sweet decay. I light a fire, watching spiders scatter manically from the wood, and see the bats swing leisurely above, fur-cheeked and toothy, Robin's halfway smile. I shoo a pigeon from the armchair, and sit, eyes closed, imagining them here.

Tomorrow, I will choose my four: the next four, after us. I'll do it in her name – Robin's name – and the names of all those who've come before.

And I'll teach them all I know, all my predecessors have known – the power of angry women, the fates we hold and furies we possess. I'll let them stretch their wings and claw at the eyes of those who stare; teach them to burn with righteous fire and cleanse the world with learning. I'll teach them beauty, revenge, madness, and death, and if they burn it all, and start again, the more the better. For they'll be fearless, becoming bold, just as Annabel wanted for me. For the four of us, though we're split apart; for the Fates' thread still remains.

'No matter what,' Robin said, that last night, while the cool air sang and we danced in white, 'we'll always be together.' The scar in my palm burns, and I look down from the tower, a shadow rocking on the swing.

'And when the end of the world comes, we'll be here,' she said, and we danced, and I smile, now, knowing she was right.

Acknowledgements

Thanks are owed to so many people for helping to make this book what it is.

To my incredible agent, Juliet Mushens, whose belief in these four wicked girls gave them life, and made them real.

To my editor – and, I am lucky to say, my friend – Natasha Bardon, whose vision and love for this book gave it magic beyond anything I could have crafted alone.

To the team at HarperFiction, including Jack, Jaime, Fleur, Hannah, and Fionnuala, as well as my copy editor, Verity, and my proofreader, Linda. Your passion and talent for what you do is awe-inspiring.

And to Micaela Alcaino, for the cover. It is a thing of beauty. I can only hope the words inside live up to it.

To the many authors and scholars upon whose work I have drawn to varying degrees as part of the 'syllabus' of this book. Much is pulled from a variety of online resources, often without citations – so to those unnamed: thank you for your generosity with your knowledge and learning. I hope I've used it well.

And, of course, to the teachers who inspired the book – for better, and for worse.

To the powerful women I am privileged to know, and blessed to call my friends: Caroline Magennis, Natalie Houlding, Mallory Brand, Laura Bligh, and Emma Maisey. Without you, I would fail more, and laugh less. The girls in this book are yours.

To the accidental patrons of the arts at Mash, a team I am lucky to call both colleagues and friends: Chris Wareham, Phil Edelston, Davinia Day, Lynn Booth, Jennie Tubbritt, and the rest of the team, both in the office and the field.

And, to my family.

To Jim Lowe, with whom I could happily talk into the early hours, forever. Your constant support, enthusiasm and inspiration made this book what it is. Without you, I wouldn't be a writer.

To Cathrine Lowe, whose love and strength I am grateful for every day, and who made me the woman I am. Without you, I wouldn't be a reader.

And to my sister, Becky. I'm so proud to know you, and so grateful to have your music and laughter in my life.

Finally, to girls everywhere. You are more powerful than you think.